The Porter's Wife

First Edition Design Publishing

The Porter's Wife
Copyright ©2014 Lisa Brown

ISBN 978-1622-874-03-0 PRINT
ISBN 978-1622-874-04-7 EBOOK

LCCN 2014931045

January 2014

Published and Distributed by
First Edition Design Publishing, Inc.
P.O. Box 20217, Sarasota, FL 34276-3217
www.firsteditiondesignpublishing.com

This book is dedicated to my husband, Jeff.
I could not have written it without your constant reassurance,
support and never-ending patience.

The Porter's Wife

By

Lisa Brown

December 1901

The light from the oil lamp flickered in the darkness. The flame licked the inside of its glass home, leaving a thickening layer of black. Despite its foe, the light escaped and danced on the walls, bringing them to life in a room that seemed otherwise devoid of it.

Sarah sat at the old, wooden table, her eyes fixated on the flame. But she didn't see it. Her vision blurred to the thoughts she fought so hard to suppress. She breathed the stale air in a slow and methodic rhythm, the empty room echoing with each raspy breath.

It had been a fortnight since Thomas left their home for the infirmary. He fought the cough the best he could, but his strength was stolen by an enemy he could no longer fight. He had fought the same enemy four months past and had emerged victorious. But this time was different and Sarah knew it. For Thomas, every breath he took felt like it could be his last. Exhaustion permeated every fibre of his being and its consequence became too much for Thomas to bear.

Throughout his thirty-eight years, Thomas Berry had worked with an intensity most were incapable of. Arduous was the common thread that bound them, and despite the difficulty, Thomas never lost hope. He never believed the position he found himself in was a matter of fate, but one of a temporary nature that divine providence would guide him beyond when God was good and ready. And he hoped God would be ready soon.

Thomas longed to break free from the physical agony of his work. There were days where Thomas could barely stand up. His elbows and shoulders ached with every movement. The summer months provided some relief, but it was the dreaded winter months, where the cold, damp air seemed to make its home in the deepest parts of Thomas' joints, that were the worst.

As bad as it was, Thomas knew it could be worse. His eldest son, Thomas Samuel, carted away factory waste and sewage for his pay. Some days, Samuel, as he was known, worked throughout the day clearing the factory where his father worked; others he worked through the night clearing midden from the courtyards outside the factory worker's homes. The pay was poor and the work unimaginable, but it was work and it meant he could be a man and contribute to the family.

But on one August day in the year prior, a day when the sky was dark and the air filled with an unyielding spray, Thomas set out to improve his circumstance. It was only Wednesday, but Thomas was impeccably dressed in his Sunday best. He was dapper in his dark suit, waistcoat and dotted tie. His shoes were worn, but the sight of his noble attire concealed any inferiority his shoes betrayed.

Thomas appeared as finely dressed as any gentleman, and all because of his wife. Sarah was an extraordinary seamstress and could sew anything with the utmost skill. It was this skill that masked, to the outside world at least, Thomas' true standing in life.

Thomas had worked beyond his duty late into the evening prior, and he committed to doing so the following night as well. It was all to secure some precious daytime to go in search of better work. That he was even able to trade the time for extra work was a testament to his relationship with his supervisor. That type of bartering would be unheard of with any other employee.

Thomas lived equidistance from both the Ardwick Station and the London Road Station, both of which would take Thomas to Manchester Central. Leaving from the London Road Station meant one less stop and a lower fare, but that day the London Road Station was blocked by a factory that had burned down days before. Its charred hull was still smouldering and remnants of the walls that once supported the building were now lying haphazardly wherever they had fallen. Firemen worked to snuff out the remaining embers, but time was all that would silence it for good.

The London Road Station was a principal railway station in the Manchester area. It was a constant hub of activity, receiving and delivering a flurry of passengers from electric and horse drawn trams on the lower road and from personal carriages and cabs on the upper. The Ardwick Station, in contrast, was no such hub, with only single service going in either direction.

On that fateful day, Thomas stood in the mist of the Ardwick Station with his ticket in hand. A dozen or so people stood alongside him on the track, destined for some place other than where they were at that moment. And the truth was most people in Ardwick wanted to be somewhere other than where they were at that moment.

Thomas mused about the purpose for which they would find themselves in the same place and at the same time as he did. And his thoughts gave way to Sarah, and of his beloved children, and how he could not fail them on this bleak day.

As the train pulled up to the platform, Thomas felt a burst of nervous excitement. It must have been evident on his face for the usual dull faces that greeted him now bore a look of gratitude for the cheer that his bestowed.

The train came to a stop and the doors opened. Only a few passengers disembarked at Ardwick. Most of them were off to London Road and points beyond. Passengers that were not in need of assistance boarded the train with their luggage and tickets in hand. A small and neatly uniformed man rushed around helping those that remained. His brow was awash with perspiration and he looked harried and ineffective, despite his best effort. As a matter of course, Thomas remained back, waiting for others to board first.

An elderly woman, deep in a struggle with her luggage and handbag, caught Thomas' attention. Her face was blushed with effort as she bent down and fought for breath. Thomas rushed to her side to assist. Her relief and appreciation were apparent, and she thanked Thomas with the coin that she had reserved for the porter who was nowhere to be found.

Bearing witness, the uniformed man rushed to their side to continue to the aid of the woman. He was unaware of who Thomas was and was fearful he was someone who would bring to light the unfortunate circumstance of his kind deed. As the man carried the woman's luggage onto the train, Thomas followed behind and inquired as to the whereabouts of the porter. Clearly, this man was no porter…a supervisor, perhaps?

A deep sigh gave way to a hesitant admission. The porter had abruptly left his post but an hour earlier and it was now vacant.

Thomas took full advantage of this unexpected opportunity, disclosing that he was currently on his way to Manchester Central in search of employment. He was able bodied and ready to start working immediately. He assured the man he would be a sterling porter, the best in fact.

The supervisor was perplexed by Thomas. He was a fine dressed man, but one in need of employment. Most dressed as finely as Thomas were not. But still, he was in a bind, and he had seen firsthand the gentleman that Thomas was.

Thomas would need a uniform, but there was no time for that at the moment. The next train would be along in a half hour and it was in need of a porter. Thomas could hardly breathe for his good fortune.

The supervisor reviewed the rules and expectations. Thomas was given a hat and uniform. He would wear the hat when the next train arrived, but the uniform would have to wait until the following day, until Sarah could tailor it appropriately. So, for that day at least, he would be the best dressed porter that Ardwick had ever seen.

There was no comparing the joy Thomas felt with his newfound freedom. The previous day he was breaking his back in a factory and today he was moving freely across the platform, assisting passengers as he saw fit. Throughout the day, Thomas never stopped. He quickly moved from passenger to passenger, helping those who needed his assistance both on and off the train.

The supervisor, Mr. Linley, appeared numerous times throughout the day and he would tip his hat to Thomas as Thomas worked. It wasn't a complicated job, but one that could be managed to varying degrees of effectiveness. A good porter had to move quickly. He had to be pleasant. He had to be knowledgeable of the routes and local area. In other words, he had to be many things to many people, and all at the same time.

The loud whistle and plume of ashen smoke that billowed upwards from the train marked another successful departure, and at six o'clock in the evening it meant the end of Thomas' first workday at the Ardwick Station.

As procedure dictated, Thomas stepped into Mr. Linley's office to announce his departure. Mr. Linley was a slight man, about three inches shorter than Thomas' five foot nine inches. He was well groomed and clean shaven. He had a demeanour that was gentler than one would expect in a supervisor, and certainly more so than Thomas was accustomed to. Thomas was grateful for the blessing.

Mr. Linley thanked Thomas for his efforts and Thomas assured him that he would be ready on the platform, in full uniform, at the first train's arrival the next morning.

As Thomas left the station, he reflected upon his old job, and how, God willing, he would never have to do anything like that again. But Thomas knew beggars couldn't be choosers and he had Samuel in mind for his old position. At fourteen, Samuel was a tall and strapping lad. He already stood an inch taller than his father and had broad shoulders and a thick, solid chest. He would be able to do the work with little difficulty, and there was no doubt in Thomas' mind it would be an improvement for his son.

Samuel worked for Mr. Arbuckle, a large man with an angry disposition, a man who respected no one. His labourers worked under continual threat of abuse, both physical and verbal. It was disgraceful, but it continued without dispute because divisiveness was not tolerated; and a dreadful job was infinitely preferable to no job at all.

William Markley, on the other hand, was less harsh with Thomas. He was strict, but treated those who did their jobs to expectation with respect. His father, Charles, owned the factory. And his sister, Eleanor, had been a childhood friend of Sarah's and the two had remained close.

Thomas had been grateful to William for his job, as it provided the family with an income and a home. But it was hard work and the pay was poor. The elder Mr. Markley was a frugal man, and while the working conditions he provided were superior to most, his payroll was not. A porter's salary was no better, but a porter could hope to augment his twenty-three shilling per week salary with tips. And, at the end of Thomas' first day as a porter, he had collected a few coins and was very pleased with the result.

As Thomas walked, he passed by one factory after another. His eyes burned from the pungent air and he constantly wiped his handkerchief across them. His cough rasped, and the soot that coated his lungs made its way back out, attaching itself to the dirty cotton fibres. Progress had permanently discoloured the handkerchief, as it had most things in Ardwick.

Within the city limits, and especially alongside the rivers where the factories were the densest, the air was smoky and ash fell from the sky like snowflakes in winter. The River Cornbrook was so heavily polluted that it had been referred to as the "Black Brook." Its water was so thick with waste that what was dumped into it would disappear from sight the instant it broke the slick, black surface. The smell was overwhelming. One never got used to it. The heat in the summer months only made matters worse.

At one time, Ardwick had been a beautiful garden community where parks were plentiful and the air was fresh and clean. But, sadly, with modernization Ardwick had become better known for its filth than its beauty. Things were improving in Manchester, but for most people life was still barely tolerable.

Chapter 2

For Thomas and family, home was four rooms. On the main floor, there was a kitchen in back, a sitting room in front, and two bedrooms upstairs. A cellar had been built below to prevent the endless bursts of drenching rain from settling into the main level living quarters, but the dankness and mustiness remained despite the accommodation.

Charles Markley was the landlord. The dwelling was in one of many buildings that surrounded the two factories that he owned. One manufactured sewing machines and the other wove fabric and made clothing. It was his three hundred or so workers who filled the buildings.

The two factories sat side by side. Behind them there were two rows of houses running the length of the block. They were separated by a narrow alleyway. There was a break in the houses that spanned the width of five of those houses and it provided a small courtyard area for the communal use of the tenants.

While there was a great movement to bring housing standards up to modern levels, the cost to retrofit older homes with modern plumbing was not something that most landlords would entertain, and that included Mr. Markley.

Private privies lined the alley, one to each house. Each privy was three feet by three feet by six feet high. It had a private door, with a bench seat that had a hole in the middle of it. Inside the hole sat an ash pit that would be cleaned once or twice a week. Beside the privy sat an open box where all other waste could be placed.

There was no running water in the houses, but the tenants did not have to go far. There was a pump on the north side of the courtyard, on Francis Street. It provided clean drinking water for the tenants and anybody else who wanted it and was willing to stand in queue for it. Thomas and Sarah lived only four houses from the courtyard.

Fortunately for his workers, Markley was more benevolent than most. He insisted on as clean a working environment for them as he could manage because he realized, and quite rightly, that this would ensure healthier, happier, more productive employees. But, in the end, if benevolence was not profitable, it wouldn't be a virtue he would have counted as one of his own.

Unlike Markley's housing, most employer-provided housing was built back to back. There was no garden area, and the only part not connected to another house was the front door. They were poorly built, without controls or regulations to ensure the minimum of quality. They were dark and damp places. The walls were single brick and the rain seeped through, causing moisture and mould to mark the walls. Communal cesspits would be shared by as many as fifty people. There was no running water in these horrid places, and in most cases community water was not close enough to motivate people to seek it out. It was easier not to bathe, and the stench was not a strong enough deterrent.

Mr. Markley's employees were fortunate and they knew it. They worked hard for the simple reason they didn't want to risk losing what they had.

On that morning, Thomas had left with the hope of securing better employment, without any knowledge of what it would be or if it would be anything at all. And, at the end of the day, he arrived home successful and happy and it was clear to Sarah something good had come of his efforts.

Mary was sitting on the floor rolling a ball that Thomas had made from fabric scraps and twine. She looked up when her father entered and she jumped up and ran to him as quickly as her chubby little legs would carry her. Thomas so loved his children. They gave him unsurpassed joy.

He picked her up and wrapped his arms around her. She buried her face into his bristly cheek with an affection that melted Thomas' heart.

Sarah looked up from her pot and smiled at Thomas. People at that time married for all sorts of reasons. They married to escape their present circumstance, to appear more mature and responsible, to honour the results of uncontrolled lust, and occasionally for true love. Sarah and Thomas married for two of those reasons.

As an eighteen year old, Thomas had been an errand boy for a market in Stretford. He would deliver to the better-off residents of the area. Sarah's mother, Elizabeth, was a market gardener and cultivated produce destined for that very same market. Elizabeth's father, Samuel, had been a market gardener prior. He died when Sarah was twelve, and in order to support her family, her mother carried on in his place.

Market gardening was one of many agricultural jobs in Stretford, which had been predominantly an agricultural village prior to industrialization. It was still a large gardening area, producing much of the produce for sale each week in Manchester.

Sarah did not carry on in her parents' footsteps. At sixteen, she was a maid for one of the residents who Thomas delivered to. It was there that their paths would occasionally cross.

Sarah was exquisite; her skin was fair and flawless, her lips plump and pink. Wisps of her auburn hair would fall out of her bonnet and brush the sides of her face as she looked away. Her shyness made her all the more alluring to Thomas and his heart beat like drumfire whenever he gazed upon her. Thomas was smitten and he had eyes for nobody else.

Sarah thought Thomas was the most handsome man she had seen. He stood tall with an air of self-confidence. His broad shoulders seemed to invite an embrace. His eyes bore a kindness that was warm and comforting to Sarah. She burned with an admiration and lust that she could not stifle.

For the first year or two after they had become aware of each other, they barely spoke. Their paths wouldn't often cross, and when they did, there always seemed to be something in the way that would stop what would inevitably happen. If it wasn't Sarah's employer, it was Sarah's mother.

It wasn't until Sarah turned nineteen and became a woman in her mother's eyes that she was given the freedom she had longed for. And time helped her to overcome her shyness. Eventually their eyes would connect and she would not turn away. There was a spark between them that couldn't be denied.

Thomas had every intention of marrying his sweet Sarah, and he knew he needed to leave that job to search for one more befitting a married man. So Thomas moved on to factory life. He would come to unload stacks of coal from the train, coal which was destined for ovens that melted glass for stained glass windows. The hours were longer, which meant that he would see less of Sarah, but the pay was better, albeit only slightly. He focused on the additional money as a way to forget about his aching back and burning lungs.

Their time spent together was brief and usually entailed a walk, arm in arm, on a Sunday afternoon. On one particular Sunday afternoon, a day unusually warm for the month of May, Thomas and Sarah met in front of the market just as they had done the week prior. Thomas appeared unusually nervous and Sarah's thoughts grew fearful.

There weren't many places where one could go for privacy, but Thomas managed to find one.

They walked along Trafford Street, barely speaking. They took a detour at the river. As they stepped away from the street and made their way down a narrow dirt path, Thomas reached out for Sarah's hand to guide her. After a few moments, Thomas pulled in behind a section of thick bush, where a small clearing emerged. To Sarah's surprise, there was a blanket laid out with a covered box at its edge.

Thomas stopped, turned Sarah around, and pulled her into his arms. Thomas had never embraced Sarah with such voracity, and Sarah's legs weakened.

Thomas kissed Sarah's forehead with a tenderness that only a man deeply in love could do. He put his hands on her waist and pushed her away just far enough that he could look at her face. Sarah was embarrassed by her shyness and looked away so Thomas could not see the redness of her cheeks. That only made Thomas love her more.

Thomas reached up and gently guided her chin back so that she was once again looking him in the eye. And for the first time, he professed his love for her. Sarah could not breathe, let alone speak.

Thomas gently guided Sarah down on the blanket. He tugged at the ribbon to remove her hat, loosened her pulled-back hair, and gently ran his fingers through it. He ran his fingertips down the lengths of her cheeks, and over her trembling lips. He leaned into her and placed his lips on hers. Her lips were as soft as rose petals and they parted to invite him in.

Thomas looked at Sarah to see if there was any hesitance in her eyes, for he wanted this moment to be absolutely perfect. In her eyes, he found only a deep and longing desire.

In a swell of love and passion, Thomas and Sarah came together, their souls intertwined for eternity. As they lay beneath the luminous sun, they rested in each other's arms. There were no words to portray their feelings. They couldn't describe what seemed indescribable.

After Thomas dressed, he reached for the box that sat at the edge of the blanket. He lifted the lid and reached inside. To Sarah's astonishment, Thomas pulled out a single red rose and handed it to Sarah as he bowed his head. He was her prince, she thought.

Sarah took the rose and brought it up to her nose. She closed her eyes and inhaled its seductive scent until her lungs could expand no further. She did not want this memory to fade, and she promised herself she would keep this rose forever.

Thomas pulled out a bottle of wine and gently set it on the ground so it wouldn't fall over. Its cork was loosely set in the bottle and he feared it would spill. Sarah was overwhelmed with his gallantry.

Thomas handed Sarah a glass, removed the cork, and poured her some wine. It was deep crimson and Sarah could smell its earthiness. When both had a glass in their hand, Thomas made a toast. He told of his desire to make Sarah his wife, and he asked her if she would do him the honour of marrying him. As tears ran down her face, she drew in a breath and exhaled a whispered, "Yes."

Thomas kissed her tears away and then they took a drink of the wine. Sarah had never had wine before. It was a luxury that most could not afford. It wasn't a taste that she fully enjoyed, but she savoured every drop.

Thomas had assembled a feast fit for a princess, and for that day their lives were as they wanted them to be. Sarah wasn't sure that she could manage the surge of feelings. Her heart felt as though it were going to burst. And for the next hour, they ate and planned their future together.

Sarah and Thomas parted ways at the market. Sarah walked a short distance to where she knew her mother would be pulling weeds and tending to the vegetables. This was a good year for the corn. The husks were plentiful, and as the stalks reached up to the sky, they seemed to hold each other up under the weight of their bounty. The purplish tassels moved gently in unison, and as if on cue, they kept time and changed direction with the wind.

Sarah spied her mother quickly. Elizabeth noticed the spring in her daughter's step and bore witness to the glow that radiated from her. As Sarah showed her mother the perfect red rose, she shared her news. Elizabeth was overjoyed. She did not know Thomas well, but she knew that Sarah loved him with all her heart, and she knew Thomas to be kind and respectful. She couldn't ask for more for her daughter.

Elizabeth wished Samuel was still alive to share in this joyous news, but that was not to be. Samuel would have approved of the union. Of that she had no doubt.

Chapter 3

Samuel had adored Sarah. She was his baby. Sarah would sit with her father while he worked, helping him weave cotton into dazzling batches of fabric. Samuel had been a weaver, an exceptional one, until an illness had paralyzed his left side.

Sarah would take some of the pieces of fabric that were destined for the trash and would sew doll clothes for her young cousins. The dolls of the wealthiest of England were not better dressed.

Elizabeth was a good seamstress and taught Sarah what she knew, but Sarah surpassed her mother early on. Sarah hadn't simply sewn; she created. She saw form where form didn't exist. She was able to envision beautiful pieces in her mind and then make them real.

Samuel's skill as a weaver was unsurpassed and it allowed him to work for himself. He had a knack for style and colour and that kept his product in demand.

Most of the fabric was sold to John Markley, who owned the same factory where Samuel's son-in-law and grandson would eventually come to work.

On occasion Samuel would be asked to deliver custom-made batches to Mr. Markley's home so Mrs. Markley could choose fabric for her personal use. She liked Samuel's work because it was more vibrant than she could get from the shops in the area. But more importantly, it was unique and she liked to stand out like a bright flower in a sea of grey.

When Samuel visited the Markley's home, he would take Sarah. Mrs. Markley's granddaughter, Eleanor, and grandson, William, had moved in with the elder Markleys after childbirth had claimed their mother a few years before. Sarah and Eleanor became fast friends and Mrs. Markley was thankful for her granddaughter's happiness.

Sarah and Eleanor remained the best of friends through their teens, despite the pronounced disparity in their social standing. Any differences between them, material or otherwise, simply never occurred to them. In their minds, they were one and the same. They were equally strong-willed, bright, and idealistic, though perhaps Eleanor wanted gender equality more and romance less.

After her own mother, Eleanor was the first person who Sarah shared her news with. Eleanor was at her cutting table when Sarah arrived, which wasn't at all surprising to Sarah.

Where Sarah could make stylish garments and sew from what she envisioned in her mind, Eleanor would engineer the patterns from the end result. Eleanor was less creative and more structural. She could take designs and create the exact patterns so they could be replicated over and over. Sarah made unique and Eleanor made mass. Mass is what made money and Eleanor no doubt had a head for business like her grandfather.

Eleanor was thrilled for Sarah. She was pleased with her happiness, but could not understand the desire. Eleanor was expected to become a wife, but managing to other people's expectations was not something that Eleanor fancied, not in the least. She saw herself being a respected businesswoman and had no desire for romantic frivolity.

One month after Sarah's engagement, Eleanor's grandfather passed away. As expected the business passed on to his eldest son, Eleanor's father, Charles. Unexpectedly, Eleanor's grandfather left a provision in his will for a piece of property to be provided for Eleanor, along with a small sum of money. While he didn't dictate how the property was to be used, Eleanor knew her grandfather was proud of her work and of her desire to be a success in her own right. He would have intended it for a dress shop and she was thrilled.

At the time, Eleanor's world wasn't the only one changing. Sarah began having difficulty doing her work; her exhaustion became debilitating. Sarah had no appetite and what little she ate, or her mother forced her to eat, she couldn't keep down. Her mother thought the worst. Living in the city meant an endless supply of diseases, all of which had crossed Elizabeth's mind.

Elizabeth had buried a husband and two children and the thought of losing Sarah was more than she could bear. But the fright of disease was soon replaced by shock as Sarah's bosom began ripening like an apple at harvest. With its ampleness, it became abundantly clear that the wedding would need to be moved up.

Sarah and Thomas were married at St. Matthews in Stretford four Sundays later. Eleanor, and Thomas' brother, John, stood with the happy couple as they exchanged their vows. Sarah was married in a magnificent dress of her own creation. It was an elegant ivory colour, with a loose fitting waistband of mauve accent. It hugged the floor with a delicate lace trim that was adorned with pale pink fleur-de-lis. The lace was a wedding gift from Eleanor.

Six months later, Thomas Samuel was born. He arrived without drama or incident, born by candlelight in the early hours of a cold February morning. He was known as Samuel from the start and her father's namesake brought an indescribable joy to them. Sarah's love was profound, and deep, and fiercely protective.

Thanks to Eleanor's assistance, Thomas had both a job at the Markley factory and a place for his expanding family to live. Thomas' new job wasn't unlike his last. He still shovelled coal into the ovens, but instead of melting glass it melted metal for sewing machine parts. It was hard work, but the accommodations were a blessing.

Up until they moved into their new home, Thomas and Sarah had lived with Sarah's mother and siblings. It wasn't ideal, but it was a better solution than Thomas' family home, which was far more crowded.

Shortly after Eleanor's grandfather passed away, Eleanor moved into her property. It was typical by Ardwick standards, including the flat above the shop where Eleanor would live. She was never one drawn to pomp and circumstance, nor was she one to surround herself with more than she needed. It suited her perfectly.

Sarah started working for Eleanor soon after her shop opened. It was a few blocks from the factory and Sarah and Thomas' home. It was ideal.

Before Samuel was born, Sarah would go into the dress shop daily. She designed custom dresses for well-to-do women who were looking for original designs. Together Sarah and the buyer would pick the material, discuss the shape and design, and then Sarah would draw a sketch. Once the buyer agreed, Sarah would sew it. Eleanor designs became even more coveted as they garnered wider-spread attention.

Sarah had no desire to have her name on the design. She was happy to have the work, and that the work was with her best friend had a value greater than any monetary one. It was unheard of that a woman would make what a man did, but Eleanor paid Sarah a percentage of the profits from what she designed, and when business was good, Sarah did better than she could at any other job.

Eleanor proved her mastery of business early on. Sarah's designs soon filled Eleanor's catalogue, and patterns were constructed to make them available to the masses.

Eleanor was good about giving Sarah freedom to work around Samuel, and that included working from home. When Sarah had to go to the shop for fittings, the seamstresses were all too eager to sit with Samuel. He often slept soundly in his bassinette as the sound of the sewing machines whirred and their melody lulled him off to a peaceful place.

Sarah did her sewing at home. Eleanor provided Sarah with a sewing machine, but a good deal of her sewing was still done by hand. She preferred it. It was familiar and comfortable, and allowed her flexibility she could not get with modern machines.

Samuel was followed by James Frederick in 1889, Margaret in 1890, Elizabeth Ellen in 1894, Sarah Agnes in 1895 and eventually Mary Jane in 1897. Elizabeth died of fever at two, the year that Agnes was born. Sarah was devastated, but the chaos of a house full of children and her sewing helped distract her from the immense pain.

Sarah's mother passed away the year that her daughter Mary Jane was born. No one knows what ultimately took her life. Her time in a lucid state had become rare, and taking care of her needs became a full-time job for Sarah. Sarah loved her mother with all her heart, but there was some relief when she finally passed on.

Sarah's brother, Bertie, had married and emigrated to Canada in 1894. There were promises of free land, and it was too exciting and inviting for Bertie to pass up. Bertie would write often of his adventures. He was six years older and had always more fatherly than brotherly, especially after their father died. He was beholden to Sarah for taking care of their ailing mother and he vowed he would take care of her should she ever need him.

Bertie said the country was beautiful, and the people hard-working and full of desire for a better life. It was all that he had wished for. And as much as it sounded like heaven compared to Ardwick, she could not imagine taking her family on such an arduous journey.

Immediately after Thomas had secured his new position as a railway porter, he had been successful in managing the transition for Samuel to his old job. It was big step up for a young man and it wouldn't have been possible if not for Eleanor.

But, with Thomas leaving his job at the factory, their home was to be lost. Samuel was still a boy and not eligible for family housing. This was a rule that even Eleanor was not able to influence. To Thomas and Sarah, it was a move worth making, and they made it despite the hardship.

The Berrys moved into a house a few streets over from Francis Street. Fresh water was no longer available just outside their door, nor was a private privy. They had to make the five minute journey to secure the water they needed to cook and bathe. They took turns and they collected rain water in between trips to supplement their supply.

The courtyard was overrun with filth and communal cesspits. Five cesspits were shared by two hundred and fifty. Relieving themselves in such a degrading way was simply not acceptable, and they chose to create their own private privy, of sorts, inside. It consisted of a portable box with a seat. Inside the box housed a basin that would be emptied out into the courtyard. Thomas vowed this was only temporary, until they could find   a   better   home.

Chapter 4

As the smoky and hazy August days began to be replaced by darker and mistier ones, a different kind of cloud settled over Ardwick. Death became as prevalent as the piles of waste in the streets. It came slowly, torturing poor souls with an agonizing pain and suffering that lingered beyond what any human was built to endure. For a lucky few, it came quickly, unleashing its devastation in a wave of unbridled fury that would last no more than a few days.

Death came in many forms, but there was no escaping it. And like the coward that it was, it targeted those who could fight back the least.

Thomas' journey was of the long and torturous variety. He was an easy target as he greeted travellers from all walks of life. He had no way to protect himself. He was exposed and death took full advantage.

Thomas began to tire more easily. A deep and rough cough rattled his chest like thunder. He ignored the annoyances for a few months. The fever and night sweats began to worry Sarah, but it was the blood that accompanied the smoky cough that caused the greatest concern.

When he no longer had the energy to work, Thomas found himself at the doors of the Withington Workhouse Infirmary. His admission was permitted due to new provisions that had been made for the working poor, those that weren't destitute enough to enter the workhouse as residents, but those who could not afford medical care.

Tuberculosis patients were quickly diagnosed and separated from the rest of the hospital community. Outside visitors were allowed only on the first Saturday of every month and every precaution available was taken to reduce the likelihood the disease would spread.

While Sarah waited for her Saturday, she spent every moment wondering if Thomas would walk through the door or if she would be told of his untimely passing. It was agonizing. The emotional toll it took on her aged her profoundly. Her auburn hair now showed streaking of grey, and faint lines began to bore their way into her beautiful, porcelain skin.

Without Thomas' income to support them, Sarah needed to work more often. Eleanor was happy to have more of her dear friend, but Eleanor had hired additional seamstresses as her business grew and there just wasn't the volume of work that was needed to fully support another.

Samuel continued to work and contribute to the family, as did twelve-year-old James, who had become an errand boy for a local market as his father had done years before. But it was still barely enough. Sarah was fiercely proud and would not take handouts, especially from Eleanor.

And on one bright Sunday morning, almost one month after he left the family home, the heavy burden of Thomas' absence was lifted in one glorious swoop when he walked through the door. He was mobbed by his family, who would not leave his side. They were the greatest medicine to Thomas and he drank in the comfort, letting not a single drop waste.

Sarah soon realized that he was still not well. On first glance, he appeared healthy. He was well nourished and rested. But it was merely a shell. Inside he was destroyed and she feared the consequence. For the good of her family she fought desperately to maintain her strength and optimism.

Thomas struggled to make his way to the station the following day. Mr. Linley's compassion was not enough to heal the pain of the loss of his position. Thomas understood Mr. Linley needed to fill it, but Thomas had desperately hoped the new appointment would have been temporary.

As Thomas made his way from the station, he watched the new porter tending to his passengers and his heart wrenched with pain.

Thomas spent the next month cleaning Eleanor's shop. It wasn't full-time work, but it was the best Eleanor could manage. Her shop was successful by local standards, but it wasn't a large enterprise, by any means.

Thomas didn't have the physical strength to go back to Markley's factory. He was appreciative of Eleanor's work, both for the opportunity and for the compassion that came with it. Eleanor's heart broke for Sarah as she watched Thomas toil with the broom. He was clearly unwell and getting more so by the day.

By November, Thomas' skeletal frame shook with every cough and gasp for breath. Exhaustion doubled the effort and time it took to manage even the simplest task.

One cold and damp evening, Thomas awoke coughing, unable to breathe. Sarah sat up, placed Thomas' head in her lap, and gently stroked his sweat-soaked hair. The night felt eternal, and when the sun rose and Thomas was still with her, it was a miracle.

Sarah cared for Thomas at home for three more weeks. She spent her days tending to the family, completing the few dress orders she had, and her evenings comforting her beloved. Passion and pain kept Sarah in motion.

When it became clear that Thomas was not improving, Sarah helped her husband make his way back to the infirmary. They spent a few moments on the bench outside the hospital. They held hands as emotion flooded Sarah. A single tear landed on her wrist as she lowered her head. Thomas tenderly lifted her hand and kissed the tear away. His parting words were of a man deeply in love, but a man broken and destroyed. She was his angel and he told her so. He would always be there for her, in spirit if not in body. His only hope in life was for her happiness.

She stood at the door as they took her Thomas away in a wheelchair. And, for the first time, Sarah collapsed in grief.

At home, the quiet knock on the door brought news of Thomas' passing. A young messenger boy handed Sarah the envelope, then quickly fled.

Sarah fixated on it and held it in her hand before she could bring herself to open it. The hospital's mark was prominent on the front and there was no denying what was inside.

Sarah's three daughters could not ignore their interest in the visitor. They were far too curious about the intrusion. They emerged from the back room and quickly noted their mother's expression and the envelope in her hand. With trepidation they inquired as to its content.

Sarah sat down at the table where she did her work. Her long, slim fingers gently pulled at the flap of the envelope until it lifted from inside. She removed the card and read it slowly, focusing intently on the words. They blurred and made no sense. Sarah became paralyzed with grief.

At eleven, Margaret could read. She took the card from her mother's hand and eagerly read it. It dropped to the floor as her hands shot up to her face. She covered her eyes as if to make the horrible scene disappear. She voiced her own pain with a piercing scream that shocked Sarah back into reality. Her two sisters looked on in horror.

The card read – *I beg to inform you that Thomas Berry, late an inmate of this house, died on December 12, 1901. If you desire to make any arrangements with respect to the funeral of the deceased, please let me know on or before December 16th.* It was signed by the workhouse master.

Sarah composed herself quickly. She embraced her girls one by one and told them of their father's love for them. Through their tears, Sarah assured them all would be fine because their father was now with their Lord, and was watching over them from heaven, protecting them from above.

"Margaret, I need you to care for your sisters until I return. I must visit the infirmary to make arrangements for your father."

Margaret was still a girl, but was mature beyond her years. Instinctively she, too, reassured her sisters. She led them upstairs to play so that her mother could prepare for her visit in peace. There was an obedient "Yes, Mama" and a kiss on the cheek and then Sarah was alone in the room.

Sarah inhaled as though it were her last breath. She walked over to the cabinet that sat in the corner of the room. From inside she pulled out a small box. It had a sliding lid that, when pulled back, revealed a dried, red rose.

Sarah gently pulled out the rose and held it to her cheek. She studied it intently, as if willing it back to life. Underneath the rose was a piece of wrinkled paper. Sarah unfolded it and read the words out loud:

>Life is but a journey, and one that I take with pride. God shall guide me.
>
>Life is full of challenges, all of which I accept with purpose. My heart is pure and my head held high.
>
>Life is difficult, but it only makes me stronger. God protects me. Nothing can break me.
>
>Life is painful, but its lessons teach us to feel. And I feel from the depths of my soul.
>
>I am Sarah. I am strong. I am proud.

She had written it the day her father passed away. It comforted her when she was in her deepest despair and today it did as well. Sarah placed the paper and rose back in their resting place. She gathered a few items and put her hat and coat on, then was on her way.

Chapter 5

The infirmary was over four miles away and more of a foot journey than Sarah could manage that day, so she made her way to Ardwick Station. As she approached the platform, she saw the sign for Mr. Linley's office. As she entered through the open doorway, Mr. Linley stood from his chair and lowered his head with respect. "Madam, how can I be of service?"

"Mr. Linley, I presume?" On Mr. Linley's nod, Sarah continued. "I am Mrs. Thomas Berry."

Mr. Linley straightened up and held out his hand to shake Sarah's. Sarah took his hand and attempted a smile.

"Mrs. Berry, how is Thomas?" Mr. Linley asked hesitantly.

He dropped his head upon seeing Sarah's sad expression. "My Thomas went to be with our Lord a few days past, Mr. Linley. And now, I find myself in need of your assistance."

"Most certainly, Mrs. Berry. Thomas was a good man and I shall do what I can. How may I be of assistance?"

"I just received word of his passing and I need to make arrangements with the infirmary. Thomas spoke of your good nature. He had a great deal of respect for you. Today I come to ask for your assistance with passage to Chorlton. It is not charity; I assure you. I shall cover the cost when I am able. You have my word."

Mr. Linley saw a strong woman, but one suffering. He was moved by Sarah.

"My dear Mrs. Berry, Thomas never collected his final day's pay. I have been keeping it. It will cover your passage to Chorlton."

Mr. Linley walked through a door into another room. Sarah could hear a drawer open and the clanking of coins. Mr. Linley emerged, with hand held out. He offered the coins to Sarah. Mr. Linley's generosity was a gift from God, as Sarah knew that Thomas was owed nothing.

"You are very kind, Mr. Linley. May God bless you always."

Sarah hurried from Mr. Linley's office over to the ticket window. In a rush, she placed the coins on the counter and requested a ticket.

"Where you be going on this fine day, Mum?" The ticket clerk had a crooked smile, but it was his bright blue eyes that caught Sarah's attention. They were the same colour as Thomas'.

"Chorlton, please."

"The next train be along in fifteen. You've got plenty of time. You want that track there," he said pointing his finger. "Or else you be in Ashbury's before you know it," the clerk quipped.

Sarah stood on the platform waiting for the train. She noticed the porter standing alongside the station building waiting for the next arrival, and she pictured Thomas in his uniform. She pulled the bag closer to her chest for support and drew in a deep breath to stay whole and keep from collapsing under the weight of the emptiness and helplessness that engulfed her.

As the train pulled up, the passengers readied themselves for boarding. The doors opened and a few passengers disembarked. Sarah had no large baggage or parcels with her on that day so there was no reason for her to be approached by a porter.

As the train pulled away from the station, Sarah looked out from the grime-covered window unfocused on anything but the vision that played out in her mind. Buildings passed by in a blur and blended into each other like a firework streaking through the night sky.

She thought of the man she fell in love with so many years ago, the man who made her feel whole. He was the best part of her. The fire of passion had been replaced by a numbness that was paralyzing. The thought of him dying alone in that dreadful place was devastating and she closed her eyes to change the scene playing out in her mind. Today there was no time for sorrow. There was business to take care of. She had arrangements to make, a funeral to plan.

More than for herself, her children needed to say good-bye to their father. When Sarah's own father had died, her mother had made sure that she could say a proper good-bye. It helped Sarah process her grief and move on. Her children would also need that and she fully intended to provide that for them.

Sarah had to change trains at London Road and Man Central. When she arrived in Chorlton-cum-Hardy, she had a short walk to the infirmary.

In the distance, the workhouse stood like a walled palace, with its giant courtyard and its tower rising high into the wintery sky. It was a stark contrast to what lay inside.

In the workhouse, paupers and lunatics filled its spaces. The despair was incomprehensible. The ghastly moaning and wailing that filled the hallways blended together into a single, constant disturbance that was indistinguishable as to its origin.

The Withington Workhouse had been lauded as revolutionary in its approach to care and organization, but only so much could be done for its residents, many of whom were beyond any hopes for improvement.

The empty bench she and Thomas sat on as they had said their good-byes stood before her like a lonely grave stone. She paused at it, but did not sit down. Instead she reached out and ran her hand over the cold stone surface, hoping to feel something. She felt nothing but numbing cold.

She walked up to the infirmary gate and waited. Like the gates of hell, it kept the outside world from the horrors beyond. Today Sarah would experience her own personal hell, and as she waited she asked God for the strength to see her through.

The workhouse porter approached. "Visiting hours are on the first Saturday of the month, Mum. You best be leaving. There is nothing for you here today."

If only there was someone to visit. The thought seared in her chest.

"Sir, I am here to see the master. Arrangements must be made."

"Ah, I see. Somebody passed on, I be guessing. What a shame." He paused as he opened the gate and stepped aside for Sarah to enter. "You best come this way then."

The porter led Sarah down a walkway beside a large courtyard. If not for the time of year, it would have been lovely. It was winter and the grass was brown, the bushes barren, and the flowers but a mess of soggy, wilted stems.

They turned along a path and entered the master's office from the outside. He was sitting at his desk, focused on a large pile of official looking papers. The porter announced Sarah and the master looked up and nodded his approval. He waved her over to a seat next to his desk.

"Who is the deceased?" he asked bluntly. The coldness caught Sarah off guard. She still didn't think of her beloved Thomas that way. She stumbled as she searched for words. Her mouth was numb and nothing came out.

The master looked at her, lowering his head, and looking over the top of his spectacles. He waited for a moment and asked again, "The deceased's name, Madam?"

Sarah still could not speak. She could not draw in enough breath to exhale the words. Instead she reached inside her bag and handed over the death notice. The master took the card, noted the name, and walked over to a record book.

He ran his finger down the page, scanning the records. "Ah, here we have it. Mr. Berry died two days past. Do you have plans for his burial?" The coldness and finality continued to torment Sarah.

"Sir, we do not have the means to afford the burial my Thomas deserves." Sarah choked on the words. "I need to understand what options lie before me. If you would be so kind as to tell me, I would be most appreciative."

"Mrs. Berry, the Guardians shall provide for a basic burial. Unless you direct otherwise, Mr. Berry will be interred here on the workhouse grounds in a common grave with no marker."

To the master, this was business as usual. To Sarah, it was worse than her own death. The thought of Thomas being buried with complete strangers made Sarah's blood run cold. For a brief moment, she wished she had died with Thomas. This could not be happening. It couldn't be real.

"No, Sir, that will not do. Thomas shall not be buried on the workhouse grounds." Sarah was adamant about that.

"Well, Madam, we also have the option of Southern Cemetery just outside the workhouse grounds. The Guardians shall cover the cost of a similar burial. Cremation and markers have an additional cost."

Thomas' mother and father were both buried in Southern Cemetery. They had died of fever within days of one another and were buried together. It was a common, unmarked grave, but at the very least they were buried together. It gave Sarah some comfort that Thomas would be buried in the same cemetery as his parents.

Sarah could not afford a fancier casket, nor could she afford an engraved headstone. Sarah had to be practical, despite the agony of doing so. There was little money, and what money was available had to provide subsistence to Samuel, James, and the girls. To spend their money on anything other than basic needs would have been seen as irresponsible by Thomas.

"Thomas shall be buried at Southern Cemetery, Sir."

"Very well, Mrs. Berry," the master said agreeably. He reviewed another record on his desk, noting its contents with a nod.

"There shall be two others from this infirmary along with Mr. Berry. The interment will take place the day after next. If you go see your way over to Southern Cemetery and seek out a Mr. Barton, he shall provide you with the specific details."

The offer was not made to see Thomas. Sarah was unclear of the rules of such matters. In her heart, she could not bear the thought so it was just as well. She wanted to remember Thomas the way he was, not in the state he found himself at present. Her Thomas was gone. He had left the moment he passed. His soul and spirit were now with their Lord, in peace, and despite her own suffering, she was happy for him.

"Sir, I would like to make a request of you, if I may," Sarah questioned. "I would like my Thomas to be buried in his uniform. I have brought it with me." Sarah held out the bag and placed it on the master's desk.

"That could be arranged, Mrs. Berry." The master held out his hand in request of the garments. Sarah opened the handbag and handed him a smaller paper bag that sat inside. He took it and looked inside to note its contents and then placed it on the floor beside his desk.

Thomas' personal effects were handed over in a similar bag. "This is all that Mr. Berry came in with, Madam." Upon the final transfer, the master signalled for the porter to take Sarah to the gate.

"My condolences to you and your family, Mrs. Berry. May God speed your healing."

Sarah was not offended by the coldness and routine nature of his sympathies. She was so numb to the day's events that nothing could move her from the dark place that she found herself in.

The porter reappeared and ushered Sarah out the same door she entered from mere moments earlier. But, in those few moments, the reality of her circumstance formed the acknowledgement that she was no longer a wife. She was now a widow.

Sarah had watched her mother transform from wife to widow. She had watched aunts, cousins, and neighbours do the same. Each woman endured the tragedy of a lost love, but the emotional toll, the indescribable loneliness, was pushed back to the depths of their being. They could not mourn, for mourning was a luxury that few could afford.

Some prayed to God for support and some cursed God for their hardship. But, through it all, they fought for survival. The fine line between subsistence and absolute poverty couldn't be crossed. There was no going back.

Sarah left the gates of the workhouse, thanked the porter, and did not look back.

The day had turned bitterly cold and sleet fell from the sky, stinging Sarah's face and eyes. Her hat did little to stop the assault. The roadway was slick and walking became treacherous.

Sarah's feet ached as the icy wetness filled her boots through the seams. Any grip they may have once possessed was long gone and they slipped on the uneven surface, forcing her to catch herself every other step.

Sarah turned down Nell Lane. The vast expanse of the Southern Cemetery soon came into sight. Sarah made her way down to Barlow Moor and approached the main cemetery gate.

A layer of icy snow covered the wrought-iron top of the surrounding wall, which disappeared into the distance. The cemetery office was located inside the main gate. The stone building was befitting a place of death, with its dark, gothic feel. Its steeply pitched roof was as harsh as the reality of Sarah's circumstance. The tower and spire stood as a marker for the entrance to eternity. It wasn't warm and inviting, but rather cold and unforgiving.

Sarah approached the building and entered the front door. She was greeted by an elderly lady with pale, wrinkled skin. The old woman moved slowly but deliberately, as if playing out a well-managed routine.

"Good afternoon, my dear. How can we be of service to you on this blessed day?" Her calm and cheerful manner was surprisingly comforting to Sarah and she found herself relax ever so slightly.

"I wish to see Mr. Barton, if I may," Sarah replied with a half-smile.

"Yes, of course. Please take off your wet coat so you can warm up, Love. I'm Mrs. Barton. I will show you to my husband after we get you nice and comfortable." Mrs. Barton clearly had a way with the bereaved and her goal was to make this part of the journey as comfortable as possible.

Mrs. Barton held out her hands in anticipation of Sarah removing her coat, which Sarah did gladly. It felt good to remove the damp weight. It was placed on one of the ornate hooks that hung on the heavily papered walls. Bright yellow sunflowers and daffodils adorned the walls in an attempt to bring some cheer. It was a stark contrast to the cold, dark winter outside.

"May I offer you a cup of tea, Miss…?" Mrs. Barton said, hesitating as she waited for Sarah's name.

"I'm very sorry. My name is Sarah Berry. I'm here to see Mr. Barton to make arrangements for my husband, Thomas." Sarah rubbed her hands together in an attempt to warm them.

"My dear Mrs. Berry, I am so sorry to hear that. You are far too young to be a widow. But God works in mysterious ways and we have to trust His judgement, for it is never wrong."

Sarah choked back a tear and Mrs. Barton reached out to touch Sarah's shoulder. "Oh dear, let's get you some tea and a seat by the fire."

Mrs. Barton led Sarah through a door into an office. Her husband, Sarah presumed, sat behind the desk, which was heavy and ornate. It would have been built in the room because it was far larger than the doorway that Sarah had just walked through.

He was deep in thought, focusing on the papers on his desk. His concentration didn't break, and Mrs. Barton ushered Sarah over to a large, oversized chair in front of the fireplace.

Flames crackled and danced and gave off a warmth and glow that filled the room. Sarah thanked Mrs. Barton and took a seat, sinking back into it as though it had no form or substance. The flames were mesmerizing and Sarah's body began to relax.

Mrs. Barton returned with a cup of tea and Sarah accepted it happily. Sarah was left to drink her tea, and, as if on cue, Mr. Barton emerged as her cup was almost empty.

"Mrs. Berry, I understand you are here to make arrangements for your husband. We are most honoured that you have chosen Southern as Mr. Berry's final resting place."

"You are both very kind, Mr. Barton. The infirmary master sent me here. Mr. Berry died two days past and it is my wish that he be buried here at Southern. Both of his parents are buried here," Sarah offered. "We are of simple means, Sir, and cannot afford the burial that I would like for my Thomas, but his children and I shall be here to say our final good-byes."

It was clear the idea of poor did not register well with kind Mr. Barton. He abruptly stood up and cleared his throat. "Well, I see" was all that he could manage. Clearly Sarah's well-tailored clothing masked her status as effectively as Thomas' had.

He walked over to his desk and reviewed his register. "The Guardians shall provide for a common grave. They shall have Mr. Berry delivered the day after next. Transport occurs between eleven in the morning and noon. It is your right to be present for the interment."

Mr. Barton stopped his speech long enough to inquire as to the Berry's religious affiliation. Armed with that information, he continued.

"Interment shall occur in the M section of the cemetery. It is located at the north end, just alongside the central path. At this moment, we are looking at grave 377, but that could change in the next day depending on how quickly it fills. Now, Mrs. Berry, shall there be anything else?"

His abruptness caught Sarah completely off guard. She was dumbfounded.

"Well, good day then, Mrs. Berry." And with that, Mr. Barton returned to his desk and resumed his work.

Sarah stood there speechless. "Mrs. Berry, you shall find your coat on the hook where you left it."

Sarah turned and headed toward the door. "And, Mrs. Berry, morning chapel services are held at 10:30 and 11:00."

Sarah remained facing the exit as Mr. Barton spoke, and then without looking back continued through the door.

Sarah looked around for Mrs. Barton, but she was nowhere within sight. Sarah put on her coat and left the building. The sleet continued unabated and home could not come fast enough.

Chapter 6

As Sarah arrived at home, the sun was just setting in the western sky. Despite the daylight, darkness had loomed all day as the thick clouds hung over the city surrendering what they could not carry.

Upon hearing the door, Margaret came to the front room, wiping her hands on her apron. She walked up to her mother and started to unbutton her coat. She struggled with the buttons as moisture had stiffened the material. She removed it and hung it in its usual place. Water dripped from its bottom, forming a puddle on the floor beneath it. Sarah removed her hat and placed it on the table where it sat wet and wilted.

Margaret retrieved her mother's slippers and motioned for her to sit down. Sarah obeyed, too tired to do otherwise. Margaret unlaced the wet boots and pulled with all her might to remove them. As they broke free from Sarah's swollen feet, Margaret fell backwards and landed on her derrière. The tension in the room was lightened with a giggle.

She removed the stockings and dried Sarah's feet. She placed slippers on her feet and then laid her head in her mother's lap. Sarah put her hand on Margaret's head and gently stroked her hair. No words were spoken.

Agnes and Mary emerged from upstairs. "Mama," they squealed with delight and ran to Sarah. Margaret had kept them busy to isolate them, keeping their thoughts carefree. As Sarah embraced her girls, she noticed the aroma emanating from the kitchen.

"What is that I smell, Margaret? You have been a busy girl, it would appear." Sarah beamed with pride through her exhaustion.

"Yes, Mama, I have made a pottage for supper. I used what I could find in the pantry and James brought home some scraps from the market. I made some bread also."

"Thank you, Margaret. This is an unexpected treat." Sarah made her way into the kitchen to check on Margaret's work. The stew was simmering in an iron pot on the coal stove. The bread was cooling on the table.

Occasionally, as was the case today, James was able to pilfer some meat scraps that were destined for the local feed house. It was James' job to deliver what the market considered waste, and he was able to separate the good from the bad and share what he could with his family.

James arrived at home shortly after six. He greeted his mother with a kiss on the cheek.

"Did you see the scraps I brought?" James was proud of his accomplishment and never viewed it as stealing. It was destined for animal feed, and the animals wouldn't miss it, he figured.

"We shall eat well tonight and I have you and Margaret to thank for that," Sarah said, too tired to smile any further.

As they sat down at the table, Sarah spooned pottage into small bowls. She ripped off pieces of bread and shared them with her children. They all bowed their heads and Sarah thanked God for the food placed before them. She wasn't ready to pray for Thomas yet.

The pottage consisted of the pork scraps that James had retrieved, along with potatoes and corn from the last harvest. Margaret had shucked the corn of its kernels earlier that day and let them simmer in the pot to attempt to return some of their original tenderness. By December they became terribly stale and chewy.

Sarah purposely kept the conversation light. James spoke of his fifteen deliveries around Ardwick. The slushy roads made riding his bike difficult and at one point he had tumbled of his bicycle, spilling his delivery on the wet ground. He was terrified he would be reprimanded, but Mrs. Taylor had been understanding and said nothing. The market owner, on the other hand, had no patience for accidents, however truly accidental they were.

Margaret had tidied the house and cooked the meal. Her sisters were behaved for the most part, and it was the first time that Sarah noticed how mature Margaret was becoming.

The wind whistled through the crack in the window frame and the breeze moved across the room. It encircled the flame of the lamp causing it to flicker and sputter. Nothing of the meal remained, with the exception of bread, when all had filled their bellies. For the moment, they were content.

Margaret cleared the table and wiped the bowls with a wet rag. James took the potato peelings and corn husks, which were sitting in a waste bin, out to the courtyard for dumping. Waste was strewn in small piles, and James made his contribution to one of them. The cold was uncomfortable, but were it not for the unrelenting chill the smell would have been unbearable.

The family retreated to the sitting room, where each kept busy. Sarah sewed while the girls read and played. James whittled a piece of scrap wood that he had found. His skill was extraordinary.

At about half past seven, Sarah took Mary and Agnes upstairs to dress for bedtime. With the exception of what was needed for breakfast, the last of the daily water supply was used to bathe. Sarah took a cloth and wiped down their faces. Full baths were only permitted once per week.

Sarah placed the girls in their bed and pulled the covers up to their faces. Sarah gave each girl a kiss and then sat on the side of the bed.

"Where is Papa?" Agnes inquired. Her daughter's simple question bore a hole in Sarah's heart.

Sarah hesitated, wondering if she should tell them again or wait until the morning came. Sarah did not want to have that conversation with the girls tonight, but tomorrow she knew would not be any better.

"My dear, sweet girls, your father has gone to heaven to be with the angels. He shall always be with us in spirit, but he won't live with us any longer."

Agnes looked awestruck. "Do you mean Papa has wings like the angels?" she asked.

Mary was caught up in her sister's excitement even though she didn't understand what her mother was saying.

"Yes, Agnes, just like that."

They did not understand and reality would set in soon enough. With that the girls each got one more kiss and Sarah left them to sleep.

Sarah carried the lamp out of the room and joined James and Margaret downstairs. At half past eight, Samuel arrived home dirty, wet, and tired. Sarah greeted her eldest son with a warm embrace.

Once Samuel had removed his wet coat, he went into the kitchen and stood next to the coal stove. The coals were still hot from supper. Samuel opened the door and held his hands out to warm them. Sarah reached into the cupboard and pulled out some of the bread from the meal, spread on a thin layer of preserves, and handed it to her son.

Sarah called James into the kitchen from the front room. When both boys were sitting at the table, Sarah spoke of her day.

"My boys, I have some sad news I must share with you. This morning I received word from the infirmary that your father died two days past."

The boys stared at Sarah emotionless, the lamp light creating shadows on their faces that made it difficult for Sarah to see their reaction.

After a moment of silence, Sarah continued. "Your father loved you both very much. He was proud of you beyond words. As you know, it is not for us to question God's will. It was God that decided your father should join him in heaven, and we must abide by His plan. We shall miss him tremendously, but we shall endure."

The boys did not move. They could only stare at their mother in shock.

James was the first to speak. "Mama, what shall we do? How shall we live?"

"James, your father worked hard. Everything he did, he did to give us a better life. It was your father's dream that you and your brother could rise to a place better than he found himself in. That is every father's wish.

Your father shall not be here to see you grow into men, but you still owe him your best. You owe your father the best life that you can give yourself. He shall be watching down from heaven and he shall accept no less, nor shall I. Do you understand?"

Both boys acknowledged their mother's words and nodded in agreement. "Yes, Mama. We shall make our father proud of us. You have our word. We shall also take care of you and our sisters."

Once the children were all in bed, the house became eerily quiet. Sarah was alone with her thoughts and she could not turn them off. Thomas' love had touched her so deeply and had filled her with a completeness that she had never known before. He could never be replaced and she knew that she would never feel that way again.

Sarah stood at the cabinet eyeing the wooden box. But, instead, she reached out and removed a ceramic flask. A cork sealed its contents.

Sarah walked to the table and placed the flask down as she sat in her chair. She studied the vessel as though it were the first time she had laid eyes on it. Its round body had a broad base and tiny circular handle. The name on the front acknowledging its origin had become worn. In the dark, Sarah could not read it. The scotch that filled it had been a gift to Thomas from Eleanor on the day of Samuel's birth, and he had coveted his prize as though it were filled with the last drops on earth.

Every year on Samuel's birthday, he would allow himself a few small sips. He was rationing it until Samuel was old enough to share with him what remained. Sarah dropped her head in sadness at the thought that day would never come.

Sarah removed the cork and lifted the flask to her nose. She inhaled the essence and shuddered. It wasn't the liquid she smelled but Thomas. He would kiss her after he swirled the earthy liquid in his mouth and Sarah would enjoy the remnants that had lingered on his lips.

And, on this unbearably cold and dark night, she succumbed to her urges. She lifted the flask to her mouth and let the liquid pour until her cheeks were full. And, before her tongue started burning, she swallowed. She gasped for breath, sputtering until she was able to inhale again. She licked her lips quickly, careful not to waste any of it. Then she lifted the flask to her mouth once more.

Sarah turned her eyes to the oil lamp, and as her body warmed from within, she became entranced with the dancing flames. The scotch transformed her and she so desperately needed to numb the pain.

After a short while, Sarah replaced the cork, returned the flask to the cabinet, and made her way upstairs. She climbed into bed with Margaret, and as she put her head on the pillow she felt as though she were floating. The scotch's effects had not yet abated and she was glad for it. But Sarah succumbed quickly, caught in an eddy of motion, dizzying, falling swiftly, waiting for an end. She commanded, but her body did not obey. Walking by a river, she saw the brightest blue sky she had ever seen. The water was crystal clear. All that stood before Sarah was bathed in a warm light that seemed to come from nowhere, and yet it was everywhere. It was endless and ethereal.

She recognized the path by the river, the one where she and Thomas walked every Sunday before they were married. She continued along the path studying the flowers of every colour that so abundantly and brilliantly lined it.

"Sarah," she heard in a whisper.

Sarah turned around, not seeing where the voice was coming from. It was familiar but made no sense.

"Sarah, my love," the voice repeated.

As Sarah turned around again, Thomas stood before her. He was framed by a warm glow.

"I have missed you, my darling," he said softly.

Thomas didn't move. It was inconceivable to Sarah how he could be standing before her. "Thomas, I don't understand," Sarah said in a state of wonder.

Thomas' smile was reassuring to Sarah, and as she revelled in the moment he held out his hands. Sarah walked toward Thomas and she took his hands in hers. He felt as real to her as the air she breathed. Thomas embraced Sarah and she melted into his arms. *This can't be real*, she thought, but she so desperately wanted it to be, needed it to be real.

"Sarah, my love, I shall always be here for you. But my journey is over. You have a great one that lies before you yet. It shall be arduous, but it shall bring you tremendous joy. You must persevere."

Thomas gently pulled away from Sarah and took a few steps backwards. She didn't understand what was happening. Thomas told Sarah that he loved her, and then he began to fade, dissipating from the unimaginable scene, blending into a garden of colour. Sarah began to panic at the thought.

"No, Thomas, you can't leave me," she begged.

"My darling Sarah, you know that our love is eternal."

The haunting whisper of Thomas' voice filled the room as Sarah awoke. The sound echoed in her ears. She heard it as clearly as the gasp that escaped from her beating chest. Consciousness brought a realization that something had happened to her that she could not explain. Thomas was as real to her as he had been every day of their life together.

Sarah played the scene out in her mind, and something he said took her breath away as she thought of it: *Our love is eternal*. Sarah had written those very words on a piece of paper before placing it in the pocket of his porter uniform.

It felt like an eternity before Sarah fell asleep again. But eventually she succumbed to the heaviness once more. By the morning, her memories were only of a vivid dream. Sarah thought it might be wise to stay away from scotch in the future.

Chapter 7

James and Samuel arose early to fetch the water they would need for the next few days. Saturday night was the time set aside for the weekly bath, but the previous night hadn't been a routine one for them. So both boys went to the community pump to gather what they needed. They took two trips, unloading the water into a large copper pot between visits.

After Sarah warmed the water, the children bathed and dressed for church. Oldest to youngest was the routine, Sarah being the exception. And when all were squeaky clean, James and Samuel removed the bath water and took it outside while Sarah made potato pancakes. They ate in silence, each deep in their own thoughts.

They walked the five blocks to church together. Away from the sun, the morning was cool and crisp, coating the store windows in a foggy dew. But, in the sun, a warm glow blanketed the street. Sarah smiled at the memory.

The vicar announced Thomas' passing and the parishioners who knew Sarah turned toward her. A few looked on sadly, but most were apathetic. They were too busy trying to survive themselves and there simply wasn't any energy left for sympathy.

As they exited the church, Sarah remembered they were to have dinner with Eleanor. It had completely escaped her mind. At first she thought she could not endure a visit, but Eleanor was her dearest friend and she would be hurt if she was not told in time to attend the burial.

The boys headed directly home and the girls stayed with Sarah, who had planned on visiting the Jewish market. It was open on Sunday and Sarah had not been able to purchase what she needed the day before. Flour, lard, butter, potatoes, onions, cheese, dried peas and salted pork were on the list. Sarah and Margaret shared the load on the journey home.

When they arrived, the children undressed from their Sunday best and changed into their everyday clothes. Sarah resumed her sewing, while the two youngest played beside her. James shovelled coal into the stove and Samuel worked to repair a cabinet door that was loose on its hinges. Margaret spent her time making pease porridge for their evening supper.

At about half past one, the family dressed for Eleanor's. The sun was fully hidden behind the thick grey clouds and the air was moist. There weren't many people out and about during the ten minute walk to Eleanor's house. Shops were closed and generally it was the beggars who milled around.

Sarah and her family were clean and well-dressed so they were targets for the street urchins. The adults were more apt to shelter themselves in the alleys while the children were sent to scour the neighbourhood. They would beg, and what they couldn't beg for they would try to take if the opportunity presented itself. Agnes and Mary were taunted by the young street walkers, many of whom were roughly the same age. Their clothes were torn, tattered, and filthy, and their stench was beyond compare. They were constantly on the hunt for their next mark. You never walked alone after dark for fear you would be outnumbered in an assault and unable to defend yourself.

And while the locals viewed these children as an utter nuisance, Sarah felt their pain. She understood how easy it would be for a child to end up like that. Her own children were only one parent away. The thought of them having to beg for food on the street made her quail.

There was a separate entrance to Eleanor's flat, the door for which was beside the shop. Sarah rang the bell announcing their arrival and Eleanor appeared within a minute. She wore her disappointment plainly when she didn't see Thomas.

"Oh Sarah, Thomas is not home yet. I'm so sorry. You must miss him so."

Tears welled up in Sarah's eyes, and in unison the oldest children all dropped their heads. Their suffering was too apparent for Eleanor to misinterpret. She threw her arms around Sarah and began to cry. Sarah stifled her own cry as she comforted her friend, and the children stood there, still as statues.

When Eleanor had regained her composure, she took Sarah's hand and led the family upstairs. Eleanor lived modestly, and as such the children were not aware of her family's status or of the life that she lived as a child. Her furniture, while more substantial than they enjoyed, was understated and well worn. It had been her grandparent's furniture. When her grandfather had died, her father sold that property and had built an estate outside of town. He gave the furniture to Eleanor so that his new wife could buy pieces more befitting a country estate. Eleanor had no need for such frivolity and it suited her just fine.

The aroma of braised beef filled the air as they entered the flat. The children were always excited about dining with Aunt Eleanor. They sat in the sitting room, with a fire blazing. As was usually the case, James and Margaret sat at the chess board, prepared to duel until the death. Samuel picked at Eleanor's collection of books. As his godmother, Eleanor had been close to Samuel from the beginning. She shared her love of books with him and would give him a new one, one to be treasured and read over and over, every year on his birthday. Mary and Agnes sat down to play with the dolls that she kept just for them.

"My dear Sarah, please share the details with me so that I can be of assistance," Eleanor offered with sadness and concern.

"I received word from the infirmary yesterday and the arrangements have since been made. The burial shall be tomorrow morning." Sarah trembled as she spoke, looking down at her hands, which were playing with the lace on her dress.

Eleanor spoke quickly. "I shall arrange for my father's carriage for the morning. It shall be at our disposal. A train ride simply won't do."

Sarah was grateful and relieved. She dreaded the idea of the train ride, and she hadn't yet thought of the cost.

They sat down to Eleanor's meal and enjoyed the braised beef, biscuits, mashed potatoes and tangy cabbage slaw. And, as delicious as the meal was, it was what followed that they were most excited about. Eleanor had made a warm banana pudding, and they savoured every bite of the exotic treat.

Sarah and Eleanor picked at their food. Neither one had much of an appetite, but in contrast the children ate heartily. The children cleaned up after the meal as Sarah and Eleanor enjoyed a cup of tea in the other room.

With all the modern amenities, it never felt like a chore to clean Eleanor's kitchen. It had a gas stove and running water as all the newer homes did. It also had an indoor toilet, which was absolutely fantastic.

As the afternoon wound down, the children bid their farewells to Eleanor. Unbeknownst to Sarah, Eleanor had snuck her way down to her shop like a thief in the night and had rung her father. A carriage was arranged for the following day, as was a day of mourning for Samuel.

Eleanor's shop was one of only a few hundred in Manchester that had a telephone line. It was so new a service, and incredibly costly. Sarah's father had installed a line at his factory and another at his estate in the country, and he decided that Eleanor's shop should have one as well. It wasn't all over fatherly concern for his daughter's well-being. Truth be known, it was more for business and Eleanor had no illusions to the contrary.

Sarah thanked Eleanor and said her good-byes. Sarah was forever grateful for her friendship with Eleanor. It had spanned most of their lives and they had become like sisters. With Bertie in Canada and Thomas now gone, Eleanor was all she had beyond her children.

They awoke the following morning to wet and heavy snow. The children were fed and clothed in a manner befitting the final good-bye of their father. Sarah also packed James' work clothes as he would be dropped off at the market on the way home.

The carriage arrived at quarter past nine. It was about five miles to the cemetery, about an hour's journey. On the way, they stopped at the market.

Sarah prepared herself to exit the carriage when Eleanor insisted it be her. Sarah was too preoccupied to question her and she sat back down. A short time later, Eleanor exited the market with her purse in hand.

"James, you do not have to work today. Your employer has generously agreed to allow you a day of mourning," Eleanor said, smiling at him as she sat back down.

The ride was a long one. All seven squeezed into the carriage. Agnes and Mary sat on Sarah and Eleanor's laps. The two youngest had not experienced a carriage ride prior. They could not sit still, trying to see outside to catch a glimpse of the horses. To them, this was a thrilling adventure.

"My dear girls, please sit still. Mary, you are going to crush your dear Aunt Eleanor's knee with all that bouncing about."

Eleanor embraced Mary tightly from behind. "But, Mama, this is a great adventure and I cannot sit still," Eleanor said, teasing Sarah. Mary nodded in enthusiastic agreement while Sarah could only laugh at her friend's playfulness.

They arrived at the cemetery in time for the service. The chapel was empty except for Sarah, Eleanor, and the children. There was no music or ceremony, no greeters, and no flowers. There were no words spoken of Thomas and the man who he was. But the vicar did approach Sarah to express his sympathies for her loss, and Sarah appreciated the gesture.

Eleanor did not normally attend church, but she was moved by the vicar's words of challenge, redemption, and life ever after. When Eleanor's mother died, her family stopped going. And it wasn't that she closed herself off to God; she just stopped thinking about Him. Today the simple message touched her deeply. When the service was finished, Eleanor placed a generous gift in the offering box.

The carriage remained at the front of the property while they walked to Section M. Eleanor had begged Sarah to let her contribute to the burial, but Sarah would have no part of it.

Thomas was a proud man and he would have said that one should not waste money on things that do not matter. He would have said that a body is still a body no matter where it lay or what box it lay in. No amount of money or fancy headstone would bring you back.

Sarah did not fully agree, at least not in her present state of mourning, but she wanted to honour who he was.

They made their way down a long pathway, which was lined with tall trees on both sides. Through the trees, evenly spaced headstones covered the ground. A few had bouquets of silk flowers placed on them to brighten an eternal resting place. Brightly coloured petals were crushed under the weight of the ice and snow, and others lay there limp and damp from the misty air.

Sarah headed to the back of the cemetery, along the north wall. As they approached the end of the pathway, they could see a high mound of displaced earth. It was the only one like it in the area that Mr. Barton had directed them to.

Sarah's chest tightened as she saw the vast hole in the ground. The boys, being the curious lads they were, approached the hole to look inside. Sarah swiftly grabbed them by their sleeves and pulled them back.

The ground was hard and the grass encrusted with ice. The group stood close to each other for warmth. The wind whistled through the trees, and without their blanket of leaves there was nothing to stop the wind's power from numbing those in its path.

The girls shivered and whimpered as the occasional gusts unsteadied them. Sarah and Eleanor reassured them that it would be all right and they would soon be on their way. The boys remained stoic.

The cart that would bring Thomas to rest was not yet in sight. There was nothing to do but wait. As the moments dragged, Eleanor broke the silence by singing *Amazing Grace*. Despite the wind, the words hung in the air, as though fuelled by a power greater than any of them.

As they continued to sing, the horse and cart appeared in the distance. The clicking of the hoofs and rolling of the wooden wheels rose to a crescendo against the sweet sound of the music. The wagon came to a stop at the grave. The horses whinnied. The steam from their breath dissipated into the heavy winter air as the driver pulled back on the reins and set the brake in place.

Four men stepped off the wagon, two of them pulling the cover off the load in the back. Three basic coffins lay side by side. Sarah's knees buckled and Eleanor reached around her waist to steady her.

"Which one's yours?"

Eleanor spoke to spare Sarah the grief. "Thomas Berry was the beloved husband of our Sarah," she said gesturing to Sarah, "and the treasured father to these wonderful children."

The words had no impact on the man. He had no capacity for empathy. He announced, "Mr. Berry is second in line today. He'll be down there," he said, pointing to the hole, "with one below him." He patted the first coffin twice and said, "She'll be first."

Sarah cringed at the crudeness of his remarks. Her heart was breaking and Thomas was being treated like a dead animal.

The men lowered the first coffin into the ground. It was simply made, plain flat boards with no texture and lid securely nailed. The wood creaked as the ropes rubbed against its sides, much like the tall trees as they swayed in the wind.

The men grunted, straining under the coffin's weight. When it reached its resting place, they turned back for Thomas. As they pulled his coffin off the wagon, Eleanor spoke: "The Lord is my Shepherd I shall not want. He maketh me to lie down in green pastures. He leadeth me beside the still waters...."

She spoke those words to offer some comfort to Sarah and the children, but with enough power and conviction to ensure the men who were lowering Thomas to his final resting place felt something for him.

Agnes and Mary did not need comforting as they didn't fully grasp the finality of what was happening. James stood by them ensuring they did not move from where they stood. Margaret wept uncontrollably as Sarah tightened the grip on her daughter's shoulder. Samuel stood behind his mother. He was now the man of the family and he would make sure she was cared for as his father had done before. As Thomas was lowered into the ground, Eleanor finished reciting the Twenty-third Psalm.

As the men returned to the wagon for the last coffin, Eleanor ushered Sarah and the children away. There was no need for them to stand there any longer. The ground would not be filled in. There were more coffins yet to be added that day.

As they walked up the path back to the carriage, they passed a funeral in progress. A priest presided over the ceremony. More than a dozen people stood around the coffin, which was shiny and ornate. The priest's voice carried across the cemetery as he committed the dearly departed back to the earth, to a final resting place which would be shared with no one. Eleanor kept the pace quick to lessen the blow of the cruel contrast.

They boarded the carriage and made their way home, leaving Thomas behind forever. Sarah's thoughts turned to the words that he spoke to her in her dream. He said that she had a great journey before her. Sarah could not reconcile great journeys at the moment. She simply wanted to survive the day.

December 1903

It was four o'clock. Dinner was finished and James was waiting impatiently at the door as Margaret gathered what she needed for the week. James escorted Margaret to the train every Sunday afternoon, and he had done so every Sunday since young Victoria Mathews was found. Sarah was being fiercely protective, but she refused to let Margaret journey to the tram depot on her own in the dark.

This was Margaret's thirteenth summer. She was still a child in every way that mattered, but physical and emotional immaturity could not keep life's circumstance from consuming her and stealing her innocence. Even the death of her father had not adequately prepared her for the harshness that had become her every day.

Margaret had not wanted to leave school, but her family's financial situation had made the additional income a necessity. It was heartbreaking to her as she had been a diligent student and loved to learn. She had longed to become a doctor. But her mother was pragmatic and unmistakably clear in her thoughts. "You must have both want and will or your desires are merely childish dreams. They will occupy your mind and leave room for little else," she would say.

This dream was too special to have trampled so Margaret chose to share it with the only person who would understand. With Eleanor she could escape practicality and indulge in the ultimate pleasure of what could be. It was that indulgence that kept her from feeling completely powerless, trapped in a world where every aspect of her life was governed and her fate was not of her own making.

Margaret had both will and want, but what she lacked was means, and in the world she lived means were a curse that enslaved her in subservience and social inferiority.

"Hurry up, Margaret. You have woken up a sloth today." James stood at the door tapping his foot with impatience.

"Oh, bugger off, James," Margaret replied uncharacteristically.

Sarah entered the room hearing the exchange and voiced her astonishment. "Margaret! We do not speak such words in our home. I did not raise a foul-mouthed girl."

Margaret dropped her head in shame, and muttered a dutiful "Yes, Mama."

Sarah gestured to her daughter to come to her, and she did as commanded. Sarah softened. She caressed Margaret's chin while she held up her head so that she could look into her eyes.

"Margaret, my dear, I pray for your good fortune and well-being, and that the good Lord brings you back to me at week's end as you stand before me now."

Sarah wrapped her arms around her daughter and hugged her as she always did, as though that hug would be her last. With a kiss on the cheek, a whispered "I love you" in her ear, Margaret said, "Yes, Mama," and was through the door.

As Margaret and James stepped out onto Robinson Street, the sun had just set behind their home. It was getting darker by the moment and the grey landscape was blending into the dusk, making it difficult to distinguish.

They turned south, heading toward Manor Street. The half mile walk to the tram stop was an unpleasant one for Margaret. Margaret's personal sadness was amplified by the tension that permeated the town. Ardwick was on edge, and the tension was as thick as the smoke that choked it.

The residents, most of whom had grown indifferent to the violence that had become so commonplace, were now fearful for their safety and the safety of their children. Young Victoria Mathews was not yet ten when she died. By all accounts and recollections, she was an obedient girl with nary an ounce of trouble in her short life, and her good-natured disposition made her disappearance all the more troubling. As a baby, Victoria's father had died of typhoid, and her mother struggled to support the family on a woman's wages. Victoria was watched over by her siblings while her mother worked, and they did the best they could, but they were only children themselves.

Victoria was missing two days before she was found battered and lifeless in Ardwick Green, her body discarded like trash behind a row of bushes. Death and disease had become as much a part of life as breathing, but Victoria's death hit the town hard because it was at the hand of a vicious and invisible monster.

Ardwick Green had been converted to a public space some thirty years earlier when the city acquired it and turned it into a public park. It was an oasis amid unpleasant surroundings, but the pond and greenery couldn't hide the fact that a monster was amongst them.

As they progressed down Manor Street, the officers made their presence known before Margaret and James laid eyes upon them. Their shouts of solidarity rang through the streets with force and authority. They were there to protect, but the ominous tone that their calls evoked cast a frightening chill.

The Peelers were lined up on the south side of Ardwick Green, forming an impenetrable wall. In unison they marched like soldiers heading into battle. Their red uniforms blended together in a sea of colour, bringing an ironic vibrancy. They passed Margaret and James, focused on their march, and oblivious to their surroundings.

Vagrants stepped aside to make room for the procession. It took a few moments for the officers to pass, as they stood eight wide and ten deep. It was a shocking display.

Margaret and James walked the full stretch of Ardwick Green, approaching the tram depot where Stockport and Hyde Roads met. It was the main depot for Manchester Corporation Tramways, the largest of the tram companies in operation in Greater Manchester.

Margaret had been taking the tram every Sunday at this time for the past year. Catherine Markley insisted that she arrive by six o'clock so as to not disrupt her household. She insisted this of all the servants who did not reside full time at Amberley House.

Sarah did not like Margaret travelling in the dark and Margaret did not fancy it either, but leaving earlier meant less time with her family and for Margaret leaving later was worth the discomfort.

"James, this is all rather frightening. When is this going to stop?"

Margaret felt incredibly vulnerable. She reached out and looped her arm through her brother's for some comfort and warmth.

"Can't say. I suppose when they track him down. All I know is he's got to be a nutter. Nobody in their right mind would do that. I should go looking for 'em. Follow the clues and you'll find the answer. They always leave clues. The answer is right under your nose. That's what Samuel always says."

"Are you daft?" Margaret said incredulously. "As you said, he is probably a nutter. He probably lives in a cellar and eats rats and snakes and only comes out in the dark."

The officers had been present for the past week, marching at dusk as if to warn those who lurked in the darkness. They started when a second child, a boy, had gone missing. He had not yet been found.

Margaret reached the tram stop with the usual sadness. The lost look in her eyes broke James' heart. She gave him a massive hug and a kiss on the cheek. He was sombre as Margaret boarded the waiting tram, waving good-bye to her brother.

"Well, hello, Miss Margaret. How are you on this chilly evening? Looks like we could get some snow. I hope you've packed your woollies."

"Hello, Dennis. I am well, thank you. How is Charlotte doing?"

"She is well. Thank you for asking. Little Virginia lost her first tooth last week."

Dennis loved his family. Charlotte was his only child and he spoke of her with the greatest affection. With the exception of the day his wife died, which was a few months past, Dennis had been the driver on Margaret's Sunday journey each week. Their conversations made the forty-five minute journey bearable and helped keep her mind off the coming week.

She bypassed the fare-paying passengers and took her usual seat in the first row behind Dennis. Charles Markley was part owner in the Garden Tram Company and Margaret rode to Levenshulme at no charge.

The Garden Tram Company, which was based in Stockport, operated beyond greater Manchester, but had some overlap with Manchester's peripheral boundaries. Beyond the Stockport and Hyde Depot, which was the electric terminus, travellers were forced to transfer to horse-drawn trams to continue their journey. Margaret loved the horses and preferred the horse-drawn trams to the electric ones anyways so it suited her just fine.

The Markleys lived on eight acres just outside of Burnage, a quaint little village on the outskirts of Levenshulme. Charles Markley had commissioned Amberley House for his new wife, Catherine, who went on to spend the better part of two years appointing it with extravagance and excess. The property wasn't as large as he would have liked, or felt he was entitled to, so he made up for it with the grandeur of the architecture. To gain further favour with Catherine's father, the estate was named after Catherine's childhood home in Yorkshire, and where her father still held vast holdings.

When Margaret was past the age of mandatory schooling, she was put to work. As good fortune would have it, Eleanor was able to take full advantage of her family connections. She arranged for Margaret to be a maid at her father's home. There she would be safe, well-fed, and, with Eleanor's ties to the estate, checked on periodically. But, despite the fortunate position she found herself in, Margaret still needed to live away from home five to six days a week, which was difficult for her.

The sky was now dark and the air strikingly brisk. The chill wasn't enough to hide the smell of the horses, but Margaret didn't mind. She loved horses and dreamed of living like the Markleys. They had a stable full of horses, but most were used only for the carriages. Margaret considered it a tremendous shame. Horses should be loved and nurtured and not treated like machines.

As the horses whinnied, steam burst from their mouths. They shook their heads as if to try and extricate themselves from the harness that bound them to the driver and tram. Margaret wanted to set them free, but, just like her, they were imprisoned with no hope of escape.

The tram moved along Stockport Road. There was a constant drone as the metal wheels rolled over the track. There wasn't much activity out and about on Sunday evening. Most were home having a late dinner or early supper. Margaret watched the odd person milling around.

"Miss Margaret," Dennis shouted over his shoulder, "did you enjoy your time with your family?"

Dennis was a kind man who went out of his way to make Margaret's journey more pleasant. He had been a foreman in a brickworks factory for many years until a stack of bricks fell on him, mangling his leg. It broke in three places and he was never able to walk the same again. Fortunately, as a driver, he didn't have to move much. The pulley boys did most of the moving around. They notified the driver with a bell signal at the stops and helped the passengers on and off the tram.

"Thank you for asking, Dennis. Mama finished her work early on Saturday and we went with Aunt Eleanor to the dress shops in Salford. It was glorious. The dresses were so pretty." Margaret couldn't hide her girlish enthusiasm.

"That sounds wonderful. My Annie loved looking in the windows." Margaret could see the smile from Dennis' half turned head, but she didn't have to look to hear the suffering in his voice. The pain of her passing was still strong, and Margaret tried to steer the conversation to pleasant memories of Annie as they always made him happy.

"She was beautiful, just like my mama."

From behind, Margaret could see Dennis sit taller at the comparison, drawing his shoulders back as he beamed with pride.

Annie would sometimes ride the tram Sunday evening with Margaret. They would sit together in the front row behind Dennis. Their daughter Charlotte lived in Levenshulme with her husband and their grandchildren, and Annie would occasionally spend a few days a week helping out with the little ones. Margaret enjoyed her conversations with Annie, and she, too, felt a loss with her passing.

The trolley boy signalled from the upper deck that the next stop was approaching and Margaret looked on, as a matter of course, for Dennis' son-in-law, who would meet Annie at the stop when she was visiting. Today there was no son-in-law and Margaret knew Dennis' thoughts were in the same sad place. Two passengers alighted onto the street and then the tram was moving again.

The street lights flickered in the darkness, creating ghostly shadows. It was such a stark contrast to the lively hustle and bustle of the daytime when the motion of the people cast a constant, disorganized energy. At any point, there was no clear beginning or end. It continued on unabated.

On Sunday evening, by contrast, the stores were dark and empty. There were no business transactions taking place, apart from illegitimate ones, and no street-side conversations. It was as though the world went to sleep.

The tram continued down Stockport toward the edge of Levenshulme and the border of Heaton Chapel. Margaret's stop was High Lane, which sat as the transition between the two.

Margaret picked up her bag and made her way to the top of the stairs. Dennis smiled at her and tipped his hat.

"Evening, Miss Margaret. We shall see you in a week's time. May the good Lord bless you."

"Thank you, Dennis. And you as well."

And with that farewell, Margaret was on foot. A cold breeze kicked up and tugged at her hat, tightening the ribbon under her neck. She tucked her chin into the top opening of her coat to conserve her warmth.

Margaret turned off Stockport Road, heading west on High Lane. Between Stockport and the road to Amberley House, there were no buildings that immediately fronted the street. Lights could be seen in the distance, but the walk turned suddenly dark. There were markers at the rail crossing, which was a short distance off Stockport, but they didn't enhance the visibility. Margaret's heart always started racing as she stepped away from Stockport Road. It was the same week after week, and in this instance familiarity did not breed comfort.

It was roughly a half-mile journey down High Lane to the entrance to the Markley estate. It sat just before Stockton Farm. Charles Markley had purchased the land from his wife's father, Philip Armitstead, who had wanted to sever all his financial ties to the area. Philip had experienced some difficulties from past business dealings and had retreated in a cloud of embarrassment to his vast estate in Yorkshire.

Stockton Farm was part of that transaction, but there was a long-term lease on that section of the property. Ten years remained and Charles Markley was waiting that legal obligation out. In the interim, he was profiting nicely from the lease revenue.

It was about a fifteen minute walk from the tram stop to the entrance to Amberley House. High Lane was rough and extremely pitted from repeated carriage travel and it made for a rather precarious walk in the dark.

Margaret tried to remain in the centre of the lane to avoid the slope and loose earth at the lane's edge. The slope served to steer the water from forming puddles, but it made walking difficult. Margaret focused on the lights in the distance to guide her, but she occasionally stumbled in a pit.

There were a few estates ahead of the Markley's which, like the Markley's, were illuminated at their entrances. They served as her guide on High Lane.

The estate's private road leading up to the house was nearly five hundred feet long and not well lit. Thankfully, it was relatively straight. On this particular evening, the sky was clear and the stars bright. The moon was almost full and provided enough light to illuminate her path. Margaret was unaware of the exact time, but there had been no delays so she was confident she would arrive in time.

As Margaret approached the halfway mark, the distinctive sound of horse hooves on the road filled the air. Margaret instinctively stepped to the side as she turned to face the sound. Despite the dark, Margaret recognized Catherine's carriage. It was the one that Catherine preferred in the winter months as it was enclosed but had a front window that would allow Catherine to see what was in front of her. The moonlight blanketed the carriage, and the lantern beside the driver acted as a beacon of warning.

Margaret stood still as the carriage passed her. She recognized the driver, Reuben, as he sat alone on his seat up front. He warmly tipped his hat to her and Margaret nodded her head in acknowledgement. Margaret had seen Catherine through the front window as the carriage approached, but Catherine turned and momentarily locked eyes with her through the side door window. She was accompanied by the children's governess, Cecily, who also happened to be Catherine's niece.

It was clear to Margaret that Catherine did not like her. She often wondered if the dislike was for Margaret specifically, if she disliked all servants, or if it was dislike by association. Eleanor had asked her father to allow Margaret to join the staff and that infuriated Catherine who, aside from that insistence, was fully responsible for the household. She did not like being overruled, and she tolerated it only begrudgingly. Margaret believed it was association, but Margaret could also see that Catherine was pleasant to very few.

The carriage continued on, unabated, leaving Margaret as she was. Margaret paid the passing little thought. She recognized it was a matter of hierarchy and wishing it away was of no use.

Margaret continued toward the house. The garden lighting brought the grounds to life. As much as Margaret had no desire to be there, she was always awed by the sight. In the distance, it was a magical castle.

Over a gently rolling landscape, flickering gas lanterns illuminated a maze of winding pathways, as if beckoning visitors into a dark abyss. At night, it would seem there was no end. But it was not ominous; in fact, quite the opposite.

Beyond the front gardens, the house was alive with a warmth that emanated from the windows, silhouetting the elaborate draperies that adorned them. Lanterns stood at the base and top of the entry stairs like guards protecting the castle.

Every inch of the house was designed to impress. The brick was not local. It came from Russia. The marble was Italian. The fixtures were finished with a brushing of Welsh gold, from a supply close to where the Royal family sourced theirs. And the gardens were architected by the top landscapers England had to offer.

Electricity was not yet available in the Burnage area, and it was Markley's biggest frustration. Existing country estate homes were being retrofitted with electricity and, for those country properties with no access, it was produced on the property directly when it could be.

The property around Amberley House did not have a large enough water supply to produce the electricity needed to even partially power the home, but Stockton Farm did. For Markley, electricity would have to wait.

As Margaret approached the house, she stepped onto the path that would take her to the servant's building. It sat on the east side of the main house and was sheltered from view by massive English Oaks and dense ornamental bushes. Catherine was clear that she did not want to see the servants except when they performed their duties, and even then she wished they could do so invisibly.

The servant's building had seven rooms, four of which were bedrooms, two were toilets, and the remaining one a room for household supplies. At present there were eight full-time servants employed in the Markley household. There were two house maids, a stable manager, a stable boy, two drivers, a chef, and a scullery maid. The gardener was seasonal.

Margaret shared a room with the other maid, Agnes, and the scullery maid, Beatrice. Agnes was in her twenties and was like an older sister to Margaret. Agnes lived on the property seven days a week because her family could not afford to house and feed her. Even with that abandonment, she dutifully sent most of her earnings to her parents.

Until a week prior, there had been three house maids in the household. Catherine Markley had caught Lydia with the stable manager and had promptly fired her. The stable manager remained in her employ. For the life of her, Margaret could not understand that particular discrimination.

Jonathan was the stable boy. He was fourteen and the son of the driver, Reuben. Jonathan's mother had died during childbirth, and he had been sent to live with his aunt in Liverpool. Reuben paid for his care and, when he reached working age, he was brought to the Markleys. He was a good boy and a hard worker.

Jonathan was a year older than Margaret and the two had become good friends. There was nothing untoward about their relationship, certainly nothing that Catherine Markley could take issue with. Jonathan lived at Amberley House full time and he had no other friends his age. He appreciated Margaret's companionship as they had one significant thing in common: a love of horses.

Jonathan didn't live in the servant's house. He slept in the loft above the stables. Michael, the stable manager, on the other hand, had a room in the stable. It was here that his trysts with Lydia played out. Catherine had stumbled upon them while looking for Reuben one afternoon. She saw Lydia coming out of Michael's room. Her hair was tousled and she was straightening her skirt. It was clear to Catherine what had come before and it infuriated her.

Lydia had finished her shift for the day – for the week, in fact – so Catherine's anger could not have been based on any disregard of duties. Instead, Margaret surmised, it was based on jealousy, plain and simple. Lydia was attractive and men tended to take notice, and Catherine's own husband was no exception.

When Margaret returned to Amberley House the following evening, Agnes told her about the incident. Lydia had burst into the room, crying inconsolably. She didn't speak to Agnes. She gathered her things and was gone.

Agnes went in search of answers. She was aware of the relationship with Michael. Lydia had spoken of him with great affection. It appeared that affection was mutual because Michael was truly bereft at her departure. He told Agnes of the confrontation with Catherine Markley and how she went absolutely mad with anger. Michael said he didn't know what he would do. He was in love with Lydia and now she was gone.

So, for the time being, Margaret had only two roommates. She was the youngest, with the least seniority, so her bed sat directly underneath the window. While it was pleasant to look up at the stars when she lay awake at night, it was uncomfortably draughty.

Lydia's bed, in contrast, had been on the opposite side of the room. Margaret felt horrible for benefiting from Lydia's misfortune, but it would have been silly to have let the moment pass.

Both of the drivers and the gardener were considered senior members of the staff and were each given their own rooms. Not surprisingly, they were also men. They were housed on the second level and shared a common bath. The exception was Nicolas, the chef. He had a room on the main level of the main house. The Markleys paid him handsomely and he was afforded certain privileges. The only thing worse than not having a notable chef in your employ was having one and then losing him to another family.

The women were on the main level next to the storage. They, too, shared a single bath. For Margaret, the plumbing was such a luxury. There was running water, toilets that flushed, and a tub that she could fill without having to cart water in.

There wasn't much for Margaret to do in the evening. She filled her time reading books that Eleanor had given her, knitting, and visiting the horses in the stable.

On that particular Sunday evening, Margaret decided to visit the stable. When she arrived, Jonathan was grooming Napoleon, a soot black Arabian stallion. Napoleon was a pet of Philip's, the Markley's youngest son. He had been a gift from Catherine's father.

Jonathan acknowledged Margaret's arrival with a smile. Margaret noticed Philip sitting on a bale of hay as she entered the stall.

"Hello, Philip. Did you have a nice day?"

Margaret enjoyed engaging Philip in conversation. He was nine years old and a sweet boy, but terribly lonely. He was unlike his older sister, who was an absolute shrew. Margaret often mused at how these two could have come from the same family.

"I did, thank you, Margaret. I caught a rabbit on the back of the property. Mum told me to drop the filthy animal, but it didn't look filthy to me. Jonathan made a home for it," he said as he pointed to a cornered off area of the stall. "We'll have to move it so it doesn't spook Napoleon."

Margaret walked over to the rabbit and took a closer look. It was snow white and didn't seem bothered by all the attention. Its only interest was in the carrot it was voraciously chewing. "What shall you name it?" Margaret asked.

"Snowflake, I believe. It suits him, don't you think," Philip asked as he looked for validation.

"It absolutely does, Philip. It's perfect."

Margaret picked up a grooming brush and started to brush Napoleon. He whinnied and turned his head toward her. At the acknowledgement, Margaret took a few steps forward and scratched under Napoleon's chin.

"Well, aren't you a happy boy this evening?" Napoleon nuzzled into Margaret's head and she melted with the affection. Nothing compared to the love of an animal.

"I must go inside for dinner. My mother will come looking for me if I'm late. Good night." Philip said, and as he walked off Jonathan reassured him he would move Snowflake to a place where he would be safe for the night.

The Markleys ate their main meal around seven in the evening. The servants, excluding Cecily of course, ate their main meal earlier. Dinner for them was at two.

Jonathan and Margaret finished brushing Napoleon. They tied him up to a post in the main area of the stable while they went up to the loft and made a temporary home for Snowflake. Together they sectioned off a small corner of the loft with bales of hay. Jonathan tossed in the remaining carrots that Philip had been given by Beatrice from the scullery.

"I think that shall work," Jonathan said approvingly. "He looks comfortable enough. Philip'll be happy."

Margaret thought about the prison that Snowflake now found himself in and it bothered her. But the happiness that it would bring Philip outweighed any discontent it would cause the rabbit, she thought, easing her conscience. Philip was starved for companionship and this would do nicely.

"It is getting late. I must get to my room. I'll put Napoleon in his stall on my way out," Jonathan said to Margaret as she stood up to leave.

The loft room that Jonathan slept in was built of thick timber for support and insulated with straw. Straw did a reasonable job keeping the wind and cold out. A few heavy wool blankets covered the bed that he slept on and they kept him warm on the cold winter nights. There was a modern toilet beside Michael's room that Jonathan was able to use, but in the dark of the night it was tremendously difficult to get up and down the ladder stairs. There were a few late night tumbles and Jonathan learned that a couple of well-placed bales of hay would help cushion any fall.

Chapter 9

Monday morning, as with all mornings at Amberley House, began at half past six for Margaret. Beatrice was up an hour before, hard at work in the scullery.

Margaret and Agnes dressed and were in the kitchen promptly at seven, when they joined the others at the table for breakfast. Beatrice served bread and preserves and a pot of porridge and then sat down herself. Beatrice was the scullery maid, and she also provided the servants with their meals.

"Jonathan, how did Snowflake fare last night?" Margaret questioned.

"Well, I believe," Jonathan said. "He didn't seem too out of sorts. He ate his carrots and looked as though he was ready for more."

The others were happy to have something new to discuss, as there rarely was. Conversation, while friendly, tended to be mundane.

"Snowflake is a rabbit that Philip found at the back of the property yesterday. We made a home for him in the barn and fed him some carrots that Beatrice shared with us."

Beatrice was happy to offer up the scraps, as she, too, liked young Philip. "I have some more vegetables that I put in a bucket for you to take to the stable after breakfast."

"Thank you, Beatrice." Jonathan enjoyed having the extra company in his room nearly as much as Philip enjoyed having a new pet.

Margaret left the room at half past seven, ready to begin her full day of chores. Their household responsibilities were decided by Catherine Markley and weren't necessarily divided fairly, but Margaret persevered. Complaining would only make matters worse, and deep down she believed her situation temporary.

Agnes stayed behind to help Beatrice clean the breakfast dishes from the kitchen and Margaret made her way up to the bedrooms. The Markleys were down in the dining room by this time having their breakfast and there was little chance of running into them in their private rooms.

Margaret ascended the staircase, which was a stunning mixture of stone, wrought iron, and gold leaf accents. It was blanketed with an intricately designed, hand-woven rug of pale green and yellow silk from India. The walls were covered in oil paintings that spanned the centuries. Most were recently purchased at auction specifically for Amberley House.

Markley's parents had been only moderately wealthy, and they were not ostentatious. There had been nothing of significance to pass down. Catherine's parents were still alive, and with Catherine being the youngest of ten children, there was little likelihood she would receive anything more than the family connections that Charles had married her for.

The long hallway that led to the bedrooms was lined with more paintings, each one more beautiful and finely detailed than the last. Markley had met a French painter named Paul Gauguin when he was younger and had purchased two paintings. He wasn't overly fond of them, but when Gauguin died and the painting's value soared he gained a newfound appreciation for them. Margaret was taken with their vibrancy, of the life that sprang from their canvases, and the stories they told. She studied each one up close and from a distance, amazed at how their intricacy teased the eye, and their colours blended so beautifully.

Philip's room was the last room in the hall, and the one that Margaret cleaned first. It was a handsome boy's room, full of the earth tones of the English countryside and of horse imagery. His bed, which was the centre point of the room, was an elaborately carved sleigh bed. It was covered with a duvet that was emblazoned with an armoured knight on horseback. The horse was high up on his rear legs, preparing for charge.

Above his bed was a painting of Philip and Napoleon that his grandfather had commissioned. Brass gas wall sconces hung on either side of the painting and an eighteen light gothic gaselier hung from the centre of the room. A carved rocking horse stood in the corner.

Philip's room faced the back of the estate. He had a clear view of the stable and the servant's building, which he enjoyed.

Margaret looked forward to making the beds. As she ran her hands over the wrinkles to smooth them out, the silkiness was beyond anything her imagination could have dreamt. She couldn't fathom sleeping in such luxury.

On Philip's bedside table were photographs of the family at the country home in the Lake District. But most importantly to Philip, there was a horse that James had carved for him. On occasion, before Margaret went to work for the Markleys, Philip and Anabel would visit with their sister, Eleanor, and she would invite Sarah's children over. Philip had taken a liking to James, and James had made a carving of Napoleon for him. It was one of his favourite possessions.

Anabel, on the other hand, took a liking to very few. She had no time for those she perceived as inferior. To a certain extent, she thought her older sister inferior as well. To live in such deplorable conditions was appalling, but to do so willingly was absolutely mad.

Anabel's room was as Margaret would have expected. It was a room fit for a princess. The four poster bed had pale pink organza from China draped over the cross beams. The linens were similar to Philip's, but were covered in a heavy woven brocade of lilies and maiden's breath. The painting that hung over her fireplace was of herself, alone, sitting on a blanket beside Esthwaite Water, alongside where the family's summer home sits in North Lancashire.

Anabel's room glowed with white and pretty pastels, but Margaret preferred Philip's more masculine stable and leathered look.

Across the hall from Philip and Anabel's room sat Catherine and Charles' room. It spanned the length of both their children's rooms. It was French in design, with elaborate English rococo inspired wainscoting. The bed was a Chippendale, and the bed coverings were woven silk of black, red, and gold from China. The remainder of the furniture that filled the room was a mixture of Thomas Johnson and Chippendale.

Over the fireplace hung a large tapestry depicting Marco Polo's exploration of Asia in the thirteenth century. It had been given as a gift by Sir Claude Maxwell MacDonald, British Ambassador to China, whose parents were friends of Philip Armitstead. The ambassador was a relationship that Charles Markley had earned through his marriage into the Armitstead family. Sir Claude had become a business acquaintance of Charles Markley and was advising him on expanding his business dealings into Asia.

Both Catherine and Charles had separate dressing rooms and water closets. Both were elaborately shelved and filled with richly designed clothing and outerwear. The furniture was very much an extension of the bedroom's furniture.

It took Margaret a considerable amount of time to finish the Markley's bedroom as neither of them was overly tidy. The linens were laundered twice per week, and the water closets cleaned daily. It was the same routine in the children's rooms. The guest rooms, which lined the west hallway, were only cleaned as required.

After Margaret finished cleaning the family's bedrooms, she made her way down to Catherine Markley's study. Catherine was not in the home as she had taken the train to London to complete her Christmas shopping. Christmas was only a few weeks away.

As with all of the rooms upstairs, the study belonging to the lady of the house was filled with impressive furniture and artwork. The main desk was a Louis XIV and was considerable and ornate. The painting that hung over the fireplace was a Louise Élisabeth Vigée Le Brun portrait of Catherine's great grandparents, who had been friends of Élisabeth. It had been given to Catherine by her grandmother. Margaret studied the painting as she swept the floor. The colours were captivating and Margaret never tired of it.

Margaret's next room was the library. It was here that the children received their daily lessons. They had attended boarding school in Cambridge until recently, but Charles decided it was too great a distance. Catherine was searching for suitable alternatives.

Margaret was careful not to disturb the group as she entered. She began her work dusting the furniture on the far side of the room. The tutor, Miss Stockwell, was deep in a math lesson. Philip looked up at Margaret and was promptly scolded. And, as Margaret stoked the fire, Agnes entered the room and announced that luncheon was being served in the dining room.

After Margaret finished cleaning Catherine's study, she made her way to the kitchen for her own meal. All the servants were sitting down to dinner, with the exception of Reuben, who was running errands for Charles Markley, and Beatrice, who was busy serving the meal.

The salty smell of braised ham hocks filled the kitchen. Beatrice brought out the meat, along with cheese, bread, and boiled potatoes and then joined the table. They drank apple juice that Beatrice had canned the previous summer. The household budget provided for canning supplies and Beatrice canned all sorts of produce in season so that it could be enjoyed during the winter months. The servants also drank ale, milk from Stockton farm, and water from the well.

Catherine had created a list of servant meals that could be prepared by Beatrice. The meals weren't all that different from what Margaret ate at home with her family.

The servants were also permitted a supper meal, one later in the evening after the Markleys had finished their dinner. It usually consisted of soups or breads left over from the Markley's dinner. Catherine's generosity generally stopped there, though. She would rather the *plat principal* be discarded than enjoyed by the servants. Margaret added it to the growing list of things that made no sense to her. Throwing away food was an utter crime as far as she was concerned, especially food that delectable.

Margaret liked the social aspect of mealtimes, but most importantly she liked the fact that the kitchen was the only room in the house that Catherine never entered. It was completely beneath her to set foot in there. She particularly enjoyed seeing Jonathan and Reuben interact. They had a close relationship and it reminded her of home. On that day, as they ate their braised ham hocks, Margaret watched Chef Nicolas prepare the Markley's evening meal. Chef Nicolas had been trained at the Sorbonne in Paris and his mastery of the cooking arts was exemplary.

Nicolas winked at Margaret as he covered the pheasants with a specially prepared herb and sea salt mixture. He always said that food needed to be nurtured. Food worth eating required care and attention, and most of all it required a love of creative risk. No two meals were the same. Slight nuances in flavours made each meal unique.

Margaret enjoyed watching Chef Nicolas when she was afforded the opportunity. She took a keen interest in what he prepared and how he prepared it. The smells were fantastic, and occasionally Chef Nicolas would allow her to sneak a taste of the sauces. Tonight's sauce was a port wine, tarragon, and Dijon reduction. Simply divine.

Nicolas was not an arrogant chef, not in the least. He genuinely loved cooking and experienced tremendous joy when his meals were enjoyed. Nicolas encouraged Margaret's interest and he was happy to explain his work. Nicolas also taught Beatrice the fine art of spices, and taking the poorest cuts of meat and braising them into the most succulent of meals. It was all in how you prepared them, he would say. All the servants were grateful for his tutelage.

"Margaret, do you have any plans for your birthday on Saturday?" Agnes asked inquisitively.

Jonathan was caught off guard and appeared annoyed with himself that this was news to him. "Margaret, I did not know it was your birthday on Saturday."

"The Markleys shall be at home this weekend so I must work on Saturday, but at the end of my day I shall visit with my Aunt Eleanor. She has invited me to stay with her overnight. I shall have an opportunity to try what I have learned from Chef Nicolas." This time it was Margaret's turn to wink at Nicolas.

With the exception of Agnes, the other servants were not aware that Aunt Eleanor was, in fact, Eleanor Markley. Margaret did not want them to know for fear it would cloud their judgement of her or have them believe she was getting preferential treatment, which it was quite clear she was not.

"What are you going to prepare for dinner, Margaret?" Jonathan asked.

"I am making a roasted chicken. I am quite excited." But, Margaret didn't need to speak of her excitement. It was written all over her face.

"Margaret, a chef's greatest gift is enthusiasm. It propels you to create and invent. I look forward to hearing the result on Monday." Chef Nicolas was pleased and proud of Margaret's passion.

"Beatrice, this meat is superb today," Margaret complimented. "You are becoming an impressive chef yourself."

Beatrice beamed at the compliment. When they were finished, they carried their dishes into the scullery and resumed their afternoon chores.

Monday was the day the servant's building was to be cleaned, and it was Margaret's responsibility. She would spend the remainder of the day sweeping and dusting the rooms, cleaning the water closets, and scrubbing the tile floors in the rooms and hallways. The servants were responsible for making their own beds.

It was altogether common for the servants to sleep in the attic, but Catherine did not want them in the main house. She won that battle with her husband, but he insisted the servant's building be appointed with the same flooring and fixtures as the main house so that Amberley House, if sold, would retain its value. She begrudgingly agreed. It pained her to think that the servant's accommodations exceeded the level she felt they deserved.

The workday ended after the dining room was cleared of all remnants of dinner. It was then that the servants sat down for their supper about eight. The younger servants, the ones with the most arduous jobs, were exhausted and hungry by day's end. The conversations at this meal were never as lively, nor was the laughter as abundant.

With Christmas fast approaching, Margaret needed to complete the wool scarves that she was knitting. She had already completed wool gloves for the boys. She had purchased the yarn in Burnage with a few coins that her mother had allowed her to keep in preparation for Christmas. She regularly stayed up and knit by lamplight until the early morning hours.

The week passed without much ado. Catherine Markley arrived home on Friday afternoon from London just ahead of her husband. The carriage was overflowing with parcels. Reuben had brought the parcels to the kitchen door and Margaret carried them into a closet in Catherine's study.

Saturday arrived and Margaret was bursting with anticipation. As she arrived at breakfast, the other servants began wishing her a happy birthday. Margaret was blessed to have such good friends.

As Margaret sat down at the table, Beatrice placed a plate of pastries on the table. Margaret looked dumfounded.

"What are these, Beatrice?"

"Chef Nicolas wanted to celebrate your birthday with a traditional French pastry. He made these croissants this morning. They are fresh and still warm," Beatrice said happily.

Margaret arose from the table and went to Chef Nicolas and gave him a hug. "Merci, Chef Nicolas. Merci beaucoup."

Margaret was the first to try a croissant. At Nicolas' suggestion, she pulled one apart and then spread butter and preserves on each half. She could feel the warmth on her fingers as she pulled it apart and the smell was overwhelming. She took a bite and hummed a contented melody.

As she finished her first bite, she enthused, "C'est tres bon, Chef Nicolas. Vous êtes très amiable." Nicolas was impressed, as were the others around the table. They didn't know what she had said, but they all nodded in agreement.

The croissants weren't on Catherine's "list," but Nicolas didn't think twice about serving them. He had made them for the Markley's breakfast and Catherine would never know.

As Margaret got up to leave the kitchen, she thanked Chef Nicolas again. Nicolas handed her something wrapped in paper.

"What is this?" Margaret asked.

"Veuillez ouvrir pour voir," Chef Nicolas said.

Margaret gently pulled open the paper to reveal a small jar. The label read "Meaux moutarde avec le vin blanc."

Margaret squealed with delight. "Whole grain mustard with white wine. Thank you so much. Where did you get this? Dinner will be superb," Margaret said enthusiastically.

"A chef must keep some secrets, Margaret," Nicolas teased. "I hope your birthday is très fantastique."

Margaret again hugged Nicolas and returned to her room quickly to store her gift. She was floating on air and could not remove the smile from her face if she tried.

Chapter 10

The day seemed endless. Margaret simply needed to make it until four that afternoon and then she would be able to leave for home. She made her way through her list of chores and tried to maintain her focus.

The children did not have lessons on Saturday and Margaret had come upon Philip on a few occasions. She had a nice conversation with him in the library as she cleaned. He noted her happy demeanour and she had confessed it was her birthday. She told him of her evening plans and he was pleased for her.

As half past three approached, Margaret was still cleaning the library, her final room of the day. It took a substantial amount of time to dust the books and shelving, which went on and on. She pulled out the books, one by one, and dusted underneath. As she focused on her task, Anabel entered the room.

"Margaret, you seem rather distracted today. You need to be mindful or you will be replaced by someone better suited for the position." Anabel was a horribly rude girl who took pleasure in exercising her social superiority over most others. This was especially true of Margaret, who was a year older, and that only added to the insult.

Margaret tried to ignore Anabel and continued with her dusting. "Margaret, you are a servant. You do not ignore me. Do you understand?" Anabel said smugly.

Margaret turned to Anabel and said yes quietly. It was enough to satisfy Anabel, who then turned and exited the room. A few moments later, Catherine entered the room.

"Margaret, you have done an unacceptable job in Anabel's room. She tells me her bed is not tidy and her floor has not been swept properly. You may leave once you have tended to her room to her satisfaction."

"But, but I...." Margaret stopped herself as she knew it would do no good and she could not afford to anger Catherine Markley. Margaret curtseyed and spoke a quiet "Yes, Ma'am."

The tram left Stockport and High Lane promptly at twenty past four. She had to be on her way by four to arrive at the tram on time. It was now ten of four and Margaret feared she would be late.

She took her broom and dashed upstairs to Anabel's room. Anabel was sitting in her chair looking at a book. She acknowledged Margaret's entrance with that same smug expression that made Margaret cringe.

Margaret looked at the bed and it appeared as though it had been jumped on. It certainly was not in the state that Margaret had left it that morning. The floor was clean, immaculately so, and she could not understand how it could be seen as otherwise.

Margaret straightened the linens on the bed, being careful to do nothing to fuel Anabel's fire.

"Margaret, I told you downstairs, just moments ago in fact, that you need to be more diligent in your duties. This is exactly what I spoke of."

Margaret was amazed at what a parrot Anabel was. She sounded exactly like her horrible mother. They were cut from the same nasty cloth.

"My young brother told me it was your birthday today and that you have to hurry to catch your tram. You best be hurrying then."

When Margaret looked up at Anabel, her nose was in her book. She didn't even have the nerve to look Margaret in the eye as she tormented her. Margaret took a deep breath and continued cleaning.

It was now five past four. Margaret felt panicked.

Margaret took another deep breath. "Anabel, is this acceptable to you?" she asked calmly. It was difficult to speak when one was biting one's tongue.

"I suppose." Anabel paused for a moment and then motioned for Margaret to leave with a dismissive sweeping of her hand.

She was in her room, dressed in her regular clothes, inside of three minutes. It was now approaching ten past four and she had ten minutes to get to the tram.

She dashed out of her room without a good-bye to anyone. She ran down the estate road and turned onto High Lane. It was above freezing, which meant no ice. Margaret was grateful for that, at least.

Gasping for breath, Margaret continued to run. Her heart was pounding and she felt nauseous. She could not run any faster and she felt at any moment she would faint. But she continued.

She crossed the train tracks. Thank goodness there was no train in sight. She approached Stockport, and as she readied herself to cross the road she saw the back of the tram moving in the distance. She had missed it by a minute at best, but it might as well have been an hour.

Margaret bent over as she tried to catch her breath. She could not hide the tears, nor did she care if anyone could hear her. This was her birthday, and it was turning into a disaster. There were a few people in the street watching her with curiosity, but Margaret paid them no attention. The tears continued as Margaret frantically gathered her thoughts.

The next tram would come along in thirty minutes time. By then she could make it most of the way to Ardwick if she hurried. She determined moving was better than standing still and she made her way up Stockport.

Margaret continued to wipe her eyes with her coat sleeve. The wool irritated her skin, but the cold numbed the pain. She ran as far and as fast as she could and then transitioned to walking when she could run no more. Her feet throbbed with each step. All along the way, people stared at her, wondering what she was running from.

Margaret stopped and pulled out her pocket watch. It had been a gift from Eleanor for her last birthday. Eleanor said that she needed to keep time so she would not keep her loved ones waiting. That was the only thought in her mind at the moment.

It was now a few minutes of five and she was still another ten minutes from the tram stop where James would be waiting. If James was not finished his deliveries by that time, he would break long enough to see Margaret home. She could not keep him waiting.

Darkness had fully set in, and the street lights illuminated her path. She could not run any more. Each step was more excruciating than the last.

As she approached the tram stop, ten minutes past the time her tram arrived and departed, she could see James waiting. She ran the few remaining steps and then collapsed in his arms. She couldn't spare the breath to speak. The tears continued.

Gasping for air, she managed to say, "I am so sorry, James. Mrs. Markley made me stay and I missed my tram. I came by foot."

"Well, that is obvious," James teased.

Margaret couldn't help but laugh through her tears. She was relieved he was not cross with her.

"This is not the first time she has made you miss your tram and I am entirely certain it won't be the last. I would have waited for the next one and then gone off after you."

"Thank you, James. I don't know what I would do without you."

"Oh, and happy birthday." Margaret had completely forgotten it was her birthday. She smiled at the thought.

Together, they headed home. It was a short walk, but it felt like an eternity to Margaret. She looked forward to getting her boots off and resting her feet.

As they arrived home, Agnes and Mary came running to the door. "Happy birthday, Margaret." Both girls embraced their sister at the same time, almost knocking her over.

"Well, hello, girls. I have missed you so this week." Margaret scanned the room for her mother. Sarah and Eleanor came out from the kitchen and Margaret ran to them.

"Yes, happy birthday, my dear girl. I hope your day wasn't too difficult." Sarah noticed her swollen eyes and irritated cheeks. What on earth happened to your face?" Sarah kissed her daughter's cheek.

"It was nothing, Mama. All is well." Sarah stared at her daughter, trying to determine if she should let it go or if she should persist. She saw through her deception, but she chose to let it go, determined to not cause her daughter any more of whatever grief reddened her face to begin with.

It was two years to the day since Thomas had passed away. Margaret's birthday was a bittersweet day for all, especially Sarah.

"We shall see you for dinner after church tomorrow," Sarah said cheerfully, trying hard to hide her sadness. Sarah and the children would be joining Eleanor and Margaret for dinner and they would celebrate her birthday as a family then.

Margaret removed her coat and the satchel that hung over her shoulder. It was filled with her pay. She placed it dutifully in her mother's hand. Sarah acknowledged it with appreciation.

"Well, Margaret, we must go now if you are to prepare a feast for me. I have been dreaming of nothing else all week."

Margaret and Eleanor headed for the door. "Please say hello to Samuel for me when he gets home. I love you all very much." And with that, Margaret and Eleanor were gone.

The ten minute walk was a pleasant one for Margaret. Eleanor was her sunshine. Eleanor adored the children and she had an extra special relationship with Margaret, being the oldest daughter.

"I had a new customer come into the shop today with an order for three dresses, all to be designed by your mother. I was chuffed to bits," Eleanor said excitedly. "Your Mama shall be very busy before Christmas."

"That'll be as easy as anything for Mama." Eleanor loved Margaret's childish optimism.

As they approached Eleanor's shop door, a couple of men were having a row outside. Clearly, one of the men was drunken, staggering and slurring his speech. Eleanor put her arm in front of Margaret to stop her. Instinct prevailed.

"Aunt Eleanor, he is absolutely kalied," Margaret quipped. Eleanor couldn't disagree.

As the men continued their argument, the more drunken of the two locked his eyes on Margaret. "Well, what do we have here, Petey?" he blathered. "I thinks me might be having a bangin' good time tonight."

As Eleanor and Margaret stood in their place, the man started to walk toward them, obscenely motioning with his hands. Margaret gasped in horror and Eleanor pulled on her arm so hard she stumbled. Eleanor didn't wait until Margaret had her proper footing before she pulled her out into the street. They barely missed a wagon, whose driver cursed at them when one of his horses stumbled and he fell forward, almost losing his grip of his reins.

As Eleanor looked back, the drunken man was still approaching. His row mate was stumbling in the other direction, clearly drunken himself. Eleanor picked up her pace as they crossed the street. As Eleanor looked for a route to take, she noticed two Peelers on the other side of the street. Her fast pace turned into a trot, as they approached the officers. It seems the drunken man also noticed the Peelers and did an about-face and headed off clumsily in the other direction.

One Peeler caught sight of Eleanor and Margaret and, seeing there was some franticness about them, waited for them to approach. Eleanor pointed at the man as he staggered down the street and the officer told her that he had been giving him trouble all day.

"It would seem the bloke won't be causing you any more concern, Ma'am. What is your destination?"

Eleanor pointed across the street.

"Let us escort you two ladies to your door so you won't be bothered again," the officer offered graciously.

"Thank you. That is kind of you, Sir."

After Eleanor latched her door, she turned the lights on as she entered the flat. Margaret sat down and removed her boots. She had forgotten how sore her feet were and she grimaced in pain as she removed her boots. The pain helped take her mind off the unpleasant experience outside.

"Margaret, dear, let's prepare the chicken and then we shall soak your feet while it cooks. You deserve a rest, especially on your birthday." Margaret delighted in the thought.

Margaret entered the kitchen and turned on the gas oven. She took out the jar of mustard that Chef Nicolas had given her. The Dijon that Eleanor had bought her was on the counter and she mixed the right amount of each in a bowl. She chopped some fresh rosemary and added it along with some minced garlic. She blended it all until it was smooth and even. She scooped some of the mixture and slathered it on the chicken. She sprinkled some sea salt and crushed pepper on it, placed some potatoes that had been quartered, salted, and brushed with oil around the chicken, and then placed it all in the oven. She peeled and cut up some carrots and placed them in a pot with water and some sprigs of thyme, but it was too early to turn them on.

"Margaret, dear, come sit down and relax," Eleanor summoned from the sitting room.

Margaret joined Eleanor in the sitting room. As she sat in her favourite chair, Eleanor brought a basin of warm water with Epsom salts and a drop of rose oil. Margaret removed her stocking and dipped her feet in the water. Her eyes rolled upward under her closing eyelids.

"Thank you, Aunt Eleanor. This is absolutely divine."

"Now tell me, Margaret, how was your week?" Eleanor inquired.

Margaret sat silently for a moment as she tried to control a sudden rush of emotion. It proved stronger than she. She broke down in uncontrollable tears. She tried to end the flow by holding her breath, but one by one the tears fell on her cheeks.

"Oh dear, was it that bad?" Eleanor asked, feeling completely responsible.

Margaret had no reason to hide the truth from Eleanor. She never wanted to worry her mother, but Eleanor was the one person she could share her feelings with and not be judged or pitied.

"My week was the same as always, until today. Anabel knew it was my birthday and she purposely messed her room so I would have to stay late and miss my tram. I ran home all the way from Amberley House. It was awful. Why is she like that? I have done nothing to her." Margaret whimpered like a wounded animal.

Eleanor knew very well what her younger sister was like. She was appalled by her behaviour. She also knew that the apple didn't fall from the motherly tree.

When her own mother passed away, Eleanor was only a few years old. Her mother had died in childbirth and neither mother nor child could be saved. Her father had always been determined to elevate his status in society and he buried himself in his work even more after that point. William and Eleanor moved in with their paternal grandparents and they raised the children.

Charles Markley remarried at the age of forty-five. Charles was wealthy by that point, having inherited his father's business and having grown it nicely. But, what he didn't have was the other thing he craved, perhaps more than money: social status.

Charles Markley met Philip Armitstead when Charles purchased some land in the Lake District. He purchased it from an acquaintance of Philip's who invited Charles to a party at Philip's home. From there their relationship began. Philip was impressed with Charles' drive and business acumen. He thought Charles would be a good match for his daughter, Catherine. Most importantly, he knew that the relationship would benefit both families nicely.

Catherine was thirty-three and had no prospects for marriage. She was an unattractive woman, and her father also knew her to be a bit of a self-conscious and dim-witted girl, and one who possessed an angry temper. He had no hopes of her finding a suitable husband on her own.

Philip made a deal with Charles Markley that should he marry his daughter, he would be introduced into his social and business circles. It had been a long time since Charles had been married and he didn't have the time or desire to look for a wife himself, so he agreed.

Charles was hopeful there would be some attraction, but it wasn't a requirement for him. And it was a good thing it wasn't, because he thought she looked like a bit of a horse's ass.

The wedding took place in Yorkshire, at the Armitstead estate. Both William and Eleanor attended. Neither of them cared for Catherine and the feeling was undoubtedly mutual. Catherine was incredibly rude to them both and didn't try to hide her insecurities in the least.

Charles purchased the Burnage property from Philip, and five years after they married Amberley House was completed and they moved in. In the meantime, Catherine joined Charles at the house in town. Both Anabel and Philip were born there. They were the only children of Charles and Catherine, and Eleanor was convinced it was because his father was drunk both times and had temporarily lost his wits.

The smell of the mustard filled the air and made Eleanor's mouth water. "My, my, Margaret, that does smell divine," Eleanor said. "I am so looking forward to dinner."

Margaret took her feet out of the basin and dried them off. She slipped her feet into her slippers and went into the kitchen to turn on the carrots and inspect the chicken. She opened the oven door to see her chicken browning nicely. It was twenty minutes or so from being finished and was time to turn on the carrots. She was hungry and looking forward to tasting her creation.

Margaret slipped back into the sitting room and sat down in her chair. Eleanor went to her cabinet to retrieve something. Margaret paid attention with keen interest, knowing that Aunt Eleanor would never forget to buy birthday gifts.

Eleanor handed Margaret a parcel wrapped in a piece of red silk fabric and gold ribbon.

"Aunt Eleanor, it is so pretty. Thank you so much."

"You are most welcome, my dear. Happy birthday." Eleanor bent down and kissed Margaret on the forehead.

Margaret tugged on the bow and the ribbon gave way. She pulled at the silk fabric to reveal a book. It was a biography on the life of Florence Nightingale. Margaret opened the cover enthusiastically and read the inscription:

There is no more noble or greater a calling than one that helps the weak and the poor and the suffering.

With love and affection, Aunt Eleanor

She embraced Eleanor so tightly that Eleanor coughed mockingly.

"Thank you, Aunt Eleanor. I love you with all my heart." For Eleanor, the feeling was mutual.

The chicken was ready and Margaret took it out of the oven. The mustard had browned perfectly, as had the potatoes. Margaret sliced the chicken breast against the bone so that the entire breast came off in one piece. Chef Nicolas had taught her how to do this. She positioned a breast on each plate, along with some potatoes and carrots and then placed the plates on the table.

Eleanor sliced into the chicken and took a bite. The taste was exquisite. The rosemary and mustard were a sublime combination, and the garlic added a layer of complexity that enhanced the experience.

"Margaret, I am impressed with your cooking. Chef Nicolas has been teaching you well. You could serve this at the finest of restaurants." Eleanor was not teasing. She was truly impressed and believed that Eleanor could have a future as a chef if she chose not to become a doctor.

Both Margaret and Eleanor were exhausted and readied themselves for bed soon after dinner. Margaret was now used to modern plumbing so it wasn't the treat it used to be. But her mother constantly reminded her that they didn't have it and were still perfectly content. The older Margaret got, the less she believed it.

Chapter 11

In the morning, Margaret woke early. She had to prepare the puff pastry for dinner before they left for church. It needed time to rise. After the pastry dough was made, she sautéed the chicken livers from the previous night's chicken with garlic, mushrooms, and herbs and ground it with the back side of a fork until it was smooth. She placed the paté in the icebox to keep it fresh for later. She could never prepare something like that at home because they did not have an icebox and food would spoil.

Eleanor had made apple muffins the day before and they ate those for breakfast. Eleanor was a good cook in her own right, but she didn't stray too far off a traditional path when it came to what she prepared.

After breakfast they bathed and dressed for church. Eleanor had been going to church regularly with Sarah and the family since Thomas had passed away. She found it nourishing and it became a routine part of her week.

As they walked, the sky was black and a sleety rain fell. The damp cold was uncomfortable, but Margaret enjoyed the patter of the rain on the top of their brolly. They could see their breath as they exhaled into the cold air.

Sarah and the children were already at the church when Margaret and Eleanor arrived. They took their places at the end of the pew. Mary bounced in her seat at the sight of them and Sarah placed her hand on her shoulder to calm her down.

The service started shortly after they arrived. Today's sermon was on the need for forgiveness. Both Eleanor and Margaret thought about Anabel and Catherine and knew that they could both benefit from some themselves.

After the service, the entire group made their way back to Eleanor's home. The sleet had abated, but the cold was still bitter. The ground was covered in a slushy mess that kicked up whenever a step was taken. The bottoms of their pants and skirts were a wet, sloppy mess.

When they arrived, they each used a towel to dry off the excess moisture from the bottom of their pants and skirts. As they got themselves comfortable in the sitting room, Eleanor started a fire and Margaret made her way into the kitchen. Sarah followed.

"It smells remarkable in here, Margaret," her mother said proudly. "You have become such a good cook. It seems working at the Markley's was a good choice for you."

"Yes, Mama," Margaret said agreeably, but rather unconvincingly.

Margaret took a small knife and sliced the puff pastry into equal squares. She took a small dollop of the pâté and placed it on one side of the square, folding the other side over, and pinching the edges. The chicken carcass continued simmering on low heat in the large pot on the stove, as it had been doing for the past four hours, and was ready to remove.

Margaret lifted the pot and placed it in the sink. The contents were very hot and she was careful to not splatter the hot broth. Sarah watched on, impressed with her daughter's skill.

Margaret used a large slotted spoon and fork to remove the carcass from the pot of broth. She placed it in a bowl to cool down so she could separate the good meat from the bones. She ran the broth through a colander to separate out the bones and cartilage that had settled in the pot. When the broth was clean, the pot was placed back on the stove.

Margaret took the corn and carrots that had been sliced and added them to the pot, along with the chicken pieces. She added a dollop more mustard, some rosemary, and salt and pepper. She was so focused on her activity that she didn't notice her mother's gaze. Sarah was awestruck at the ease with which Margaret moved around in the kitchen.

The puff pastries looked as though they had come from a bakery window. They were placed in the centre of the table. Margaret ladled soup into each bowl. They had eaten soup their entire lives, but this was not like any soup they had eaten before. Samuel didn't look up from his bowl.

"Samuel, good grief. Take a breath while you eat." The table erupted in laughter and Margaret relaxed knowing that she had done well.

"Margaret, these pastries are superb," Eleanor enthused.

"Chef Nicholas taught me how to make puff pastry and I made up the filling with what we had here," Margaret said. She had gone from following instructions to creating. It was a proud moment for her.

Every morsel of food was consumed. As Margaret got up to remove the dishes from the table, Eleanor motioned for her to sit down.

"Today we celebrate your birthday and you have done enough. Sit, Margaret, sit."

Eleanor and Sarah removed the remaining dishes from the table and returned from the kitchen with a chocolate cake. On the top was a single lit candle.

"May the light guide you through the year, Margaret," Sarah said, full of love and hope for her daughter.

"It looks delicious. Where did you get it?" Margaret asked.

"Chef Nicolas offered me some tips, my dear. I made this yesterday before you arrived home." Eleanor was pleased with the expression on Margaret's face. "Now let's eat this cake and pray it tastes as good as it looks," she said, hopefully.

Eleanor extinguished the flame between her wet fingers. And, as she sliced the cake and dished out the servings, Margaret soaked up the love she felt in the room. She could not feel more contented than she did at that moment. This was the best birthday that Margaret could remember.

"Well, look at you two little chocolate ghouls," Sarah teased as she wiped a swath of icing off Mary's face with her finger. Agnes took a big swipe with her tongue, only to push the chocolate farther away from her mouth.

"Margaret, we have one other item to attend to," Sarah announced as she picked up a parcel from the corner.

"Oh my, it is so heavy. Mama, what is this?" Margaret asked.

"Open it, my dear, and you shall see."

Margaret pulled back the paper to reveal a long, black wool, crepe frock coat. Margaret stood to open it up and then held it against herself.

She was speechless. "It is exquisite, Mama. This is the most incredible coat I have ever seen." And Margaret meant that sincerely.

The coat had embroidered piping along the lapel and on the pockets. It was gathered at the waist and elegantly flared at its length.

"Well, try it on," Agnes said impatiently.

She put the coat on. Margaret noted the ornate buttons as she pulled them through the button holes. It fit perfectly and it felt wonderful. It had more weight to it than her current one did and it was infinitely more elegant. She felt like a woman in it.

"You have outgrown your old coat, and you are now thirteen, almost a woman. You can now dress like one," her mother said with a wink.

"Thank you, thank you, thank you, thank you, thank you," Margaret said as she kissed her mother all over her face.

"You can thank Aunt Eleanor. She provided the material for the coat. I simply made it."

Margaret looked at Eleanor, who was smiling in the corner. "But, Aunt Eleanor, you already gave me your gift yesterday," Margaret said, surprised.

"What did she give you, Margaret? You must show us," Agnes demanded.

Margaret picked up the book from the table in the corner and handed it to her mother. Sarah reflected on the cover, opened it, and read the inscription. It was general enough that it did not betray Margaret's secret, but personal enough to have deep meaning for her.

"Margaret, these are words to live by. We could all benefit from demonstrating a bit more kindness and empathy in life," Sarah opined.

"Well, we must be on our way. Margaret, my dear girl, we need to get you to Amberley House." Sarah stood up and straightened her skirt.

Eleanor cringed every time she heard the name "Amberley House" as it reminded her of Catherine. She would like to feel sorry for her father, but how could you feel sorry for someone who knowingly and willingly walked into their circumstance? You simply could not.

"I shall be seeing you all in a few short weeks for Christmas. I'll be counting the minutes," Eleanor said with genuine excitement.

Eleanor would not be going up to Yorkshire with her father, Catherine, and the children. Instead William would be joining his sister and Sarah and her children. It was just as Eleanor had wanted it.

"Thank you so much for my book and for the enchanting evening. I could not have hoped for a better way to spend my birthday."

Margaret loved Eleanor like no other.

Eleanor did not need to put her new coat on. She had not taken it off. She put her boots on and picked up her bag and was ready to go. Together the family set off for home. It had been a good day.

At home Margaret quickly exchanged her dirty clothing for some clean clothing and was ready to depart again.

"We have had such a short time with you this week. I am happy that you enjoyed your birthday, but I do miss you so," Sarah said sadly.

"Mama, you are always in my thoughts." Margaret did not want to deepen her mother's suffering so she chose not to speak of the utter despair she felt when she left on Sundays.

"We have Christmas to look forward to." Sarah tried to cheer her daughter, and herself. "We shall have three days to share, and in just a few short weeks."

Christmas Day fell on a Friday this year. Most businesses closed for Christmas Day and Boxing Day. The Markley factory was no exception. They would have the two holiday days and then the usual Sunday. They would all be together as a family and there could be nothing better in the world.

As Samuel and Margaret approached Ardwick Green, the Peelers came into view. They were out as they had been the previous week and showed no signs of losing intensity.

"Did you hear another one is gone? That's three now," James said. "And I don't suppose they are getting any closer to figuring out who did it. Still haven't found two of 'em."

Margaret had nothing to say. The chill she felt in her spine was not from the cold. There was a constant sense of helplessness that pervaded Margaret and it was utterly exhausting. Her spirit was weakened, like a bird with a broken wing. There was more to life. There had to be, she thought.

Margaret said good-bye to her brother with a quick kiss on the cheek. There was so much sadness and she could not muster any more affection. What good would it do other than making her feel worse?

The tram pulled up to the stop shortly after they arrived. As she made her way up the stairs, she waved good-bye to James.

"Well, hello, Miss Margaret. I want to hear all about your birthday," Dennis said cheerfully, lifting Margaret's spirits.

It felt like it had already been a lifetime since Margaret's birthday. But, when she thought about it, it warmed her heart.

"It must have been a good one. Your smile is as big as the moon."

"It was, Dennis. I spent the night with my Aunt Eleanor and we had a splendid time. She bought me a book about Florence Nightingale, and my mama made me this exquisite coat."

"You look very becoming in it, Margaret. You are a fortunate girl to have a family that loves you so," Dennis remarked. "So many spend their entire lives without ever experiencing the love you are constantly surrounded by. I had that with my Annie, God rest her soul."

Margaret knew Dennis was right. She was fortunate. As she walked away from the tram, she said her good-byes to Dennis and then made her way down High Lane.

As Margaret crossed over the train tracks, that familiar feeling enveloped her. She turned her thoughts toward Christmas and the three days she would have with her family. She needed no gifts. Being with her family was the greatest gift.

The sound of horse hooves behind Margaret forced her to the side of the road. Deep in thought, she lost her footing as she stepped back abruptly and into a pit at the lane's edge. Margaret landed on her derrière with a thud. The carriage stopped in front of Margaret and she could see it was Reuben.

"Madam, are you all right?" Reuben asked as he placed the brake on the carriage and stepped down the ladder.

Margaret picked herself up off the ground and wiped off the back of her coat. "Hello, Reuben. It is me, Margaret. You caught me in a daydream. What a nilly I am."

"Hello Miss Margaret. Let's get you to Amberley House."

Reuben helped Margaret up to the empty seat beside him.

"Thank you, Reuben. I am rather clumsy. It is a good thing I am not carrying eggs from the market. That would have been an utter mess," Margaret said with a laugh. "What are you doing out at this time on a Sunday?"

"Mr. Markley sent me out to pick up a parcel."

"Really? What is it?" Margaret asked with keen interest.

"It is a painting, but I do not know what of. It is wrapped," Reuben said showing no interest whatsoever.

Reuben pulled into the barn. Margaret stepped off the carriage and thanked Reuben for the ride. As Reuben began untethering the horses, Margaret made her way to the servant's building. Agnes was sitting on her bed writing in her journal when Margaret entered the room. Beatrice was elsewhere.

"Margaret, how was your birthday?" Agnes asked. "Do tell."

"It was perfect, Agnes. It really was." Margaret's head dropped slightly.

"Well, why so glum?"

"I do not want it to be over."

Agnes spied Margaret's gift. "Look at that coat. A birthday present?"

"My mama made it for me. My Aunt Eleanor got her the material from her dress shop and my mama made it. It is exquisite, isn't it?" The joy returned to Margaret's face. "But I had a bit of a slip on the road and landed on my arse. Is it dirty?" Margaret asked as she turned around.

"You have a bit of mud back there, but nothing that won't brush off when it dries. No damage done," Agnes said as she admired the coat.

Agnes walked around to Margaret's front to get a better look. She ran her fingers over the piping on the waist pocket. "Margaret, this is one of the finest coats I have ever seen. I really mean it. It is exquisite."

Margaret took off her coat and hung it on the hook to dry. She had only a few more weeks to finish her Christmas presents so she sat down to her knitting. She had no appetite so she continued knitting through supper.

Chapter 12

The morning brought a blanket of newly fallen snow. From the window, Margaret could see the cover of white illuminate the darkness. The sky had cleared since the snow had fallen and the stars twinkled high over the peaceful scene.

Margaret and Agnes dressed and made their way to the kitchen. The snow cushioned the sounds. It was deathly quiet, and the only sounds that filled Margaret's ears were her own breath and the squeaking as her boots packed down the perfectly untouched snow.

Margaret and Agnes kicked off the snow that clung to their boots before they entered the kitchen. "Beatrice, you were as quiet as a mouse this morning. I did not even hear you wake up."

"You were knitting late into the night so I didn't want to disturb you."

"Thank you for that. I don't know how I am going to get it all finished in time for Christmas," Margaret wondered.

Beatrice brought the steaming pot of porridge to the table, along with some biscuits that were baked fresh that morning. Margaret loved porridge and could eat it every day. It was so comforting to her. It reminded her of her mother.

"Jonathan, how is Snowflake doing?" Margaret asked. She hadn't seen Snowflake in a couple of days.

"He eats non-stop. I don't know how he doesn't burst. I took his carrots away at night because the sound was very annoying and it kept me awake. But, other than that, he is a good mate."

Margaret thanked Beatrice for breakfast and then left to do her chores. She could hear the family in the dining room engaged in lively conversation as she made her way down the hallway. Philip's voice rose above the others and Margaret could hear him talking about building a snowman after lessons were done. Philip was the only Markley, with the exception of Eleanor of course, who could put a smile on Margaret's face.

When Margaret was done with her work upstairs, she made her way to Catherine Markley's study. She could hear the sound of the piano coming from the conservatory. The music would break and Margaret could hear Cecily admonish Philip for his sloppy style. "Philip, you can do so much better. Pick up the pace. One, two, three."

It was important that Margaret be finished in Catherine's study by one to avoid contact. Catherine routinely went to her study after luncheon. As

Margaret tidied and dusted, she could hear a presence behind her. Her heart skipped a beat as she waited for her master's shrill voice to fill the room. Instead it was her master's daughter.

"Margaret, what have you done with it? I demand you return it immediately." Anabel was clearly furious and Margaret had no idea why.

Margaret swung around. "Return what? I'm not sure what you are talking about."

"You know very well, you thief. How dare you steal my necklace? How dare you take something that does not belong to you? Return it at once and then leave." Anabel's voice was now at full scream. She was hysterical with anger.

Margaret was trembling. She had taken nothing. She did not know what Anabel was referring to. The commotion brought Catherine to the door.

"Anabel, what is the problem? I could hear you all the way from the conservatory." Catherine gave Margaret an icy stare, making the assumption her daughter was justified in her anger.

"This thief stole my necklace. She took it from my room. And now she stands there unwilling to admit it. I demand she return it and then leave this house immediately."

Anabel was no more than a hysterical child throwing a tantrum. She could not think straight for the venom that was oozing from her.

Margaret was fully in tears by this point. "Mrs. Markley, I swear I did not take anything from Anabel's room. I would never do that. Please believe me," Margaret begged.

"Stop your blubbering, Margaret. I'll get to the bottom of this," she stammered.

"Anabel, what necklace are you referring to?" Catherine asked her daughter.

"The emerald one you gave me for Christmas last year. It was on my nightstand yesterday and now it is gone. She took it," Anabel said pointing at Margaret.

"Anabel, if you remember, your emerald necklace had a loose stone. I sent it to the jewellers this morning to have the stone properly set so you could wear it for Christmas."

Through her anger, Anabel tried to understand what her mother was saying. She paused long enough to catch her breath.

"Oh, I guess I forgot," she said rather flatly.

"It is time for your piano lesson. Cecily is waiting for you."

Anabel turned and gave Margaret an icy stare, as if in warning. There was no apology, no regret. She simply walked past her mother and left the room.

Catherine turned and followed her daughter, leaving Margaret in the room, utterly destroyed. Margaret stood there for an eternity before the reality of the situation set in. When it did, she dropped to the floor and completely broke down. Her chest heaved with every breath and the tears would not stop.

Catherine stood in the doorway. "Margaret, the entire household can hear you. Pick yourself up and get back to work. This is entirely unacceptable."

Margaret looked at Catherine through her tears, wiping them with her sleeve. She stood back up on her feet and turned to continue her work. Margaret was numb. She felt so alone.

At dinner, her eyes were still red and puffy. She was questioned as to why and she felt obliged to quell her friends' curiosity. They were horrified and disgusted. There was no love lost on Anabel by any of the servants.

Chef Nicolas thought a change of subject was needed and inquired about her birthday dinner. "How did the meal turn out, mon ami?"

Margaret could not get excited about the one thing that always excited her, and it broke Nicolas' heart. "Do tell…what did your aunt think of your creation? It was a triumph, I am certain."

"She loved it very much. Thank you." Margaret's spirit was broken and there was nothing that was going to make her feel better at that point, absolutely nothing.

After dinner Margaret finished her chores. During supper Margaret visited the stables. She was not hungry. Jonathan had left the lantern on for Snowflake and Margaret climbed the ladder to check in on Philip's new friend. Snowflake was sitting in the corner where Margaret had seen him last. She bent over and petted him. His silky soft fur was comforting. He seemed to enjoy the attention. There was no struggle to try to escape the intrusion.

"Snowflake, how does it feel to be a prisoner? Not good, I know. You must miss your family. I miss my mother." Margaret's tears started again. And, for a brief moment, Margaret's senses left her and she thought about running home.

As she got up to leave, a noise startled her.

"Margaret, you weren't at supper tonight. Are you feeling all right?" Jonathan looked worried.

"Yes, I am fine. I was not hungry."

As Jonathan came closer to Margaret, he could see that she had been crying again. "Come sit, Margaret." Jonathan took Margaret's hand and sat her down beside him on a bale of hay.

"I know how hard it is to be separated from your mother. After my mother died and I went to live with my aunt, I thought I would die myself. It was so lonely. You are not alone here. We are your family. We all care about you and that includes me." Jonathan leaned over and gave Margaret a kiss on her cheek. Her face flushed with warmth.

Margaret liked the kiss, but was taken aback. "Thank you, Jonathan. You are a good friend."

"You do not deserve to be treated that way. Would you like to help me brush Napoleon? I think he needs some love as well," Jonathan said boldly.

"I would. Then I have to get back to my room to finish my knitting."

The two of them descended the stairs and made their way to Napoleon's stall. Napoleon seemed happy to see them both and acknowledged their presence with a whinny. Margaret wrapped her arms around Napoleon's neck and gently ran her hand down his back. She grabbed a carrot from the bucket and he took it from her enthusiastically.

"How shall you be spending your Christmas this year, Margaret?" Jonathan asked.

"Spending the day with my family and my Aunt Eleanor and her brother, William."

Jonathan knew that Eleanor wasn't a real aunt so it wasn't a surprise to him when Margaret described William that way. There was still no connection to the Markleys as there had been little interaction with Eleanor and William.

"I'm sure you shall have a wonderful time."

"And what about you? Are you going to visit family with your father?" Margaret wondered.

"No, we shall be staying here this year. The Markleys are going up north and the house shall be empty so we'll be staying in my father's room. It looks like everyone else'll be leaving too. Michael was able to find Lydia, and he'll be joining her for Christmas in Stretford."

"Pardon me? Did you say that he found her? Do tell me more." Margaret was dumbfounded. That was such welcome news.

"Beatrice remembered hearing Lydia say her father was a tailor at a shop on Chester Road. She told Michael and he went to every shop on Chester Road until he found her father. It seems that her father was duly impressed with his diligence. It just may work out after all."

"Maybe happy endings do exist," Margaret said hopefully.

"Yes, perhaps they do." Jonathan agreed. "As for everyone else – Beatrice is going home to her parents, Chef Nicolas is visiting friends in London, and Gerald is accompanying the Markleys to Yorkshire."

Gerald was the Markley's other driver. He had no family and was happy to be occupied through the holidays.

Margaret was pleased that Jonathan would be with his father at Christmas, but was saddened by the fact that they would be spending it here, where they spent every day. That just didn't seem right.

The week progressed with no more than the usual drama. As Saturday arrived, Margaret found herself homesick. She could not wait until the day ended so she could be home with her family. The following week would be a shorter week, as Friday was Christmas Day and the Markleys would be leaving Thursday for Yorkshire. It seemed too good to be true.

Mid-afternoon Margaret was sweeping the foyer floor. She was facing the back wall and she caught a glimpse of Anabel coming down the stairs. She didn't let on that she saw her and she continued with her sweeping. Anabel passed Margaret on her way to her mother's study, making enough commotion to let Margaret know she was there.

When Margaret did not acknowledge her, Anabel became annoyed. She cleared her throat as if demanding acknowledgement. Margaret continued to sweep, unwilling to give in to Anabel's ridiculous rudeness.

"Margaret, you are such a sloppy maid. You are fortunate that my father agreed to hire you. My mother, with her good judgement, certainly would not have. She would like to see you gone, as would I."

Margaret still did not look at Anabel. She would not give her the satisfaction.

Suddenly and unexpectedly, the front door opened and Margaret turned to see who it was. It was Eleanor, and she could not contain her excitement.

"Aunt Eleanor!" Margaret yelled, reacting by instinct, not thinking about the ramifications.

"She is not your aunt – you need to remember your place, Margaret."

Eleanor sighed, acknowledging the familiar hopelessness that always accompanied visits to her father's home. Eleanor narrowed her focus and locked onto the reprehensible child that riled her so incredibly. Anabel was her mother in every way and their presence turned her father's home into a den of prickles and vinegar.

Condescending to the child, Eleanor spoke with her own air of superiority. "Well, Anabel, my young sister, you must never forget that choice is a gift. And oftentimes the family we choose is far preferable to the family we do not."

Eleanor knew moral lessons were lost on those who could not see beyond themselves, but it felt too good to say nevertheless and Eleanor simply could not help herself. Once again, the subtlety escaped Anabel. She shrugged off the comment and walked away under her usual cloud of juvenile arrogance. And, while the comment missed its intended target, it hit another one of far greater value to Eleanor.

Catherine entered the room with her own squint and exhaled disgust. "To what do we owe this honour, Eleanor?" The disingenuous and amusingly pretentious greeting made Eleanor laugh.

"My father sent for me," Eleanor replied equally as smugly.

None of the drama was lost on Margaret. She had learned it was all carefully played on both sides. Catherine's insecurities drove her need for position and authority. Eleanor's contempt for the abuse of those same things drove her need to exercise a certain level of moral superiority. And, if for no other reason than Eleanor couldn't care less about positioning herself against Catherine, and much less her obnoxious daughter, it would seem Eleanor always had the upper hand.

"Your father is in his study," Catherine directed. "What business is it you have with him today?"

"You shall have to ask him yourself." Eleanor was out of patience.

"And, Margaret, I'll be accompanying you home today. We shall be leaving at four sharp. I will meet you in your room."

Margaret nodded, speechless. She could see Catherine turn to look at her out of the corner of her eye, but she did not look back. It would only annoy Catherine, and she knew it.

Eleanor left the room and made her way to her father's study. Catherine turned and left the room as well, leaving Margaret incredibly uncomfortable.

At four o'clock Eleanor knocked on Margaret's door. She was dressed and ready to go. Neither Beatrice nor Agnes was there so there was no need for any introductions or explanations.

"Are you ready to go home, my dear?" Eleanor asked unnecessarily.

"Very much so," Margaret replied, eager to leave.

Together they walked down the road, arm in arm. This was a treat for Margaret. Usually, this journey was taken alone.

"I have a question for you, Aunt Eleanor."

"What is it, Margaret?" Eleanor asked in anticipation.

"You know Reuben and his son, Jonathan?" Eleanor nodded. "They shall be here alone at Christmas while your father and Catherine are away. I hate the thought of them spending Christmas in Reuben's room. It isn't right. Could they have Christmas dinner with us? I know your flat is small, but we can make it work," Margaret implored.

"Margaret, you are a sweet and thoughtful girl. Unfortunately, my home is barely big enough for us. There would not be enough room for two more."

Margaret's head dropped, saddened by what she knew to be true. "I understand," she said quietly.

"I do have a suggestion, though," Eleanor offered. "When I was meeting with my father, he offered for us to have Christmas at Amberley House. They shall be gone and this massive house completely empty. Seems a shame, doesn't it? Of course we won't have Chef Nicolas to cook for us, but I am sure we can make do." Eleanor winked at Margaret.

"Really? Is it true?" Margaret could not contain herself. She jumped in front of Eleanor, facing her. "Really? Really?"

Eleanor nodded. Margaret launched herself at her and wrapped her arms around Eleanor's neck.

"Let us leave it as our little secret. How about that? I would imagine Catherine would drop if she found out." Eleanor was entertained by the thought.

Margaret knew what she meant. Catherine would make life intolerable for Margaret if she knew. But the thought of Catherine dropping certainly had some appeal. It was a secret she would have no problem keeping.

"Reuben shall be picking me up, well us really, on Christmas after church. We shall let Reuben and Jonathan know they are welcome to have dinner with us then. How does that sound?" Eleanor didn't have to ask because the tight squeeze around her chest was her answer.

"It cannot get any better than this," Margaret gushed.

As they arrived at the tram stop in Ardwick, Margaret looked for James.

"I told James I would be bringing you home. He had no need to come."

When the two of them arrived, Margaret took off her boots and coat and sat down. Eleanor asked for a quick word with Sarah in the kitchen.

Mary jumped on Margaret's knee and, for the first time in a long time, Margaret felt completely relaxed. It was home and there was no better place.

Eleanor emerged from the kitchen. She said her good-byes to everyone. "We shall see you in a week's time for our Christmas celebration." She winked at Margaret as they walked through the door.

James had brought home some end pieces of beef and Sarah had made a stew for their evening meal. They waited until James and Samuel were home so they could eat together as a family. In most cases, it only happened once a week, but it was important to Sarah.

After dinner Sarah got Mary and Agnes ready for bed, and Margaret and Samuel played a game of chess as James whittled at a piece of wood.

"Check," Samuel said, feeling entirely unchallenged.

"Well, if you think it is that easy, my dear brother, then you are sadly mistaken," Margaret said as she made her move. "Check, yourself."

Caught off guard, Samuel let out a grunt. He surveyed the board and let out a deep sigh.

"Not nearly as confident now, are you?" Margaret said jokingly.

James laughed in the corner as he occasionally looked up from his carving.

"Confidence is overrated, dear sister. It makes you weak and leaves you vulnerable," Samuel said with a laugh. He made his move and then it was Margaret's turn to pause.

"Hmmm, it would seem that my opponent has been practicing. But is it enough?" Margaret asked sarcastically.

"I'd say so," Samuel replied as he took her knight.

"Ouch, that one hurt. But this one shall hurt more," Margaret said, taking his queen.

This was much too much fun for James to ignore. He put down his carving and focused his attention on the game. Samuel grunted at the loss. How would he recover? He had never lost to Margaret before, and he would not allow himself to now.

Samuel moved his rook to block his king, but Margaret was one step ahead of him. She moved her knight so it was in direct line of fire. His king was blocked by his rook and his bishop. He had done himself in.

"Checkmate, my dear brother. Checkmate." After Samuel had completely surveyed the board, he waved his red flag in surrender and dropped his head in disgust. How could he have allowed himself to be beaten by his younger sister? He could never overcome that. For James, it was a treat to witness.

As Sarah came down from putting the girls to bed, she walked in on the tail end of the competition.

"Do my eyes and ears deceive me? Did someone beat the great Samuel Berry at chess?"

Margaret sat silent. She would not be the one to rub salt in the wound. She would let James do it for her.

"Mama, it was so exciting. Margaret was one step ahead of Samuel the entire game. She toyed with him and then, when the time was right, she went in for the slaughter." James was very animated as he described the attack.

Samuel shook his head in disgust and Margaret simply laughed. Sarah was content knowing that her entire family was together and happy under one roof.

"Congratulations, Margaret! That is an accomplishment to be proud of. Our Samuel is a formidable chess player. He has taught you well." Sarah had a way of praising one, while lessening the defeat of another. "I hear that we shall be joining you at Amberley House for Christmas. Eleanor tells me that we are invited to spend the holiday there while her father is away. How do you feel about that?"

"I am excited beyond words," Margaret answered with ardent enthusiasm. "I am pleased that Jonathan and Reuben will attend Christmas dinner with us. I am sure you shall like them as much as I do."

Sarah sadly recalled the last time she met Reuben. He drove them to say their final good-byes to Thomas. This would be a happier occasion, undoubtedly.

"What is this about Christmas at Amberley House?" James asked before Samuel had an opportunity to.

"It appears that Eleanor's father and his new family are in Yorkshire for Christmas and he has agreed to allow Eleanor, William, and their guests to enjoy Christmas at Amberley House," Margaret said excitedly.

"I suppose we are the guests, and I assume that the mistress of the house is unaware of the invitation?" Samuel questioned.

"Right on both counts," Margaret said with a laugh. "Catherine Markley would literally explode, and her head would pop off her shoulders if she knew."

"Margaret, that is not a kind thing to say about the woman who pays your salary." It was not a complete admonishment, as Sarah knew well enough of Catherine Markley's disposition.

Margaret did not argue with her mother on the point, but she did not apologize either. She kept silent, which is something she had become good at.

"It is late, my dear children, and I think it is time that we all went off to sleep." Sarah stood and the children followed. All said their good-nights, completed their nightly routines, and then went to sleep. Margaret had only one thought on her mind...four more days.

Chapter 13

The week before Christmas felt longer than any week Margaret had ever experienced in her life. Her chores seemed never-ending, and sleep eluded her as the excitement was too much to bear.

Anabel bounced around the house, excited as well about the impending holiday. Anabel seemed less concerned with her usual torment of Margaret and Margaret was thankful for it, whatever the reason. Nothing was going to ruin this Christmas, absolutely nothing.

As Thursday approached, the house was abuzz with activity. Trunks were filled and parcels were packed. Margaret was shocked at the volume that was to be taken to Yorkshire. The one thing Margaret was certain of was that they could not leave soon enough.

As Margaret was tidying the sitting room, young Philip shuffled in. He didn't seem as excited as his sister to be leaving Amberley House.

"Well, hello, Philip. Why so glum? I would think this is an exciting time of the year for you."

"I do love Christmas, but I do not want to go to Yorkshire. It is all rather stuffy. "'Don't do this' and 'don't do that' and 'sit up straight.' It isn't much fun, to be honest. I would rather be here with Snowflake and Napoleon," Philip said sadly.

"Jonathan shall take good care of Snowflake and Napoleon. Don't you worry."

"Well, I must be going. We shall be leaving soon. I hope you have a terrific Christmas." Philip startled Margaret with a hug.

"Philip, I wish you a wonderful Christmas as well." Margaret gave Philip a kiss on the cheek.

He was so very lonely and it saddened Margaret. He seemed like a child who did not fit into his life. Margaret could empathize.

Before the Markleys departed, all of the servants were asked to meet in the main house foyer. They stood end to end, as if soldiers awaiting inspection by their king. But their king was Catherine Markley. She handed each one of them a small box and wished them a Merry Christmas. Some smiles were forced more than others, it was clear, but Margaret paid no attention, completely focused on the box. Could this be a gift?

Catherine would have preferred to have provided nothing to her servants or, at the very least, to have been selective in choosing what and for whom. But this was another example of husband over-ruling wife. He would simply not have those in his employ being treated less than fairly. How would that look?

Catherine was able to maintain her dignity through the giving, though. As she wished them well, she was adorned in fur and spoke of her incomparable Christmas memories at her father's estate in Yorkshire. There was no denying social superiority, not at all.

As the carriage door closed behind Catherine's robust derrière, the servants jumped for joy. They hugged each other and wished each other well. Jonathan's sad expression broke Margaret's heart. He did not know what Christmas Day would bring and she could not tell him; at least, not yet.

"What do you suppose is in the box, Margaret?" Beatrice asked.

"I've no idea. When I shake it, it sounds like coins."

"Coins? Money would have to be pried from her dead fingers. And she looked very much alive to me before she left," Agnes said giggling. Margaret could not contain her laughter either.

"Well, I suppose Mr. Markley had a hand in it. He is far more generous than that old trout. I can't imagine what he sees in her."

"Nor can I," Agnes admitted.

"Are you excited to be seeing your family, Agnes?" Margaret asked, unsure. It had been a while since she had seen them.

"I am looking forward to seeing my brothers and sisters. I have missed them so. And my mama and papa, as well, I should think." Margaret noted the tone in Beatrice's voice. Beatrice was the oldest, and Margaret understood her parent's predicament, but understanding did nothing to lessen the pain.

"I imagine you shall have a marvellous time and I look forward to hearing all about it on Monday," Margaret said hopefully.

As Margaret arrived in Ardwick, James was not waiting as he usually did. He was working until later that evening, as it was a regular Thursday workday for him, despite it being Christmas Eve. For the first time in a long while, Margaret was able to walk home on her own and she did not mind one bit.

As Margaret opened the door, she was bombarded by siblings and the smell of her mother's cooking. Mary and Agnes pounced on her as though it had been a year since they had seen her. It was exactly what she needed and it made her feel so happy.

"Margaret, you are home. We have missed you so." Sarah shooed her daughters away so she could welcome Margaret home. She melted into her mother's arms.

"Is Aunt Eleanor coming over this evening?"

Margaret turned to the sound of rustling in her bag. "Girls, get out of there. If you keep looking, your gifts shall turn to coal." In full pout, the girls stepped away from the bag.

"Yes, Eleanor shall be over shortly," Sarah announced.

As a tradition, gifts were exchanged on Christmas Eve. It had been that way for Sarah since she was a young girl. Her mother had always joked it was because the children lacked the patience to wait until Christmas Day. The truth was no one really knew why. Sarah had always thought it best to not mess with tradition.

James arrived home at six, and Eleanor shortly after that. Samuel arrived last at seven. By that time, Mary and Agnes were bouncing off the walls in anticipation.

Much to the children's chagrin, the Christmas Eve traditions also included sharing a meal together before the gifts were to be opened. This particular meal celebrated Eleanor's family's Scottish heritage and included bridies, savoury pies filled with minced meat. They were followed by a dessert of shortbread. Sarah had spent the afternoon baking and the house smelled heavenly.

"Samuel is finally home. Mama, Samuel is finally home. Can we eat now?" Agnes begged.

"Yes, let us eat now," Sarah answered.

They bowed their heads and Sarah said grace. She thanked God for the many blessings He had bestowed upon the family that year, for the family's health and well-being, and ultimately for the love that they had for one another. They all nodded their heads in unison and dove into the meal. The bridies were warm and moist and the shortbread crumbled in silky perfection in their mouths. At that moment, there was nothing in this world that could have tasted better.

"Can we open our presents now, Mama?" Mary begged. "I cannot wait any more. I am bursting."

Sarah laughed and nodded in agreement. The family all moved into the sitting room, each in possession of the gifts they wished to share.

Eleanor began. To Mary and Agnes, she gave dolls. To Margaret, she gave a pair of elegant black gloves. "I shall wear them with my new coat. Thank you so much, Aunt Eleanor. I love them."

To Samuel, she gave an engraved pocket watch that said, *To Samuel, I am very proud of the man you are becoming. With all my love, Aunt Eleanor.* Samuel beamed as he read the inscription.

To James, she gave a new whittling knife and a large piece of burl. James was so excited. He knew burl to be rare and expensive. He was happy beyond words.

"And, to Sarah, my best friend in the world, I give you my heart." Eleanor handed Sarah a heart-shaped pendant on a chain. Sarah was speechless.

"Open it. Please open it," Eleanor coaxed.

Sarah opened the heart and inside it was a small photo of Eleanor and Sarah. "I shall have you in my heart forever, and now you shall have me in yours," Eleanor said.

Stoic Sarah, a woman who rarely showed emotion, could not hide what this meant to her. Without a word being said, Sarah embraced Eleanor. It was a love that was deeper than blood. It transcended social class and wealth. It was pure, without pretence, and without expectation.

To Eleanor, Sarah gave a quilted blanket embroidered with her name. The blanket was made with pieces of fabric from Eleanor's shop. Sarah had collected them from the beginning.

"This blanket shall keep you as warm as an embrace, for the times that I am not with you."

Eleanor wiped the tears with her fingers and said, "That is enough of my blubbering. Let us move on."

After the remaining gifts were given, the family shared some hot mulled wine and sang some Christmas carols and hymns. It had been a joyful evening, one that they would all remember fondly for the rest of their lives.

"I forgot. Mrs. Markley gave me this," Margaret said as she handed her mother the tiny box.

"Well, open it, Margaret. It is for you," Sarah said.

Margaret took the lid off her box. Margaret looked at the contents and shrieked with excitement. "Look, Mama, it is a half week's wages! But I was already paid. Is this a gift?" Margaret asked.

"Yes, Margaret. It is a gift for you. It is yours. You have earned it, my dear. You work hard. It is yours to spend as you wish, whenever you wish."

Eleanor breathed a sigh of relief. It wasn't overly generous, she thought, but it was better than what she feared. She thought her father must have had a hand in this because Catherine certainly wouldn't have been generous willingly and without pressure. Margaret was ecstatic. She had never had her own money. Never.

Chapter 14

Samuel and James walked Eleanor home while Sarah got the girls ready for bed.

The morning arrived as perfectly as the last evening had ended. Samuel, James, and Margaret did not have to work, nor did they have to prepare themselves for work. It was to be a day of family and of divine blessings.

The family sat down to breakfast and were discussing the day's events when there was a knock at the door. Sarah rose to see who the visitor was. To her surprise, it was a uniformed Peeler.

"What can I do for you on this Christmas morning, good sir?" Sarah asked of the intrusion. Mary was standing behind her peeking out.

"I am inquiring into the whereabouts of a young child, a ten-year-old boy by the name of John Andrews, to be exact. He has been missing since yesterday," the officer said as though it had been the hundredth time he had said those words.

Sarah shuddered at the thought of another child unaccounted for. She noted to herself that meant three now remained missing. The thought sent chills down her spine.

"No, Sir, we have not. We have not been out of our home since five yesterday," Sarah said holding Mary close to her.

"How many people live here, Mum?" the officer asked.

"I have two young girls, a daughter thirteen, a son fifteen, and another son seventeen."

The officer cocked his head slightly. "Is the older one here now?" he inquired.

"He is. And why might you be asking?" Sarah asked defensively.

"Might I have a word with him?" He continued to push Sarah.

"I need to understand why you...." Sarah was cut off by Samuel's entrance into the room.

"It is all right, Ma. What do you want to know?" Samuel asked. By this time, James had joined him in the room.

"Might I ask you where you were yesterday afternoon?"

"I was working at the Markley factory until half past six. I arrived home at seven and have been here with my family since that time."

"And what about you, lad? Where were you?" he asked James.

James hesitated, frightened by the authority and questioning.

"I had my deliveries until half past five. I arrived home at six." James was shaking and the officer took notice.

"Why so fidgety, lad? Might you have a reason to be nervous?"

"My son is a good boy. There is nothing unlawful going on. Why are you asking so harshly?" Sarah turned the questioning around, but the officer did not answer.

"Where do you deliver?" he continued probing.

"Market Street to Robinson Street," James answered. "I had five deliveries yesterday."

The officer hesitated, narrowing his glance on James. It was apparent something James had said reduced any suspicion the officer may have had, but he wasn't willing to admit it yet.

"Thank you, Mum," the officer said to Sarah. "That shall be all for now, but I may be back." Clearly, intimidation was his target, and he succeeded handily.

Sarah closed the door as the man walked away. The visit had chilled the room as much as the cool draught. Sarah did not speak to what was on everyone's mind. She thought it better to move on and focus on the day.

After they finished their breakfast, they prepared themselves for Christmas service at church. The visitor had extinguished the smiles and brought a sombre mood to the morning, and Sarah hoped to return the atmosphere to what it had been.

As they walked to the church, Sarah shared her thoughts with her family. "We are all truly blessed. Every day the good Lord guides us and protects us and blesses us immeasurably. We have each other to offer support and guidance as well and there is no greater gift in the world, absolutely none. No matter which path He chooses for us in life, we must take it with full hearts, and God's light shall always guide our way."

The children all said, "Yes, Mama" in unison as they continued their walk. Standing outside the church was Eleanor, and to Sarah's surprise, her brother William.

"Merry Christmas, William. What a splendid surprise to have you join us for Christmas service." Sarah was happy for Eleanor to have her brother with her on this day.

"Thank you, Sarah. Merry Christmas to you as well. I have been looking forward to sharing the day with my sister and all of you," William said sincerely.

The group entered the church and took their place on a pew.

"My name is Mary," Mary said as she sat down beside William.

William was smitten with her preciousness. "Well, hello, Mary. You look lovely today. Thank you for sitting beside me."

The sound of the church organ filled the room. The organist brought to life a sound that was both haunting and beautiful. The pipes rose to the frescoed ceiling dispersing each note through the church like fireworks in the sky.

The congregation was asked to pray for the children of Ardwick, and in particular those who were separated from their families that Christmas. They were told that it was not for them to understand God's plan, and that God's wisdom was infinite.

"We are all faced with challenges in life, and it is how we manage those challenges that we shall be judged by God. We are all special in His eyes and we each have our own purpose, our own destiny. And, on this day, on the anniversary of the birth of Christ, we come together to give thanks for what He has given us: the gift of life."

As the organ music continued to play, they stood up in their pews and began to make their way outside the church, which had not had an empty seat. It was clear there was a need for some spiritual healing and Sarah felt today's message served that purpose well. It was uplifting without being dismissive or disempowering.

"Reuben shall be arriving shortly at your home. We best be going," Eleanor directed.

"I have a surprise for you both," Sarah revealed to Mary and Agnes

"A surprise? Oh, Mama, what is it?" Mary asked clapping her hands.

"I think I shall let Aunt Eleanor tell you."

All but Mary and Agnes knew of the surprise, and now they waited impatiently for it to be revealed.

"We are going on an adventure today. We are going to spend Christmas Day at my father's home in the country. Would you like to see some horses, Mary and Agnes?"

"Can I pet a horse, Aunt Eleanor?" Agnes asked with her voice full of excitement.

"Yes, of course you may pet a horse."

Sarah wanted her children to experience the beauty of the country, the wide open spaces, and the horses, but it was her greatest fear that the children would question the life that Sarah was able to provide for them. Was it irresponsible to show them something that could never be theirs?

As they all walked to Sarah's home, the children showered Eleanor with questions. William walked behind the group and Sarah held back to walk with him.

"It is kind of your father to allow us to spend Christmas at his home with you both. And I appreciate your generosity as well." Sarah spoke from her heart and it touched William.

"I have known you since we were children, Sarah. Eleanor thinks of you as a sister, and I, too, think of you as family. My own family has changed over the years and I have learned family is what you make of it. I would not want to spend the day in any other manner." Sarah felt a tenderness that she had not felt from him before. It indeed felt like family, and it was a sense of belonging and a feeling of overwhelming peace that had eluded her for so long.

William was very much like his sister. He was kind-hearted and had a good soul. He was always good to Thomas when Thomas worked for him, and he treated Samuel with the same respect. And, much like Eleanor, William was never drawn to the extravagances that wealth can acquire.

William never married, and Sarah felt that the loss of his mother had played a large part in that. He dutifully took care of his grandparents until the end of their days and transferred his attention to his sister thereafter. There was a strong sibling bond between the two, and while Eleanor would never admit it, she needed her brother.

As they arrived at Sarah's house, Reuben and carriage were waiting outside. Agnes and Mary could not contain their excitement and were bouncing about like bunnies in the snow.

"Hello, Miss Markley, Mr. Markley, and Mrs. Berry. Merry Christmas to you all."

"Hello, Reuben, it is so nice to see you today. And thank you for coming to take us to Amberley House," Eleanor said. "We are all excited to spend the day in the country."

Reuben nodded his head in acknowledgement and moved toward the door of the carriage.

"I shall fetch the bags I packed for the evening. Just a few moments," Sarah said.

When Sarah returned, all were seated comfortably in the carriage, with the exception of James, who was sitting on the seat up top.

"James, what on earth are you doing up there?" Sarah asked.

"It is all right, Mrs. Berry. I look forward to the company," Reuben said.

"Well, if you say it is all right, then I am fine with it. And, please, Reuben, call me Sarah." Sarah was uncomfortable with Rueben's formality. She was of no higher standing than he was.

Reuben blushed. "I will. Thank you, Sarah."

Reuben stowed the bags and helped Sarah into the carriage. William smiled at Sarah as she sat down.

"Mama, Mr. Markley was telling us that there are deer at Amberley House, and that his brother, Philip, has a pet rabbit." Agnes was trying to be a little lady, but she could not hide her excitement. It was torturing her.

"Maybe we shall be fortunate enough to see them." Sarah was nervous and hesitant. It was a different world, and she was unsure of how she felt.

"We are all spending Christmas together. Please call me William. You may call my father Mr. Markley, but I am William. Can we all agree on that?"

Mary and Agnes nodded, but Samuel could only look out the window. This was uncomfortable for him. William Markley had been good to him, but much like Sarah, processing the reality of the day was proving to be challenging for Samuel.

As the carriage made its way down Stockport Road, the sun shone down warming the air to well above freezing. It was a welcome change from the cold that had hung in the air for the better part of a month. The sky was clear and blue and, as they distanced themselves from Ardwick and the towering smoke stacks, the smell of ashen smoke dulled. It was an exquisite day to be out.

It was much quieter than a usual Friday. Most places of business were closed, and there was no need to be out and about unless you had a specific place to go. There were no boys selling newspapers on the corners, and there were few beggars because there was no one to beg from. It felt like a Sunday evening on a Friday afternoon.

They turned down High Lane, and the sullen mood that usually accompanied Margaret at this point was absent. It was a different set of circumstances. It was not dark, and she was not on foot and alone. The Markleys would be gone and Margaret was overjoyed.

"We are here," Eleanor said, adjusting herself in her seat.

Agnes looked out the window and gasped. Amberley House could be seen in the distance, and it was a castle fit for a princess.

Mary jumped off Eleanor's lap to get a better look out the window and stumbled as the carriage turned onto the estate. William reached out to Mary to steady her.

"Careful, Mary, you will hurt yourself," Sarah said sternly, drawing a look of reassurance from William.

As they made their way up the road, Margaret caught sight of Jonathan and grew eager with anticipation at the thought of his presence at Christmas dinner.

Reuben pulled the carriage up to the front of the house. He stepped down from his seat and opened its door. He helped Mary and Agnes out first and then Eleanor and Sarah.

Agnes and Mary could not contain themselves. They feasted their eyes on everything they could take in from where they stood. It was a fairy tale in a book come to life. It really was the adventure that Eleanor had described.

"Margaret, is this where you work?" Agnes asked in wondrous disbelief.

Margaret nodded and beamed. "Mama, I shall take our bags to my room. You and the girls shall sleep with me," Margaret directed.

"That sounds lovely, Margaret," Sarah agreed, following her daughter's lead.

"Let's leave the bags in the foyer for now," Eleanor suggested. "We shall have plenty of time to get them to their proper places. For now, I propose that Margaret and I go to the kitchen to prepare a luncheon for us all. James and the girls, you can join Jonathan and Reuben in the stable. I think you would all enjoy watching them take care of the horses. If you are good girls, perhaps Jonathan can show you Napoleon."

Mary and Agnes bounced enthusiastically at the thought.

"William, perhaps you would like to show Sarah the grounds. It is a beautiful day for a walk. And, Samuel, I would think you would greatly enjoy the library." Eleanor had everyone accounted for.

"Sarah, if you are interested in a stroll, I would be happy to show you the grounds," William offered.

Sarah hesitated, uncomfortable with the attention. "I wouldn't want to impose."

"No imposition whatsoever," William countered. "None at all."

"Well, I would like that then. Thank you," Sarah said, not wanting to offend her hosts.

"Before we do that, I would like to show Samuel to the library myself. Samuel, I hear you are a great lover of books. Are you interested in seeing my father's library?" William looked on in hopeful anticipation of Samuel's response.

"Thank you. I would like that," Samuel said, also trying to be positive.

Jonathan introduced himself to James and the girls and walked them toward the stable. There was no hesitation. They were feeling nothing but excitement with the events as they were unfolding.

"I'll put your bags in the foyer then," Reuben said.

"Thank you, Reuben, but I think we can handle them. We shall be having luncheon in about an hour's time. We would welcome Jonathan's and your company."

Reuben was taken by surprise. "Thank you for the kind offer. I have no doubt that Jonathan would like that." Reuben beamed at the inclusion. He then drove the carriage, following the children to the stable.

"Mama, let me show you the kitchen while Mr. Markley shows Samuel to the library." Margaret began to make her way down the path leading to the back of the house when Eleanor stopped her.

"Margaret, we'll go in the front door. It is the fastest route to the kitchen." Eleanor winked at Margaret. Margaret hesitated at the break in protocol, but followed Eleanor's lead.

Eleanor picked up a couple of bags and Margaret did the same. Sarah reached for one and William took it from her.

"Let me take that for you, Sarah. Here, Samuel, why don't you take this last one?" William handed the last bag to Samuel.

Sarah thanked William and followed Eleanor and Margaret up the stairs. It was the first time that Margaret had walked up the front stairs. She had spied them as she made her way up the estate road, but had never actually walked up them. As simple as it was, it was exhilarating.

Eleanor opened the front door and entered. It was an entirely different experience for Margaret. The staircase was grander than she had remembered. The Bernini sculpture was larger and more lifelike and the painting on the back wall more vibrant. Entering from the front door, it felt real. Usually, she saw it from the inside, and she suddenly realized it was as though she had seen it from the pages of a book, as an observer. Now it was tangible, and more incredible than she could ever have imagined.

"Samuel, put that bag there, and I'll show you the library."

Samuel placed the bag down beside the others and followed William to the library. The library was twice as large as their kitchen and sitting room combined. It was filled with dark mahogany wood shelves that went from floor to ceiling. Rows upon rows of books filled the space, and the smell of their binded covers filled the room. Samuel closed his eyes and soaked it in.

"Samuel, I sense your discomfort. Is it with me or with Amberley House?" William asked.

Samuel was taken aback by the question and the words bounced around in his head. The silence was excruciating as he tried to formulate a response. William was patient and waited for Samuel to speak.

"I must say, a bit of both, actually," Samuel answered honestly.

"Hmm, I thought that might be the case." William paused while trying to find the right words to express his own feelings.

"I have always liked you, Samuel. You were a good boy and you have turned into a good man. The truth is, I have always thought of you as the son I wished I had. I don't want you to see me as your employer. The respect I expect from you is no more than I would expect you to give any other person. I am no better than you, no worse. In my eyes, we are equals." William paused for Samuel's reaction.

Samuel had been looking at the ground as William was speaking. After a moment or two, Samuel looked up. He looked William in the eyes and fixed his gaze on him. He was letting the words settle as William reached out his hand. Samuel continued to look at William. William was determined to hold out his hand until Samuel took it. Samuel finally did.

William tried hard not to show his relief. No words were spoken. William walked out of the room leaving Samuel on his own.

Eleanor, Margaret, and Sarah were in the kitchen preparing a luncheon for the group. Margaret went into the scullery to see what was available to prepare. As she opened the icebox, she noticed an extraordinarily large turkey.

"Aunt Eleanor, what is this doing in here? Should your father and Catherine have taken this with them to Yorkshire? Did they forget it?" Margaret asked.

"I am certain that they shall have their own turkey. This is my father's gift to us all this evening."

Margaret was speechless. It was perfect.

"All we are required to do is to put it in the oven. I believe it is already stuffed."

Margaret took a closer look and noted stuffing bursting from the bird.

"We'll just need to make some accompaniments, and I do believe there is no one better than you for that task." Margaret was bursting like the turkey.

As Margaret moved the turkey aside, she spied a platter of sandwiches, the kind that Catherine was served. They were all identical sizes, cut in pointy triangles with their crusts removed. The platter sat next to a lidded pot. Margaret lifted off the lid to see what was in it. It appeared to be a soup or a sauce of some variety.

"Aunt Eleanor, why would Chef Nicolas have made these sandwiches if he knew your father and Catherine would be away for Christmas?"

"Perhaps, because he made them for us," Eleanor teased. "How about we warm up the soup in the pot?" Eleanor suggested.

As they walked from the scullery, a whistling William entered the kitchen.

"Are you ready for me to show you the grounds, Sarah?" William asked hopefully.

"Go on, Sarah. We shall have our luncheon ready for your return. Go and enjoy the day," Eleanor nudged.

Sarah walked with William toward the front foyer. William helped Sarah with her coat and the two made their way outside. They walked down the front steps onto the pathway leading to the front gardens. The pathway meandered through ornately sculptured hedges and ornamental bushes. They walked in silence. William was uncomfortable, unsure of what to say.

They approached a pond at the edge of the property. There were two grand, white swans floating elegantly in the water. They looked like moving art, neither of them bothered by the pair's intrusion.

"They are delightful, aren't they? We don't see many of them in Ardwick."

"You are right. I have yet to see one." They both laughed at the thought. "And, yes, they are spectacular, so graceful," Sarah added.

They paused to watch the swans. Sarah was taken with the effortlessness with which they glided in the water. They were so smooth, leaving barely a ripple in their wake. Beyond the pond, at the edge of the property, were trees that soared into the sky. They were bare from the season, but it did not diminish their beauty. They looked like soldiers protecting the property, providing a boundary with which the unwelcome were kept out.

As they continued on the path, they flanked the main house and moved toward the back of the property. A latticework pavilion, with lush vines woven through its open spaces, caught Sarah's eye. Sarah's thoughts turned toward Thomas and how he would have loved such a place. He was an incurable dreamer, and what place could be better to dream? As her thoughts came back to the moment, she felt the sting of the memory.

William sensed her discomfort. "Are you all right? Are you too cold?"

"I am quite comfortable. Thank you for asking."

"How have you been, Sarah? I have not seen you in a while. It has been too long. I often think of you and hope you are well." Sarah sensed William's nervousness.

"We have been well. Thank you for asking. Margaret seems to be doing well with her work here. Samuel is most grateful for the job he has at your father's factory. James is growing like a weed, and the girls are happy and healthy. We most certainly cannot complain."

William hesitated, pulling his words together carefully. "I am glad to hear your children are well. I am most interested in how you are. I know Thomas' passing was very difficult. You are a strong woman and you have managed your family brilliantly." William paused, taking a deep breath. "I don't mean to be presumptuous or invasive, but I am interested in knowing if you are, um, well, if you are happy." William stammered on his thoughts.

Sarah was taken aback. Not only was she not expecting the question, but she did not know the answer. Her happiness had never crossed her mind. She had never allowed it to cross her mind. She had been too occupied with the lives of her family that anything beyond her basic needs were not thought of, nor indulged in.

"I am fine. Thank you for asking," Sarah answered softly.

William was not content with the polite response. He understood her hesitation, but he so desperately wanted to understand what was in her heart.

"Thomas was a decent man. I had deep respect for him. He was a hard worker. He was honourable and cared for his family more than anyone I have ever known. I, too, was saddened when he passed. He was taken from you far too soon and it was an immeasurable loss. I have never been in your position directly, but I remember the loss of my own mother. It pained me immensely. But, over time, I learned to deal with the loss the best I could."

Sarah was touched by William's heartfelt thoughts. They were comforting to her.

"Thank you, William. You are a dear friend."

William felt a hesitation, that there was more to come, and he sensed it was not what he wanted to hear.

"My Thomas was my life. He was my soul and I shall miss him always. I do not fear that I cannot move past the loss. I am fearful that it should be possible. He is in my heart as though he is standing next to me at this moment. I pledged my love to him once and I cannot imagine my heart belonging to another. I simply cannot." Sarah stopped, took a deep breath and held it. She slowly exhaled to release the pressure of her sorrow. The tears were waiting and she was not prepared to see them fall in front of William.

Sarah's sorrow became William's. He wanted to ease her pain and he did not know how. It was clear to him that she was not ready to move on. He cared for her deeply. He always had, and would support her any way he could.

"The love you shared was beyond measure. And the children you created are a testament to that every day. God may have brought Thomas home, but it does not mean that you were ready to let him go. It shall take time for you to grieve. He could not have asked for a better wife. Sarah, you are an exceptional woman, and I am honoured to call you my friend. I shall be here for you always, should you ever need anything."

They continued to walk down the path. William looked at Sarah and noticed tears falling down her cheeks. She was deep in thought and didn't seem to notice them.

She stopped walking and turned to William. "You are a kind soul, William, and I pray with all my heart that you find love as I have. And I pray that it is eternal, as mine is. You are the best of men and I am so proud to call you my friend. I cannot imagine my life without you and Eleanor."

The sentiment was bittersweet for William.

"Let us get back to the kitchen. I am sure that they are waiting on us," William said, eager to move past that moment.

Chapter 15

In the stable, Mary and Agnes bounced through the hay, studying the horses one by one. The work horses – Star, Stormy, Clover, Puddle, Tommy and Tiny – were all in their stalls. The girls fed them carrots and giggled as the horses chomped hungrily.

"How do horses sleep?" Agnes asked Jonathan.

"Horses sleep lying down, just like you do. They sleep in their stalls in the wintertime, and in the summertime they sometimes sleep outside in the field." Agnes was very excited to see the animals in the barn, learning about how they lived. It was something the girls had never experienced before.

Jonathan gave each girl a brush and showed them how to groom the horses. They reached as high as they could and stroked their bellies and flanks. Puddle nibbled mischievously on Mary's hat as she brushed her, causing Mary to use her stern voice. Reuben looked on, smiling at the innocence he had not seen in so long.

Jonathan showed James how to pick out mud, hay, and stones from the horses' hooves with a hoof pick. James mastered the skill quickly and impressed Jonathan.

"It is quite like carving," James said. "I'm pretty good with a knife. It certainly helps. I'll bet you could whittle yourself. I'll show you some time if you'd like."

"I'd like that. Thank you," Jonathan said, appreciatively. He longed for something to do to pass the time.

"I think it is about time that we head over to the main house. I think we have a meal waiting for us." Reuben directed the children out of the barn.

"Thank you so much for showing us the horses. I love horses." Mary nodded in agreement with her sister.

"Well, how about we show you Napoleon after lunch? He is young Philip's horse and he is out in the field right now getting some exercise and fresh air." Both girls nodded enthusiastically.

The group from the stable arrived at the back kitchen door. Margaret and Eleanor were placing the food on the table, and they all eagerly removed their shoes and coats and took their seats. Samuel came in from the library and followed along.

Margaret poured hot apple cider into the glasses and spooned soup into bowls. The sandwiches were arranged on a tray and placed in the centre of the table.

"Margaret, this soup smells sooooooo good," Agnes said. "Did you make it?"

"I did not. Chef Nicolas did."

"Who's Chef Nicolas?" Mary asked.

"Chef Nicolas cooks all the tasty food that Aunt Eleanor's father eats here at Amberley House."

Mary looked on wide eyed at the explanation. It was just another piece to the amazing story that was unfolding in front of her.

William and Sarah were the last to arrive. "Mama, how was your walk?"

"It was lovely, Margaret. The grounds are stunning. I saw two swans swimming in the pond." Margaret was so pleased that her mother was enjoying herself. It meant the world to her.

William said grace and then the group devoured their meal. They were all famished from the day's activities. The children were taken with the tiny, crustless sandwiches. They were unlike any they had had before, and they ate them until they were bursting.

"Mama, can you make sandwiches like this? These are my favourite," Mary asked her mother, wide-eyed and hopeful.

Sarah laughed at Mary's question. It warmed her heart to see her family together and happy, and she tried to put aside the circumstance and simply focus on their joy.

"Samuel, did anything catch your eye in the library?" William wondered.

"There are so many interesting books in there. I could spend the rest of my life reading and not get to all of them. Your father must love books to have collected so many."

William laughed. "Well, surprisingly he doesn't like to read at all. He is a collector, and I guess it doesn't really matter much what of. Could be art, could be books, could be anything, really. Seems silly, I know. I could not imagine collecting something that I was not absolutely passionate about. Could you?" William posed the question to Samuel.

"No, I suppose not." William was pleased to see Samuel opening up.

Jonathan remained quiet. He was focused on Margaret, pondering the impact of her secret relationship with the Markleys. Was this omission a forgivable deceit? He chastised himself. He should have known. But then again, how could he? There were no signs, none at all. There were no special privileges, and in fact, it was quite the opposite. He had seen how Catherine Markley had treated Margaret. And now the only privileges he had ever witnessed her enjoying he was enjoying as well. He had come to care too much for Margaret. She was a devoted friend, generous and gracious. He decided then and there he would not let it come between them.

A tempting aroma began to fill the room. It teased their nostrils as they tried to discern its origin.

"What is that smell, Margaret? I am stuffed beyond belief, but it could make me eat again," James joked.

"Turkey and herb stuffing. Mr. Markley was kind enough to provide it for Christmas dinner."

"And Reuben and Jonathan, we would be honoured if you would join us for dinner this evening," Eleanor offered.

Jonathan looked at Margaret for her reaction. She grinned knowingly and nodded with approval. Jonathan blushed a crimson hue and looked back down at his empty plate, feeling nothing but nervous excitement.

"This is unexpected. Thank you. We are honoured to be included and look forward to it. Please let us know if there is anything we can do." Reuben was grateful for the opportunity for his son to experience Christmas with as close to a family as he had had in a very long time. Jonathan's happiness was worth the world to him.

"Dinner shall be at seven. Does that sound good to everyone?" Eleanor asked. One by one, they all nodded in agreement. "And, before we go, there is one last gift to give," Eleanor offered, piquing everyone's interest. "Before Philip left for Yorkshire, he asked me to give Margaret his gift as he could not be here to do it himself."

Margaret was surprised and was at a loss for what Eleanor could be speaking of.

"Philip wanted to give you something that you would like very much. He knows how much you love Napoleon and he wanted for you to ride him."

Mary and Agnes squealed with delight and Margaret sat stunned.

"He knows we are here?"

"He does. I shared the news with him before he left. He was eager to stay with us all, but he knew it was not possible," Eleanor explained.

"Really? I can ride Napoleon!" Margaret could feel the excitement building up inside her. She had never been on a horse before. But her excitement was squashed with a single thought.

"What would Mrs. Markley think of that?" Margaret asked.

"Napoleon is Philip's horse, not Catherine's. She is not here, and she does not know we are so we have nothing to worry about, now do we?" Eleanor said, unable to hide her contempt. "But it might be best if this stays our little Christmas secret." Eleanor winked at Margaret, who was having difficulty staying in her seat.

"Jonathan, could you take Margaret to the stable and prepare Napoleon for a ride? Margaret, your mother and the girls and I shall tidy up the kitchen. Samuel, perhaps you would like to spend some more time in the library. William, you could show Samuel our father's collection of Sherlock Holmes books. He does love a good detective story." Eleanor was being Eleanor, making sure that everyone was busy and content.

Margaret and Jonathan made their way to the stable, following a few paces behind Reuben. The sun was getting lower in the mid-afternoon sky, and was a ball of fiery glow. Everything that stood in its path basked in the orange hue, creating a surreal landscape that took Margaret's breath away.

"The day could not be better, could it, Jonathan? It is spectacular." The air was still. There was no hint of a breeze.

"I'm sure Napoleon'll be as thrilled as you are. He loves the company."

Jonathan walked out to the paddock where Napoleon was grazing. Margaret stayed at the fence to keep the mud off her dress. As Jonathan walked toward Napoleon, the animal looked up from his meal and took notice of his two visitors. He started walking toward Jonathan. Jonathan took hold of his bridle and walked off toward Margaret and the stable.

Margaret fed Napoleon a carrot while Jonathan outfitted Napoleon with his riding gear. Napoleon was in an especially friendly mood today, nuzzling up to Margaret as she scratched under his chin.

"All ready. Why don't you come around this way, Margaret?" Jonathan directed.

Margaret walked around to Jonathan and waited for his directions. Nervousness surged in her and she was having second thoughts about getting up on Napoleon. Jonathan sensed her trepidation and attempted to pacify her fear with humour.

"Just imagine Napoleon is Catherine Markley...but I guess that is an outright insult to poor Napoleon. Just imagine it is her and get up there and show her who's boss," Jonathan teased.

Margaret laughed and chided Jonathan for his disrespect, as humorous as it was.

Jonathan held out his hand for Margaret's foot, which she placed in it. She hoisted herself up as she had seen Philip do many times before, and placed herself on the saddle. She pulled her free foot rather clumsily behind her stirrupped foot so that she could sit properly. She could see why more riding was done by men. It wasn't very easy to remain elegant while trying to get up on a horse in a skirt.

"Are you comfortable?" Jonathan asked. He put his hand on her leg to make sure that she was steady.

Margaret blushed at the contact. She had not been touched by a boy like that before and it made her legs tingle. Jonathan noticed her flushed cheeks and blushed himself.

"Yes, I am comfortable. Thank you for your help."

Jonathan led Napoleon out of the barn. His long gait forced a fluid up and down movement that was a strange sensation for Margaret. It was relaxing while at the same time unsettling in its insecurity. There was no harness to hold her in place. She simply sat there with her legs hanging precariously over the side. If Napoleon was to bolt, it would be horrible. Jonathan picked up his pace and Napoleon began to trot.

"Jonathan, what are you doing?" Margaret said, panicking slightly.

Jonathan laughed at Margaret's concern. Ultimately, she lacked control in that situation and that is what bothered her the most. He was in control now and it gave him a great sense of pleasure to see their usual roles reversed.

"Would you like to hold the reins yourself, Margaret?"

Margaret hesitated at the thought. It was all a bit frightening for her. She loved Napoleon and could not imagine him hurting her.

"Napoleon, we are friends, are we not?" Margaret said as she rubbed his neck. "I would like to take you for a walk and I need for you to be gentle with me. Can you promise me that?"

Jonathan handed the reins to Margaret and she took them in her hands. Napoleon backed up slightly and Margaret panicked.

"Margaret, you must relax. Do not hold the reins too tight. Let Napoleon do the work," Jonathan chided.

Napoleon began walking slowly toward the paddock where he spent most of his days. Margaret did not guide him; she just let him lead as Jonathan watched on protectively.

Being atop such a wondrous creature was exhilarating. If the day ended at that point, she would have wanted for nothing more. Never in her wildest imagination could she have ever seen herself in this position and she was fearful that she could not go back.

Napoleon honoured Margaret's request and was an absolute gentleman. She teased the reins, guiding him to all corners of the paddock. Under the backdrop of the setting sun, the rolling hills of the estate were afire with warm light. To see something so differently, a perspective as new and alien as to cause one to question one's perception, was beyond comprehension to Margaret.

As Margaret guided Napoleon back to the paddock gate, she focused on her friend. Jonathan was her best friend. He provided her with comfort when she was feeling melancholy. "Melancholy be damned," he would curse, pretending he was slaying what ailed her with a sword. It never ceased to make Margaret laugh. He was very thoughtful that way. Margaret never realized how thoughtful until that moment. Appreciation aside, she was seeing Jonathan differently that day.

As she approached Jonathan, he held out his hands to take Napoleon's reins.

"Well, how did you enjoy that, Margaret? Napoleon seemed to be enjoying himself."

"It was marvellous. Absolutely marvellous. It was very kind of Philip to think of me that way. I am very touched."

"It is easy to do nice things for nice people."

Margaret smiled at Jonathan's sentiment.

Margaret's mood became serious as her thoughts turned toward the guilt she felt for not telling Jonathan about her relationship with Eleanor. It had been weighing heavily on her. He had not said much to her all day and she was concerned he was angry with her.

"Jonathan, I hope you'll forgive me for not telling you that my Aunt Eleanor was Eleanor Markley."

Jonathan stopped in his place, caught off guard by the request. He turned to Margaret and saw the concern on her face.

"I never meant to deceive you. I really did not. I did not want you to think of me any differently. I did not want you to think of me as different than you. I am not. I am afforded no special treatment. None at all." Margaret pleaded with Jonathan.

Jonathan did not say a word as he turned and continued to walk toward the barn.

"I wish you would say something, Jonathan. If you do not forgive me, it shall hurt me beyond words."

Jonathan looked back at Margaret with a look of understanding. "I do not need to forgive you. There is nothing to forgive. I understand why you kept it from me. I am sad that you thought I would think of you differently, but I am not angry. I have often wondered why Catherine Markley is harsher with you than the others and now it is clear why. It is very apparent that Eleanor does not like Catherine and I'm assuming the feeling is mutual. I also assume you have your job here because of Eleanor's father and not her stepmother."

"And I am thoroughly confident Eleanor planned the day here specifically because she knew it would drive Catherine mad if Catherine was aware we were here. I am very glad she did. Spending Christmas with you and your father like this has been wonderful."

Jonathan brought Napoleon to a stop and helped Margaret down.

"I, too, am enjoying myself," he said locking eyes with Margaret. "It has been the best Christmas I can remember."

As Jonathan took off Napoleon's riding gear, Margaret brushed him. She imagined it would feel good after getting off the blanket and saddle. Napoleon whinnied with gratitude.

"I should be getting back to the house or else they'll think Napoleon ran off with me. We shall see you in a few hours at dinner."

"I look forward to it," Jonathan said happily.

In the kitchen, Eleanor, Sarah, and the girls were sitting at the table having a cup of tea. The girls were engaged in animated conversation about Snowflake, and were pressing their mother for a rabbit.

"How was your ride, Margaret?" Eleanor asked hopefully. "Was it what you hoped?"

"It was, and much more. I adore Napoleon. He is magnificent." Margaret was radiating joy. "The turkey does smell fantastic. I cannot wait to eat it," she continued.

"I have peeled the potatoes and placed them in the pot of water on the stove. We have made the dough for cranberry bread and it is rising in the corner. Let's see, mmhhh, have we missed anything?" Eleanor asked herself aloud.

"What about a sweet dessert? There are eggs and cream, and I believe I saw some cocoa powder in the scullery. I could make a pudding." Margaret offered.

"I love chocolate pudding. Yes, please," Mary said enthusiastically.

"Well, chocolate pudding it is then," Eleanor decided. "Margaret, why don't you look in the scullery to see what else you could use to dress it up?"

Margaret hesitated, causing Eleanor to remind her that Catherine was not there. She assured her there was nothing to concern herself with. It was Christmas and they were going to enjoy their meal.

"Mary and Agnes, would you like to help me make the pudding?"

They both jumped up out of their seats as an answer to Margaret's question. Margaret led them into the scullery to obtain the supplies they needed. She handed Agnes the eggs and cream, and Mary the cocoa and sugar.

"Girls, please take these things out to the kitchen. I shall be there in a moment."

Margaret searched the cupboards for items to spice up the pudding. She saw a jar of canned black cherries, pieces of Swiss chocolate, and some dessert biscuits and she brought all of them with her into the kitchen.

Mary and Agnes helped with the egg cracking, cream pouring, and cherry smashing. Margaret warmed up the cream, eggs, and sugar on the stove, thickening the mixture to the right consistency. She added the cocoa until it was nice and chocolaty and then she removed the mixture from the stove. She held out the wooden spoon for Mary and Agnes to taste. Both offered their approval without hesitation.

"We must wait for it to cool and then we shall finish it off," Margaret explained. "And, in the meantime, I think I will go to the library to see how Samuel and James are doing."

Sarah nodded as Margaret left the kitchen. In the library, Samuel was sitting in a large, plush chair with his nose in a book. James sat in the corner working at his piece of burl and William stood, fixated, in front of a map of the world. Not one of them noticed Margaret as she walked into the room.

Margaret cleared her throat to make her presence known. William turned around, but the other two were far too engrossed in what they were doing to pay attention.

"Hello, Margaret. How was your ride?" William inquired.

"It was thrilling, absolutely thrilling. Philip's horse is amazing."

William laughed at Margaret's enthusiasm.

"Have you ever placed on a map where your Uncle Bertie lives?" William asked. "Come here and let me show you."

Margaret walked toward William and the large map that covered the wall. It was very intricate and detailed. Margaret had only seen small maps in textbooks in school. She had never seen anything this elaborate.

"This is where we are right now," William said pointing to Manchester on the map. "And this is Winnipeg, Canada," he said pointing to the centre of Canada. "From what I understand, that is where Bertie lives."

"I believe that is true," Sarah said, entering the room. "I would like to see myself, if I may."

William once again turned around and caught Sarah's eye. He was happy to see her and his expression showed as much. As Sarah walked toward the two of them, William stepped aside to let Sarah in between himself and Margaret.

William again pointed out Manchester and then traced his finger on the map to Winnipeg. "It is an enormous distance. There is no doubt about that. If you look past Winnipeg, and at the lines here, they represent elevation. All along here sits vast mountain ranges unlike anything we have here in England. I have read about these mountains. From what I understand, they are very similar in splendour to the mountains in the Alps of Switzerland and France."

Sarah surveyed the room and was taken with the remarkable masculinity. And despite its lack of feminine ambience, it was warm and inviting as the glow of the lantern light blanketed the dark wood and the sound of Vivaldi's "Four Seasons" played quietly on the gramophone. Through the window, Sarah could see the circular entrance to Amberley House, with its towering fountain and illuminated lamp posts.

Sarah could never let herself sit long enough to relax, but she could imagine herself sitting on the heavy, plush chairs sewing or embroidering. As she allowed herself such thoughts, she watched her two sons who were engaged and contented with their own activities.

"This room is quite something, William," Sarah said. "I don't believe I have seen so many books in one room before. I cannot imagine one could read even a fraction of them in a lifetime. Then again, I suppose one would never *need* a house this grand either," Sarah said very matter-of-factly.

William was taken with Sarah's practicality. He had always admired that about her. For her it was not about wealth or poverty. It was about common sense, and common sense was something that Sarah possessed in abundance.

"Dinner shall be ready shortly. I must handle the final preparations. I shall let you all know when it is ready." Margaret excused herself and left for the kitchen.

Chapter 16

Mary and Agnes were drawing pictures at the table as Margaret entered.

"Margaret, look at what I drew. It is a picture of Snowflake," Mary said, holding up her work.

"Very nice, Mary. It looks just like Snowflake."

"Girls, would you like to help me with the pudding?"

Mary continued her drawing, but Agnes joined Margaret at the counter. Margaret added the crushed cherries to the cool pudding and gently folded them in. Margaret handed the biscuits to Agnes and explained how to position them around the inside rim of the bowl. When she was finished, Margaret handed her curled slivers of chocolate to place on top.

"It's a masterpiece," Agnes said proudly.

Eleanor walked by and admired the work. "I would agree. Perhaps we should eat dessert first."

"I don't think Mama would like that," Agnes said surprised at the suggestion, completely missing the playful tone.

"No, I don't suppose she would, Agnes," Eleanor said, clearly amused.

Margaret took the turkey out of the oven. It was a golden brown and the smell was indescribable. Steam was pouring off the stuffing and Margaret put it aside to rest.

"Aunt Eleanor, I'll set the table and then we shall call everyone to dinner."

"Margaret, I have something to show you," Eleanor said. "Follow me."

Margaret wiped her hands on her apron and followed Eleanor out of the kitchen. Eleanor directed Margaret to the dining room. Margaret had been in the dining room only a handful of times because it was predominantly Agnes' responsibility.

As Margaret entered the room, the smell of fire filled her nose. Margaret stopped in her place as the realization of what was in the room overtook her. There was a fire burning in the fireplace, and the table was set with the good china, stemware, and linens. A stunning Baccarat chandelier crowned the room. The table looked as though it was ready to receive the king.

"What is this?" Margaret asked incredulously. "Aunt Eleanor, what is this?"

"We are eating in here tonight, Margaret. It is Christmas and I would like a fire."

Margaret was speechless. She stared at the table, which was elegantly set. This couldn't be real, she thought. It must be a dream.

"Well, we must bring the food in here before it gets cold," Eleanor suggested.

Margaret snapped out of her stupor and looked wide-eyed at Eleanor. Eleanor was radiant, as contented as she had ever been in her life.

As Margaret and Eleanor were entering the kitchen, Jonathan and Reuben arrived. They were dressed in their best clothes and impeccably groomed.

"It smells delicious, Margaret," Reuben complimented. Margaret emanated happiness.

"Agnes, you carry the potatoes and cranberry bread, and Mary, the stuffing. I shall carry the turkey. Margaret, it would be most helpful if you could bring the gravy and cranberry sauce."

Jonathan looked confused. "Where are they going with the food?" he asked.

Margaret did as she was told and picked up the gravy and cranberry sauce. "Come with me," she directed.

Jonathan and Reuben's reaction to the dining room was no different than Margaret's. They stood at the door and did not move. When Sarah arrived, there was a full blockage.

"Are we going to stand here or are we going to sit and have dinner?" Eleanor asked playfully.

Eleanor took the lead and took her seat. Margaret followed, leaving a space. After a pause, Jonathan looked at his father and then took a seat beside Margaret. Reuben followed and sat beside his son.

"Agnes, Samuel, and James, why don't you sit on that side?" Eleanor said, pointing across the table. "Mary, you can sit here between Margaret and me."

"William, perhaps you would do us the honour of choosing a wine for this lovely meal," Eleanor continued.

"Absolutely," William said. "Sarah, would you like to help me choose a wine?"

Sarah followed William to the door that led down to the cellar. William held up the lantern to light their way.

"Please watch your step. These steps can be tricky."

As they got to the bottom of the stairs, William turned on a few more lanterns to illuminate the room. It was beyond compare. Rows and rows of bottles of wine filled their view. Sarah tried to comprehend the number and could not. It appeared to be thousands, but that would be ridiculous, she thought. It must have been the lighting.

"As you can see, my father likes to collect wine," William said with a hint of apology. "I know what you are thinking, and you would be correct. No person could ever drink this much wine in their lifetime. For tonight, we shall not judge, only enjoy. Can we agree on that?"

Sarah focused on William's words. This was not the time for judgement or condemnation. This was the time to enjoy the generous gift that had been placed before her.

"Of course, William," Sarah agreed.

"Good, then. Why don't you choose the wine?"

Sarah suddenly felt a panic. The last time she drank wine was the only time she had drunk wine. The moment quickly played out in her mind.

"Sarah, it is all right. You cannot make a mistake," William said supportively.

Sarah brought herself back from her memory, and into the cellar. She surveyed the shelves of wine and did not know what to do.

"We are having turkey, so I would suggest a nice light pinot noir from Burgundy." William moved toward a row of shelves and stood there.

"Sarah, these wines would go well with turkey. Please choose one." William pointed to a section of wines and then stood there waiting for her to select one.

Sarah hesitated. With no knowledge of what she was doing, she pulled a bottle off the shelf and handed it to William.

William held the bottle up to the lantern and looked at its label.

"Perfect," he said. "Very nice choice." He also pulled the bottle off the shelf beside it, holding the two bottles in one hand and the lantern in the other.

"Sarah, if you could please turn off the lanterns, I would very much appreciate it." As they entered the dining room, everyone else was seated.

"Sarah, please take a seat while I open the wine."

Sarah did as she was directed, taking a seat beside James. William opened both bottles of wine. He placed one on the hutch, which was an elaborately carved Louis XIV, and proceeded to pour the other. He took a smell of the open bottle, but didn't bother to taste it. Nor did he bother to let it breathe. He father would have been horrified, but it didn't matter that evening.

William first poured wine into Sarah's glass, and then Eleanor's, and then Reuben's. "Samuel, you are old enough to drink wine. Would you care for any?"

William looked at Sarah for approval and Sarah nodded. "Yes, please," Samuel said with keen interest.

"Sarah, would it be all right if I gave Margaret and James a tiny bit to taste? Did you know in France it is customary for children to start drinking wine with meals when they are twelve or thirteen?" William said coaxingly.

"If they would like some, that would be fine with me."

William poured half the amount into Margaret and James' glass, not waiting for their confirmation.

"Reuben, would the same be all right for Jonathan?" William looked to Reuben for his approval.

Jonathan sat up in his seat, waiting in anxious anticipation.

"Yes, and thank you for the offer."

William poured wine into Jonathan's glass. Jonathan could not hide his excitement. He had never felt this confident and mature. William filled his own glass, placed the empty bottle on the hutch, and then took his seat beside Sarah.

"I would like to make a toast," William offered. And as he raised his glass, the flames brought the crystal to life, sending dancing beads of light around the room. The miracle of the moment was not lost on anyone.

"Tonight, as we come together as family and friends to celebrate the birth of Christ, our Lord, we are truly blessed. We are blessed for the food that sits before us, we are blessed for our health, and we are blessed for the people who are in our lives." William acknowledged everyone at the table, but his gaze lingered longer on Sarah. "And tonight I raise my glass to each of you as we come together. It is an honour to share a meal with you. May the good Lord bless you in the coming year."

"What a lovely prayer and toast, William. Thank you," Sarah said, acknowledging his words. William took a drink of the wine and everyone else followed.

The wine was nothing like Sarah remembered. Her memory was of something harsher, less desirable in flavour. This wine, on the other hand, was velvety and smooth. It was luscious.

Eleanor started the food around the table, and when everyone had filled their plates they began to eat. The turkey was moist and flavourful. The stuffing and cranberry sauce added a palette of colours to the plate that was as appealing to the eye as it was to taste.

The food was delicious to Sarah, but she could not have imagined how incredible the wine would be. As she took a sip, she noticed William hold the glass up to his nose. He inhaled deeply and then took another sip. Inexperienced with wine, Sarah followed William's lead. She smelled a sweet and earthy scent.

William watched Sarah drink in the bouquet of the wine and was so pleased that she was enjoying it.

"Sarah, what do you smell?" William asked.

Sarah was taken aback, and slightly embarrassed by being called out. She hesitated as she formulated her thoughts. She took another smell and then said, "My nose must not be working properly this evening. I smell vanilla, and currants, and oddly enough, earth," she said with a laugh.

"It is not odd in the least. Your nose is quite good. That is exactly what I get as well. That is the terrific thing about wine, especially French wine. It can be exceedingly complex, with many layers. If you take your time and allow yourself to, you can pick them out."

"Margaret, what do you think of the wine?" William asked.

"It is different than anything I have had before and I really like it. Thank you."

The fire continued to snap and crackle at the end of the room, bringing a dancing light to the walls inside the fireplace. Dinner was being enjoyed by all and disappearing at a good pace.

"I have been to the wine cellar myself. I helped carry wine down when it was delivered once," Jonathan revealed. "I cannot imagine how many bottles are down there. It would be interesting to count."

"My father does like wine," Eleanor said. "And I believe he may like Chef Nicolas for his wine connections in Paris almost more than his cooking."

William emitted a hardy chuckle. "I would agree with you on that, Eleanor."

Sarah was particularly enamored with the wine. She could taste its richness with her entire body. Her tongue came alive with the flavours and she felt her body relaxing more with every sip. She had not felt so vibrant and alive in a very long time. And, as she watched the fire, she was mesmerized by the hypnotic flames.

Eleanor watched her dear friend and could see the transformation. It was heartwarming to see her relax and enjoy herself. It was far too infrequent.

"I shall clear the table and then bring the dessert in."

"Let me help you, Margaret," Sarah said, preparing to stand.

"You shall do no such thing, Sarah. Sit and relax." Eleanor looked on in mock sternness.

"Yes, Mama, listen to Aunt Eleanor. This is your time to relax."

Sarah knew she had been defeated and sank back into her chair.

"Let *me* help you, Margaret," Jonathan offered.

Margaret became warm and flushed as she nodded, but it went unnoticed in the dimly lit room. They worked together to clear the dishes, brushing against each other as they circled the table. Margaret cleaned off the plates into the bin and stacked them beside the sink. Jonathan watched Margaret work, organized and with purpose. He was impressed with her. He had always been. Whatever she did, she did perfectly.

Margaret and Jonathan returned to the dining room with the pudding, and Margaret placed the bowl on the hutch. She spooned the pudding into the bowls that were sitting out. She carefully placed two biscuits on the edge of each bowl, filled the bowls with pudding, added a sliver of chocolate and then placed the bowls in front of each person.

Margaret took her place at the table and then waited for someone to take the first taste. William obliged.

"Margaret, this is fantastic. I am very impressed." William paused long enough to offer his compliments and then he continued to enjoy his dessert.

The children inhaled their dessert, not even pausing to breathe. Margaret ate with reserve, as did her mother and the other adults. Jonathan watched Margaret and tried hard to do the same, fighting hard his urge to satisfy his desire.

"I must thank you both for your generosity in including us for this meal. We have both enjoyed ourselves immensely, and we shall leave you now to continue with the rest of your evening." Reuben stood to leave and motioned to Jonathan to do the same.

"I would very much like to help Margaret tidy up, if I may," Jonathan said hopefully.

Margaret again blushed with the offer. Reuben told his son to come back as soon as he was done, fearing that he would linger and overstay his welcome.

Eleanor moved to the other end of the table to sit across from Sarah and William. She picked up the bottle of wine and poured generously. Sarah's better judgement told her she should stop, but she was enjoying herself immensely and was unable to bury the urge.

The girls helped with the clean-up and James and Samuel retreated to the library. Sarah's attention turned inward. The conversation she was having with herself was mildly amusing to her. *Sarah, you should not have let yourself drink so much. You must have more control over yourself... But I was offered the wine and it would have been rude to have turned it down.*

The wine brought a warmth to Sarah that she felt deep inside. It was a silent embrace, and one that brought forth a sense of peace and belonging. The tingling she felt on her tongue was intriguing and altogether delightful to her. Sarah was basking in the new experience, desiring to enjoy every piece of it.

Eleanor revelled in Sarah's smile. It was completely spontaneous, purely contented.

"Eleanor, it has been such a good day. Please thank your father for allowing us to enjoy his magnificent home. It is an experience the children and I shall cherish forever."

Optimism engulfed William. Was there hope? Was she finally allowing herself to relax and move on?

"I only wish Thomas were here to savour this day as I am. He loved you so, Eleanor." Sarah reflected.

With those few, heartfelt words, William's optimism turned to despair. At that moment, he realized that Sarah was not ready to move on and his heart broke. He loved Sarah, but there was no denying her heart still belonged to Thomas, and he was fearful it always would.

Eleanor loved her brother and the look that transformed his face hurt her deeply. She loved both of them and she wanted only for both of them to be happy. She could not do anything to lessen the pain for either. It was an impossible situation and she felt utterly helpless.

"I am so happy that you are enjoying yourself, Sarah. We are as well, aren't we, William?"

William forced a smile and nodded in agreement. Sarah was deep in her own experience and noticed neither William's desire nor his disappointment.

In the kitchen, Margaret filled the sink with warm, soapy water and began to wash the dishes. Jonathan took his role of drying the dishes seriously. He wanted to impress Margaret, and to do so with a task that he was wholly unfamiliar with.

"Jonathan, I do believe that plate was dry about ten minutes ago," Margaret teased.

Jonathan was so focused that her comment did not immediately process in his mind and he stared blankly at her. Margaret was amused by his reaction, and spontaneously and without thought flicked soapy water at Jonathan, hitting him squarely on the chin.

Margaret shocked herself with her behaviour. What would Jonathan think? He stood there, somewhat surprised. He paused for a moment, placed the plate on the counter, and then did the same thing back at Margaret. But, this time, rather than a flick of water, a large splash catapulted from the sink onto Margaret's chest, leaving a large, wet spot.

Margaret and Jonathan both gasped in surprise. Jonathan was horrified and could not speak, even to apologize. Margaret looked down at her dampened clothes. She reached into the sink, scooped up a handful of water, and sent it flying through the air, directly at Jonathan's face. The water hit its intended target with aplomb.

Margaret's smirk acknowledged her successful attack and Jonathan knew he had been beaten. Margaret took the dish towel from the counter and slowly wiped the water from Jonathan's face. He let her continue to dry his face and did not attempt to take the towel from her. They locked eyes in a moment of connection that was broken when Margaret took the towel and snapped it on Jonathan's leg.

"I surrender, Margaret. You are a formidable opponent and I am defeated," Jonathan said, throwing his hands into the air in mock surrender.

"Thank you for helping me with the dishes, Jonathan," Margaret said, feeling her shyness overcome her.

"Washing dishes? Is that what you call it? I call it an ambush," Jonathan teased. "I must be getting back. I enjoyed myself immensely today. Thank you for including us. I know it was all your doing," Jonathan said, lightly touching Margaret's arm.

Margaret walked Jonathan to the door and closed it behind him. She walked over to the window and watched him walk away. As he did, he turned back and she waved another good-bye. Margaret was exhilarated with the rush of new feelings. She turned off the lights and closed up the kitchen.

Margaret returned to the dining room to find it empty. Smouldering embers radiated in the fireplace, providing no substantial light, but offering an incandescent afterglow as a reminder of the unforgettable evening.

The table was bare and Margaret presumed that they had taken their wine glasses to the library. Samuel and Jonathan were alone, busy with their activities, but looked up long enough to acknowledge Margaret. Margaret's next thought was that the others were in the sitting room and she made her way there, crossing the vast foyer. As she approached the room, she noted that the lights were on, but the room was empty. Partially filled wine glasses sat on the table, but there was no one there to drink from them. It left Margaret perplexed. Where could they be?

As Margaret tried to consider the possibilities, William descended the grand staircase.

"Hello, William, do you know where my mother is?"

"Yes, she is putting your sisters to bed."

Margaret's bewildered look prompted an explanation. "They are sleeping in one of the guest rooms, as will your mother, and I do believe yourself as well. Your mother and Eleanor shall be down momentarily, but you may go up now if you wish."

"Thank you," Margaret said, still confused. "I think I may."

Margaret ascended the staircase as William headed off in the direction of the sitting room. As Margaret made her way down the long hallway toward the guest rooms, the sound of voices guided her. Eleanor and her mother were sitting on a bed, telling a bedtime story to her sisters. The girls' yawns signalled a successful transition from the day's activities and Eleanor and Sarah stood up to leave. Eleanor turned off the lights and motioned for Margaret to leave the room with them.

In the hallway, Margaret requested an explanation.

"We are all staying in the main house this evening. And that includes you, Margaret. Tonight you'll sleep in Anabel's room."

Margaret asked for Eleanor to repeat herself, which Eleanor did without any indulgence in explanation or clarification.

"I cannot do that. Anabel would simply go mad if she knew that I slept in her room." Margaret looked dumfounded at the suggestion and even more so that Eleanor would have offered it.

"You can, my dear, and you will. It does not make sense for you to sleep in your room alone. I would not feel comfortable with that, nor would your mother. The other rooms are accounted for this evening and it makes good sense."

Once Margaret had fully thought through the arrangement, she looked at Eleanor with a look of "I see what you are doing." Margaret was entertained by Eleanor's childishness and she knew that she could not say no. Eleanor made no attempt to hide her true intent, and it showed Margaret that maturity sometimes eludes even the strongest of characters.

"James shall sleep in Philip's room, and your mother shall sleep with me in the next room. Samuel and William shall each take one of the other guest rooms." Eleanor almost dared Margaret to find issue with the arrangements. Margaret would not do that. She thought it best to indulge Eleanor.

"Margaret, you may end your evening now, or you may join us downstairs in the sitting room," Eleanor offered.

Margaret was exhausted and decided it was time to retire for the evening. "I think I might go to sleep. I am tired. Thank you so much for all that you have done. I will remember this day forever." Margaret hugged Eleanor and kissed her cheek.

"You are most welcome, my dear. And I would guess that I was not the only one who made your day memorable. It is up to each of us to seize the moment, and it is up to each of us to be happy."

Eleanor's words were meant as much for Sarah as they were for Margaret.

"Your bag is in Anabel's room. I wish you the sweetest of dreams, my dear."

Margaret hugged her mother and then made her way to Anabel's room.

Chapter 17

As Margaret closed the door behind her, she closed the door on reality. The sense of trepidation she felt was overwhelming. It didn't feel right that she was in the position she was. This room, while pleasing with its decoration, did not exude warmth for Margaret. Anabel had tainted its beauty with her contemptible behaviour, and that feeling lingered for Margaret.

Margaret undressed and changed into her bed clothes. She used the toilet inside Anabel's room. It was the first time she had done so and it was just another in a long list of surreal experiences for that day.

Margaret turned off all the lights, with the exception of the lantern beside the bed. She took her Florence Nightingale book out of her bag and placed in on the table. She pulled back the covers on the bed and focused on what lay before her.

Margaret slipped into the pink linens, pulling the heavy brocade duvet over her. The bed was softer than she could have imagined. It was as though she were lying on a cloud. The linens were silky and her hands ran over them like a hot knife spreading butter, melting away until there was nothing left. The pillow enveloped Margaret's head, caressing it with a softness that left her unable to move. It was pure bliss.

Margaret looked up at the wispy pink organza that hung on the cross beams and wondered what Anabel thought as she looked at it. Could such a nasty person recognize beauty? Could she truly appreciate it?

As Margaret basked in the enchanting experience, she was shocked back into reality as she caught Anabel's eye. Anabel looked at Margaret from her framed position on the wall, disapprovingly acknowledging Margaret's presence in her room. And while she did not speak, her loathing of Margaret was clear. In the darkened room, Anabel appeared to scowl at the intrusion and it made Margaret shiver with uneasiness.

Margaret moved her glance away from the portrait, and instead focused on the book on the bedside table. She was enthralled with Florence's perseverance and dedication to improving conditions for the sick. Her devotion was admirable, and Margaret wanted to impact the world just as she had.

Margaret tired to the point where comprehension began to elude her, and she placed the book back on the table and turned off the light. Her thoughts turned to Jonathan and to her new feelings. Jonathan had always been a dear friend, but now her feelings were different. They had become intensely physical and emotional. She savoured the thought of him, looking to tomorrow when she could see him again. One thing was very clear. She could not go back to how things were before. They had changed forever and Margaret was unsure of what that meant.

Margaret drifted off into a deep and peaceful sleep. As the night continued, the house was silent. But, suddenly, Margaret was thrust from her slumber by a horrific sound.

"What do you think you are doing in my room?" shrieked Anabel. "Get out of my room at once. Do you hear me! AT ONCE!"

The sound of Anabel's high pitched screeching pierced Margaret's ears like a knife through her heart. Margaret was utterly horrified, completely paralyzed with fear.

Margaret gasped for breath and bolted up in the bed. It took her a moment to realize where she was, and then another to realize that she had just had the most frightening dream. Margaret surveyed the room as she tried to get her bearings. The moonlight came in from the windows, illuminating Anabel's portrait. Margaret could not help but feel that Anabel actually knew she was in her room, and it frightened her to death. Margaret was a logical girl, and she tried to tell herself that it was not possible.

Margaret eventually fell back asleep until the morning light coaxed her out of her peaceful slumber. It was a bright and agreeable morning, and as Margaret looked around the room she realized she was awake, but that her reality had become a dream.

She readied herself for the day, dressing and tidying the bed. She took one last look around the room, knowing the next time she entered it the circumstance would be entirely different. As she walked toward the door, she glanced up at Anabel. For the first time, she felt as though she was in full control. She spent a day in Anabel's world as an equal and Anabel could do nothing about it. Margaret grinned as she walked out of the room.

Downstairs in the kitchen, Sarah, Eleanor, and the girls sat at the table enjoying muffins and tea.

"Well, good morning, Margaret. You had quite the sleep. How are you doing this morning?"

Margaret breathed in the smell of the warm muffins and coffee. "Wonderfully. Thank you."

"James is helping Reuben and Jonathan secure the carriage for the ride home. Perhaps you would like to go and assist." Eleanor was amused with her mild meddling. "But, first, eat a muffin."

Margaret took a seat at the table and devoured her muffin. "I didn't realize how hungry I was," Margaret explained.

Eleanor knew better, and her face playfully revealed her disbelief. Margaret looked away as her cheeks flushed with embarrassment, but she was not deterred.

Margaret headed over to the stables, trying with all her might to maintain her composure and walk like a lady. Inside the stables, James was helping Reuben harness the horses and ready them for the carriage. James was intently engaged placing a bit in one of the horse's mouths, but it was stubbornly clamping its teeth together. Reuben was amused as James became exasperated. He knew James would work through it and he held back, allowing him to figure it out for himself. Jonathan was nowhere to be seen and Margaret's heart sank. She looked around casually, trying hard not to draw attention to herself. Perhaps he was still in his room. There was nothing for her to do so she decided to visit with Napoleon. Napoleon lifted his head as Margaret entered his stall.

"Well, hello there, beautiful. How are you doing today?" Margaret asked, scratching under his chin.

"I'm doing well. Thank you."

Margaret spun around to see Jonathan standing behind her. He was smiling slyly as his curly brown hair fell softly on his forehead. Margaret had not realized how handsome he was until that moment. Her knees felt weak and she leaned against Napoleon to steady herself.

"Didn't your father tell you it is rude to sneak up on someone?" Margaret said in her best stern voice.

Jonathan laughed. "I wasn't sneaking. I just happened to be in the same place as you, only slightly behind you. Purely coincidental, I would say."

Margaret regained her composure, trying hard to appear in control. As Jonathan stood in front of her, she was tongue-tied. She was definitely not in control, not in the least, and it frightened her. How could she allow herself to be in his presence when she couldn't function in the most basic ways?

"Did you have a good sleep?" Jonathan asked.

"I did. Thank you. And you?"

"Yes, thank you." The polite conversation was running its course and Margaret was unsure of what to say next.

"There you are, Margaret." James stood at the stall entrance. "It is time to leave."

"All right. I'll be right there," Margaret answered, relieved to see her brother.

"Goodbye, Napoleon," Margaret said, stroking his neck.

"I suppose I shall see you tomorrow evening," she said to Jonathan.

"Yes, I suppose you will," he replied. "Napoleon shall meet his new mate tomorrow, in the afternoon, I believe. You might enjoy it," Jonathan stammered, "uh, um, if you wanted to come a bit early."

"That sounds like fun. It would be nice to see Napoleon's new friend. I do hope it is a good match. He deserves a companion. I would imagine he gets very lonely all by himself." Jonathan nodded in agreement and then motioned for Margaret to leave the stall. He secured the door behind them and then they walked back to the carriage.

"Margaret, you can get yourself seated inside the carriage and I'll drive you over to the house. Jonathan, I'll be back in a few hours," Reuben directed.

Margaret took her seat in the carriage and Reuben closed the door. As the carriage pulled out of the stable, Margaret looked back and waved at Jonathan. The butterflies in her belly were as strong as they had been the previous evening, and for the first time Margaret found herself wishing that she was not going home.

As the carriage pulled up in front of the main house, Eleanor and Sarah emerged. Margaret opened the door, stepped down, and made her way up the stairs to the front door.

"I must retrieve my bag," Margaret announced.

"I have it here, Margaret," Sarah said. "I do believe we have everything. We are ready to go home."

Everyone took a seat in the carriage, with the exception of James, who took a seat beside Reuben. The ride home was bittersweet. It had been a magical Christmas and they were sad to see it end.

Reuben stopped at Sarah's home first. "I cannot thank you both enough for your kindness and generosity. We all enjoyed ourselves immensely and it was an experience that shall live in our hearts and one we shall never forget."

Sarah gave Eleanor another hug, and then reached out and gave William one. William hid his anguish, but as soon as Sarah turned to walk away, his face dropped with a sadness that could not be suppressed.

"Dear brother, I am sorry for your pain. I know you care deeply for Sarah. It is my hope that one day she shall be able to move on from what holds her back and come to see you in the same way you see her. You are impeccably matched. My two favourite people together. I could not imagine anything better."

William said nothing. He continued to look out the window as the carriage rolled along. Reuben stopped at William's home next. It was but a few short blocks from Eleanor's. William motioned for her to stay sitting, but Eleanor would have no part of that. She embraced her brother tightly.

"William, you are a good man. I don't know what I would do without you. You have been my support for as long as I can remember. I do love you so."

"Take care, Sister," he said as he exited the carriage.

Chapter 18

Margaret arrived at Amberley House with Christmas still fresh on her mind. She was able to convince her mother that she was needed mid-afternoon, and was able to leave earlier than usual. She could not get back fast enough and her heart raced as she neared the estate.

When she arrived in her room, Agnes was lying awake on her bed.

"Hello, Agnes," Margaret said, excited to see her. "How was your Christmas?"

"Unfortunately, I have not been feeling my best. I am getting better, but I am still a bit weak. Should be fully well by tomorrow."

As Margaret walked up to Agnes' bed, she noticed she was frightfully pale. Margaret felt her forehead. She was very warm. She sat down on the bed beside her.

"Can I get you anything? Food, water?" Margaret offered.

Agnes put her hand to her face as she sneezed. "Bless you, Agnes. I hope you aren't too uncomfortable. Please let me know if I can get you anything. Soup always makes me feel better. Perhaps I can bring you some back tonight if there is any for the evening meal."

"I'm afraid I do not have much of an appetite. I'm sure I shall be hungry enough to eat an entire cow tomorrow, but for now I think rest is all I need."

Agnes squeezed Margaret's hand appreciatively.

"I shall be back later to check on you then. I promised Jonathan I would help him with Napoleon."

Margaret arrived at the stable as Napoleon's new mate was being unloaded. She was nearly as large as Napoleon and every bit as dark. Her sleek, black profile stood out prominently against the bales of hay that towered behind her. She initially followed where Michael led her, and then without warning reared up, aggressively kicking out her front legs. When she fell back down, Michael pulled tight on her lead and rubbed her neck to try and calm her down.

Margaret stood back to avoid getting in the way. She was focused on the visitor and did not notice Jonathan watching her from the side. As the path became clear, Jonathan approached her.

"You made it. I wasn't sure if you would want to leave home early. I know how much you enjoy your time with your family."

"I do, but I could not pass up the opportunity to see Napoleon with a new friend," Margaret said, pleased with her answer.

"They shall put her out in the paddock with Napoleon for a short period to let them get acquainted. We can go out there and watch if you would like."

"Yes, I would." Margaret would have gone anywhere with Jonathan, but she was truly interested in watching Napoleon meet his new friend.

Philip was standing in the paddock with Napoleon. Napoleon continued to look back toward the barn at all the commotion, as though he knew the commotion was about him. As Michael led the new horse toward the paddock, he directed Philip to come out.

Philip noticed Jonathan and Margaret standing behind the fence and he went to greet them. Michael rubbed her neck one last time, removed the lead, and then closed the gate. She stood there, not moving. Initially, Napoleon did not move either. He looked on at the intruder, unsure of what to make of her. Eventually, Napoleon began to slowly make his way to the paddock gate where she stood. As he approached her, she trotted off, avoiding him.

"It is a bit of cat and mouse, isn't it?" Margaret said.

"I think it is just an example of a sly female making her suitor's job more difficult," Jonathan said. "Don't you think, Margaret?" Jonathan grinned.

"Patience is a virtue, and it is something that most men lack," quipped Margaret.

Philip ignored the banter, making no sense of it. The visitor stopped halfway up the paddock. Napoleon watched intently and then decided to try again. He made his way toward her and stopped a few feet short. She started to move again. This time she moved more slowly, as if to say, "I'm not going to give in quite yet."

"Her name is Storm," Philip explained. "She belongs to my cousin, and she is ready to become a mother. We are hoping she likes Napoleon."

Napoleon continued to approach Storm, getting close enough to smell her. It appeared he liked what he smelled because he did not move away. Storm stood there allowing Napoleon to become familiar with her and then the two of them playfully trotted around the paddock together, watching each other constantly and never getting far from the other.

"Well, I'd say we have the beginning of a successful courtship," Jonathan said triumphantly.

"Napoleon deserves a mate. Unfortunately, this one shall be taken from him at some point," Margaret said as she watched Napoleon nuzzle Storm. "And that saddens me."

All three continued to watch the two horses become familiar with one another. They really were no different than people, Margaret thought.

"Philip, I must thank you from the bottom of my heart. You gave me one of the best Christmas presents I have ever had. It was an experience I shall never forget."

She leaned forward and gave Philip a kiss on the cheek. Philip blushed and looked down at the ground.

"You are welcome, Margaret. I am so glad that you enjoyed yourself. I have wanted to do that for some time now, but I had to wait for the right time." Margaret knew exactly what he meant.

"How was your Christmas in Yorkshire?" Margaret asked.

"Very, very boring," Philip said with an exaggerated roll of his eyes. "Too many old people and nothing fun to do."

"I'm sorry to hear that. It is very nice to have you home." Philip beamed at Margaret's sentiment.

"How were your Christmases?" Philip asked, addressing both of them.

Margaret and Jonathan shared a glance that said more than any words could. They both hesitated, waiting for the other to speak first.

"Very nice," they both said at the same time.

They laughed, clearly amused by each other. Philip sensed something was different. He was happy to be with his friends again and whatever had changed was not important, so long as it didn't take them away from him.

"Jonathan, I need you to put Napoleon back in his stall," Michael called from the paddock as he was placing a lead on Storm.

"I shall see you at supper tonight, Margaret," Jonathan said as he set off toward the gate. "And I hope to see you tomorrow, Philip."

Margaret said her good-byes to Philip and then went to check on Agnes. Agnes was asleep when Margaret arrived in the room. She entered quietly so as to not disturb her. Margaret sat on her bed, turning on her lantern for some light. The cracking and rattling of Agnes' breathing filled the room. Every few breaths, Agnes would sputter and cough, but she remained in a deep sleep.

Margaret decided to read to fill her time until supper. She reached into her bag to look for her book. She didn't feel it. She removed her clothing to place in her drawer and looked into her bag once again. Her book was not there. Where could it be? She had not removed it from her bag at home. She hadn't read since Christmas evening. A single, horrendous thought entered her mind and she gasped in horror, forgetting Agnes was sleeping.

Agnes stirred in her bed, momentarily bringing Margaret back. Margaret remained still as she tried to think, covering her mouth with her hand to prevent another outburst. She finally exhaled slowly when she was convinced that she had not woken Agnes. Then it struck her again. Could she have left the book in Anabel's room? Her chest tightened and she could feel moisture building under her arms. Small beads of sweat formed on her forehead, and she wiped as them before she buried her face in her hands.

What would she do? How would she explain it? She would surely lose her job. Anabel would have her head for this, that she was sure. She would have to leave. Her family needed the money and her mother would be so disappointed. She would never see Jonathan again. That thought continued to play over and over in her mind. Tears welled in her eyes.

She could not go to supper. Not only had she completely lost her appetite, but the thought of running into Anabel was simply too distressing. She supposed it didn't matter. She would run into her at some point and then it would be all over.

Margaret did not sleep at all that night. She tossed and turned and lay awake listening to the changes in Agnes' breathing. As the night continued, it stabilized, becoming more regular and less hoarse.

When Beatrice arose, Margaret still lay awake. Sleep had completely eluded her and her eyes burned with the painful recognition. As Beatrice left the room, Margaret remained in her bed, unmoving, paralyzed with fear. Agnes began to stir and Margaret knew she didn't have much time.

Agnes sat up in bed and rubbed her eyes. She looked over at Margaret, surprised to see her lying there. Usually, Margaret was up and ready to go before her.

"Margaret, are you awake?" Agnes whispered.

Margaret contemplated not answering, but she determined it would do no good. She responded "Yes" and then sat up in her bed as she turned on her lantern.

"Good morning, Agnes. How are you feeling today? I thought you might have been hibernating until Spring."

Agnes laughed at Margaret's teasing. "I don't recall ever being that exhausted. I slept and slept, but I feel so much better now. I am ravenous beyond belief."

"Well, that is good. It means you were able to sleep your sickness away."

"Margaret, you look like you haven't slept in a week," Agnes said, noticing Margaret's puffy eyes. "Are you all right?"

Margaret was burdened with terrible anxiety and she needed to talk with someone. Her chest was tight and she could not breathe. She decided to tell Agnes everything.

Agnes listened in awe as Margaret revealed the details of her Christmas. She spoke of riding Napoleon and of spending Christmas in the main house with Eleanor and William Markley, and of her absolute fear that she had left her book in Anabel's room. Agnes was happier for her friend than she was fearful of the consequence, and she couldn't understand how Margaret could be be otherwise? Things like that rarely happened to people like them.

"I shall say that I put the book in her room before I left for Christmas. I'll say I thought it was hers and that I wanted to ensure it did not get lost."

Margaret pondered the thought for a moment and believed that it might actually pass for a plausible explanation. She had absolutely nothing to lose. In order to execute the plan, though, Agnes would need to see Anabel before Margaret.

"Thank you so much, Agnes. I would be indebted to you forever if you would do that for me," Margaret said, her voice filled with relief.

"You shall not be indebted to me in any way. I am your friend and I would do anything for you, anything at all."

Margaret and Agnes dressed and then made their way to the kitchen in the main house. When they entered the kitchen, Beatrice had already placed the porridge on the table, and Reuben and Jonathan were well into their meal. Jonathan looked up at Margaret, very happy to see her. He was taken aback by her appearance. She looked haggard and pale.

"We missed you both at supper last night," Jonathan said, wanting desperately to understand why Margaret hadn't been there.

Margaret half-smiled at Jonathan. It was all she had the energy for.

"Agnes was ill yesterday and I wanted to ensure she was going to be all right so I stayed with her throughout the evening," Margaret explained.

"Margaret, you are a good friend. Thank you for that," Agnes said.

Margaret did not have much of an appetite and she played with her porridge, eating none of it. Jonathan watched her with worry, not believing her explanation.

At the end of the meal, Agnes and Margaret got up to tend to their chores. Outside the kitchen door, Agnes assured Margaret she would seek out Anabel. Margaret should not encounter Anabel herself as Anabel was in the dining room at that moment and then she would be going to the library for her daily lessons. Hopeful, but not entirely comfortable, Margaret went up to the children's rooms.

Margaret cleaned Philip's room first. The children had been away for a few days so his room was already tidy and did not require much effort. When she finished, she went to Anabel's room. As she walked in the door, her heart raced. She made her way over to the bed, hoping to see the book on the bedside table. It wasn't there. Where could it be? Perhaps she didn't leave it in there after all. Relief flooded Margaret and she breathed a sigh of relief.

"Are you looking for this?"

Margaret spun around to see Anabel standing in the doorway. She had one hand on her hip and the other hand holding up her book. She was clearly on a mission and Margaret trembled with fear.

"What was this book doing on my table?" Anabel asked accusingly.

Margaret stood there, not knowing how to respond.

"I asked you a question. I expect an answer. I would be happy to get my mother to ask you if that would make the question clearer for you."

Anger was beginning to override Margaret's fear. She loathed being spoken to so condescendingly by that spoiled brat.

"Do not try and hide it. I know exactly what you were doing."

Margaret was waiting for the sword to pierce her. It was only a matter of time until it was over. She merely needed to wait for the final blow.

"You are a servant in this house and nothing more. You are paid to work, not read. If you want to read, you do so after your day is done. Is that clear?"

Margaret was not sure if she was more flabbergasted by Anabel's unabashed rudeness or by her sheer stupidity. Clearly, intelligence was no more a trait of Anabel's than it was of her mother's. If she'd had a brain and used it properly, she would have realized it was not possible that Margaret could have left a book in her room while cleaning. Anabel was in there after Margaret. Margaret breathed a sigh of relief again.

"Yes, it is," Margaret said, trying hard not to laugh out loud.

Anabel continued to hold up the book. "Florence Nightingale?" Anabel remarked with disdain. "What menial drivel."

Margaret attempted to hide her own contempt. What a rude, self-absorbed creature. She was fearful of her mounting disdain for Anabel. One could only bite one's tongue for so long before the pain reflex would drive's one's mouth open.

"But I understand your interest in her. You identify with her, being a servant yourself."

The anger welled up in Margaret. She held her breath, hoping Anabel would grow bored and leave her alone. Margaret was not that fortunate. The assault continued unabated, leaving Margaret no choice but to attack.

"Yes, I can see how you would be off-put by a desire to help others. It requires the ability to think of someone other than one's self. Florence comes from a family that is every bit as wealthy as yours, if not more so, so clearly wealth and class can accompany each other on occasion."

Anabel huffed at the blatant insult. She threw the book at Margaret and then turned and left the room. Margaret knew this would not be the end of this, but she was relieved that the truth was still a secret.

By the end of the afternoon, Margaret could barely stand. She was completely exhausted and wanted only to sleep. She ate very little for her dinner again and offered the explanation that she had not slept well the night before. She made it through to the end of her workday and then collapsed in her room. Now that her concern over her missing book was gone, she believed she would sleep soundly and then awaken the next day feeling much better.

Chapter 19

Margaret woke up in a pool of sweat. Her bed linens were soaking and her stomach was turning in circles. The room was dark and Agnes and Beatrice were still and quiet in their beds. Margaret did not know what time it was, but she knew that morning was painfully distant. She drifted in and out of sleep for the next few hours until Agnes woke her for the day.

"Wake up, lazy," Agnes joked.

When Margaret didn't move, Agnes repeated herself with exaggeration. Margaret remained as she was. Agnes went to Margaret and shook her shoulder to wake her. Margaret stirred with a moan that sounded as though Agnes had woken death. Agnes became frightened and shook Margaret again, more aggressively.

"Margaret, what is wrong?" Agnes begged.

Agnes rolled Margaret over and could see that she was pale and ashen. All colour had drained from her face and her cheeks and forehead appeared moist with sweat. Margaret looked at Agnes, but didn't speak.

"Good Lord, Margaret." Panic began to set in. Margaret looked horrific.

Margaret tried to clear her throat, which was swollen shut. Her chest rattled when she coughed, and she winced uncontrollably.

"Let me get you a glass of water," Agnes said, filling the glass on her bedside table from the pitcher that sat nearby.

Margaret sat up slowly and reached for the glass. She held the glass up to her lips and took a few sips. Within seconds, the swirling in her stomach reached a nauseous crescendo and she ran for the toilet. Her movements were slow and unsteady. She made it just in time to release the contents of her stomach. Agnes had followed behind her, watching in horror.

"You must get back into bed at once. I shall tell Mrs. Markley that you are unwell."

"No, no, you mustn't do that. I am certain that Anabel has poisoned her further with unkind thoughts of me. I shall be fine. I just need a few moments to gather myself. I shall be down after breakfast. I feel better already," Margaret said unconvincingly.

Agnes recalled what Margaret had told her happened in Anabel's room and she was afraid Margaret was right.

"All right," Agnes agreed, "but the moment I think you are too unwell to work, I shall bring you back to bed." A nod was all Margaret could muster.

Agnes left and Margaret returned to her bed. She was shivering and pulled the bed covers up to her neck to warm up. Her limbs were aching and she could not imagine working the entire day. But she had no choice. After a short time, she got up out of bed and slowly dressed herself. As she lifted her bed clothes up over her head, her muscles ached with pain. She was weak and had to sit down momentarily to regain her strength.

When she was fully dressed, she walked to the main house, draining herself of the remaining energy she had. She entered the kitchen, having waited until everyone had left, and sat down until she was ready to continue. She didn't want Jonathan to see her like this, and she didn't want to be dishonest and tell everyone she felt well when she clearly did not.

In Philip's room, she continued to move slowly. Tuesday was the day to remove the linens. The bed cover felt like a lead weight. Margaret finally managed to pull it back so that she could remove the linens underneath it. With every movement, her head throbbed in agony. She piled the linens in the corner until she was ready to take them to Beatrice in the scullery.

When she entered Philip's water closet, the room began to swirl and she fell to the floor. The cold tile on her hot cheek felt like heaven. As she lay there, she focused on the underside of the cabinet, analyzing every angle and marking. She did not know how she was going to move from the spot where she lay. Her world was now limited to her own myopia, to the thoughts of her aching limbs, to the drum beat in her head, and to the deafening pulse that she believed could stop at any dark and empty moment that lay before her.

She drifted off to sleep and was unsure of how long she had been out when she awoke. She sat up on the floor and a surge of nausea overtook her. She did not try to get up, and instead steadied herself by leaning against the wall. She would not be of much use to anyone today. That she knew. But she needed to get the linens off the other two beds at a bare minimum or she would undoubtedly pay, and pay far greater than she was paying at the moment. Surely, she was being punished for speaking to Anabel the way she did and she had no one to blame but herself.

Eventually, she found the strength to stand and walk back into Philip's room. She bent over to pick up the sheets and moaned in agony. She did the same in Anabel's room and, as she was exiting the room, she looked up at Anabel's picture and said, "I'm sorry" in a broken and defeated whisper.

After she removed the Markley's linens, she rolled them in a ball and held them under her arm. She used her free arm to steady herself as she walked down the heavy stone stairs. At the bottom, she caught her foot on a corner of one of the sheets that dangled free and she stumbled forward, falling from the last step. She landed with a thud. The bedding softened the blow, but the jolt sent a shock through her body that felt like she had been hit by lightning. No one was there to see and no one was there to help. She was completely and utterly alone in her agony.

Margaret picked herself up and dragged herself to the scullery. Beatrice was busy working on other laundry. She was cranking the wringer, relieving the items of their excess water.

"I was going to come find you straightaway. Almost done here," Beatrice said.

When Margaret didn't respond, Beatrice looked up at her and was aghast at the sight.

"Margaret, you look terrible, like death, actually." Beatrice stopped herself, feeling downright awful for her bluntness. "Margaret, really, you don't look well."

"I will be. I am sure I shall feel better before long," Margaret said, but Beatrice was not convinced.

"Sit down," Beatrice demanded, pointing to the chair behind where Margaret stood.

Margaret obeyed without fight. She was relieved. She needed desperately to sit down. But more so, what she desperately wanted to do was find a small, dark corner and crawl into it. The light was painfully bright and the slightest noise amplified like an explosion in her head.

"You must go to bed."

"I cannot. Mrs. Markley has no tolerance for excuses."

Sadly, Beatrice, too, realized that Margaret was right.

"Please let me know if I can do anything to help you."

"Thank you."

Margaret slowly stood, and her legs buckled under her weight. Beatrice reached out to steady her.

"You are definitely not fine, nor shall you be anytime soon."

Margaret pulled away from Beatrice and walked out of the room. She had a few remaining tasks left in Anabel's room and then she would be done upstairs until the linens were ready to be put back on the beds.

The stairs may as well have been ten miles long and straight up for all the energy that it took her. At the top of the stairs, the hallway stretched on for an eternity and Anabel's room was close to the end of that eternity. Margaret's impulse was to sit down on the floor, but she held back on the urge, frightened by the prospect of someone finding her.

Thankfully, Anabel's room was tidy. With the exception of a few items of clothing, nothing was askew and Margaret was able to finish in a few minutes.

The house was cleaned daily and never neglected long enough to be noticeably dirty or untidy. She was hoping that Catherine would not distinguish that day from any other.

It was the longest day of Margaret's life. It would not end, despite her wishes to the contrary. At dinnertime, she made the decision to go back to her room to rest for the hour rather than go to the kitchen. All day she wavered between intense heat and trembling chills and when she was back in her room she was neither comfortable on top of her bedding nor under it.

Margaret had not eaten or had anything to drink for a day, and she still had no appetite to do so. Her head throbbed and her throat was on fire. Moment by moment, she worsened, her strength being sucked out of her with unending voracity.

Agnes burst into the room. Margaret was asleep and did not move.

"Margaret, you must wake up immediately," Agnes said in a panicked tone.

Agnes shook her in her bed as she had done that morning, and Margaret finally awoke. She was not immediately aware of her surroundings, but the feeling in her head brought her back straightaway.

"Mrs. Markley is looking for you. She is in a downright foul mood."

Margaret moaned, unable to form words.

"You must get up, Margaret. Let me help you."

Agnes put her hand around Margaret's arm and helped her to sit up in bed.

"You can steady yourself on me. I shall not let you fall."

Margaret stood up with Agnes' help. She had not taken her coat or boots off so there was no need to put them on. Agnes wrapped her arm around Margaret's back and held her up as they walked. Halfway to the main house, Margaret bent over and retched uncontrollably. There was nothing to come up and the acid burned her throat with an intensity that made her cry out in pain.

"Oh dear. What are we doing to do?" Agnes felt helpless.

As they arrived at the main house, Agnes straightened Margaret's skirt and smoothed out her hair. She ran her hand tenderly over her cheek and gave her a hug.

"Best of luck, Margaret. I shall say a prayer for you."

Margaret assumed Catherine would be in her study having tea so she made her way there. As she approached the door, she took a deep breath and tried to focus. She mustered all the strength that she could and she entered the room. Catherine sat at her table, managing household papers.

Catherine looked up at Margaret as Margaret tried to quietly clear her throat. Rather than waiting for Catherine to speak, Margaret attempted to lessen the severity of the anticipated reaction.

"Mrs. Markley, I am so very sorry for being remiss in my duties. I am not well today, but I am sure that I shall be better tomorrow. I will do extra to make up for what I have missed today. I beg your forgiveness."

Catherine Markley stared at Margaret, squinting with an intense anger that frightened Margaret. Catherine looked off to the side of the room and Margaret followed her gaze. Anabel was sitting in the corner with her usual satisfied, smug expression. Margaret knew she was done and she didn't care. Nothing could make her feel worse than she already did.

Margaret barked a deep, rattling cough and it sent Catherine recoiling in disgust.

"You may take your sickness and leave my home at once. I have no patience for the shirking of duties. I do not pay you to be sick. You have a job, and I expect it completed to my satisfaction. I shall consider your return when you are well. You may leave now."

With that, Catherine lowered her head and resumed her work. Margaret looked over at Anabel, and Anabel was basking in the satisfaction of a job well done.

With nothing further to say, Margaret turned and left the room. She didn't encounter anyone along the way to her room and she didn't seek anyone out. After sitting on her bed for a moment to gain some strength, she put her things in her bag and made her way home.

The estate road appeared insurmountable to Margaret. She thought she couldn't possibly make it to the tram. She would have to, though. She had no choice.

The cool air felt soothing, and as the breeze gusted in different directions she turned to catch it so that it would hit her cheeks just right. Halfway up to High Lane, Margaret could go no farther. She kneeled down on the side of the road and placed her head on her bag, which was lying on the road in front of her. She contemplated staying like that, but her better judgement triumphed and when she felt rested enough she continued walking. She turned onto High Lane and then took another rest, pausing long enough to regain the strength she needed to continue.

A carriage drove by, kicking up dust and surrounding Margaret in a cloud. She inhaled the dust, bent over, and retched again. There was nothing to retch, but her body convulsed with the movement.

A wave of heat enveloped her and she unbuttoned her coat to let some cool air in. She walked along High Lane, the wind blowing her coat fully open, each side noisily flapping like a Union Jack at full mast.

The sound of a train's whistle blew as she approached the train tracks. Margaret felt the ground rumble as the train rolled down the tracks. She knelt down again to wait for the train to pass. The shrill of the whistle pierced her ears over and over and her agony continued unabated.

After the train passed, Margaret crossed the tracks. She didn't have much farther to go to get to the tram stop. She merely had to cross Stockport and walk a few feet. She had made it this far. Surely, she could make it a bit farther, she thought.

Crossing Stockport was chancy. She could not move quickly in her sluggish state and the traffic was not sympathetic. As the sun was setting, visibility was growing more difficult and she narrowly escaped being crushed by a carriage. But neither the near miss, nor the rage of the driver had any impact on her.

As she stood at the tram stop, she shivered uncontrollably. She stumbled as she waited, drawing curious looks from those who waited alongside her. As the tram stopped in front of her, she stepped onto the street, losing her balance, and stumbling to her knees. She rubbed the dirt off her hands and retrieved her bag, which had been thrown forward in the fall. Tears welled up in her eyes and she comforted herself with thoughts of her mother.

As she looked up, she noticed Dennis looking at her in horror. She was happy to see a friendly face. She had not expected to see him. She felt so alone and seeing Dennis gave her strength.

"Rupert, please help this young lady."

Rupert was the trolley boy. He had noticed Margaret before Dennis had and didn't need to be told.

"Thank you," Margaret whispered, as Rupert latched onto her arm.

Rupert held Margaret up the stairs and he placed her on the seat behind Dennis.

"Miss Margaret, what ails you?" Dennis asked, concerned.

Margaret could not speak loud enough for Dennis to hear her. He turned and strained himself, but it was no use. He continued to look back at her to see how she was faring. He was concerned, but grateful that she found herself on his tram.

Margaret leaned against the tram wall. She closed her eyes to block out the lights. The whir of the wheels on the tracks lulled her to sleep. When the tram arrived at Margaret's stop, Margaret did not move. Dennis looked back at her, waiting for her to open her eyes. She did not. Dennis hobbled back to Margaret and tapped her on the shoulder. She slowly opened her eyes, trying to focus on Dennis.

"Margaret, this is your stop. I know this is not the time you usually go home. Will you be able to make your way by yourself?" Dennis asked, doubtful.

Margaret cleared her throat and said she would. "Thank you, Dennis. I am not feeling well today, but I shall be fine. I shall see you on Sunday," Margaret said smiling.

Dennis was not sure if she was trying to convince him or herself.

"Margaret, I am at the end of my shift today. I have to pull the tram into the depot and then I shall be free to help you home. If you wait for me, I shall help you."

Margaret looked at Dennis, but did not hear what he was saying. The ringing in her ears was far too loud.

"Rupert, please help Miss Margaret off the tram and to the side of the road."

Margaret made it to the side of the road, but was confused as to where she was. She tried to get her bearings as she scanned her surroundings. In a moment of lucidity, she determined that she needed to get to the park. She lived on the other side of it.

When Dennis arrived at the tram stop, Margaret was not there. He looked up and down Stockport and did not see her. He surveyed the crowds and she was nowhere to be seen. He did not know where she lived so he could not go after her. He could only pray that he would see her on Sunday.

The darkness had fully set in and the lights were a blur to Margaret. She stumbled toward the park, bumping into a woman who hit her with her bag. Margaret felt nothing.

When Margaret arrived at the park, she could go no farther. As she was about to sit on the ground, she noticed a park bench a few feet beyond the entrance. She walked toward it, lost her footing, and fell to the ground. She hit her head with a thud and then all went black.

Within minutes they appeared, slithering out of the darkness like snakes in the grass. They lived in the park after dark. They were safe there because no one would dare enter, unless by accident. And if they did, they paid dearly for the intrusion.

The first one looked Margaret over, poking her with his foot. He couldn't have been older than ten. He was scruffy and tattered from head to toe, and encrusted with a permanent layer of dirt.

"Nigel, you got to see this. Look at this 'ere bloke. What do you make of 'er?"

"I'd say she be deader than a doornail. That's what I say. And we all know dead people ain't be needing their coats and boots. Ain't that right, Mickey?"

"Well, if she ain't dead, soon she be."

They both laughed as if it were the funniest thing they had ever heard. Then, as if by routine, Nigel rolled Margaret over. When she didn't move, he pulled each arm out of its sleeve. He rolled her over once more, yanking the coat out from under her. Mickey untied her boots and pulled them off. When they were done, they both rolled her over a few times until she stopped under the bushes. Now she was out of sight, and they disappeared with their spoils, slithering back into the darkness from whence they came.

Margaret remained comatose throughout the night, unprotected from the cold, and entirely hidden from the world.

Chapter 20

After breakfast Philip took a quick visit to the stables before his lessons. He skipped happily, without a care in the world. When he arrived, he said a quick hello to Napoleon and then he looked for Jonathan. Jonathan was mucking out the work horse's stalls.

"Jonathan, have you heard how Margaret is?"

Jonathan looked up, eager to know the answer to the question himself.

"I'm sure that Agnes or Beatrice can give us an update. I believe she is ill yet and in her room."

"No. My sister tells me that my mother sent her home yesterday afternoon."

Jonathan was surprised by this. He had not heard.

"Would your father be able to ask Samuel how she is doing?" Philip asked hopefully.

"Come with me. Let's ask him."

Both boys walked toward the back of the stable. Reuben was tending to some carriage repairs when he noticed the boys coming at him in a hurry.

"Why the rush, you two?" Reuben asked.

"Pa, Philip tells me that Mrs. Markley sent Margaret home ill yesterday. We would like to inquire as to her condition. Could you ask Samuel when you go to the factory?"

"I'm due to leave in a few minutes. I shall ask Samuel when I arrive."

"Thank you," Philip said. "I hope she is feeling better."

Jonathan began to worry. He had not seen Margaret in a few days and knowing she had been sent home when she was unwell was troubling. He did not feel good about this.

Reuben finished his repair, secured the horses to the carriage, and was off. When he arrived at the factory, William was in the administrative office.

"William, would it be possible to have a word with Samuel?" Reuben asked. "Philip and Jonathan would like to inquire as to Margaret's condition."

"What is wrong with Margaret?" William asked, surprised.

"It seems that Mrs. Markley sent her home yesterday. I believe she was ill. We would like to ensure she is better so that we can ease our minds."

"Of course. I'll go get him."

Moments later William returned to the office, accompanied by Samuel. Samuel was dirty from head to toe, his face covered in grease.

"Hello, Reuben. How are you today?" Samuel asked.

"Fine, thank you. I have come to inquire about your sister's condition. Philip tells me that Mrs. Markley sent her home yesterday afternoon, ill with fever. We are hoping she is feeling better today."

Samuel looked shocked. Charles Markley walked in at the same time.

"My wife did *what*?"

Reuben felt a sudden panic. He was merely inquiring as to Margaret's condition and he suddenly felt as though he were in the middle of something he should not be.

"Mrs. Markley sent Margaret home yesterday, ill with fever, Sir. Philip was inquiring as to her condition. He was concerned about her."

"I don't understand. My sister did not come home yesterday or last night."

"What do you mean she did not come home? Where could she be?" William asked with mounting concern.

"Reuben, take the carriage. Take Samuel and go to Eleanor and Margaret's mother. Find her!" Charles Markley ordered.

Reuben and Samuel ran out of the factory. Reuben directed the carriage to Samuel's house at full gallop, skilfully manoeuvring in and out of traffic.

Samuel jumped off the carriage and ran in the front door of his home. Startled, Sarah jumped up.

"Samuel, what on earth...?" Sarah said.

"Ma, Margaret left the Markley's yesterday. She was sick with fever and Mrs. Markley sent her home. She did not come home last night. Where could she be?"

"Slow down, Samuel. What are you talking about?"

Samuel repeated himself more slowly after taking a deep breath. Sarah was overcome with fear. Her knees gave way as she thought of the unimaginable.

"No, no, no, no, no. Not my Margaret. Dear God, not my Margaret." Sarah began to shake with panic.

"Reuben is outside. He and I shall go to Eleanor. Perhaps she went there. You need to stay here in the event that Margaret comes home."

Sarah nodded. Samuel ran out the door and jumped on the carriage. Reuben dashed over to Eleanor's shop. They both ran in hoping to see Margaret sitting there. She was not.

"Samuel, what are you doing here in the middle of the day? Is everything all right?" Eleanor could see from Samuel's face that it was not and her mind began to race.

"Mrs. Markley sent Margaret home yesterday with a fever. She never arrived. It has been an entire day and we do not know where she is."

Eleanor gasped and tried to gather her thoughts.

"Samuel, please go looking on foot. Reuben, would you be so kind as to take me back to Amberley House? Perhaps she is resting, hiding away in some part of the house."

"Of course."

"Samuel, please check back in with your mother regularly. She'll be absolutely sick with worry," Eleanor pleaded.

Samuel nodded as he dashed out the door.

Eleanor put her coat on and left with Reuben. Reuben pushed the carriage as hard and fast as he could. As they raced down Stockport, Eleanor scanned the street looking for any signs of Margaret. There were none.

As they arrived at Amberley House, Eleanor laid out the plan.

"Reuben, I shall check the servant's house and then the main house. Please check the stable."

Reuben agreed and both went their separate ways.

Eleanor entered Margaret's room. It was empty. Her bed was tidy, and nothing was amiss. She ran to the main house, entering through the kitchen. Chef Nicolas was in the kitchen and Beatrice was in the scullery.

Eleanor was out of breath and could not speak right away. Nicolas looked on in surprise.

"Miss Markley, are you all right?"

"Margaret?" Eleanor took a few gasps of air so that she could speak. "Have you seen Margaret?"

"No, I have not. Is Margaret all right?"

Beatrice heard the commotion and came into the kitchen.

"What is wrong with Margaret?" she asked.

"Margaret left here yesterday and she did not arrive at home."

Beatrice gasped. "What do you mean she did not arrive at home? Where could she be?"

"Where is Catherine? Where is she? I need to know right now!" Eleanor's anger was bubbling like a boiling pot whose lid was about to blow off.

"She is in her study right now. She is having tea with Mrs. Stanton. I just took it to them," Beatrice announced.

Eleanor turned and ran through the door. It was a short distance to Catherine's study and she was there in a split second. She burst into the room causing Catherine and her guest to look up abruptly.

Catherine looked surprised, but tried to appear unaffected. She continued to sit starched and superior, waiting for – and dreading – the reason for the rude interruption to reveal itself, but the insecurity that thrived deep within her seized the moment and allowed her face to contort with paralyzing fear. Eleanor did not make Catherine wait long.

"Is Margaret here?" Eleanor asked, out of breath.

"I sent her home yesterday. Her vile disease was not welcome in my home," Catherine said, appearing poised and in control. "Should she recover, I shall consider her return."

Catherine looked at her guest and offered a quick nod to affirm her superiority over the intruder. Her guest nodded primly in response. Catherine drew Eleanor's ire. She was furious that Catherine had sent Margaret away when she was ill, but even more so that she could even remotely consider that Margaret might not recover. Eleanor burst into a rage, completely devoid of any control, driven purely by protective, animal instinct. She inhaled deeply and screeched like a wild animal. Catherine and her guest cowered in their seats.

"'Consider' is a luxury for those who are in possession of choice. In this instance, my dear stepmother, you are not. I may *choose* to like you, but I do not. I would wager at this point my father merely tolerates you and the sight of you stirs the bile in the depths of his belly. As for vile disease, the only thing vile in this home is you. I bid you good day, Madam."

Catherine's guest sat stiffly, adorning all that Eleanor had shunned so fervently throughout her life. She now sat wide-eyed and gaping-mouthed, moving only her eyes to lock on Catherine. Upon her stepmother's gasp, Eleanor tugged her skirt, and turned and exited the room with a flurry that altered the balance of power, unmistakably and forever.

Eleanor ran out to the stable where Reuben was waiting. Jonathan sat pale faced and sombre beside the driver's seat.

"She is not in the main house and Beatrice does not know where she is. We must keep looking."

"Jonathan would like to help."

"Of course," Eleanor agreed. "The more help, the better."

Reuben opened the carriage door and Eleanor stepped in. Before Reuben closed the door, Eleanor shared her thoughts.

"We need to retrace her steps. If she was weak with fever, she could have collapsed anywhere. Please drive slowly down High Lane. I shall look on this side," Eleanor said, pointing. "And you look on that side. Perhaps we missed her. And we must drive slowly up Stockport. Look between buildings. Please, we must find her," Eleanor pleaded.

Reuben could see the panic on Eleanor's face and he felt helpless.

"Eleanor, we will find her. We *will*," Reuben said emphatically.

Eleanor smiled as tears welled up in her eyes.

"As God is my witness, yes, we shall."

As directed, Reuben drove slowly down High Lane. Eleanor stood in the carriage, steadying herself by holding on to either side of the door. She scanned the roadside and saw nothing. The temperature was warmer than usual, but still brisk. The thought of Margaret helpless in the cold caused Eleanor to writhe in pain.

Eleanor scanned her side of Stockport, looking at every face. Against a building sat a woman hunched over in a black coat that looked similar to Margaret's. She sat on the ground, with her head down. Her hair was the same wavy, sandy brown of Margaret's. Eleanor could not see her face. In a panic, Eleanor banged on the wall and yelled at Reuben to stop. Reuben stopped abruptly, causing the horse behind them to rear up.

Eleanor opened the door and ran to the woman. She lifted her head to see that it wasn't Margaret but an old woman. She scoffed at Eleanor.

"Piss off you," she blathered, either intoxicated or a lunatic, or perhaps both.

Eleanor's heart sank. She turned around looking in all directions, wondering what to do next and hoping to find some answers. There was nothing. She returned to the carriage and they continued on.

Chapter 21

Samuel returned to the streets with no clear plan. He decided to travel the route to the tram stop. If she had made it to the stop, she could be somewhere along the way.

As he ran down Robinson Street, he called out Margaret's name. He searched the alleys and the garbage heaps. There was nothing.

"Maaaaaargareeeet," he screamed, his voice cracking. He did not stop screaming, nor did he stop running.

"Shuddup, would ya? Ain't no Margaret round here."

Samuel ran by the old man, paying no attention to him.

"Trouble be the whole lot of 'em. Be glad she's gone," he yelled in Samuel's direction.

Samuel continued to run alongside the park, drawing the attention of a Peeler who was patrolling on foot. He held his truncheon tightly in his hand as Samuel ran by. Samuel was dishevelled, dirty clothed, and greasy faced.

Samuel passed the park and ran to the tram stop. He searched every inch of the area around it. Nothing. Not a trace. He was running out of options and was unsure what to do next.

He began to run down Stockport, away from the park, when he spotted a tram coming in his direction. He stepped in front of it, frantically waving his arms.

The tram stopped suddenly, causing the trolley boy to lose his footing and fall over.

"What the hell? Are you a lunatic?" the driver yelled at Samuel.

Samuel ran up to the stairs and addressed the driver. "Do you know where Dennis is? I urgently need to speak with him."

"You are insane. No, I do not."

The driver started the horses up again, and Samuel ran alongside keeping stride.

"My sister is missing. I need to find her. I need to find Margaret."

Defeated, Samuel stopped running.

"Margaret, did you say?" the trolley boy yelled.

Samuel looked up and started running to catch the tram. "Yes, Margaret," he answered, hopefully.

"I worked Dennis' tram yesterday. She was on it. End of my shift, about five o'clock. Quite ill, she was. Helped her off myself. Last I saw of 'er."

Samuel stopped in his tracks, watching the tram move on. What did this mean? He had to walk the route again. Surely, she must be along it somewhere.

He crossed over Stockport, in the direction of the park. As he passed the park entrance, he stopped. Could she have taken a shorter route and crossed through the park? Surely, she wouldn't do that in the dark. She knew better.

Samuel turned and faced the park entrance.

"Maaaargareeeet," he yelled once again. Nothing. "Maaaargareeeet."

As he took a few steps into the park, he heard a muffled sound. To Samuel, it sounded like a cat skulking through the bushes and he dismissed it and called out again.

"Maaaargareeeet."

The sound continued and Samuel instinctively looked in its direction. He saw what looked like a foot sticking out of the bushes. Samuel quickly lifted the brush and saw that it was a person. He dropped to his knees and wedged himself farther in and saw it was his sister.

"Margaret! Noooooo!" Samuel pulled Margaret by her arm, sliding her out from under the bush.

She had a gash on her forehead, which was covered in blood. She was moaning, which meant she was still alive. Relief flooded through him and gave him a strength that he had never experienced before. He picked her up and began to run through the park toward home. Her head and arms dangled loosely, bobbing up and down as Samuel ran.

The Peeler now stood at the entrance to the park. He saw Margaret's head and arms dangling beyond Samuel as though there were no life left in her.

"Stop! Stop immediately!" the Peeler shouted. Samuel heard nothing.

"Stop, I say! Stop or I will shoot!"

Samuel continued to run. He was sobbing and gasping for breath, hearing nothing but his own breathing.

"I said, STOP!"

As Samuel continued to run, the Peeler raised his pistol and fired, catching Samuel in the back of the leg. Samuel dropped to his knees in shock and agony. Margaret rolled out of his arms, landing on her belly. Samuel screamed out in pain, falling on his sister as his momentum carried him forward.

The Peeler approached, with his pistol drawn.

"Do not move," the Peeler ordered.

Samuel did not listen. He picked up Margaret and turned toward the officer.

"My sister," he sobbed, "she is ill. I need to take her home."

Margaret moaned and whispered, "Samuel."

"Yes, Margaret, I am here. We'll get you home."

Samuel stood on one leg as the searing pain in his other leg was unbearable. The officer appeared utterly horrified. The smell of gunshot hung in the cool, damp air. The officer lowered his pistol and placed it back in its holster.

Manchester Peelers didn't routinely carry pistols. But since Victoria Matthews had been found in that very park, not far from where they stood, they did and they were ready to use them.

The officer looked at Margaret and could see that she was at death's doorstep. Her cheeks were sallow, her lips blue, and her hair matted and wet with perspiration.

Having heard the gunfire, another Peeler came running toward them with his truncheon raised. The Peeler who stood with Samuel held up his hand to stop him.

"Edward, stop," he yelled.

The officer lowered his arm and surveyed the situation. Blood was pooling on the ground behind Samuel as he bled from his wound. He was barely hanging on to Margaret. His arms were weakening and trembling under her weight.

"Edward, fetch the prisoner wagon. We'll transport them to the hospital. They need medical attention. This lad cannot walk."

The officer walked off about a hundred feet and turned to face a park exit. He blew his whistle and motioned to the driver of the wagon. The wagon pulled up to Samuel and Margaret and the Peeler opened the back door. The wagon was empty.

"No, I must take my sister home. I must take her to my mother. She is sick with worry," Samuel pleaded.

The officer's guilt was overcoming him. Samuel would not be injured if the officer had paid closer attention. His unintentional misstep caused a bad situation to be much worse.

"The wagon driver will take you both to the hospital and then he will retrieve your mother." The officer took out his notebook and captured Sarah's name and address and provided it to the driver.

"Lie her down in there. You can travel with her. He'll transport you both to the hospital now."

Samuel did not ask any questions. He simply nodded. Before the door was closed, the officer voiced his regret.

"Given the circumstances, the choice was not mine."

Ancoats Hospital was a ten minute journey. Samuel held his sister's hand as she lay motionless, eyes closed. Her hand was hot and damp.

Samuel was terrified. He knew her condition was dire. He had to tell his mother. He needed to get home.

The ride took an eternity. Margaret's head struck the floor of the wagon with every bump. Samuel watched his sister's head bounce like a hammer on a nail, and that she did not acknowledge the pain only made his torment worse. Samuel reached down and placed his hand under her head to try and soften the roughness.

Samuel felt the back of his leg. It appeared the bullet entered to the left side, directly above the knee. There was no exit wound so the bullet remained lodged in its place. Samuel could smell the blood and he could feel it exiting the wound.

As they arrived at the hospital, the driver opened the door. Samuel picked up his sister and limped off the wagon. He entered the main door. Inside the entrance was an administrative window with a long, winding line of people extending from it. Above the window was a sign that stated "Patient Check-In." Beside that was the door for the "Out-Patient and Accidents Waiting Room." Samuel dismissed the line and hobbled into the waiting room. In it sat two hundred or so men, women, and children, all in various degrees of unwellness, all waiting for their medical care. There were three nurses bustling about the room.

As Samuel hobbled into the room, he shouted for help. The crowd all turned to see what the commotion was. The nurse who was closest to Samuel arrived at his side in a whirl.

"Do you have your paperwork?" she asked.

"No, my sister will die before I get through that line," Samuel pleaded in desperation.

The nurse felt Margaret's forehead and responded with visible consternation. She motioned to an orderly, who arrived with a wheeled stretcher. The orderly took Margaret from Samuel and placed her on it.

The nurse noticed blood pooling on the floor and looked at Margaret for signs of blood.

"Where is that blood coming from?" the nurse asked, bewildered. "It's not her forehead."

"My leg. It was a bullet," Samuel said matter-of-factly. "I am fine. *Please* tend to my sister."

The nurse looked at Samuel, horrified.

"What on earth?" Her mind raced with the possibilities and she instinctively stepped back.

"My sister... is she going to be all right?" Samuel asked, with what little energy he had left.

"How did she find herself in this condition?"

"She had a fever. She collapsed, I believe, and spent the night in Ardwick Green. I found her like this. No coat or boots."

"Oh dear. We shall need to have a doctor evaluate her. She has a very high fever. That leg will also need tending to."

The orderly pushed the stretcher to the back of the waiting room and Samuel followed the nurse. Margaret was wheeled into a room with six beds. Three were occupied and three were empty. A doctor stood over a patient listening to his chest with a stethoscope while the nurse watched on. The room was brightly lit and stark white. It smelled sweetly pungent.

The orderly motioned to another orderly for assistance in moving Margaret to a bed. Samuel felt helpless.

"We need to tend to your leg. You are still bleeding."

The nurse wrapped a linen bandage around Samuel's leg to slow down the bleeding until the doctor could examine it. Samuel winced in pain as pressure was applied.

An administrative clerk approached Samuel as he waited for the doctor.

"Are you a subscriber to this hospital?" she asked.

Samuel stared blankly at her.

"A subscriber. Are you a subscriber to this hospital?" she asked again. "And this is clearly not a workplace accident," she said, looking at Margaret. "Is yours?"

Samuel continued to stare blankly at her.

"Who is your employer?"

"I work at the Markley Factory in Ardwick," Samuel replied.

The clerk perked up. "Markley is a large subscriber to this hospital. His employees are covered for workplace accidents. But these are clearly not workplace accidents. You'll need to pay for your care. Are you able to do that?"

Samuel responded the only way that would help his sister at that moment.

"Yes, we can pay for care."

The clerk looked unconvinced, but chose not to question. The hospital's policy was not to turn anyone away, but the clerk's job was to collect fees and sometimes the two clashed.

"Very well, then. I shall complete the paperwork for you to sign."

The clerk took Samuel and Margaret's name, ages, mother's name and address before she left the room.

The doctor began to evaluate Margaret. He looked at the gash on her forehead, dabbing at it with a cloth. He checked her lymph nodes, and checked her for spots or discoloration. He opened her mouth, held her tongue down, shined a light in her throat, looked in her ears, and opened her eyes to check for pupil dilation. When he was done with his initial observation, the nurse placed a thermometer under her tongue and held her mouth closed. After a few moments, the nurse pulled it out of her mouth and handed it to the doctor.

"Your sister has a fever of one hundred and five. She is non-responsive. It is primarily due to her fever, but the gash and swelling on her forehead would indicate she was either hit or she fell and hit her head. Either way she is very ill. Having stayed out all night without a coat may have helped her more than it hurt her, as it kept her temperature from rising any further. We need to wrap her in ice to bring her fever down. If she survives, there is a chance of damage to the brain. My initial diagnosis is influenza. With her exposure last night, there is a significant risk of pneumonia."

Samuel was stunned. This could not be happening!

"I have to go to my mother immediately. She'll want to come. She is sick with worry. She doesn't know I have found my sister. There are people desperately looking for her."

"You cannot leave until we look at that leg of yours. Why don't you lie down on this bed, face down? I'll assess the damage," the doctor said.

Samuel did as he was told. He got up and placed himself on the bed. The doctor cut Samuel's pants off with scissors, just above the wound, and then pulled off the bandage.

"I can see the bullet. It has grazed the muscle. I have to remove it. Your biggest risk is infection. If it is kept clean, you'll be no worse for wear before you know it. There shouldn't be any lasting damage."

While one nurse was packing Margaret in ice, another asked Samuel to lie on his side. She placed an ether dome over his mouth, and as he began to inhale the room began to dance. An immediate feeling of lightness, a sensation of floating, overcame him. The nurse prepared the area with an iodine solution. The doctor pressed a pin into Samuel's leg. When he did not react, the doctor removed the bullet and put in a single stitch to close the wound. The nurse bathed the area in iodine solution again and wrapped the wound with bandages. When the procedure was complete, the nurse removed the ether dome and handed Samuel the bullet.

"You shall be as good as new before you know it," the nurse said.

Samuel sat up in bed, and a wave of nausea overcame him. He grasped at his mouth in a reflex to the threat of vomiting. The nurse placed a basin on his bed.

"Thank you," Samuel said as he placed his mouth over the basin.

"You have had ether. You'll be dizzy and nauseous for a while. It is not safe for you to be walking about so soon. You should continue to lie down."

The nurse could see the dread on Samuel's face and she felt bad for him.

"You cannot do anything for your sister at the moment. She needs to rest, as do you. You do not want your leg to become infected."

The nurse was kind to Samuel and he was thankful. As Samuel lay on the bed, he studied the bullet. It was marked and pitted, and there was blood caked in the graze marks. As he focused on it, exhaustion overcame him. His eyes burned and became unbearably heavy, and he drifted off to sleep.

The wagon driver arrived at Sarah's home. She answered the door, hoping that it was Margaret, even though her better judgement knew that Margaret would not knock.

"Mrs. Berry?"

"Yes."

"I am a wagon driver with the Ardwick Constabulary. Your son and daughter are at the Ancoats Hospital and I am to take you to them."

Sarah stared at the driver as she tried to understand what he was saying.

"The hospital?" she said, incredulous as to his words. The impact of them finally hit her. "Samuel found Margaret." Sarah's mind was racing in every direction. "The hospital. Oh, no. My dear girl."

"I'll take you to them. Please come with me."

"Certainly," Sarah said. "James, please get Mary and Agnes from school. Take them with you to finish your deliveries. When you are done, please come home and wait. I need to go to Samuel and Margaret. When Eleanor comes back, please tell her we are at the Ancoats Hospital. Can you do that for me?"

James looked fixedly at the driver, struggling to fathom what his mother was asking of him. He was still merely a boy, only fourteen and not nearly mature enough to grasp the seriousness of the situation.

"James, can you do that for me?" Sarah repeated.

James turned his gaze to his mother. "Yes, of course. I shall do that."

With haste, Sarah put on her boots and coat and was out the door. The wagon was waiting out front. The driver opened the back door and Sarah hesitated, uneasy and unsure.

"Apologies, Mrs. Berry. I will get you there as expeditiously as I can."

"Of course. I appreciate your help. Very much I do." Sarah said, feeling bad for appearing ungrateful, which was not at all the case.

As Sarah climbed into the back, the sight of blood on the floor and seat made her gasp. She took a seat on the opposite side. What poor, wretched soul caused that mess, she thought with sadness.

Sarah was sick with worry. Where had Margaret been? What state was she in? How had Samuel found her? Was he all right? Sarah nervously tapped the floor of the wagon with her foot and prayed for the ride to end.

The wagon came to a stop and the back door opened up. The driver held out his hand for Sarah.

"Thank you for your kindness. I am most appreciative."

"You are welcome, Mrs. Berry. Best of luck to your children."

Sarah panicked at the thought. Her children. She needed to get to them. She turned and ran to the door.

Chapter 22

As James walked up Robinson Street, Catherine Markley's carriage came toward him. Reuben and Jonathan saw him and stopped.

"James," Jonathan yelled.

James looked over and saw Eleanor jumping out of the carriage.

"James, where are you going? Where is your mother?"

"A police driver came and took Mama to the Ancoats Hospital. I am to go and get Mary and Agnes from school and then finish my deliveries."

"Ancoats Hospital?"

"Yes, I believe the driver said that Margaret and Samuel are at the hospital. The driver took Mama there. I do not know any more than that."

"Go and finish your deliveries. When you are done, go home and wait. I shall get Mary and Agnes from school and then go to the hospital and see the situation there. We shall be home as soon as we can. Are you all right with that?"

"Yes, I'll go home as soon as I am done."

In short order, Eleanor and the girls were beyond the school and off toward the Ancoats Hospital while James frantically finished his deliveries.

Inside the hospital, Sarah saw the long line in front of the patient check-in window and refused to wait. She burst into the waiting room, hoping to see Samuel and Margaret directly. Once in, she quickly surveyed the room and ran up the main aisle. A nurse approached her and asked her to take a seat.

"I am not here for myself. I am looking for my children. I was told that they are here and I do not know where."

"If they are not in this room or in a treatment room, then you must be mistaken."

Sarah started to panic and began raising her voice.

"I am not mistaken. The officer told me that they were here. They must be here."

"Madam, please quiet down. This is not a football grandstand," the nurse replied harshly.

"You do not understand. My daughter was missing and my son has found her. The officers brought them here."

As Sarah continued to plead with the nurse, Eleanor entered the room. She quickly saw Sarah talking with the nurse and she ran to them both.

"Sarah," Eleanor called as she was running. She had one girl on each hand.

"Eleanor, thank heavens," Sarah said. "The nurse is trying to tell me they are not here. They must be."

"My father is a very large benefactor and subscriber to this hospital. If I do not see some assistance immediately, I shall advise that he stop being so, and I shall do so without hesitation. Do I make myself clear?"

The nurse was not used to being spoken to this way and she huffed and put her hands on her hips in a show of disgust.

"How dare you?" she said before being cut off by an orderly, who had stepped in to assist the nurse.

"What seems to be the problem?" he asked.

Sarah, Eleanor, and the nurse all began speaking at once, each talking over the other.

"One at a time," the orderly directed.

Eleanor jumped in quickly and restated why they were there.

"I know the two that you refer to. They are both in the in-patient room. I can take you to them."

Sarah's knees buckled at the news, and Eleanor dropped Mary's and Agnes' hands and reached out to Sarah.

"Yes, please take us to them. Thank you very much," Eleanor said to the orderly.

Sarah picked up Mary, who had started to cry.

"Mary, my dear girl, there is no need to cry. All is well," Eleanor said reassuringly and kissed Mary on the cheek.

Sarah took Agnes' hand and squeezed it tightly. Together all four followed the orderly through a set of doors at the end of the waiting room. As they entered the in-patient room, Sarah quickly spotted Samuel. She put Mary down and ran over to the bed. He was still lying on his side, but was awake and looking at her. He sat up quickly to greet his mother, but the pain of his leg and the constant dizziness forced him to lie back down.

"Samuel, what in heaven's name is wrong?" Sarah beseeched. "And where is Margaret? Where is she?"

Margaret was on the bed that was to Samuel's back. Based on the position of the wound, it made lying on the other side problematic for him.

"She is behind me, Mama."

Margaret looked over at the other bed and ran to it. Margaret was not recognizable. She was wrapped in blankets, which held in a layer of ice to keep her cool. Her face was completely colourless and her lips were blue.

"Eleanor, what could have happened to my dear, sweet girl? What is wrong with her?" Sarah was frantic. She could not stand still. She started pacing beside the bed. Eleanor tried to calm Sarah down, but it did no good.

The doctor arrived at Margaret's bedside.

"Doctor, please tell me what is wrong," Sarah pleaded.

"Are you her mother?" the doctor asked.

"I am. I am desperate for answers. Please tell me."

"She is experiencing complications from influenza. The influenza brought on a very high fever, causing weakness and delirium."

"If she was just brought here, where has she been since yesterday?" Sarah wondered out loud.

"From what I understand, she spent the night in Ardwick Green," the doctor offered.

Sarah gasped. "What do you mean she spent the night in Ardwick Green? How is that possible?" Sarah tried to understand, but the words made no sense. She frantically scanned the room as though the answer might appear somewhere.

"You need to ask your son. He located her and brought her here. We have fixed his leg and he shall be fine. Your daughter is gravely ill. Her biggest threat is her fever. If we cannot bring it under control, shock shall be the threat. And, if that is the case and she still survives, she'll most likely experience damage to her brain. There is also a risk of pneumonia, which is common with influenza patients. We have her packed in ice at the moment to keep her temperature down. Now we must wait. We stopped the bleeding from the gash on her forehead, and the swelling from that is down. If she survives the night, it shall be a miracle. You should prepare yourselves and say your good-byes."

Sarah began to wail in denial. Eleanor wrapped her arms around Sarah's waist to hold her up. This could not be happening. She was young and healthy and had her life to live.

"We removed the bullet from your son's leg and disinfected the area. There should be no long-term damage," the doctor continued.

"*Bullet?* This is making no sense." The anguish in Sarah's voice was palpable.

Sarah walked around to Samuel's face.

"Samuel, what has happened? Bullet? I do not understand. Please tell me," Sarah pleaded. "Please tell me."

"I found Margaret in Ardwick Green underneath a bush. It was only by the grace of God that I found her. She had no coat or boots. She was bleeding from her forehead. I could not wake her. I tried to bring her home. I did." Samuel was crying as well. "The next thing I know, a Peeler shot me in the leg. He thought I was hurting Margaret, I suppose. I was simply trying to bring her home to you."

"My dear boy," Sarah said, kissing her son on his forehead. "You are a good son and a good brother. Thank you for finding your sister. I am so sorry you were put in harm's way to do so. How are you feeling? Does your leg hurt?" Sarah asked.

"I am still feeling a bit ill. My leg doesn't hurt that much."

Samuel slowly sat up in bed, adjusting himself so that his knees were bent and there was no pressure on the back of his leg. The room had stopped moving and the nausea was weakening.

Sarah held Margaret's hand while she stroked her cheek.

"Margaret, we all love you so. You must come back to us. We could not bear life without you. I pray you can hear me." Sarah hoped for a sign that Margaret could hear her, but she gave none.

The rattling of her breath was the only sign of life. She had no facial colour and there was no movement in her eyes. Sarah studied her face, noting every line and every mark. She wanted to commit it all to memory, forever.

"Mama, is Margaret going to be all right?" Agnes asked.

Sarah was caught up in her own reality and did not think of her other daughters. What must they think? They must be terrified, not understanding what was happening.

"Yes, she is resting now." They were too young to understand the gravity of the situation, Sarah thought.

As she spoke to them, she looked for Eleanor, who was on the other side of the room speaking with the doctor. When Eleanor returned to Sarah's side, she spoke of her plans.

"Sarah, our family doctor is one of the finest in the area. I would like to arrange for him to care for Margaret at home."

Sarah could sense there was something more.

"What did the doctor say?" Sarah asked, more frightened by what Eleanor was not saying.

Eleanor did not want to discourage Sarah, nor did she want to give up hope, but she knew the situation was very dire and she did not want Margaret's remaining time to be spent in a hospital.

"The doctor said that there is nothing more they can do here that Dr. Ward could not do for her at home. She shall be considerably more comfortable there, as shall you."

"Eleanor, we cannot afford to pay for a private doctor. You know that." Sarah looked helpless and hopeless.

"That is not for you to worry about, Sarah. You must resign yourself to the fact that you are not in control here. No one is. We need to manage the best we can, and we cannot think of ourselves. Margaret is like my daughter and I shall do what I can to ensure she gets well. I shall do anything." Eleanor was not asking.

Sarah knew Eleanor was right. It was no time for pride. It was time to do what was best for Margaret. It was time to accept help.

Reuben travelled to the factory to provide an update to William and Charles Markley. William returned with Reuben and Jonathan. They waited outside while William went inside to understand the situation and to see how he could assist.

Eleanor walked over to her brother when she saw him enter. She was surprised to see him. She wanted to talk with him away from Sarah. She would need to speak truthfully and that would be more than Sarah could bear.

"William, how did you know we were here?" Eleanor asked.

"Reuben came to the factory. He told us that you were here. I came at once," William said. "What happened?"

William listened, aghast, as Eleanor explained.

"I shall arrange for Dr. Ward to accompany Margaret home, and he shall care for her there. It is dire, William. It does not look good at all. I shall not allow what happened to Thomas to happen to Margaret. It is bad enough to lose someone you love. I shall not allow Sarah to be separated from Margaret the way she was with Thomas in the end."

"Please let me help. Let me take Mary and Agnes home to James. I will go get Dr. Ward and bring him here. You should stay with Sarah."

"William, thank you so much. I'll go get Mary and Agnes."

"Girls, go with William. He shall take you home to James, and then we shall follow promptly. Please mind James until we do."

Eleanor walked the girls over to William. Sarah was focused on Margaret and did not notice them leave.

"Hello, girls. It is nice to see you again. Would you care to go for a carriage ride?" William asked.

"Yes, please," Mary said enthusiastically.

"I'll be back shortly, Eleanor," William said, addressing his sister.

William took both girls, leaving Eleanor to return to Sarah.

Samuel was sitting up in bed in the same position, but his colour had returned. He was on the mend, and he was ready to get up. Sarah insisted he stay in bed until they leave. There was no need for him to be up. It would serve no purpose.

Margaret's condition remained unchanged. Sarah continued to hold her daughter's hand, praying silently for her prayers to be answered. Margaret's fever persisted at one hundred and five and the nurses continued to place ice around her body in an effort to keep her cool.

Sarah broke from her concentration and looked around for Mary and Agnes. Overcome by hysteria, she called out for the girls.

"Sarah, William took the girls home. James is there and he shall watch them until you arrive. They were getting tired and there is nothing for them to do here."

"William was here?" Sarah questioned. "When was he here?"

"He left a few moments ago with the girls. He is going to return with Dr. Ward. We are securing the hospital ambulance to transport Margaret home."

"William is a good man," Sarah said. "Please remind me to thank him."

The hospital clerk returned to the room and handed Sarah paperwork.

"Here is a listing of the services rendered, including the ambulance that has been requested. It is all paid in full and the account is now closed," the clerk explained.

"I do not understand. What do you mean 'paid in full'"? Sarah asked. "We have made no such arrangements. Eleanor, did you do this?"

"I did not," Eleanor responded, bewildered herself.

"It was paid in full by Mr. Markley," the clerk said.

Sarah looked at Eleanor, surprised. "William paid the bill?" Sarah asked.

"No, Madam, it was Mr. Charles Markley who paid the bill in full. He was in a short time ago and he settled the account."

The clerk walked away leaving Eleanor, Sarah, and Samuel in stunned silence.

"I shall find a way to repay your father," Sarah said, trembling. "I will. I promise."

"I will ask for additional hours and I will pay it off myself," Samuel offered.

"You shall do no such thing, either of you. As surprised as I am that my father settled the account, the fact is he did. He would not have done so if he expected anything in return."

Eleanor was flabbergasted. She could never have imagined that her father would do such a thing. He had never done anything like this before. Perhaps what he had told her before Christmas was genuine. Perhaps she had misjudged him.

The nurse returned to take Margaret's temperature. It was one hundred and four. The ice had brought it down slightly, but it was not enough. The nurse removed the ice and wrapped Margaret in a light blanket for the journey. She took a final look at the wound on her forehead and changed the bandage.

The doctor returned to speak to Sarah. "Her temperature has dropped slightly, which is good, but is not enough yet for us to be optimistic. Long-term heat exposure is damaging to the brain and other internal organs. The longer she stays at this temperature, the more damage will occur. Eventually, her organs will begin to shut down. She may never wake up, and if that is the case her passing will be pain free. It will be a blessing."

Sarah's silent tears fell swiftly. Her love for Margaret was infinite, as was the pain that ripped at her heart. She was going to lose her daughter, and it was because of her own pride and stubbornness. If she had allowed her friends to support her from the beginning, Margaret would not have found herself in that position. At that moment, Sarah cursed herself.

"We cannot keep ice on her any longer. Her chest is becoming more congested and I fear pneumonia. You can keep her cool with a cold compress. Beyond that all we can do is to wait. I wish your daughter a miracle, Mrs. Berry. God does provide them. I have witnessed them myself."

"Thank you, Doctor," Sarah said acknowledging his reassuring words.

Chapter 23

William arrived with Dr. Ward. While he conferred with the hospital doctor, William joined Sarah and Eleanor at Margaret's bedside. Sarah took enormous comfort in their presence.

"Thank you for coming, William. You are a good friend."

"How are you doing, Sarah? Can I get you anything? You must be exhausted," William declared.

"I am fine. Thank you. Is that Dr. Ward?" Sarah asked, looking in the stranger's direction.

"Yes, he is arranging for the ambulance. We shall leave shortly."

William turned his attention to Samuel.

"And you? I hear you are a hero. Getting yourself shot? There are easier ways to get a day off work," William joked, bringing out a laugh in Samuel.

"I suppose you are right."

"And before you worry, because I know you will, your job will be waiting for you when you return. Do not fret for one moment." William's look turned serious and he patted Samuel on the shoulder.

"Thank you."

Samuel was taken aback by William's generosity. William had always been fair, but work had been a difficult place and he had never been treated any differently. William managed to his father's expectations. And Charles Markley had been a task master, driving out every last drop of effort from his employees, always pushing for profits. He had noticed a change in Charles Markley over the last few weeks. Something was different and he was curious as to why.

Dr. Ward arrived at Margaret's bedside along with the hospital doctor. Dr. Ward did a quick inspection of his patient and gave his approval for transport. The nurse summoned the orderly, who wheeled over a bed that was specifically designed for the ambulance. Two orderlies carefully transferred Margaret to the new bed. The nurse covered Margaret in a blanket, tucking it under her at both sides. Belts were secured around her so that she would not move about in the ambulance.

The orderly pushed the bed to the waiting ambulance at the side entrance of the hospital. William walked around to the front where Reuben and Jonathan waited, and summoned them to the side to join the others. The raindrops fell cold and heavy from the sky, and the fog hung like a shroud, blanketing all that was in its path. It was stifling. It was an unpleasant day, made much more so by the circumstance.

The ambulance was a longer version of a carriage. The orderlies released the latches and lowered the bed down on its folding legs. They placed it onto the rollers that sat on the ambulance floor and pushed the bed forward, locking it into place. Dr. Ward and one of the orderlies stepped up into the ambulance and each took a seat beside the patient. The remaining orderly closed the ambulance door behind them.

"Reuben is waiting to take us to Sarah's now. The ambulance has been directed to follow us," William said.

Samuel hobbled along with the cane that the hospital had provided for him. Aspirin helped with the pain, and did not bring about the nausea or dizziness that the ether had. He had regained his strength and could put his weight on his left hand to support himself. Agility, on the other hand, was a different story. William was right handed and managing the cane with his left hand proved to be challenging.

Reuben and Jonathan were waiting at the carriage. Reuben stepped down to open the door. Jonathan remained up beside the driver's seat. He looked tired and pale and didn't address anyone.

"Reuben, thank you so much for all your help today. You have made the day much easier for us and I am grateful," Sarah said.

"Mr. Markley has freed me up to be at your disposal. And I am happy to do so," Reuben offered.

Once the carriage was loaded, Reuben headed off toward the Berry home. The ambulance followed behind. To the outside world, it looked like a funeral procession. The mood inside the carriage was not much different.

The carriage pulled up front. Jonathan stayed up in his seat, focused on the road ahead. The day had been an emotional whirlwind and it was far from over. He was numb and could not speak. He had not seen Margaret. He knew it was bad, but did not know how bad. He felt destroyed. His world was being crushed.

The ambulance driver opened the door and Dr. Ward and the orderly stepped down. The bed was unsecured from its locks and the bed was rolled out. The driver and the orderly lifted Margaret out of the ambulance and were waiting for instructions on where to go next.

"Please follow me," Sarah said.

As Margaret was being transported toward the door, Jonathan turned his head to catch a glimpse. He saw Margaret lying on a bed, motionless. She looked as though she was ready for burial and the image caused him to lose control of the little control he was holding onto. He turned his head when he could look no more.

The orderly and driver pushed Margaret inside, stopping near the spot where James and the girls stood waiting. James could not believe what he was seeing. He was stupefied by the sight of his sister in such a state. The girls did not understand what was going on. They were simply happy to see their mother.

The bed that Margaret lay on was to be returned to the hospital. Margaret needed to be transferred to her own bed and Sarah led the way upstairs. The orderly was an extremely large man, well over six feet tall, and as thick as a tree. He picked up Margaret as though she weighed nothing, putting an arm under her knees and another under her back. He carried her up the stairs and placed her down on the bed, as directed. Sarah covered her up and kissed her daughter on the forehead. She was still hot and damp with perspiration and it made Sarah wince.

Sarah accompanied the orderly downstairs and joined the others. The orderly and ambulance driver removed the bed and returned to the hospital. Dr. Ward went upstairs to check on his patient, taking a lantern with him to light his way.

"Sarah, you must be famished. You have not eaten all day. You should rest," Eleanor chided.

"I have no appetite or interest in resting. I can rest once Margaret is well."

Eleanor and William caught each other's eyes and acknowledged Sarah's optimism with sadness.

"James and girls, have you eaten? Samuel, you must be hungry."

All four of them nodded. They were growing children who did not lose their appetites for any reason.

"Reuben, if you could take me quickly to the market, I will pick up a few items. Eleanor and I will make something. You would be more than welcome to join us." William was trying desperately to offer assistance.

"Thank you, but upon my return from the market I need to get back to Amberley House to tend to the horses. Beatrice will find something for us to eat, I am certain."

William left with Reuben, leaving Sarah free to return to her daughter.

"Samuel, let's have Dr. Ward look at your leg and then you can put on a decent pair of pants. You look a bit silly with just one pant leg." Eleanor attempted to lighten the mood. "Let us go upstairs and see the doctor."

Samuel leaned heavily on his cane for support going up the stairs. On a few, he narrowly missed tumbling backwards, causing Eleanor to shriek.

Samuel stood in front of Dr. Ward as he knelt and removed the bandage from Samuel's leg. The bleeding had stopped and the stitch was holding nicely. He rewrapped the wound and told Samuel it was healing well.

Sarah was sitting on the bed beside Margaret, holding her hand. Sarah wanted desperately to see some sign of life, but she did not. Will was clearly not enough. It was in God's hands now.

The doctor returned to Margaret's room. "I have done all that I can do now. Her recovery depends upon the fever dissipating and then regaining some level of consciousness. She needs fluids or she will quickly become dehydrated from the fever. I'll have your driver take me to my office, and I will return tomorrow to check on her."

Sarah was distressed at the thought of the doctor leaving and the doctor could see so.

"Mrs. Berry, I do not mean to be harsh, but I must speak truthfully. Your daughter's condition could not be graver. There is nothing that can happen for the worse that I could assist with at this point. If your daughter's condition does change, you can come get me. I will leave my address downstairs. As you were told at the hospital, your family should think about saying their good-byes before it is too late."

"Thank you, Doctor," Sarah said quietly, defeated, as she dropped her head. There was nothing else to say.

Eleanor's shop needed closing for the day and Sarah insisted she not return until she had slept. She would need her rest for work. Both Dr. Ward and Eleanor were driven their separate ways by Reuben, who reassured Sarah he would return the next day to help in any way he could.

"William, there is no need for you to stay either. You have had a very long day and I cannot thank you enough for all you have done."

"I will not be leaving so you best stop worrying about it. I have put food on the table and the children are eating. You should eat something yourself to keep up your strength. It will be a long night for you."

Sarah did not have the energy to fight.

"Thank you, William. You are a good friend. I could not love you more if you were my own flesh and blood."

Those sweetly intended words stung William to the core. He understood they were not intentionally malicious, but they wounded as though they were.

William had purchased a cooked ham and chicken, a loaf of bread, and some dessert pastries from an Ardwick restaurant. The children were in the kitchen devouring the food. William was happy to see them eating and not worrying. Sarah was worrying enough for all of them.

"I shall eat later. I would like to get back up to Margaret."

"Of course."

"William, you have your own life and I do not want to keep you from it on my account. You have done more than any friend could ever expect."

Sarah's pain was destroying William. She may not have felt about him the way he would have liked, but it did not change his feelings for her.

"Go upstairs and be with Margaret. I will make sure the children finish eating, and then I will have James help Mary and Agnes to bed. I think Samuel is able to take care of himself now."

Sarah touched William on the shoulder and kissed him on the cheek. She made her way upstairs and stood at the doorway. She hesitated going inside, frightened by what she might find. As she entered the room, the lamplight cast an eerie shadow over Margaret. It was difficult to make out her features.

Sarah sat down and kissed Margaret on the forehead. She was still hot. Her bedding was pulled back and she took a cloth and soaked it in a basin with cold water and dabbed it on her face and neck. She lifted her blouse and moistened her abdomen. Margaret was still in the same filthy clothing. Her bloomers had been removed, but her dirty skirt remained to cover her lower half. Margaret placed a heavy pile of linens under Margaret to protect the bed from urine. But, as time went on and Margaret became more dehydrated, the need to change them became less frequent.

Sarah could hear James getting the girls ready for bed. When James came in to say that they were tucked in and about to fall asleep, Sarah went in and said her good-nights.

"Tomorrow shall be a good day. I can feel it," Sarah said optimistically.

"Yes, Mama," Mary said while yawning. She rolled over and fell asleep instantly.

"Samuel, how is your leg? Did you take another aspirin to help with the pain?"

"I did. It is not that bad, really." Samuel was exhausted and ready to fall asleep himself. "Please give Margaret a kiss for me and tell her I shall see her in the morning."

Sarah refused to let the kids say *good-bye* as the doctor had suggested. She let them tell her they loved her and always would, and that the Lord was watching over her.

As Sarah focused on her daughter, she remembered the day Margaret was born. Margaret came very quickly, almost falling to the floor. She was a determined child right from the beginning. When she wanted to do something, she did it. Patience was never a virtue of hers. But, as challenging as she could be at times, she was the sweetest of children, a generous soul who always took care of others before herself. Sarah thought of how horrible it must have been for Margaret to have travelled home so sick that she could have collapsed in the park. Sarah began to weep at the thought.

"I am so sorry my dear, sweet girl. I am so sorry. If I could go back, I would, in an instant. I thought Amberley House would be a pleasant place for you and instead it was exactly the opposite. I pray, one day, you can forgive me."

William entered the room, clearing his throat to acknowledge his entry. Sarah turned as she wiped her eyes. William put a sandwich and a glass of water down on the table.

"Thank you, William." Sarah looked down at Margaret and said, "No change. She is holding on. She is a strong girl."

"She is her mother," William said half laughing. "Of course she is strong."

Sarah laughed as well. Part of it was delirium and part of it was William's kind way. It was comforting to Sarah.

"It is getting late. I am sure you would like to go home."

William said nothing. He simply smiled and walked out of the room. Sarah was hungry. As she reached down for her sandwich, she noticed dirt on her hands. The basin had remained upstairs so she washed them with soap and water. She took a bite of the sandwich. It was exactly what she needed.

Margaret's breathing began to rattle and sputter and Sarah began to pray. She remembered that sound well. Thomas did the same thing at the very end. Sarah walked around to the end of the bed and climbed up beside Margaret. She pulled the covers back and lay down beside her daughter, holding her hand and burying her face in her daughter's hair. She cried until she fell into a deep sleep.

Sarah did not know what time it was when she awoke. Margaret had not moved and was still feverish. Her chest rattled like a slow drum beat. Sarah pulled herself up out of bed and went downstairs for a glass of water. When she stepped into the sitting room, she was shocked to see William asleep in the arm chair. His head was slumped back uncomfortably, but he was in a deep enough sleep to be snoring.

Sarah gently covered him with a blanket and gave him a soft kiss on the forehead. He was a good man, so thoughtful and generous, and Sarah felt blessed to have him in her life.

Sarah quietly sat down at the table with her glass of water and her beloved box. As she slid the lid back, she pulled out the piece of paper, reading her poem to herself.

"Margaret, you too are strong," Sarah whispered as she put the poem back safely in the box.

Sarah reached in and gently removed the rose. She held it out in front of the light, inspecting it closely. Sarah had not held it since Thomas died.

Those memories came flooding back and her chest tightened under the strain of emotion. Sarah held the rose to her chest and closed her eyes.

"Thomas, my love," she whispered, "please protect our girl. I need her here a little while longer with me. I am not ready to let her go just yet. Please understand that. I love you and shall see you before too long, my dear."

Sarah opened her eyes, wiping the tears from her cheeks with her handkerchief. She put the rose back securely in the box and then placed it back on the shelf. Sarah made her way back upstairs and, as she did, William closed his eyes again.

Sarah climbed into bed with Margaret. She placed her hand on Margaret's chest, feeling it move up and down with each laboured breath. The heat was radiating through her blouse like a burning log. The congestion worsened and Margaret's chest began to move more slightly. Sarah removed her hand for fear the weight was causing Margaret distress.

As she did before, Sarah fell into a deep sleep. She dreamt of a field full of flowers and Margaret was on the other side. The flowers were beautiful, but they separated Sarah from her daughter. Margaret was calling to her, but Sarah could not reach her.

"Mmmmmmmmm," Margaret moaned quietly.

Sarah shot up and, upon hearing silence, believed it was nothing more than her dream. As she watched Margaret for signs of movement, she felt her forehead. She was warm but no longer hot. Her skin was still damp with moisture but much cooler. Her fever had broken.

"Margaret, can you hear me?" Sarah asked.

Margaret's eyes began to flutter and then in one glorious moment, they opened. They looked straight up at the ceiling.

"Margaret, it is Mama. I am here, my dear girl," Sarah said, hoping for some recognition. It did not come.

Margaret's eyes closed again and Sarah collapsed on her daughter, burying her head on her belly. Sarah remembered what the doctor had said. Her daughter was alive, but may be in darkness. She may be forever.

"Margaret, please wake up, my sweetheart. Please wake up," Sarah pleaded.

Margaret opened her eyes again, still staring up at the ceiling.

"Margaret, can you hear me?"

A moment passed and then Margaret slowly shifted her eyes and looked at her mother.

"Mama, my head hurts," Margaret whispered faintly.

Sarah began laughing and kissing her daughter's forehead and cheeks in quick succession. Margaret winced in pain and Sarah stopped.

"I am sorry. I am so happy that you are awake. You gave your mother an awful fright."

"Where am I? What happened?" Margaret continued to whisper.

"There is enough time for that. You need your rest. Let me get you a drink of water."

Sarah put a clean cloth in her glass of water and squeezed some of it into Margaret's mouth. Margaret choked on the water, forcing Sarah to lift her daughter on her side and pat her back. Margaret was very congested and could barely breathe. *But she's alive,* Sarah thought. *She's alive.*

The sun had not yet risen and the house was quiet. It was as though Sarah and Margaret were the only two people awake in the world.

"Mama, I am cold," Margaret said, her voice cracking.

Sarah pulled the bedding up over Margaret. Her fever was down and there was no need to keep her cool any longer. In the dimly-lit room, Sarah could not assess Margaret's colouring. But she was awake and speaking, and that gave Sarah every reason to be optimistic.

As the sun began to rise in the sky, light trickled into the bedrooms. Sarah could hear stirring in the next room. Mary's and Agnes' voices chirped like little birds. Samuel's cane hit the floor with a solid thud.

"I shall return shortly," Sarah said. "I'll tend to your linens when I do. You need your rest, Margaret. Try to remain still."

Sarah was immune to the smell of ammonia, which permeated the room. Margaret would need to be bathed, and Sarah wanted to do so before the doctor returned.

Margaret tried to channel her energy so she could remember what brought her to this state. She was exhausted and simply could not remember. Her throat burned as though it were on fire and her chest exploded in pain with every breath. Short, shallow breaths were the easiest to manage and Margaret focused all her energy on that.

Sarah met Samuel at the top of the stairs. He lingered upstairs, afraid to enter the room. He did not know what to expect and his thoughts were focused on the words the hospital doctor said: *"Say your good-byes."* Samuel had prayed hard for Margaret when he went to bed. But, as he learned with his father, sometimes praying was not enough. God has His own plans and they were not influenced by what people wanted.

Samuel stared at his mother. He did not want to ask. His mother looked exhausted and that frightened him terribly. Sarah could sense his fear and she embraced her son.

"Samuel, Margaret's fever has broken. She has some recovery ahead of her yet, but I believe the worst may be over. Your sister is better because of you. I cannot fathom the consequences had you not found her when you did."

Relief flooded Samuel.

"Your sister needs her rest. You can see her in a while."

Samuel nodded and went downstairs with his mother. James was making porridge, while Mary and Agnes were waiting patiently. The scraps from last evening's meal were piled in the garbage basin by the door and the dishes had been cleaned and put away.

"James, thank you for tidying the kitchen. You are a good son," Sarah said.

"Wasn't me," James replied, shaking his head.

"Well, who did then?" Sarah asked bewildered.

The children all shrugged their shoulders. That left one person, and the thought brought Sarah to a panic.

"William, it must have been William," Sarah said, suddenly remembering that he had been there. "He must have gone home before sunrise."

"Mr. Markley brought us some tasty pastries," Agnes recalled, excitedly.

Sarah suddenly felt heartsick. William had done so much and then left without a word. How could she ever repay him? His presence had been so comforting, and she found herself wishing he were there at that moment.

After breakfast was finished, James emptied the waste basins, and then retrieved some water so that Sarah could bathe Margaret. He escorted the girls to school and went off to do his deliveries.

At half past nine, Eleanor arrived. Samuel was reading a book in the sitting room when she walked through the front door.

"Let me get those bags for you," he offered

Samuel stood up and took a couple of painful steps before Eleanor held out her hand to stop him.

"Samuel, please sit down. I shall put this food in the kitchen. Do not move. I shall be right back."

Eleanor returned to find Samuel sitting back down in his chair, his foot elevated on the table again.

"Dare I ask?" Eleanor questioned hesitantly. "How did Margaret do through the night?"

"My mother would be better suited to tell you the details. She stayed with Margaret the entire night. You best ask her," Samuel said.

Eleanor could not get a read on Samuel. Surely, if something dire had happened, he would be more clearly upset. Eleanor removed her coat and boots and went upstairs to see for herself. The smell of sickness filled the air and it caused Eleanor to recoil and cover her nose. As she approached the doorway, she paused. Sarah heard the footsteps.

"Eleanor, is that you? Please come in," Sarah offered.

Eleanor took an extra step so that she was standing in the doorway. Sarah was sitting on the side of the bed beside Margaret. Eleanor approached the bed and saw that Margaret's eyes were opened. Eleanor's legs buckled and she threw her hands up to her mouth to stifle the cry. She walked around Sarah to Margaret's head and kissed her forehead. Margaret managed a tiny squeak.

"Please tell me everything. When did the fever break?" Eleanor asked.

"Just before sunrise, I believe. Let us go downstairs to talk."

"She still maintains a mild fever. She is very congested and her throat remains heavily swollen. She is much better than she was initially, but a substantial recovery remains ahead of her yet, I am afraid," Sarah explained. "We shall have to wait for the doctor to assess her condition. I would imagine he should be here soon."

Just as Sarah was finishing her thought, there was a knock at the door. Sarah opened it to find Dr. Ward standing there.

"Hello, Doctor. Please do come in."

Dr. Ward had delivered both Eleanor and William. He had been the Markley family doctor for as long as Eleanor could remember and she could not imagine using another.

"Well, how is our patient this morning?" Dr. Ward asked.

"She had a very difficult night, Dr. Ward," Sarah recalled, choking on her words. "Her breathing was laboured and rattly."

Dr. Ward looked on, disappointed, afraid this would be the case.

"Her virus is very severe. Unfortunately, there is nothing we can do to treat influenza, short of making the patient more comfortable. We have done all we can."

"Please let me finish," Sarah said, her voice rising with excitement. "Just before sunrise, her fever broke. She feels warm, but not nearly to the extreme that she did before. She is complaining that her head and throat hurt, and her chest is very congested."

Dr. Ward looked as surprised as he did relieved. It was always a fine line between optimism and disillusionment. Dr. Ward fully believed that Margaret would not make it through the night.

"Well, I guess I should go up and check on our patient then," Dr. Ward said, smiling.

"Eleanor, have you spoken with William today?" Sarah wondered.

"No, I have not. What time did he leave here last night?"

"I came down in the middle of the night, before Margaret's fever had broken, and he was sleeping in the chair. I covered him with a blanket and went back upstairs. He was gone this morning. I very much need to thank him for all that he has done. His presence was so comforting." The thought of William being unaware of her appreciation troubled her.

Eleanor contemplated telling Sarah how William felt, but it was neither the time nor place. There would be plenty of opportunity. They had the rest of their lives and this would be a new beginning, Eleanor believed.

The contents of Dr. Ward's bag clanked around as he descended the stairs. His stethoscope swung back and forth on his chest like a pendulum.

"Mrs. Berry, your daughter is doing much better, but she is not free from danger yet. The virus still has a hold on her and she must continue to fight. She needs to be hydrated slowly and fed as much as she is able to take. She needs her strength. At this time, pneumonia is our biggest worry. If we can keep her chest from getting any more congested and keep pneumonia at bay, then she has a very good chance for full recovery. At this point, short of memory loss, which is to be expected, she seems to have full brain function."

"Thank you, Doctor. I am so relieved." Sarah's exhaustion was evident.

"Samuel, if you would care to drop your pants, I would like to check your bandage to ensure there is no bleeding or seepage."

Samuel was taken aback by the request and his face reddened at the thought of doing so in front of his mother and Eleanor.

"Eleanor and I shall wait in the kitchen while the doctor examines you, Samuel," Sarah offered.

"What are these?" Sarah asked of the two bags from the market that were sitting on the counter top.

"Going to the market is the last thing on your mind. This should do nicely."

She embraced Eleanor and held on for a few moments. She had said "thank you" so many times she felt as though it was losing its meaning.

"You are welcome, Sarah. You must realize by now that we are family and family takes care of each other. I am not doing anything for you that you would not do for me."

Sarah nodded and began to tear up. It was very difficult for her to let go of the control that she had fought so hard to maintain her entire life. But she realized that control without thought was often more dangerous than possessing no control at all. And she could not deny it felt good to be cared for. It was pure love, the kind that nourished your soul and fulfilled you beyond anything you could ever do for yourself.

Upon hearing the front door close, Sarah and Eleanor returned to the sitting room.

"Dr. Ward said that he would be back to check on Margaret this evening. It appears I am healing nicely as well."

"More good news. We are blessed," Sarah said.

Over the next week, Margaret's condition improved steadily. After three days, she had regained enough strength to take a few steps. Her appetite returned, and her throat healed enough to swallow without excruciating pain. Within a week, she was walking up and down the stairs with ease. She read constantly to fill her time and reduce the boredom. Eleanor had bought her another copy of the Florence Nightingale book to replace the one she lost. Inside it read simply, *You are wonderful. With all my love, Aunt Eleanor.*

Her memory from the time she left Amberley House did not return and Sarah thought it was for the best. Margaret would not be returning and that was for the best as well.

For the first few weeks after Margaret had recovered, she spent her time helping her mother run errands to and from Eleanor's shop. She also dropped her sisters off at school and picked them up. In between she helped her mother cook and clean.

During Margaret's ordeal, the missing children's case had been solved. The Ardwick Green gang had decided that there was good money to be made by selling children as slaves. They were sent to London to be shipped to points abroad. Victoria Matthews fought hard and paid with her life. Four additional children had been transported to London. Two had been recovered, and police feared that the other two had already left the country and were gone forever. Three gang members in Ardwick had been arrested, along with two in London. They were awaiting trial.

Sarah did not feel the need to provide Margaret the details of her ordeal. It chilled Sarah to the bone to think of what could have happened to Margaret in that park. She believed her grave condition may have saved her from further harm. The police believed agreed.

Chapter 24

It was a sunny April day, nearly three months after Margaret had overcome her illness. Her outside scars had healed, but her inner scars were still buried deep in memory loss. The doctor said that she may never remember and Sarah was hopeful of that.

Margaret had not returned to Amberley House. Sarah was not ready for Margaret to leave the house for any work quite yet. She wanted Margaret to be a child again, or for a little longer at least.

"Margaret, I need you to take these dresses over to Eleanor's shop, please."

"Yes, Mama," Margaret said.

She was always happy to go. It was a treat to get outdoors, and even more so to visit with Eleanor. It always involved tea and delightful conversation.

Sarah had completed two dresses that were to be picked up later that afternoon. Sarah was still working with Eleanor, but it was becoming more infrequent because the demand for custom dresses was in a slump. With Margaret not working, Sarah was forced to pick up additional work. Eleanor had offered to have Sarah work in the shop on the machines. Sarah had resisted, but the need was getting too great and Sarah decided that she would have no choice.

Margaret carried the dresses to Eleanor's. The apple blossoms were in bloom and the few trees that had not been cut down were awash in colour. They brightened the usual soot coloured town, engaging the imaginations of all who cared to look. Margaret skipped along, happy to be outside. She was well again, and for the time being didn't have a care in the world.

"How is my sweet girl doing today?" Eleanor said as Margaret entered the shop. "It is always the greatest pleasure to see you. Here, let me take those and we can go upstairs and have some tea."

Margaret agreed enthusiastically. Upstairs they sat at the table and drank tea and ate pastries. As Margaret nibbled on the sugary treats, Eleanor asked her how she was.

"I feel good today. Spring is here and it is magnificent outside."

"Jonathan was asking how you were," Eleanor said, keenly interested in Margaret's reaction.

Margaret saddened at the sound of Jonathan's name. Eleanor could see her face drop. It was as plain as day. Margaret did not miss Catherine Markley, but she surely did miss Jonathan. She thought of him often.

"Jonathan misses you so. When you were sick, he was beside himself with worry. I would imagine that nothing has changed in his heart. Time has simply preserved those feelings. Has it for you?"

Margaret realized that Eleanor was a smart and intuitive woman and there was no sense hiding any of it. Margaret missed Jonathan very much. A piece of her heart was missing since she stopped seeing him and she longed to see him again.

"Would you like to visit with him? I can arrange it."

"I would very much like to see him. He is a good friend and I would like to thank him for his kind thoughts."

"I should think thanking him for his kindness is not what he is looking for. It is very clear how he feels about you and he wants to know if you feel the same."

Margaret put her head down. There was no denying how she felt about him, but so much had happened since she had last seen him. Her life was completely different. She was not sure if she would go back, and if she didn't, would their worlds ever come together again?

"I must be getting home, Aunt Eleanor. Mama'll worry about me. She doesn't let me out of her sight for long these days." Margaret laughed.

"Well, I can understand why," Eleanor said.

Margaret kissed Eleanor on the cheek and headed out the door. As she approached the bakery, the smell of fresh bread filled the air. Margaret stopped at the window and looked inside. Through the window, she watched the baker kneading the dough, picking it up, and slapping it on the table. She closed her eyes and breathed in the intoxicating aroma. Suddenly, she missed Chef Nicolas. She missed her conversations around the kitchen table. She missed Philip and, most of all, she missed Jonathan.

The sun did not stop shining on Ardwick, and she decided to continue enjoying the day by taking the long way to the girls' school. She walked down to Ardwick Green, sat down on a bench, and studied the life that was all around her. Spring was a rebirth and this year the park seemed more vibrant and alive than in any other in her memory. The new leaves were coming in, flowers were blooming, and birds were chirping. Margaret closed her eyes and let the sun shine brightly on her face. She felt alive with energy and excitement and optimism. For the first time, she allowed herself to think about her future and she was excited about the unknown. Whatever happened, she promised herself she would not take the path that was expected of her. She would make her mark on the world and she would make her family proud.

Margaret arrived home with Mary and Agnes, who were just as happy and cheerful as their sister.

"Hello, my girls. Did you have a good day today? What did you learn?" Sarah asked, with interest.

"Mama, I learned that if you add salt to water it makes the water boil faster. I believe it lowers the boiling temperature."

"That is very interesting, Agnes, very good to know if you wish to cook like your sister. Mary, did you learn anything new?"

"I did, Mama. I learned that if I don't watch my bread closely, a squirrel could steal it."

Sarah laughed. "Yes, you do need to watch that."

The rest of the evening was spent relatively quietly. The girls made a house for their dolls, James and Samuel played a game of chess, Margaret read, and Sarah sewed a bodice on a dress.

"Margaret, I need you to go over to Aunt Eleanor's immediately after you take the girls to school in the morning. I need another yard of this black chenille fabric. Mrs. Swanson is coming in at end of day for a fitting and it must be completed. You'll need to deliver it when it is finished."

"Yes, Mama. Can I make some muffins in the morning to take to the girls?"

"Yes, you can make a double batch before breakfast."

Margaret woke up at the crack of dawn to bake bread and muffins. She made enough for breakfast and for the girls at the shop. The smell of baking oats, apple, and cinnamon permeated their home and brought everyone downstairs hungry.

Margaret had decided that she would talk with Eleanor that day about returning to Amberley House. She was ready to go back and hoped that Mrs. Markley would have her. She missed her friends, but most importantly, she didn't want her mother to have to work on the machines.

When they arrived at the schoolyard, the children were playing happily outside and Mary and Agnes joined in excitedly, waving to Margaret as they ran off. For a brief moment, Margaret missed school. She missed the learning, but she did not miss being there. Her life had changed so much and she felt as though she had outgrown her old classmates. She could not imagine she had much in common with them any longer.

Margaret made her way to Eleanor's with the basket of freshly baked muffins sitting safely over her arm. Margaret had not spoken with her mother about her desire to go back to Amberley House, but she was hopeful that her mother would support the idea. After all, they needed the money and Margaret was ready and able to work again. But Margaret did not realize Catherine Markley's culpability in her circumstance. Neither Eleanor nor Sarah was ready to forgive and forget so soon.

The sky was as blue as it ever got in Ardwick. It wasn't an intense blue. It was more of a pale blue, as the factory stacks sent up a veil of ashen smoke that dulled the sky. But, today, the smell of smoke seemed stronger than usual. It wasn't the typically pungent chemical smell, but more of a burning log.

Just before Margaret was turning onto Eleanor's street, the smell became all-consuming. As she turned the corner, she could see a bustle of activity down the block. Then she could see the smoke. It was billowing up and out of one of the buildings. Margaret began to panic. It was very close to Eleanor's.

Margaret ran down the road. She saw Eleanor's navy blue awning dangling, half-burnt, and she stopped dead in her tracks. Her arms dropped and her muffins fell to the ground. Margaret shrieked in absolute panic as she saw monstrous flames licking the front of Eleanor's building. Smoke poured out of every opening it could find, including the roof, which was all but gone. She ran as fast as she could, choking on the noxious air.

A fireman held out his arm to stop her from going any farther.

"You don't understand," she pleaded. "That is my Aunt Eleanor's shop. She lives up there," Margaret said, pointing to the burning flat.

"You cannot go any farther," he said as a blackened piece of window frame fell to the ground. "It is too dangerous."

"Where is she?" Margaret said, scanning the crowd. "Did she come out?"

Margaret was overwrought and shaking uncontrollably. *Aunt Eleanor must be down on the street. Perhaps she went to the factory.*

"The fire has been burning a while now. There isn't much left at this point," the fireman said.

As Margaret continued to scan the crowd, she noticed Lizzy, one of the seamstresses, watching the fire. Margaret ran to her.

"Lizzy, Lizzy," Margaret screamed as she approached her. "Where is Eleanor?"

Lizzy was crying and hugged Margaret for her own comfort. "I don't know, Margaret. I simply don't know. I arrived for work and this is what I found. I am so worried. I have not seen her outside."

Margaret pulled away from Lizzie and pushed her way through the watching crowd, toward another fireman.

"That is my aunt's shop. She lives above the shop. I have to find her. She may still be in there. I have to find her!"

"I'm sorry, Miss. It is too dangerous to go in. The building is destroyed."

Margaret dropped to her knees, crying out as her entire body succumbed to the agony of those words. She looked up and watched his mouth form words, but she heard nothing.

As the bystanders turned to look at Margaret, the fireman helped her up to her feet. Margaret pulled herself from his grip and turned back toward home and ran faster than she had ever run before.

The door exploded with the full force of Margaret's emotion. Sarah came running out of the kitchen to find a ghost of her daughter standing in the doorway. Margaret's body defined dread. Her eyes were as wide as saucers and her chest was heaving like a Scottish bagpipe.

"Margaret, what has terrified you so?" Sarah demanded.

"Mama, it is awful. Mama, a fire."

"Margaret, calm down, my girl. Take your time."

Margaret didn't take a breath. She could not bring herself down from her panicked state. She started wailing in agony.

"There is a fire at Aunt Eleanor's. Her shop and flat have burned. You must come right away."

"That can't be right, Margaret. You must be mistaken," Sarah said, trying to understand what the words meant. "You saw Eleanor yesterday."

"Mama, please come."

Sarah put on her coat and they both ran to Eleanor's. The fire engine continued to pull water from the cistern, shooting it in a steady stream against the building. Smoke billowed out from the holes in the roof.

The gravity of the situation suddenly became very real to Sarah and she began to well up with tears. Sarah placed her hands on her daughter to calm her down. She looked her in the eyes and told her to go to the Markley factory and get William. William needed to come right away.

Margaret nodded and ran toward the factory. In her haste, Margaret stepped into a sewer grate, and as she struggled to get her boot free, the heel broke off. She continued to run on legs of uneven length, hopping to balance herself out. She ran through the factory doors shouting for William.

"William Markley, Willllllliam!" she shouted as loud as her body would allow her.

An administrative clerk came running out of the offices to see what the commotion was.

"What in heaven's name are you screaming for?" he asked, bewildered.

"I need William Markley, NOW!" Margaret yelled.

"What on earth for? Where is the fire?" the clerk questioned sarcastically.

Margaret looked at him in horror. How could he joke at a time like this?

"At his sister's house!"

Margaret pushed past the clerk and continued to shout for William. She spotted Samuel in the factory. He could not hear her over the whirl of the machinery. She ran to him and tugged on the back of his shirt. Samuel turned to find his sister standing before him.

"Margaret, what on earth is wrong?" He could see something was dreadfully wrong.

"I have to find William. There is a fire at Aunt Eleanor's. There is nothing left. We need to find her. WHERE IS WILLIAM?" Margaret pleaded. Her face was now streaked as the tears ran down her soot-covered face.

Samuel looked horrified. He took a moment to think and then grabbed his sister by the sleeve of her coat and abruptly left his work station. William was in his office, which was at the back of the factory. Together they burst in, causing him to jump up in surprise.

"Margaret, Samuel, what is wrong? Margaret, why are you so filthy?" William asked.

Margaret began sobbing uncontrollably. She couldn't speak.

"There has been a fire at Eleanor's. It is very dire. We do not know where she is," Samuel said, answering William's question pointedly.

"Good God. That cannot be. I was just there yesterday. The shop was fine. *She* was fine."

"We need to go. My mother is there right now." Margaret continued to sob.

"Sarah?" William became concerned for both of them. "Gerald is here today. He will take us there. Go out to the carriage. I will tell my father," William commanded.

They did as they were told, putting Gerald on alert that they would need to move quickly in a few moments time. Within minutes, the factory door flew open and both William and Charles Markley emerged. William joined Samuel and Margaret in the carriage and Charles joined Gerald up front.

The children could hear Charles yelling for Gerald to go faster. William did not speak. He sat, fidgeting with his hands and nervously clearing his throat. Margaret sat with her head on Samuel's shoulder while she slowly rocked herself for comfort. The short journey ended with an abrupt stop, sending the three of them in the carriage flying forward off their seats.

William opened the door to the carriage and the three were out before Gerald had fully applied the brake. By the time they had determined where they needed to go, Charles Markley was already engaged in a conversation with a fireman. Charles was very physical, moving his arms wildly and repeatedly pointing at himself and the building. After a few moments, the fireman motioned to a colleague. It appeared to be his superior as his coat was of a different colour than the rest and his helmet was larger, with a formal looking badge on it. When the senior fireman began speaking with Charles, he became still, clearly listening intently to what the man was saying. And then in one swift instant, Charles slumped over, raising his hands to cover his dropped face.

Margaret gasped in fear and dismay. Samuel stood there numb, not moving or speaking. William looked at the crowd for any sign of Eleanor. He saw Sarah sitting on the ground with her head buried in her arms. The ground was wet from the efforts of the steam engine, but Sarah did not seem to notice or care.

William put his hand on Sarah's head. She did not respond. He called her name and she still did not respond. He got down at her level and shook her shoulder aggressively enough for her to look up at him. Her eyes were swollen and red, and her face was covered in ash. She looked at William as though she did not know who he was. She continued to whimper like a wounded animal.

William gently slapped her face and she seemed to come out of the state of shock that she was in. She focused her eyes on William and finally looked at him rather than through him. He helped her up and she threw her arms around him and began wailing.

"This cannot be, William. This cannot be happening. She must have gone somewhere and is waiting for us. We must find her." Sarah was hysterical.

The fire engine continued to spray water at the building. All of the visible flames were out, but the building continued to emit a dense smoke that choked all who were in close range. Buildings on either side of Eleanor's were damaged slightly, but remained intact.

"Your children are over by the carriage. Let me take you to them. You can have a seat and wait for me. I need to speak with my father and then I will come back to you."

William put his arm around Sarah and helped her to the carriage. Margaret rushed to her mother and embraced her with every ounce of her being. Samuel kissed his mother on the forehead and then helped them both in the carriage.

"Margaret, what happened to your boot?" Sarah asked, after noticing Margaret's awkward movements.

"My heel broke while I was running to the factory."

"I suppose you will be in need of a new pair." Sarah spoke the words, but there was no life in them.

William approached his father, who was still speaking with the senior fireman. When their conversation concluded, Charles turned to his son and told him the terrible truth.

"The fire began about one o'clock this morning. It looks like it started in the shop. They will not know where it started or what started it until they complete their investigation. Your sister would have been upstairs sleeping. She would not have been able to escape, and it is the fire investigator's belief that she would have died in her sleep from the smoke."

Charles' voice began cracking and he took a moment to compose himself before he finished.

"She would not have suffered."

William stared blankly at his father, waiting for him to tell William he was mistaken. Instead Charles looked at his son and told him that he was sorry, and for the first time that William could remember in his life his father wrapped his arms around him and began crying.

There was nothing more they could do at this point. Charles Markley was told he would be notified when the investigation concluded in a day or so. In the meantime, there was always hope, however slim the hope was, that Eleanor had not been in the building.

Gerald drove Sarah, Samuel, and Margaret home. William opened the door and helped them down.

"Perhaps she went to London to pick up supplies," Sarah said hopefully, almost cheerfully, changing her tone as if to convince herself this wasn't real.

William's heart was deeply wounded as well, and at that moment he could not offer support to anyone.

"I will return when I know more."

Sarah kissed William on the cheek and turned and walked toward her door. She looked back and watched the carriage pull away and at that moment she felt nothing but emptiness.

James had come home for dinner and had prepared himself something when he found Sarah and Margaret gone. He was sitting in the kitchen eating bread and cured ham when he heard the front door open. He walked out to see who had arrived. He saw Samuel, Margaret, and Sarah standing there, each filthier than the other. Their sullen expressions painted a worrisome picture, and James felt an overwhelming dread engulf him. Sarah looked at James blankly. He focused on each of them, waiting for an explanation.

"What is wrong, Mama?" he forced himself to ask.

Samuel spoke. "There has been a fire at Eleanor's. We are not certain at this point, but she may have been in her flat at the time. It is likely she was."

James shook his head. "No, I do not believe that." He shook his head again and turned and walked back into the kitchen.

Sarah pushed her own feelings down, as she so often did. She took off her coat and boots, which were both filthy, and went into the kitchen after James.

James was sitting at the table with his head in his hands. The sobs tore at Sarah's heart and she took the seat beside her son to comfort him. She placed her arm around his shoulders and pulled him toward her. His tears fell as though he had been collecting them his entire life. Years of pain came flooding out at that moment. The tears were for Eleanor, but they were also for his father, and for Margaret. There had been so much suffering and so much darkness.

"I know this hurts terribly. We love Aunt Eleanor with all of our hearts. She shall live there forever, as shall our memories of her."

Sarah kissed James' forehead. He looked at his mother with a look of absolute emptiness, of pain that extended so deep that there was no light that could clear the fog. Sarah spoke the words as a means of comforting him, but she wouldn't allow herself to think about what they meant to her.

When the girls arrived home from school, Sarah shared the news with them. She had thought carefully about how best to do it. They were at such a sensitive age.

"Girls, please sit down with me. I would like to speak with you both."

Margaret, James, and Samuel stood back and watched. They felt helpless. They could do nothing.

"Yes, Mama, what is it?" Agnes asked. She had not sensed anything was amiss when she walked in from school, but she could see something was not right now. Sarah's face was different, almost distorted.

"God has a plan for each and every one of us. We don't know what that plan is or will be, but we can seek comfort in knowing that there is one. And some people are called home before the rest of us are ready to let them go, and it makes us very sad. But one day, we shall see them again. And we shall stand before God and that day shall be the most glorious day. Today God has decided to bring Aunt Eleanor home."

Agnes understood what her mother was saying, and despite Sarah's efforts to focus on the positive, the reality of the situation was more than Agnes could bear.

"We shall never see Aunt Eleanor again?" Agnes asked as though it were the most ridiculous question in the world.

"Aunt Eleanor shall live forever in our hearts and...."

Agnes did not wait for her mother to finish. She did not want to hear any more. They were just empty words. She ran up to her room and threw herself on her bed. Her sobs pierced the air and echoed down the stairs.

Margaret went up to Agnes to comfort her. Each one was trying to stifle their pain by focusing on another. Margaret climbed on the bed and put her arm around her sister. She hummed a soft melody into her sister's ear and eventually Agnes' tears stopped and she fell asleep.

Mary, on the other hand, was more practical in her thinking.

"Now Papa shall have company in heaven. He won't be alone anymore."

It was a comforting thought, but it brought to light the magnitude of their sorrow.

Chapter 25

That evening William did not return, and she felt an emptiness that she could not have imagined. As the children prepared for bed, Sarah asked Samuel to stay up with her for a little while longer. She did not want to be alone.

Sarah and Samuel sat at the table in silence. They were both deep in their own thoughts, but each experienced a comfort from the other's company.

"Please go in the kitchen and get two glasses."

Samuel did as he was told without inquiry or hesitation. When he returned, the scotch flask was on the table. He understood the legacy of the bottle. He had heard about it since he was a child. It pained him to think of what it meant at this moment. He was the end of the chain, the sole living link.

Sarah removed the cork from the flask and poured what remained into each glass. She pushed a glass in front of Samuel. The smell hit his nose hard, causing him to recoil and shiver before deliberate thought could control the weakness. The smokiness brought visions of fire to his mind, and he could no longer hold back the tears. Sarah did not attempt to comfort him. She let him have his grief.

"This scotch is pure love, Samuel. Eleanor gave this to your father to celebrate you. She and your father loved you with all of their hearts." Sarah's voice cracked with emotion.

"He allowed himself some every year on your birthday. He wanted to take this last drink with you, but he is not here to do that. I am honoured to be able to do that with you. I am so very proud of you." Sarah had to stop to compose herself.

"Samuel, enjoy and appreciate what is in this glass, because when it is gone, it is gone. It shall live on in your memory, but you shall no longer be able to taste it or feel its warmth inside of you. Your memories shall have to do that for you."

Sarah held up her glass, waiting for Samuel to do the same thing. She touched her glass to Samuel's and then let the liquid slide over her lips. She licked them, closing her eyes to breathe in the experience. She knew that all too soon it would be over, and the thought made her feel as empty as the flask that sat on the table.

Samuel hesitated in following his mother's lead. He had never tasted it before, and he was afraid he wouldn't like it. He tilted the glass against his mouth. The liquid trickled down the inside of the glass, hitting his closed lips with a splash. He pulled the glass away and ran his tongue over his lips. He was surprised that he liked it. It tasted like he imagined a pipe would taste. As he ran his tongue around his mouth, he thought of the smell of the oak barrels at Amberley House at Christmas. How he loved that smell.

Both Samuel and Sarah were ensconced in their own thoughts and experiences. Sarah was the first to break free, speaking through her tears.

"Your father is here right now. He is in you. I see it more and more every day. I see it in your smile, in your laugh, in your compassion and in your unending optimism. We must enjoy and appreciate what we have, because we do not know how long we shall have it for."

Sarah sobbed uncontrollably, and Samuel moved to his mother's side to comfort her. Sarah buried her head in Samuel's chest, tightening her grip on his shirt.

"When your father died, I felt like I had died as well. Right now I feel as though I have died all over again. I have nothing left, I fear. I am supposed to be strong for you, for your brother and sisters, but I fear I cannot."

Samuel had never seen his mother so vulnerable. She was completely open, baring the depths of her soul to him. At that moment, he loved his mother more than he had ever thought was possible.

"Aunt Eleanor would want us to go on. She wanted nothing but the best for you and she would not want you to give up on life. I, too, loved her. I loved her as though she were my own mother. She cannot be replaced and she shall never be forgotten."

Samuel and Sarah cried together. Sarah eventually pulled herself back from Samuel and wiped the tears from his cheek with her hand. She took a deep breath and sat up tall.

"Let us take our final drink and be thankful for the gifts of friendship that Eleanor gave us throughout the years, for her unending support and love, and for the hope that she had for us for a blessed life. As she watches down on us from Heaven, her light shall add to God's light to protect and guide us."

As Sarah spoke her words, the wick inside the lantern suddenly brightened for no apparent reason, casting a brilliant light over Sarah and Samuel. It bounced off the ceiling and back down on them like it flowed from the heavens. Neither of them spoke; they simply looked at each other.

In the morning, Margaret got up at the crack of dawn and made muffins and bread. They all ate in silence. Samuel went off to work, as did

James. Margaret took Mary and Agnes to school and then walked over to Eleanor's. She brought muffins in a basket, as she had done the day before. She stood in front of the charred hull of Eleanor's building, staring helplessly. She fixated on the door, as if willing Eleanor to walk through it. Margaret's silent tears wet her cheeks as people walked by. They were oblivious to her pain. Margaret said a prayer for Eleanor as she placed the basket in front of the door, and then she walked home empty-hearted.

William and Charles Markley were not at the factory that day. Business continued as usual and, as tired as Samuel was, the work took his mind off his emotions. He worked the day away and did not speak to anyone.

At home there was a knock on the door just before six o'clock. William stood in the doorway as Sarah opened the door. Sarah stepped aside and invited William in.

"Can I get you a cup of tea, William?" Sarah offered.

"No, thank you. I cannot stay long. I have just come to share some information with you."

William seemed very formal. It took Sarah by surprise.

"Please do sit down," Sarah said, motioning to the chair.

"Thank you, but I will stand. Reuben is waiting outside for me. We have much to do."

Margaret desperately wanted to run outside and see if Jonathan was with his father, but she held back.

"Might we speak in private?" William asked, looking at the children.

"Of course. Children, please go into the kitchen," Sarah gently commanded.

Sarah suddenly found herself alone with William, and it was not as comforting as she would have hoped. William was unusually brusque and cold.

"We had a visit from the fire investigator this morning. They confirmed that Eleanor was found in her bed. She succumbed to the smoke in her sleep and would have never woken up. That is a blessing, I suppose." William continued as though he were giving directions at the factory. "The funeral and interment will be at two in the afternoon tomorrow. It will be at Ardwick Cemetery. Eleanor loved the springtime and I believe she would be happy with the service being outdoors. The Ardwick Cemetery is in full bloom right now."

Sarah was numb to the pain, and while inside she tensed up at the thought of Eleanor's last moments, she did not cry. William seemed devoid of emotion as well.

"I would like to escort you and the children to the service. Could I do that?" William's solid exterior crumbled ever so slightly with the request.

"We would like that very much," Sarah said. "Thank you."

William nodded. "Well, I must be going. I have much to do."

As William turned to leave, Sarah reached out and touched William's shoulder. As he turned back, Sarah asked him how he was doing.

He had so much to say and he feared that if he started, he would not be able to stop. But it did not matter. William's face said more than words could.

"I will see you tomorrow at half past one."

William turned and was gone, leaving Sarah standing in the doorway gasping for breath. There were no tears, but her chest heaved with an inconsolable desperation at the finality of what she had already known in her heart.

For the next day, the children each found something or made something personal for Eleanor, something that would show her how much she meant to each of them.

Mary drew a picture of Eleanor holding hands with an angel, looking down from the clouds. Agnes decided she wanted Eleanor to have the doll she had given her for Christmas. It was her favourite toy, and she thought it could keep her company in heaven.

James had finished carving the burl wood Eleanor had given him for Christmas, just a week before. He had spent three months carving Jesus hanging from the cross. It was intricate and spectacular. It was unlike anything he had carved before. He had shown it to Eleanor and she had been more awed by his skill than ever. She had said that he should think about apprenticing in woodworking. She had wanted to help him do so. He had planned on giving it to her, but he could never have imagined it would be in this way.

Samuel would give his oldest possession. Eleanor had given him a baby rattle when he was born and Sarah had kept it all these years. Eleanor loved to look at it on the shelf. She would always say that Samuel was her first true love, and Samuel would always blush when she did.

Margaret wrote Eleanor a letter, sharing her feelings about her hopes and dreams for the last time. Eleanor was the one person she could do that with, and it was what she would miss the most now that Eleanor was gone.

When Sarah and Eleanor were young girls, Eleanor had given Sarah a piece of amber. Encased in it was a perfectly preserved ant. It looked as though it was still alive. Eleanor had said that the ant was like their friendship – it would last forever.

Chapter 26

Just before half past one, Sarah and her children were standing in front of their home. At precisely half past one, Reuben pulled the carriage up in front of them. It was not the carriage they usually rode in. This carriage, a barouche, was more formal than Catherine Markley's landau, but was open-topped. Despite its collapsible top, passengers were more susceptible to the elements and Catherine refused to ride in it in all but the summer months.

Today it was a bright and sunny day and the top would not be needed. It was a day that Eleanor would had cherished.

Reuben tipped his hat to Sarah, but his expression was morose. Jonathan sat beside him on the bench, looking equally sorrowful. Jonathan and Margaret locked gazes for a moment's time. This was not how he wanted to see Margaret again.

William stepped out of the carriage and stood aside for the children to step in. Once the children were seated, William turned to Sarah. He was such a comfort and she was soothed by his presence.

The sun was high in the sky, brightening the clear spring day. The colourful flower boxes and blossomed trees were a stark contrast to the mourning that filled the carriage. Side by side, they sat, covered in black from head to foot. Their sullen faces cast an equal contrast to the warmth of the day.

They rode past Ardwick Green and Samuel shuddered at his memories. Sarah focused on the hypnotizing sound of the horse's hooves on the road to soothe herself and numb her pain. No one spoke on the ride.

They rode through the open gates of Ardwick Cemetery and stopped by an attendant who was directing traffic. He pointed to a corner of the cemetery where many carriages were parked. Carriages continued to enter the cemetery and pull into the places where they were directed. Sarah was shocked by the number of people. They certainly couldn't all be there for Eleanor, she thought.

William helped Sarah and the children off the carriage. Reuben and Jonathan stepped down and joined them. They followed a steady stream of mourners who were all walking toward a gravesite against the east side boundary. Charles Markley had purchased a full section when his parents had passed away. Eleanor was the next to be buried.

As they got closer to the gravesite, the sound of violin music filled the air. *Amazing Grace* gently rolled off the strings, blending into the background and sounding as though it were coming from every direction. Chairs were set up on the grass and were filling in quickly. Eleanor was not close to her extended family, but today many came out to pay their final respects to her. There were family, friends, and business acquaintances of hers and her father's. They all came out to honour Eleanor.

Charles and Catherine Markley were greeting guests. William guided his own to their seats, which were in a row at the front that had been roped off for close family. The seats were split into two sections, with an aisle running between them. Reuben and Jonathan took a seat in the row immediately behind.

The seats quickly filled and then people began to stand behind them. Sarah was shocked at the number of people. She recognized only a few – the girls from the shop, a few of Eleanor's cousins, Charles and his family, and a few of the Markley's household staff. The others were unknown to her. Based on the grandeur of the carriages and the few motor vehicles, Sarah surmised they were from Charles' business and social circles.

Charles and his family took their seats in the front row on the opposite side of the aisle. Margaret was focused on the ornate casket that sat at the front, and didn't notice Anabel glaring at her with all the smugness she could muster. Anabel was horrified that Margaret, a mere servant, could sit in the front row. It was preposterous to her.

The violin continued to play until the vicar took his place at the front of the seats. His back was to Eleanor. He greeted the mourners, speaking first of life's great contrasts and ironies. They were gathered for a sad occasion, but on such a glorious day.

"In all aspects of our lives, we must each decide whether we will choose to look at the darkness or choose to look at the light. Do we choose to focus on how Eleanor was taken from us far too soon, or on the incredible gift that God gave us by allowing us to know her and love her for the time that we did? It is up to each and every one of us to choose how we see life, to choose how we react in life. Eleanor was an extraordinary woman, and she would want us to focus on God's love and our love for each other, and not the material things that can so often blind us to the glory that is before us."

Sarah dropped her head as the tears started to fall. The finality of death hit her with a crushing blow. Eleanor was gone. She would never again hear her sweet voice or her uplifting words of encouragement. She would never again see her contagious smile or feel her warm embrace. As her shoulders began to tremble with grief, William draped his arm around her to comfort her.

"God has called Eleanor home. We can mourn our earthly loss, but we must keep in our hearts the knowledge of heaven's gain."

The vicar motioned to William and Charles, who, along with four attendants, took their places around the casket. On cue, they lifted the casket and lowered it into the ground as the violin played in the background. William placed the first shovel of earth on top of the casket as the vicar committed Eleanor's body to the earth.

William guided Sarah and the children over to where they had laid the casket in the ground. One by one, they placed their gifts into a sack, which was lowered onto the casket.

When they were done, they walked down the aisle and stood behind the crowd, and they waited for it to begin dissipating. Sarah was grasping her heart pendant, as she had been doing most of the day. She remarked about what a beautiful service it had been and William nodded in agreement.

After most mourners had departed, Sarah broke away from William and her family and walked up to Eleanor's father. Catherine was speaking to a group of people off to the side.

"I am sorry for your loss, Sir," Sarah said.

"And I for yours," he replied, placing his hand on Sarah's shoulder.

Charles Markley's face was drawn and he looked exhausted.

"You were Eleanor's favourite person and she loved you like a sister. I am forever grateful for the light you brought into her life," Charles said hesitantly, choking on his words. "I was not a good father to her. She deserved so much better."

As Charles walked away, Sarah called out. "Mr. Markley," she said as he turned back to face her again, "as parents we all make mistakes. In the end, you were a good father, and that is what she took with her."

Charles smiled at Sarah. Those few words touched him deeply, and seemed to lift some of the shame that had weighed him down so heavily. As he thought of his daughter, a single tear fell down his cheek.

"Thank you," he said.

Reuben drove the carriage back to Sarah's home. He parked it out front and waited for them to step out. William and Sarah were last, and William held back to speak with her away from the children.

"Sarah, I have something I wish to discuss with you. Would you consider having dinner with me tonight?"

The request was unexpected. William could sense some hesitation.

"I understand if you would rather not today but I do wish to speak with you at some point."

Sarah thought for a moment. She desperately needed some time where she wasn't required to be a mother, where she could just be Sarah.

"Thank you, William. I would like that."

"Wonderful. I shall be back at seven to escort you to the restaurant. For now, I need to return to Amberley House to support my father."

"Mama, could we invite Reuben and Jonathan in for some tea?" Margaret asked.

"Reuben, would you care to join us for tea?"

"Thank you very much, Sarah, but I must get William back to Amberley House. If it is not too bold of me to say, I do believe that Jonathan might enjoy the invitation himself. I will be back at seven to escort you both to the restaurant and I can retrieve Jonathan then."

"Jonathan, would you like to stay for a visit?" Sarah asked.

Jonathan grinned from ear to ear. "That would be very nice. Thank you."

He jumped down from his seat and walked toward a smiling Margaret. Sarah waved at William as the carriage drove away.

Inside, Sarah made a meal for Jonathan and her children. They all ate hungrily, finishing every last bite.

"Mama, can Jonathan and I go for a walk? It is a lovely day outside," Margaret asked.

"Yes, but please do not be gone long," Sarah said. Margaret agreed.

They walked down Robinson Street, toward Ardwick Green. The sun continued to shine, but it was dropping in the sky. Neither spoke. Margaret went back and forth on her emotions. It had been an emotional day and she was exhausted.

As they walked through the park, they stopped at a bench and sat down. Margaret took tiny pieces of bread that her mother had given her and threw them on the ground. Birds began to gather and peck hungrily at the crumbs. Margaret gave some of the bread to Jonathan, and he did the same.

"Margaret, I am sorry about your Aunt Eleanor. I liked her very much. I am happy that I was able to share Christmas with her. I will always remember that day with fondness."

Margaret nodded, smiling at Jonathan.

"I have missed you so much. Amberley House is very dull without you," he said, laughing. "And Napoleon misses you."

"I have missed you too, Jonathan. I think of you often."

"Do you think you might return?" he asked, hopeful.

"I thought I would like to. I don't know if it is possible now."

Jonathan understood.

"I suppose you are right. I do have a bit of news, though," he said, trying to lighten the mood.

"Please tell," Margaret said excitedly.

"Michael and Lydia are to be married. He is going to leave Amberley House and work for Lydia's father in his shop."

"How exciting. They must both be so pleased."

"Chef Nicolas has returned to Paris. He was given an opportunity to work at a notable Parisian restaurant. It is believed Mr. Markley gave him a strong recommendation."

"I am so happy for Chef Nicolas. He deserves it. But I am surprised that Charles Markley let him go. Perhaps he is softening with age," Margaret joked.

"And I believe that Anabel and Philip will be starting at a new boarding school for the next school year. Philip is thrilled, as he will get to play with children his own age. Anabel walks around with a scowl on her face constantly so it is difficult to tell what specifically makes that girl miserable."

Margaret laughed at that thought. Anabel was one thing about Amberley House that she did not miss.

Jonathan reached out and took Margaret's hand, causing Margaret to blush profusely.

"Margaret, I do hope you come back, but if you do not, I would very much like to see you again. I do miss you so."

Margaret kissed Jonathan on the cheek. He enjoyed the feeling and found himself wanting more.

"I liked that. I would like it if you would do it again," he said, looking deep into Margaret's eyes.

Margaret was surprised by the request, but moved toward Jonathan without hesitation. As she was about to place her lips on his cheek, he turned his head, and their lips met. Margaret pulled away in surprise, her eyes opening widely. Jonathan continued to look at Margaret, smiling as though it was the most natural thing in the world to do. He did not take his gaze off Margaret. He leaned in himself this time and Margaret did not move away. She tingled with excitement, as though fireworks were exploding within her. His lips were soft and warm and she melted into them. She opened her eyes as he pulled back, and gazed longingly at him.

The sun pulled out from behind a cloud, shining a spotlight of sun on them, and Margaret knew that Eleanor was happy for her. As they walked back to Margaret's home, they held hands. Margaret felt the comfort she had so desperately needed.

Chapter 27

At seven, William arrived with a knock on the door. Jonathan turned to look at Margaret. They both shared the same melancholy expression, anticipating the end to their visit.

"You look lovely, Sarah," William said as he helped her with her coat.

"Thank you, William."

Sarah did not eat in restaurants. It was simply too expensive, and she could never justify the cost when so many other things were needed. For tonight, she did not want to think about practicality. She simply wanted to enjoy her friend's company.

Reuben and William had arrived in the landau carriage. William opened the door and helped Sarah in. Inside, he sat facing her.

"Tonight we are going to have dinner at the Ardwick Inn. A good friend of mine is the proprietor of the restaurant. It is quaint, and not too fancy."

As the carriage pulled up in front of the restaurant, William took Sarah's hand and helped her down. William thanked Reuben for the escort and told him that he would arrange for the hotel hansom to escort Sarah and himself to their respective homes.

The façade of the inn was very stately. The large oblong windows were covered in heavy brocade draperies, and Sarah could see an enormous crystal chandelier hanging in the foyer. A doorman greeted them and held the door for them as they walked in.

The entrance to the restaurant was at the side of the hotel lobby. The double glass doors were open to a large, circular table, upon which sat the largest vase of flowers that Sarah had ever seen. The smell of Easter Lilies filled the air. They were Sarah's favourite flower and she was brightened by their fragrance. As they walked into the restaurant, they were greeted by the maître d'hôtel.

"Do you have a reservation for this evening, Sir?" he asked.

"I do. My name is William Markley."

The maître d' looked at his schedule, acknowledged their reservation, and asked them to follow him. He showed them to a table in the corner. On it was a mauve candle that burned brightly, making the gold trimmed dinnerware sparkle in its light.

William pulled out Sarah's chair, and then gently pushed it in as she sat down.

"This is lovely, William. I don't know what to say," Sarah said, truly at a loss for words.

"You do not need to say anything. You deserve...we both deserve to relax tonight, and I am happy that I can do this for us."

Andrew Lipton, the proprietor and a friend of William's, arrived at the table with a bottle of wine. William stood and shook his hand. Andrew offered his condolences and William thanked him. William introduced Sarah as Andrew poured them both a glass of wine.

"I hope you enjoy your evening. If there is anything I can do for you tonight, please do not hesitate to ask, William."

William smiled appreciatively, and then Andrew left them alone at their table.

"How are you doing, Sarah? It was a difficult day."

"To be honest, I am not yet sure," she said truthfully. "I am still feeling a bit numb. It doesn't feel real yet."

"Yes, I know what you mean."

Sarah could not imagine how agonizing this must be for William. He did not have a wife or children. Eleanor was his only sibling. He had lost his mother when he was young, and he was not close to his father or his father's new family.

"I hope you know that I shall always be here for you, William. You are my dearest friend." Sarah stopped herself short of saying, *"Since Eleanor has died"*, but the words still lingered.

William picked up his glass and held it out, waiting for Sarah to do the same. "To brighter days," he said.

They both took a drink and then read the menu. The waiter arrived and took their order; William requested the roasted duck for two.

William reached into his pocket and pulled out a piece of paper. He unfolded it and looked at it intently. He folded it back up and looked at Sarah.

"I have much to say to you, Sarah, and I am uncertain of where to start."

Sarah looked at William, trying to imagine what he could be speaking of. William's face was serious, and the wrinkles in his brow accentuated his deep thoughts.

"Just before Christmas, my father called Eleanor and me out to Amberley House. Neither of us had any idea why. Up to that point, we had interacted with our father rather infrequently. I probably did more so than Eleanor, because of my work, but it was infrequent at best and was certainly all business."

Sarah listened intently.

"He was trying to clear his conscience about some decisions that he had made and now severely regretted. It appears he had made a deal with Philip Armitstead, Catherine's father, which would allow my father to marry his daughter and benefit from all of the relationships and business dealings that would come from such a marriage, if he agreed to make Catherine his sole heir. Should she predecease him, their male children would become equal heirs. It covered all of his monies, business, and real estate holdings. Eleanor and I were to be given nothing."

Sarah was shocked by what she was hearing. How could a father do this? She could not imagine the pain this ultimate betrayal was causing William.

"It appears that his conscience had caught up with him and he was trying to determine how he could make amends, how he could make it right with Eleanor and me."

Sarah now understood Charles Markley's generosity at Christmas time, as well as at the hospital.

"When my grandfather had left my sister her property, it was kept in my father's name. And because the building remained in his name, he was the legal owner. He also maintained the insurance on the building, its contents, and on the business. He was working on a plan to transfer ownership over, but he had to be careful about how it was handled so that it didn't appear to be unscrupulous."

Sarah continued to listen in stunned silence.

"He wanted to help Eleanor, and he started doing so with small gestures, a small business contract, for example. She was to create dozens of designs for his factory. He paid the money upfront and that money was placed in her business account. But, when the fire occurred, any record or trace of the designs went up in flames. It will be assumed they were completed but not delivered. The insurance will cover the loss for my father, and Eleanor's business will keep the payment for services rendered. It is not a large sum, but it was a start for Eleanor. She had been putting all of her money back into the business, and with the fire, all of that capital investment legally goes to my father. I am telling you all of this because of what I am about to read to you."

He unfolded the paper and began.

"To the two most important people in my life, my brother, William, and my dearest friend, Sarah…"

Sarah gasped and covered her mouth with her hand. This was very painful for William and she could clearly see that. She was bracing herself for what was to come.

"To the two most important people in my life, my brother, William, and my dearest friend, Sarah, I leave you all that I have in the world. William, I could never have asked for a..." his voice trailed off, cracking.

"William, please, take your time," Sarah said tenderly, touching his arm.

William took a drink of wine, and then exhaled heavily, causing the candle to sputter.

"I don't need to read this part. You don't need to hear it."

"Please, I would like to hear it," Sarah said.

"William, I could never have asked for a better brother. You loved me and supported me my entire life. You gave me confidence and you made me strong. You have given me far more than I could ever give you. I love you with all of my heart and soul."

William wiped his eyes and took a moment to compose himself.

"Sarah, you are my sister in every way that matters. You have been my biggest grounding force. You have shown me what is important in life, and your unending faith and love have moved me to the depths of my soul. Your children are my inspiration. I am thankful to God every day for bringing them into this world, and to you for allowing me to be a part of their lives."

William paused and looked at Sarah. She was staring at the flame, tears flowing from her eyes.

"You have endured the challenges that God has placed before you with grace and dignity. I wish for you to have never-ending happiness. To both William and Sarah, I give all that I have, to share between you. It is my greatest wish that you receive it as it is intended, with the greatest love imaginable."

William placed the paper on the table. Sarah wiped her eyes, and after a moment, looked at William. They shared a look that lasted an eternity. It touched her soul and made her long for more. She missed that connection, that connection with another human being so deep that it nourished the soul.

The waiter arrived with their meals, but neither one of them was hungry any longer. They merely played with their food, but they drank their wine with vigour and reminisced about Eleanor with laughter and tears.

William regained his composure and steadied himself. He wanted to speak, and he hesitated over his words.

"Sarah, I have something I would like to say to you, and I am not entirely sure how to do so," William said, doubting himself.

His tone of seriousness brought Sarah down from her cloud. She focused her attention on William and wondered what he was thinking.

"What is it?" she asked.

William hesitated, trying to find the right words.

"We are both at crossroads in our lives," he began. "Sarah, you must know I care for you very, very deeply. I would give anything for your happiness."

Sarah continued to listen intently.

"It has been three years since Thomas passed away. It is not for us to understand why he was taken from you, but the fact of the matter is, he was. Both he and Eleanor would want for you to move on so that you can be happy." William's voice began to crack again and he looked down at his wine glass, unable to look Sarah in the eye.

"You need to move on, Sarah. You have too much life to live, too much happiness to find. You cannot move on here. Thomas is everywhere. There is not much money in the estate, but it is enough to take your family to Canada, to start a new life. I am sorry it is not more, but the circumstance is what it is."

A tear ran down William's cheek and he brushed it away with aggression, clearly annoyed with himself.

"You need to move on. You need to go to your brother in Canada. There is nothing here for you anymore."

William swallowed his pain whole, pushing it as deep as it would go. Sarah watched on in a swell of anguish, unsure of what to say.

"You have a great journey before you, and you must take it."

Sarah shot up as stiff and straight as her body could manage. How did he know the words that Thomas spoke? William was her only friend in the world at that moment, but she knew what he was saying was true. She could never truly move on unless she moved away and started anew.

Without thought or hesitation, she blurted, "Why don't you come with us? It would be a new start for you, too."

William was stunned. For a brief moment, he was ready to say yes. But his senses returned, and he realized that she was still not ready to give her heart and soul, and that was what he needed most.

"I could not leave my father right now. He needs me to help sort out Eleanor's business. Perhaps one day I will come, but for now, I cannot."

Sarah understood, and she knew it was a silly idea. But for once Sarah did not want to over-think. It felt right, and she wanted to let go and give in to her belief in what was meant to be. *A great journey.* That was all she needed to hear.

"You are right, William. That is what I need. I cannot bear the thought of being away from you, but we shall be together again, if God wills it. For now I must move on and build a new life."

William smiled, but inside he was completely empty. He was doing the right thing, he told himself. And God was telling him the same thing.

William paid for the meal and arranged for the hotel hansom cab to take them home. When they arrived at Sarah's, William turned to her and kissed her on the cheek.

"You are an incredible woman, and the man who is fortunate enough to win your love shall be the most fortunate man in the world."

Suddenly Sarah felt an emptiness that she hadn't felt before with William. She knew she would miss him immeasurably, but she also knew she had to go.

"I shall always love you, William. You are the best man I know."

With that, William knew he had made the right choice.

"I will assist you while you make the necessary arrangements, and I will escort you all to the train station."

As William got back in the hansom cab, he broke down and cried like he had never cried before. He was completely broken and he felt as though he would never be whole again.

As Sarah entered her home, all was quiet. The children had put themselves to bed and it was time for her to do the same. She took a look around her sitting room and knew that she had made the right decision. Her destiny was connected to another place.

In the morning, Sarah sat at the table with her children. She looked at them one by one. Each one felt their mother's eyes upon them and they wondered why.

"Samuel and James, you'll not be going to work today. We have much to plan for."

They both looked at their mother sideways. "What do you mean?" James asked.

Sarah paused. "We shall be going on a great journey soon, a fantastic adventure."

Mary and Agnes' eyes lit up like the sun.

"What kind of adventure, Mama?" Mary asked. "Where are we going?"

Sarah hesitated again, trying to form the words. Sarah looked at the light beginning to shine through the kitchen window, and then she looked at Mary.

"Mary, my dear, to our new home."

It had been three weeks since Eleanor was laid to rest. There was much to do to prepare for the journey, and Sarah buried herself in those preparations. The effort helped Sarah deal with the pain of Eleanor's passing, which continued unabated.

William had been lavish in his support. Sarah knew that she would not be able to take this daunting journey were it not for him. He provided reassurances when Sarah's confidence was waning. He detailed the journey for her and walked Sarah through every step. He continued to paint a picture of what her life would be like. The only thing missing from the picture, though, was William, but Sarah could not allow herself to dwell on that. She had to think of her children's future, and their future was no longer in England.

Sarah sent a telegram to Bertie, and he was expecting them in about three weeks' time. He was surprised and excited that his sister would finally be joining him. It had long been his hope. He had been gone for more than ten years now; Bertie had never even seen Agnes or Mary, and Margaret had been a small child when he left.

Bertie and Jane had no children of their own. Jane had experienced difficulties and it was now past her time. Jane, too, was excited for their impending arrival. She had been like a sister to Sarah after Elizabeth had died, and she looked forward to having a house full of children.

Eleanor's estate had been settled, and the tickets for passage had been purchased from a Manchester agent. There had been enough money for second-class passage for Sarah and the children, but there would have been nothing left over. Sarah could not justify the extravagance, much to William's dismay. He was not comfortable with Sarah and the children travelling in steerage. He understood the conditions were less than desirable, but he knew he could not sway her. Sarah was far too practical and stubborn.

They would need new clothing when they arrived, and she would need to contribute to their lodging. She was confident there would be unforeseen expenditures, and she would not allow herself to be dependent upon anyone, including her brother. She would find work when she arrived, but it would take time. Other than what little she had learned from Bertie, she knew nothing about their new home.

The day before their departure was a day for good-byes. Sarah and the children walked to Ardwick Station and made their way to Southern Cemetery. They had not been there since Thomas' passing three years prior. They had said good-bye to Thomas before, but this time was different. There was no way of knowing if they would ever return.

As they walked through the gates, it was a stark contrast to the day of his burial. That sad day was cold and wet, and the ground was hardened with frost. The tall trees that lined the pathways were barren and dormant as they slept the winter away.

On this warm spring day, the sky was sprinkled with wispy clouds, revealing the sun as it rose in the sky. Mrs. Barton was milling around outside, tending to the gardens. She smiled warmly at Sarah, clearly having no recollection of their previous encounter. Sarah was not one to hold grudges, but the recollection was stinging.

They made their way down the long pathway to the back of the cemetery. The tall trees that lined the path were full of green foliage, and alive with the season. Flowers lined the graves, transforming the sad memories into a menagerie of brilliant colours. As they approached the area where the grave lay, Sarah felt empty. There was little sadness. The grave was unmarked and Sarah was not entirely sure of the exact spot. She knew that Thomas was laid to rest here, she had witnessed it herself, but now there was no specific proof except for the memories of that distant day.

Sarah and the children stood before the spot where they believed Thomas rested. Mary tugged at Sarah's arm, and Sarah looked down at her daughter.

"Mama, is Papa here?" Mary asked, confused. "Can he see us? How shall I know if I see him? I do not know what he looks like."

Sarah's heart broke at her daughter's questions. Mary was too young to remember her father. She would grow up remembering nothing of him. Agnes would not remember either. They would only know one parent. Sarah vowed she would do her best to keep him alive in their memories.

"Yes, your father can see us, Mary. He sees us every day. He loves you with all his heart and he watches over you and protects you."

"Shall he be coming with us to Canada?"

"Of course he shall. He is in heaven and heaven is all around us."

"Even in Canada?" she continued to ask.

"Even in Canada," Sarah answered, smiling at her daughter's innocence.

Sarah was unsure of what she was expecting to accomplish at the cemetery that day. She was leaving Thomas and the thought pained her. She had loved him with all of her heart. She still did. But her life was about to change immeasurably, and likely forever. She might never stand on this spot again. Her life with Thomas still seemed real, for the places they had shared were still part of her experience. In a short time, that would no longer be the case and it felt like a betrayal. But Sarah's burden was lessened by the memory of her dream. Thomas had known and it gave her great comfort.

Sarah led the children out of the cemetery. She stood at the gates, taking one last look back. She was closing off a part of her life, the most significant part of her life so far. It was incredibly bittersweet.

They had one more stop to make. As they departed the train at Ardwick Station, Mr. Linley was standing on the platform. Sarah stopped in front of him and held out her hand. Mr. Linley was surprised, vacant as to whom this person was standing before him.

"Mr. Linley, I am Mrs. Thomas Berry."

Mr. Linley's face brightened.

"Yes, of course. My apologies, Mrs. Berry. My mind went to sleep for a moment," he said with a chuckle.

"No apologies are necessary. None at all. You are looking well, Mr. Linley. I do hope that is the case."

"Very well indeed. Is this your family?" he asked, looking at the children. "What a good-looking group of children."

Sarah smiled at the compliment. "Thank you. Well, it was very nice to see you again, Mr. Linley. I wish you well-being," Sarah said.

"And I you. Good-bye, Mrs. Berry."

Sarah guided her children away from the station, and together they walked toward the Ardwick Cemetery. It had only been a few weeks since Eleanor's service and the mound of dirt still looked freshly laid. It was blanketed with dozens of magnificent arrangements. There were flowers of every kind and every colour.

The headstone had been newly placed. It read:

Heaven has one more angel
She sings from the heavens
Of God's amazing grace
Eleanor Elizabeth Markley
August 12, 1866 – April 1, 1904

Sarah read the inscription, and her eyes filled with tears. She had been so absorbed in preparations for the journey that she had not allowed herself to think of her dear friend. The realization that she would never see Eleanor again was crushing. Eleanor had been her constant, her anchor. She could make Sarah smile during the most dire of circumstances. And in Eleanor's final gesture, with her final gift, she was giving them all a fresh start. But that gift of a new life came with the ultimate cost, and that would tear at Sarah for the rest of hers. Sarah closed her eyes and said a silent prayer for Eleanor. When she opened them, she raised her head to the heavens and whispered, "Thank you."

Margaret could not understand her own emotions. Eleanor was her best friend, her confidante. Her death left a hole in Margaret's life that was all-consuming. It altered her every thought and brought an emptiness that she never could have conceived of. How someone could be there one moment and not the next was entirely nonsensical. But Margaret would live another day, and she believed with all of her never-ending optimism that it would get better. It simply had to.

God had given Samuel two mothers. He was blessed beyond measure. He and Eleanor had shared an unbreakable bond that was not broken when she died. He still felt her presence. The sound of her voice and the sound of her laugh continued to ring in his ears. She was there. He could not explain it, but he knew she was there. It gave him a great sense of peace. And as he looked at Eleanor's grave, he knew undoubtedly that our heavenly spirits lived beyond our earthly bodies.

They all said their final good-byes to Eleanor and walked out of the Ardwick Cemetery for the last time.

At home, they spent their evening organizing their belongings and separating out what they could take with them. Only what was absolutely necessary and not replaceable would go, as would an activity to keep each of them busy on the two week journey. And it would all be packed neatly into the five leather travel bags that William had bought as a gift.

Sarah concluded that they should each have a change of clothing. In addition, they would have their Sunday best for their arrival. The thought of that first encounter with Bertie made Sarah nervous and excited all at the same time. How different would he look? What would he think of her after all this time?

Margaret decided to bring two books that she had been given by Eleanor. One was a study of human anatomy and the other was her Florence Nightingale book. She tore out the inscription pages of the remaining books, as she could not bear to leave them. Samuel would bring books as well, along with the chess set. The girls were bringing dolls, and James was bringing his whittling knife and a carving he was working on. Sarah would bring her keepsake box, along with important documentation and the few photographs that she had. Sadly, that summed up their entire lives in Ardwick, Sarah thought.

As Sarah tucked her children into bed, she talked to them about the adventure ahead of them and wished them sweet dreams. As she sat downstairs for the last time, she thought about her decision to leave, and her chest tightened with fear. This was all they had ever known. It was familiar, and familiar was comfortable, even if familiar was not always pleasant. There was nothing left here for her now but her friendship with William and her memories. Everything else was gone. It was the right decision, she was sure, but the unknown was terribly frightening.

As Sarah drifted off to sleep, she thought of her brother, and it brought her great comfort. They would not be alone, and that would make all the difference in the world.

Chapter 29

In the morning, Sarah and the children were dressed, packed, and standing in the sitting room when the knock on the door came. It was William. As the door opened, William stood before Sarah as a symbol of paradox. She struggled with her feelings of regret and hope; they tugged her in both directions, leaving her about to tear down the middle.

Sarah greeted him with a hesitant embrace. William's heart was already broken so this could hurt him no more.

"I believe we are ready," Sarah said, while she went through a mental list of all that she needed for the journey.

"We shall be off, then," William said.

With the exception of Mary, all carried their travel bags to the carriage. Reuben was waiting but Jonathan was nowhere to be seen. Margaret's heart was heavy, and despite her immense sadness, she thought it best that he not be there. She did not think she could say good-bye to him. Reuben glanced at her with a look that acknowledged the same of his son.

Their travel bags were placed in the carriage's stowage, and they all took their seats inside. Their train bound for Liverpool would depart from the Manchester Exchange Station, which sat nearly two miles from their home.

William and Sarah caught each other's glances many times, and with each glance, their feelings of hopelessness grew. William was on the edge of his seat, ready to shout out to Sarah that he could not let her leave, and Sarah was ready to give in to her fears. It was all so overwhelming. All it would have taken was one moment of weakness, but they both held strong and that moment never came.

The carriage passed the Manchester Cathedral, which stood taller than any building in its vicinity. Its perpendicular gothic design invited the eye upward, following the tower as it extended to the sky. The stunning lines of the windows were accentuated with the exquisite stained glass that filled them. It was a dramatic building and the sight of it brought Sarah to dream about what the churches looked like in Canada. Would they be as magnificent?

As they passed the cathedral, they rode alongside the River Irwell, which, on that morning, had a thick layer of fog blanketing the black waters. The children watched the Manchester Exchange Station with excitement as it appeared in the distance. At the approach to the station, they were welcomed by a large statue of Thomas Cook, which sat high up on a large stone platform and wished them well on their journey.

Reuben pulled up to the front entrance and they all stepped out of the carriage. Sarah turned to William, shaken and uneasy on her feet. She was scared they would not hold her. She searched for words, but there were no words that would suffice at such a time. Nothing she could say could convey how she felt for him or how desperately she would miss his friendship. She was leaving behind the life that she knew and was going to start anew in a far-off place. It was both terrifying and exhilarating, and it left her feeling painfully alone.

Sarah reached out and embraced William tightly. She kissed his cheek and smiled.

"William, I shall miss you dearly. We shall all miss you dearly. May God bless you and keep you well, and I pray we shall see each other again soon. I shall write to you when I arrive."

"I wish you a safe journey and a new life full of happiness." William's voice cracked as he forced a smile and looked at all of them for the last time.

"Please say good-bye to Jonathan for me and tell him that I shall write to him. I shall miss him very much." Margaret, too, tried hard to remain stoic.

Samuel shook William's hand and thanked him for his support. It was more agony piling on top of an already unbearable load. He wasn't just losing Sarah; he was losing a family.

The children said their good-byes to William and then walked toward the station's entrance. Sarah looked at William for the last time and then turned and did the same. She could not bear to look back. She just kept walking. As she approached her children inside the station, her chest heaved with grief. She gasped for breath, and her cries of anguish tore at her children's hearts.

"Mama, are you all right?" Mary asked.

Margaret embraced her mother and placed her head on her shoulder.

"Yes, Mary. I am. I am going to miss William very much."

At that moment, Sarah realized that she was going to miss more than William's friendship. She loved him more intimately than she had allowed herself to believe.

William sat down in the wagon and stared blankly out the window. As the carriage pulled away from the station, the tears, which had become all too familiar, fell silently down his cheeks. Reuben drove him away from Sarah, toward a life unknown.

Inside the station, Sarah stood looking at the signage, hoping it would offer clear direction. The sign for the London and Northwestern Railway pointed the way. A porter then directed them to the appropriate track and explained the train would be along in fifteen minutes. Third class would board at the end of the track, he advised, and then suggested they make their way down the platform.

The station was awash with activity. People were moving haphazardly in all directions as they tried to determine where they should be, but with assistance, and sometimes with luck, they all eventually found their destination.

The squeaking of braking locomotives, the whistling of steam whistles, and the whir of loud, indistinguishable voices, produced a cacophony that only added to the discomfort of the circumstance. There was no excitement, merely trepidation. Sarah could offer no words of comfort. Soon they would be on the train, and movement would become their focus.

The train pulled up to the platform and a porter checked Sarah's tickets and allowed them to pass. They stepped up onto the car, placed their bags in the overhead storage, and took their seats. Sarah continued to check her handbag to ensure all their travel documentation was there, and each time she did she felt a tremendous sense of relief.

Mary sat beside the window, impatiently waiting for the journey to begin. She watched the porter through the window, hoping that each passenger who approached him would be the last. Eventually, the last passenger made their way onto the train, the attendants gave their "all clear", and the doors were closed. As the train began to slowly make its way from the station, Mary bounced in her chair and clapped her hands. Her excitement was contagious. Sarah soon began to relax.

It was a cloudy day, but free of rain. The hour or so train ride to Liverpool went faster for Sarah than it did for the children. Sarah was deep in thought and did not pay much attention. The transfer at Edge Hill was a simple one, and as they made their way to Riverside Station, the salt water began to permeate the air as thickly as the smoke in Ardwick had.

After they exited the station, it was a short bus ride to the steamship that would take them to the docks and to begin their new lives. The Ionian was already berthed at the dock when they arrived. The steamship's black, white, and red smokestack rose majestically into the sky, shooting out smoke as it prepared its engine for voyage. The four masts stood like barren trees against the winter sky.

The cool breeze blowing off the water brought them much-needed fresh air after the train ride, which had been distressing and confining to

Sarah. The sunshine felt pleasantly warm on their faces despite the brisk ocean breeze.

The enormity of the docks was beyond compare. They had experienced nothing like it in their lives, and the fullest extent of their imaginations could not have prepared them for what lay before them. Passengers moved like cattle from the station to the ship and they laboured to keep the pace. Sarah did not take her eyes off her children for fear they would be consumed by the crowds.

It was about eleven o'clock in the morning when they boarded. They followed the crowd, which was being directed by the steward on the deck. Their initial destination was one of the large dining rooms. They stood in a line that extended outside the dining room and down the hall. The line moved slowly, and it took about an hour for Sarah and the children to progress to its head.

A doctor and a nurse examined each passenger for signs of contagious disease. The exams were quick and far from thorough – an examination of the eyes and a quick head-to-toe visual review. Those that were approved for travel were given a doctor's card and asked to continue in a line to another portion of the deck. Here they presented the two parts of their steamer ticket and were assigned to their staterooms and berths.

Sarah had heard stories about the dreadful conditions and treatment of passengers on these ships, and thus far the experience had been nothing of the sort. In fact, it had been nothing but positive. The doctor and ship personnel who they had encountered had been pleasant and polite, and the passengers were patient and orderly. Sarah's anxiety was continuing to diminish as they proceeded through the embarkation process.

They were assigned to an eight-berth stateroom in the section designated for families. It was on the bottom deck, which was the deck used for steerage accommodations. It was one deck down from the main deck and two down from the spar deck, which was the open, upper deck. While the accommodations were far from luxurious, they were substantially superior to what Sarah had expected. She had been worried that they would become separated, but that proved not to be the case. The two empty berths would likely be filled, but by whom, Sarah wondered nervously.

The stateroom was thoroughly unimaginative. The walls were white, as were the bedding, the sink, and the wooden plank floors. A mirror and porcelain washstand, which was generously outfitted with towels, stood between each outer row of berths. While lacking in anything beyond what was absolutely necessary, the room was comfortable, and for that Sarah was relieved.

There were two lights in the stateroom above each washstand, and the remaining light came from lights that were located near the ceiling in the passageways. Surprisingly, there was also an electric bell which could be used to summon a steward or stewardess if the need arose.

As they familiarized themselves with their sleeping accommodations, their stateroom companions joined them. The woman, who looked to be in her early twenties, was with a young girl, presumably her daughter. The young girl looked no older than two.

"Hello, I believe we are assigned to this room as well," the woman said shyly. "We are quiet and shall not be bothersome, I can assure you."

"It is my wish that we shall be the same," Sarah said, smiling. "My name is Sarah Berry. These are my children Mary, Agnes, Margaret, James and Samuel." Sarah pointed to each child as she said their name.

"I am Hannah Nightingale, and this is my daughter, Florence."

Margaret poked her head out from the end of her berth. "Did you say Florence *Nightingale*?" Margaret was stunned.

"I did," Hannah said. "She was named after her grandmother, who was a relation of the nurse's. Her grandmother has since passed, and the nature of the relationship isn't all that clear now, to be honest," Hannah said with a chuckle.

Margaret held out her Florence Nightingale book.

"Well, I can understand the surprise, then," Hannah said, clearly amused.

Hannah put her bag down and removed her coat, and Sarah could see now that she was heavy with child. She sat on the edge of the berth assigned to Florence and let out a big sigh.

"I seem to have much less energy with this one. It feels as though there are ten in there. I hope that upper berth will hold me."

"Nonsense. You do not have to climb up there in your condition. Why don't you take that bed," Sarah said, pointing to the berth that Agnes was sitting on. "Agnes, would you like to sleep up there?"

Agnes had been disappointed that she wasn't sleeping on a top berth so she was enormously excited to be able to do so.

"Thank you, Agnes. Florence is too young to sleep up there. I'm afraid she would fall off. What is your final destination?" Hannah asked. "We are going to Winnipeg. My husband travelled there in January looking for work. It seems he found a position with the Hudson's Bay Company. I believe that is what it is called. We are joining him."

"We are going to Winnipeg also. We'll be joining my brother."

"Well, I am grateful that Florence and I have been blessed with your company. It shall make this long journey bearable."

Sarah smiled at the sweet sentiment. "That is very kind. Thank you."

"Mama, can we go to the upper deck now so that we can watch as we leave port?"

"Yes, let's do that. Hannah, would you care to join us?"

Hannah appreciated the inclusion and nodded. She took her daughter's hand, and they all went together up to the open deck. Directly in front of the door to their stateroom was the entrance to the stairs that took them up to the main deck. The main deck housed the first- and second-class accommodations, and there was no need for steerage passengers to be on this deck beyond passing it on the stairs.

The toilets were located, rather conveniently, next to their stateroom, and the dining rooms were located near the mid-section of the lower deck. The dining room assigned to women and families was closest to their stateroom, and the dining room assigned to the men was on the far end.

They continued up to the top deck, emerging from the stairs onto a large, open landing that was surrounded by numerous large windows. The landing led to an open room that had tables stacked along a wall and a piano in the corner.

The ship had already moved away from the dock to the Landing Stage, where the first- and second-class passengers were now boarding. Many of the steerage passengers were up on the spar deck, catching a final glimpse of Liverpool. The passengers, for the most part, were smiling and jovial, but a few seemed less so, with tears flowing, perhaps for family left behind. There were people of all ages and ethnicities. On glance, nothing seemed to stand out as a common thread amongst them, but the journey they were about to take would bind them in experience for the next eleven days.

As the sun continued to rise in the sky, it brought a welcome warmth to the top deck. The salt air cleansed the senses of Manchester's smoke and freed Sarah of the remaining doubt that had burdened her so. She looked at the bright faces of her children as they surveyed the landscape with wonderment. This would be a new beginning, and she was grateful for the opportunity. Despite its hardships, life was good.

The landing was filled with family and friends, waving at those loved ones who they could see and looking frantically for those they could not. It was always more difficult for those left behind, Sarah thought. They were cursed with the pain of separation and had nothing to take their minds off it.

Little Florence was frightened by the noise, and her mother held her tight to comfort her. Sarah's children were not. Their excitement continued to build as the crowd's waves and cheers mounted. It was almost deafening, but they did not mind. They found it all very thrilling.

Sarah, on the other hand, found it quite odd that grown adults could act in such a juvenile way, and she looked forward to a peaceful journey.

The ship's whistle blew low and deep, signalling its impending departure from port. The sound only added to the frenzy, and the cheering from the passengers reached a deafening swell. As Sarah looked around, she was taken by the depth of emotion on all their faces. It was as though their entire life's purpose was to be on this ship, going to wherever they were going. From the quality of clothing that most of them wore, it was apparent that the cost of passage must have been an extraordinary burden.

As the Ionian made its way from the Landing Stage, the captain carefully manoeuvered it through the narrow passage and out to open sea. The sun illuminated the dark and still water. As Sarah watched Liverpool fade into the distance, for the first time in as long as she could remember, she felt free from burden.

Dinner, which was to be served daily at noon, was delayed an hour due to the departure. Sarah and her children made their way to the dining room, and Hannah and Florence joined them. The dining room for women and families was filled with long tables that seated ten. The tables were covered with white cloths and each setting had all the necessary utensils. The typical accompaniments – salt, pepper, mustard and bread – were situated in two places across the centre of the table, within easy reach of every seat. At the end of the table, the side dishes were placed in large bowls. On the first day of the journey they consisted of potatoes and carrots. There was also a bowl of pickles. The steward explained that they were to take their plate to the end of the table and serve themselves. Meat was served from the pantry, and they could make their way over there if they wanted some. For their first dinner on board, there was macaroni soup and Irish stew.

The steward was friendly and attentive. As the bowls of vegetables emptied, he was quick to fill them in the kitchen. Milk was provided for the young children and coffee and tea for the women and older children. At the end of the meal, a bowl of apples was brought out, along with plum pudding. The food was surprisingly good, and they all ate until they were satiated.

At the end of the meal, Hannah took Florence back to the room for a rest, and Sarah and the other children went up to the open deck for a stroll. There was still only a mild breeze and the sea was fairly calm. As Margaret walked along the deck, she ran her hands over the railing. Liverpool was far from sight, and there was nothing but sea water and sky as far as the eye could see. It felt like a dream: as though the world had been erased and it was just the ship and vast nothingness.

They picked one of the many benches that sat about the open deck and settled in for much of the afternoon. Sarah wanted them to enjoy this experience. They had nothing to do, no responsibilities other than to enjoy and appreciate the glorious day that was before them.

"Mama, I need to use the toilet. I shall be back in a few minutes," Margaret said as she stood to leave.

"So must I," Agnes said.

Margaret and Agnes made their way to the stairs that would take them down to their deck. It was a large ship, and it felt as though they were walking across Ardwick to get from any one place to another.

As they passed the main deck, a steward approached them on the stairway as he was coming up from the lower deck. He stood in the middle of the stairs, and while he moved slowly to the side, he very deliberately looked Margaret over from head to toe. It made her very uncomfortable, and she took Agnes' hand and picked up her pace.

Walter, the attendant who had served them their first day's meals, told them that steerage passengers tended to gather up on the spar deck, in the large enclosed room that they had noticed earlier. So, after the five o'clock dinner was over, they put on their wraps and made their way up top. The sun was a fiery ball of red sinking toward the seemingly endless horizon, and the stars began to dot the sky, twinkling against the heavens. It was as clear a sky as they had ever seen.

As they emerged from the stairway, they could hear music playing. There were already a dozen or so people dancing when they entered the room. An older gentleman with a bushy beard stomped his foot against the floor as he played an accordion. Others close by clapped to the lively music, while some danced around the room. Children cheered as they played a ring toss game in the corner. Some read, talked, or wrote in journals. It was a jovial and lighthearted atmosphere, and most people enjoyed themselves on the first night of the voyage.

Hannah and Florence joined Sarah and the children as they listened to the music. Mary, unlike her mother and siblings, was unable to sit still, so she danced around them. At nine o'clock, the lights were turned off and on, signalling the end of the evening. Once the room was cleared out, it was time for the stewards to sweep and wash the floors.

As they left the room, they took a final look at the night sky. The sun had completely set and the sky was black. The half-moon was bright in the sky and cast a trail of light on the dark ocean water. There were so many stars that it was difficult to focus on any one. They all seemed to blend together as though they were connected in the sky.

"Mama, I have never seen so many stars before," Agnes said in absolute amazement.

"Nor have I, Agnes. It is spectacular, isn't it?"

A multitude of luminescent stars stood out against the black sky, but more remarkable were the clusters of stars whose radiance blended together like a blanket of light. You had to focus intently to see them as individual and distinct.

"I think it is time we all returned to our room. It has been an exceptionally long day, and I believe we could all do with some rest," Sarah said while gathering the group and ushering them back inside.

The steerage passengers were descending the stairs in an orderly fashion while the stewards watched on. As they passed the main deck, the one that had troubled Margaret earlier stood on the main deck landing. When Margaret noticed him, his gaze was fixed on her, consuming her, and she felt exposed and unbearably uncomfortable.

As they continued down the stairs, Margaret looked back and saw that his stare was unbroken. She was with her family and would make sure she always found herself that way.

Florence fell asleep instantly, and Hannah was not far behind. They were all exhausted, and it felt good to lie down on the straw mattresses. They were as clean and comfortable as one could expect given the circumstance. There were two heavy, grey blankets, which were sufficiently warm, and their weight provided a welcome sense of security. Sarah kissed each of her children good night and then climbed into bed herself. Enough light penetrated the room from the hallway to take some of the edge off the darkness. It was a smooth night on the seas and they all slept soundly.

Chapter 30

At half past six, the breakfast bell rang. The steerage passengers rose from their berths and prepared themselves for the day. At seven o'clock, the breakfast bell rang again, and it was time to enter the dining room. Though they were not assigned tables, they chose the same table as a matter of habit. The same steward who had served them their meals the previous day stood at the head of the table, wearing a big smile.

"Well, good morning t'ya, Mrs. Berry. I trust you all had a pleasant evening?"

"We did, Walter. Thank you," Sarah replied. Sarah had remembered Walter's name from the previous day and was impressed that he remembered hers.

"And, young Mary, are you enjoying your journey at sea?" Walter asked as he handed Mary and Agnes slices of bread that he had carved smiling faces in. He had put preserves in the eye and mouth holes. "I was hoping you would sit at my table again," he said as he winked at them both.

"Mama, look at this," Mary squealed.

"Thank you, Walter. How clever you are," Sarah said appreciatively.

At nine o'clock, the staterooms were scrubbed and cleaned. The inspection was at ten, and passengers were encouraged to stay out of the rooms until after the inspections were completed. When breakfast was finished, they headed up to the spar deck to enjoy the morning.

It was the beginning of another marvellous, sunny day. The sky was clear, with the exception of a few wispy clouds that were being pushed about by the gusting winds. The sea was not as glassy and smooth as it had been the previous day. The waves were building and appeared to be fighting back against the wind, but not enough to sway the ship to any significant degree. It was mesmerizing to watch.

"Samuel and I would like to play chess, but it is too windy out here. We are going to go in. There are tables in there." James pointed to the room where they had enjoyed the music and dancing the previous evening.

"I'll take the girls as well. There were other children in there and perhaps they can play with them," Margaret said.

"I shall be in shortly. I would like to take a quick stroll about the deck."

As the children headed inside, Sarah walked toward the edge. As she leaned on the railing, she looked over it. Her stomach fluttered as she watched the ship tear through the water, pushing it aside. There was no land as far as the eye could see, and a feeling of vulnerability engulfed her. She continued to hold the railing, but stepped back. The wind was numbing, but the waves were hypnotizing, and the deeper Sarah's mind went into the dark water the less she felt the cold.

Her emotions were scattered, and she knew they needed to get sorted. She had pledged her eternal love to Thomas, but her feelings toward William had changed. She had realized it when they had dinner together. When she thought back to Christmas, to their walk at Amberley House, she believed, perhaps, he had felt the same way. The guilt she felt overpowered the new feelings that had invaded her heart. William had awakened emotions that had died with Thomas. There was now an ocean between them, and Sarah believed it was for the best.

Off into the distance, another ship could be seen moving with the horizon. It was comforting to know that they weren't alone out there. Sarah felt a hand on her shoulder, and she turned to Hannah, who had decided to join her on deck.

"Margaret is watching Florence. It is very nice to have a break," Hannah said.

"Yes, I can imagine it is. I forget what it is like to have a two year old. They do have a tremendous amount of energy. That one in there," Sarah said pointing to Hannah's belly, "also takes a tremendous amount of energy, but you cannot take a break from it."

Hannah ran her hand over her belly and smiled.

"This one is due in four weeks or so. Thankfully, I am not feeling as ill as I did the first time. I could barely keep anything down with Florence. I thank the good Lord every day for my health. I do not know how I could have managed without John otherwise."

The temperature turned colder as the wind changed direction and the sudden chill drove Sarah and Hannah inside. They watched the children play the morning away, as they had done the evening before. The next three days were just as unremarkable. Each was a mirror of the other in its banality, and the repetition and boredom was as confining and inescapable as the ship.

As the voyage neared its midpoint, the seas became enraged, tossing the ship around like a child's toy. The breakfast bell went off at half past six, but it was merely a formality, as most passengers lay awake in their berths, overcome by the motion. As they dressed and washed, it was difficult to maintain their equilibrium. This was especially true in the staterooms that offered no window to the outside. There was no point of reference to explain the movement, which had become violent and unyielding.

Florence stumbled toward her mother's berth as she got up from her own. She was frightened by the sensation and began to cry. Hannah comforted her until she stopped. They all stumbled about the stateroom. When they were dressed and washed, they walked to the dining room. The seven o'clock breakfast bell rang as they were taking their seats.

"Top of the morning to the Berry family," Walter said as he tipped his hat. "It is a wee bit rough today. It'll take a strong constitution to weather this one, I'm afraid. It looks as though she will be staying with us a while, too."

They took their seats at the table, and Walter poured coffee and milk. Walter could see the sour looks on their faces, and took the bowl of porridge around the table to save them all from having to get up.

"Thank you, Walter. I think it is clear that we are not entirely seaworthy," Sarah said, smiling.

Vertigo had a firm grip on the two youngest. Both Hannah and Mary were fidgety in their seats as queasiness began to consume them. Sarah's discomfort was noticeable but not overwhelming, as was the same with the others. They were all able to eat, with the exception of Hannah and Mary, and their mothers did not encourage them beyond what they could manage.

After breakfast, they went up to the spar deck as they had every morning since they boarded. As they walked up the stairs, they held onto the railings to steady themselves. The ship's motion became more exaggerated the higher they climbed. They stepped out onto the spar deck landing and away from the railing, and walked slowly, moving their arms to gain some level of balance.

The rain hit the windows from all directions. The sound was deafening. There was no going outside so the steerage passengers all went to their communal room, where they could sit and ride out the storm. The mood was not as jovial as it had been. It was clear not all were faring well with the motion.

Mary sat on Sarah's lap and buried her head in her mother's chest. Sarah continued to exhale heavily as she tried to contain her nausea. Samuel and Margaret read, James whittled away at his carving, and Agnes held her doll tightly as she looked out the window.

There were momentary reprieves in the heavy rain that thrashed the windows, and you could see the massive waves breaking into a fury of white foam. The ship would ride up a wave only to come crashing down hard on the other side. Every time it did, even the most seaworthy passengers felt a flutter, as their breakfast churned in their bellies like the water in the stormy sea.

The stewards were on hand with buckets and mops, waiting for the inevitable, and the inevitable did come. Mary was one of the first. As she retched over her mother's leg, tears welled in her eyes. Sarah was helpless and could do nothing but rub her daughter's back.

After the steerage deck inspections were completed, Sarah and the children went down to their room so that the youngest could lie down. There were two buckets in the room, and they were placed by Mary's and Florence's berths. Florence began vomiting shortly after they got to their room. She was not able to make it to the bucket like Mary was and emptied the contents of her stomach in her berth. Hannah put Florence in her own berth, pulled the slip cover off the mattress, and rolled it into a ball.

"Sarah, could you please watch Florence for a moment? She is sleeping now. I am going to find a steward so that I might obtain a new slip cover."

"Yes, of course."

Hannah was beginning to feel unwell herself, and she became more unsteady on her feet with each step. She was relieved when she came upon a steward, and she approached him and motioned for him to stop.

"Yes, Madam, how may I be of assistance?" he asked.

"My daughter has been sick on this bedcover and I was hopeful that I might obtain another in its place."

"Of course," he said. "Place it on the floor in front of your room and I'll be there momentarily with a replacement. What is your stateroom number?"

"Eighty-nine. Thank you, Sir," Hannah said appreciatively.

A few moments later, the steward arrived at the room with a clean slipcover, as promised. He also placed two additional buckets in the corner and explained that the dirty buckets should be placed in the hallway regularly and would be exchanged with clean ones. He placed the clean slip cover over the mattress himself and then inquired as to how else he might be of assistance.

"You have been most helpful," Sarah said. "Thank you."

Sarah could see that Hannah was succumbing to seasickness herself, and she was concerned for her in her present state. Florence and Mary continued to sleep, and Sarah was hopeful that both would continue to do so until the storm cleared.

As the ship continued to be tossed about in the angry seas, many passengers stayed in their rooms, unable to eat, but with the exception of Mary, Sarah's children were well enough. They sat at their usual table and were greeted by Walter, who appeared as chipper as he had with each previous encounter.

"Hello, Berry children. It doesn't look as though all of you are faring well during this mighty storm."

"No, Mary is ill and Mama is watching over her. Mrs. Nightingale and Florence are not well either, I'm afraid," Margaret explained.

"I have been on this ship since she was built. These are some of the roughest seas I have seen. This storm is a stubborn one. I think we might be in here for a few days. I don't mind, myself. It breaks up the sameness day after day."

The children ate well, although not as heartily as usual. They ate what appealed to them, which was bread and soup. When they were finished, Walter placed some bread and preserves and a few pieces of fruit in a small bag for the others.

"Thank you, Walter. We'll see you at supper this evening," Margaret said. "I'll take this food to Mama. I'll meet you all upstairs," Margaret said to her siblings.

Samuel, Agnes, and James nodded in acknowledgement. They took their activities and made their way upstairs. Margaret picked up her book and went back to the room to deliver the food that Walter had provided. Margaret passed a few passengers on her walk down the long hallway, but not as many as usual. The level of passenger activity had significantly diminished with the storm.

Sarah was awake in the room and accepted the food with appreciation. Mary was stirring and sat up at the sound of Margaret's voice.

"Margaret, I don't feel so well," Mary said.

"I know, Mary. Hopefully, the storm will pass soon and you shall be feeling better quick as a wink. I brought back some bread and preserves. They may make you feel better. Would you like to try to eat something?"

Mary nodded and sat up in her berth. Sarah took out a piece of bread, which was sticky from the preserves. She held it out, and Mary took a bite. As she chewed slowly, she focused intently on the bread. She opened her mouth to take another bite, but hesitated. In one quick motion, she leaned over the side of the berth and expelled the tiny piece of bread into the bucket. Sarah held her daughter back so she would not fall off the berth as it continued to sway violently.

"Mary, lie down. Rest is the best thing for you right now."

"Mama, you should eat something. There is enough for all of you. Perhaps the fruit will sit better when Mary has rested," Margaret wondered.

"I will. Thank you, Margaret."

Margaret kissed her mother's cheek and then left the room to join the others. The rain continued to pound the ship hard. Water crashed over the deck and slapped the windows with loud crushing blows. The wind moaned and whistled while the masts creaked under the wind's strength. Some passengers shrieked as the black walls of water exploded on the deck, while others simply wept and rocked themselves for comfort.

Margaret eventually spotted her siblings and joined them. There were more passengers than usual in the room, as the conditions outside made it impossible to be on deck. Every seat was taken, and passengers who could not find seats sat on the floor. The smell of ammonia permeated the room, and ironically what was meant to clean was more offensive to the nose than the vomit itself.

Margaret looked up from her book and glanced around the room. As was usually the case, families, single men, and single women each congregated in separate corners of the room, but due to the number of passengers crowding into the room, there was more mingling than usual and more unwelcome interactions as a result. And it wasn't limited to passengers. Some of the stewards behaved inappropriately toward the young women. Margaret was very comforted by the presence of her family and could not have imagined taking such a long journey on her own.

As Margaret looked around the room, she spotted the steward who had unnerved her so. He was talking with a pretty young woman who did not seemed bothered by his attention. In fact, it appeared the opposite. She was smiling and turning her head coyly. Margaret was sickened by the exchange, but pleased his attentions were focused elsewhere.

The Ionian continued to thrash about the rough seas. The more unsteady passengers fell off their chairs, and after failed attempts to get back up, many merely stayed on the floor. It became a decision between remaining where they sat and mustering the strength to get down to their berth. It was apparent the latter appealed to few, as most stayed put.

As the afternoon wore on, the skies became darker. Were it not for the ship's activities, one would think it was the middle of the night. Margaret became nauseous when she read, and it was simply too rough to play chess. There was nothing to do to pass the time but to sit and talk.

"Samuel, shall you work for Uncle Bertie?" Agnes inquired.

The decision to leave for Canada had been so abrupt that he had not thought about what he would do when he arrived. He found himself excited for the opportunity to start anew.

"I don't know, Agnes. I know nothing about Uncle Bertie's business. I will have to see when I get there, I suppose."

Agnes' question made them all realize that they knew nothing about their new home. They knew nothing of its environment. What was the weather like? What did the houses look like? Was it more like Ardwick or Burnage or neither? What were the schools like? They also knew nothing of its people. Did they look like they did in Ardwick? Were the people friendly? There were many unknowns, and while it was exciting to go somewhere completely new, it was also terrifying in its uncertainty.

"I shall imagine that it is a glorious place, with gardens and parks and grand houses. I shall also imagine that the sky is blue and the air smells like wild flowers," Agnes continued.

Margaret laughed. "That sounds splendid, Agnes."

"And perhaps little fairies will fly out of the flowers and sing to you," James quipped.

Samuel laughed, but Agnes was not amused. "Sod off, James," she retorted.

"Agnes!" Margaret said in shock. She had never heard her sister speak like that.

Samuel and James laughed loudly, causing those nearby to look.

"It is a quarter of five. We should go down and see if Mama and Mary will be joining us for supper," Margaret suggested.

They all agreed and made their way out of the room. It was difficult enough to walk while the ship tossed around, but it was doubly so while manoeuvring through the maze of passengers sitting and lying on the floor. Samuel lost his footing and nearly fell on an elderly lady who was either asleep or worse. Margaret and Agnes held hands to help balance each other.

They made it successfully to the stairway and then held onto the railing for support. The ship suddenly took a deeper than expected plunge, sending James and Agnes tumbling down the stairs. As Agnes landed on top of James, dishes could be heard breaking off in the distance.

Margaret was utterly horrified. Both she and Samuel raced down the stairs to the main deck landing where they lay. Samuel helped up Agnes, who appeared no worse for wear.

"Perhaps *you* can summon a fairy to help you up," Samuel said snidely as he stood over his brother.

Margaret and Agnes laughed uncontrollably. It was James' turn to be less than impressed. He stood up, brushed himself off, and shot his brother a look that could have pierced armour.

In their stateroom, they found all asleep, with the exception of Sarah. Sarah sat in her berth while Mary's head rested in her lap.

"How is she, Mama?" Margaret asked.

"The poor dear is not handling the storm very well, I am afraid. She cannot keep anything down. Sleep is the best thing for her right now."

Margaret looked over at Hannah and Florence. "How are Mrs. Nightingale and Florence doing?"

"About as well as your sister, I am afraid. Neither can keep anything down."

"Mama, you need to get some supper. I will stay with Mary," Margaret offered.

"It would be nice to step outside the room and stretch my legs. Thank you, Margaret."

Margaret settled into her mother's place under Mary's head as Sarah held it gently. Mary did not wake up. There was no reprieve from the thrashing about, and Margaret could only sit in the berth and wait. She thought of Jonathan, and she became heartsick. It felt as though it had been a lifetime already. She missed him so and could not imagine never seeing him again, but her fear had become her reality.

Chapter 31

The morning brought little relief. As the breakfast bell rang at half past six, Mary was retching into the bucket beside her bed. She had slept little through the night, and exhaustion only added to the discomfort of dehydration. She was weak and pale, and her muscles ached from the retching.

Young Florence was as ill as Mary. Hannah did her best to comfort her daughter, but Hannah's own condition was worsening and the energy she needed to tend to her was beginning to elude her. Hannah prayed for calm seas, but much to her dismay, her prayers remained unanswered.

Samuel took his turn staying with Mary while the others went for breakfast. There were fewer passengers in the dining room today, and Walter said it was expected based on the severity of the storm. Walter was his usual cheerful self, and he worked hard to bring some sunshine to the group. When the meal was over, he sent Sarah off with food as he had done the previous day.

"Take this carafe. I have put some tea in it. It may help settle young Mary's stomach," Walter suggested.

"Thank you, Walter. You are a good man," Sarah replied.

When they reached their stateroom, Mary was awake, and Samuel was telling her a story. Mary's face was expressionless. Her eyes had become sunken and the dark circles under them more pronounced. She acknowledged her mother's entry into the room with a weakened smile. A smell of stale bile filled the room.

"Good morning, Hannah. Are you feeling any better today?" Sarah asked hesitantly.

"I am afraid not," she said with no energy or emotion. "But we shall persevere. Isn't that right, my sweetheart?" she said as she kissed her daughter's forehead.

"We brought some bread and tea, and some fruit, I believe. Perhaps you should try to have a sip. It may help settle your stomach," Sarah said, hopefully.

"Thank you, Sarah. I am sorry to be a burden."

"Nonsense. No burden at all."

Sarah poured some tea into one of the cups that Walter had provided. Hannah took a sip and turned her head. The smell of the tea caused Hannah to gag, but she was able to repress the urge to retch.

"Florence, would you like to try some tea?" her mother asked.

Florence shook her head and began to cry. She was but a baby, and her innocent whimpers bore a hole in Sarah's heart. As her whimpers turned to sobs, Hannah understood what would follow. She lifted her daughter and held her head over the bucket, and Florence heaved until she collapsed on her mattress. As Hannah placed the bucket down, the smell was overwhelming and she did the same. Sarah rushed to her side and helped her into her berth. Sarah felt helpless. There was nothing she could to. There was nothing that anyone could do. Only calm seas would bring relief.

On the storm's third morning, Mary and Florence did not have the strength to sit up in their berths. Margaret carried each of them to the toilet and held them in place while they relieved themselves. They were severely dehydrated and had little urine to expel. Sarah helped Hannah to the toilet as well. Hannah was very weak, and her enlarged belly was not helping with her unsteadiness. As Sarah helped Hannah back to the room, she bent over, grasping her belly as it tensed and tightened. Hannah's moan was deep and dark and utterly primal. It sent a shiver down Sarah's spine. Nothing good could come from that sound, she thought.

Sarah continued to help Hannah back to the room. She laid her down in her berth and attempted to gather her thoughts. Helplessness was not new to Sarah, but this helplessness was needless and it frustrated her so. It was not born of disease or disaster, but of a temporary state that would right itself in due course.

"Margaret, could you please go to the ship's hospital and seek out a doctor? We must see if we can do something to ease their discomfort."

"Of course, Mama."

Margaret walked down the long corridor, steadying herself against the walls as the ship rocked back and forth. The ship's hospital was on the opposite side of the steerage deck. It was a lengthy walk that required meandering alongside dining rooms, kitchens, and engine rooms. As Margaret approached the hospital, she could see a line of passengers that extended through the door and well into the hallway.

"Yer going to be waiting a while, Missy. Looks like we ain't the only ones sick," a thin, frail, elderly man said to Margaret through his toothless grin.

Margaret wanted to see how long the line was and attempted to walk alongside to get a better look. A woman who was holding a young child began to speak loudly in a language that Margaret didn't recognize. She was wildly waving her free hand in an attempt to shoo Margaret to the back of the line. It was hopeless, Margaret thought. There were at least a dozen people outside of the hospital's door and there was no telling how many waited on the other side, beyond her view.

Having failed in her task, Margaret turned with her head lowered in defeat and frustration. As the ship lurched to the starboard side, Margaret was thrown into the wall, delivering a crushing blow to her shoulder. She rubbed it in an attempt to assuage the pain. In the distance, she could see a passenger making their way toward her, and she lowered her head, attempting to hide the tears that flowed from her eyes. As the passenger approached, she turned to her side to allow room for them to pass. She continued to look downward, watching for their feet to move past her. They did not.

Margaret looked up to see who stood in front of her. It was not a passenger, but the steward. In sheer surprise and fear, Margaret gasped.

"Why the tears? You are such a pretty young girl. There should be no need for tears," he said, as he looked her up and down.

He bit at his upper lip, as though he were deciding how to consume her. Margaret felt ill. Instinctively she smiled, trying to remain pleasant. She slid sideways against the wall, away from him. All she wanted to do was run down the hallway, but he put his hands on either side of her, locking her in. Margaret began to panic.

"Why the rush? Looks like it is just you and me," he hissed.

Margaret ducked down to try and get out from the cage he had built around her, but he lowered his hands, keeping her captive. Margaret froze in fear, and like a predator he pounced on her weakness. He leaned in and pressed his body against hers. Margaret turned her head to the side and felt his hot, sticky breath on her neck. He ran his hand over her breast and squeezed. The pain shot down her arm like lightning. The harder she resisted, the harder he pushed against her. His hand moved off her breast and down her belly. Margaret whimpered, and he let out a laugh of pleasure. As his hand came to rest between her legs, he kissed her neck, and she gagged uncontrollably, spewing her breakfast on his shoulder.

He jumped back in shock, and Margaret ran down the hallway as fast as she could. She looked back, making sure that he was not following her, and then ran into the toilet room. She splashed cold water on her face and rinsed her mouth out. She felt dirty, but as she looked at herself in the mirror, all she saw was rage. To be vulnerable, to find herself in a position where she had no control over her circumstance, was infuriating to her.

Margaret composed herself and then returned to her room with nothing of value.

"I am sorry, Mama, there is a long line waiting at the hospital. I could not get past it to talk to a nurse or a doctor. I am afraid we must wait until it clears. I will take James or Samuel with me later."

"Margaret, are you all right? You look as though you have seen a ghost. Are you feeling ill?" Sarah asked.

"Not any longer, Mama. I was sick, but I am confident it will not happen again."

"Nine o'clock is approaching and the steward will be arriving to clean the room. You may join your brothers and sisters upstairs. I will stay here," Sarah said.

Margaret nodded, picked up her book, and left the room. Sarah remained behind to tend to Mary, and inevitably Hannah and Florence as well. At nine, the steward entered the room. He was not surprised to see them there.

"Aah, havin' a hard time with the waves," he said as he scanned the room. "Well, you are in good company, I am afraid. Lots of sickness. Captain thinks the storm will break tomorrow."

"That will be nice," Sarah replied quietly. "The wee ones can't go on much longer."

"Can't do nothing about it, neither," he said. "You have to wait it out and try and keep your wits about you."

The steward got down on all fours and scrubbed the floor with a large, bristled brush. The smell of cleanser was harsh, and Sarah fought hard to suppress her own nausea. The washbasins were wiped down, and then the steward left the room to complete his assigned staterooms. At ten, the inspector arrived to view the steward's work.

"Mary, would you like to try to eat some bread?" Sarah asked.

Mary shook her head and lay on her berth, unmoving. Sarah got off her berth and walked to the other end of the stateroom to check on Hannah and Florence. Florence's eyes were closed, and Sarah touched her cheek to make sure she was still warm. Florence twitched at the touch, and Sarah stepped back, allowing her to rest. Sleep was best for her at the moment, but sleep eluded her mother. She lay awake in her berth, looking as much a child as the other two. She looked helpless and lost.

"Hannah, what can I get for you?"

"If it would not be too much trouble, would you be so kind as to help me to the toilet? I am afraid I do not have the energy to make it there myself."

"Of course. Here, let me help you up," Sarah said, holding out her hands.

Hannah mustered all the strength she could to sit up and swing her legs out of the berth. Sarah put her hand under Hannah's armpit and lifted her up to her feet. Sarah placed her arm around Hannah's waist and Hannah's arm over her own shoulder. She bore the brunt of Hannah's weight as they walked to the toilet.

"How is your cramping?" Sarah asked.

"Nothing as bad as the first one. I have had a few more, but they have been milder. I'm sure everything is as it should be. I would normally say, "It must have been something I ate," but I haven't eaten anything," Hannah said with an exhausted laugh.

Sarah did not laugh. She was worried. Hannah was in a very vulnerable state, and there was no assurance that medical care would be available.

"Here we are now. Steady on your feet," Sarah said as she lifted Hannah's dress. "I will hold you and your dress. You pull down your undergarment, and I will sit you down."

Hannah did as she was told, and Sarah used all of her strength to lower Hannah down. As Hannah stood up, Sarah bent over to flush the toilet, and noticed a light red tinge to the water. Sarah did not say anything. She didn't want to alarm Hannah, but she knew she would have to get her to her berth and then go and seek help as soon as the children came back.

The ship continued to toss about wildly in the storm. Sarah had to stop numerous times to anchor her foot so that she and Hannah did not fall over. Hannah was placed successfully back in her berth, just in time for the sound show. Thunder cracked in the sky with a deafening boom.

On the upper deck, a war raged. The darkness was overwhelming and the utter helplessness undeniable. God was in charge and nothing but prayer seemed appropriate. Margaret closed her eyes to ask for divine protection, and through the blackness she could see bright flashes of light. As she opened her eyes, lightning shot across the dark clouds, illuminating them in succession, one by one. The thunder exploded like gun fire, sending vibrations through the floor.

The constant nausea that had plagued many was intensifying, and few were immune from its effects. Scarcely any passengers were eating, and even fewer were going to the top deck in between meals. A bound and determined Russian man played the piano without falter, clearly unaffected by seasickness himself. The piano and bench were bolted to the floor to prevent them from moving about on turbulent seas, but clearly that was not the case for the person playing it. He played Mozart and Beethoven as he slid around on the bench. As the thunder rumbled and crashed, he banged the keys with dramatic fervour. It would have been a humorous spectacle were the backdrop not so terrifying.

As noon approached, they headed down to their room. Mary was awake, but in no better condition. Her eyes were dark and terribly sunken. She was a frightening sight.

"Mama, I will stay with Mary. Please eat some dinner. You have only had bread today."

Sarah nodded and got up from the berth. Her balance was shaky and she fell against the adjacent berth. Samuel rushed to her side to help steady her.

"Thank you, Samuel. I got up too quickly."

Sarah and her children went off to dinner, leaving Margaret with Mary. Margaret sat down on the mattress beside her sister and stroked her cheek. Mary whimpered.

"Mary, would you like to try and drink some water?"

Mary shook her head lightly and closed her eyes. Margaret kissed her forehead and walked over to Hannah.

"Mrs. Nightingale, can I get you anything? Would you like some water?"

"Thank you, Margaret, but I do not believe it would sit well. Florence, would you like to have a sip of water?"

Florence was asleep and did not answer. Margaret reached down to feel if she was warm. She was. She looked worse than Mary. She was so tiny. There was nothing to her. How could she take any more of this?

Margaret turned around to the sound of Hannah's long, deep moan. Hannah was curled in a ball, clutching her belly. Margaret was frozen with fear.

"Should I get a doctor? My mother?" Margaret asked, panicked.

After a few seconds, the pain stopped. Hannah took a breath and wiped the perspiration off her brow.

"I need to use the toilet, Margaret. Would you be able to help me?"

"Certainly."

Hannah manoeuvred herself to the edge of the berth and sat up with Margaret's assistance. And again, with Margaret's assistance, she stood up. Hannah put her arm around Margaret's neck, and the two walked to the toilet. Margaret walked beside Hannah and didn't notice the blood stain on the back of Hannah's dress. At the toilet, Margaret stood in front of Hannah, holding her dress up as Hannah pulled down her undergarment and urinated. Margaret reached back and flushed for Hannah as she sat, and then she helped her up.

As they entered the room, another succession of violent waves sent the ship lurching haphazardly in every direction. Margaret lost her footing as she helped Hannah back to her berth, and she fell to her knees. Hannah fell forward against the washbasin, her belly bearing the brunt of the force. Hannah screamed out in agony. Margaret jumped to her feet, catching Hannah as she fell backwards. Margaret redirected Hannah's motion and gently forced her down on the berth. Hannah's face was contorted in shock and fear. Margaret was aghast at the sight. Little Florence had awakened by her mother's screams, and began crying herself. Margaret could do nothing to console Florence. She needed to seek help.

"I shall get my mother. I'll be right back."

Margaret ran down the hallway toward the dining room. Running in the rough seas was easier than walking. The choppiness smoothed out and the movements became more fluid. Margaret did not falter. She stood in front of her mother, breathless and red-faced.

"Margaret, what on earth? Is Mary all right?" Sarah said, alarmed, jumping to her feet.

"You must come quickly!" Margaret frantically motioned her mother to follow. "Mrs. Nightingale has fallen."

"Finish your meal, children, and then go to the upper deck. Margaret shall join you shortly," Sarah directed.

Sarah and Margaret rushed hastily back to the room. Florence was crying, frightened and alone in her berth. She was unable to get to her mother.

"Margaret, why don't you put Florence in Mary's berth? Mary can keep her company."

Margaret picked up Florence. She was as light as a feather. There was nothing to her. Florence looked up at Margaret with a longing that broke her heart. Margaret kissed her lightly on her forehead and placed her on the mattress beside Mary. Florence's blonde curls blended into Mary's as they lay together on the pillow.

"Hannah, how are you feeling? Are you experiencing any pain?"

"I feel this baby is coming now. If it is God's will that it is so, I am afraid I haven't the energy to push. Sarah, I am frightened."

"Let's start by getting you more comfortable," Sarah said.

Sarah rolled Hannah to her side so she could cover her with the blanket. As she did, she saw that Hannah's dress and the blanket were stained with blood.

"Margaret, press the steward bell. Keep pressing it until someone comes."

Margaret did as she was told. Within a few minutes, a steward arrived.

"You only need to press the button once. I am not deaf. What could be so urgent?" he asked rudely.

"We need a doctor immediately!" Sarah raised her voice in distress.

"I'm afraid that is not possible at the moment. There are cases of fever amongst the first- and second-class passengers. The doctor and nurses are overwhelmed," the steward informed Sarah. "We cannot take any additional patients unless it is life or death."

"She is in premature labour and bleeding. She needs a doctor now or it just may become so."

Hannah moaned with another surge of pain. The steward stepped back, horrified at the sound. Sarah kneeled down beside the berth and stroked Hannah's forehead.

"Hannah, you must relax. We will try and get you a doctor."

The ship plunged to the port side sending Sarah and the steward tumbling toward the door. Florence began retching in the bed as Margaret rushed to get her up and over the bucket. She was not successful in timing, but there was so little in Florence's stomach, so little fluid in her tiny body, that nothing of any consequence came up.

The steward, who watched in horror, backed up. He said he would do his best to seek help, and then he left the room as quickly as he had entered.

Hannah moaned again. This time the moan was deeper. Beads of sweat began to form on Hannah's brow, as did tears in her eyes. Sarah lifted the blanket; she could see a frightening amount of blood. Her dress was saturated and it was soaking into the mattress. As she looked at Sarah, her eyes said more than her words ever could.

"Sarah, please take care of Florence if anything should happen to me. Please see that she gets to her father. His name is John Nightingale and he is with the Hudson's Bay Company in Winnipeg. And this one...." Hannah's voice trailed off.

"Nonsense. Nothing will happen to you. But, yes, of course, I would ensure that Florence is taken care of," Sarah said, fully realizing the severity of the circumstance.

"Sarah, the baby is coming," Hannah said weakly. "I cannot stop it."

Hannah's face was pale and she was scarcely moving. Her face winced in pain, but she was no longer screaming.

"Margaret, please, I need your help," Sarah implored. "You must do as I ask. Gently lift Hannah's head and position yourself under her so that her head rests on your lap."

Margaret did as she was told, without question.

"I will have to try and deliver this baby."

"Mama, you must wash your hands with soap. It is imperative," Margaret said, recalling what she learned, rather ironically, from her Florence Nightingale book.

"Of course," Sarah said.

Before she washed her hands with soap and water, she pressed the steward bell a few more times. Sarah would do what she could, but she was no doctor, and for the sake of Hannah and that child, she needed a doctor immediately.

Sarah lifted Hannah's dress and pulled down her undergarment. The blood flow was prolific, the smell pungent.

"Margaret, push yourself farther under Hannah's head. We need to raise her up a bit more. Quickly, now."

Sarah pushed against Hannah's feet so that her knees would bend.

"Hannah, we will take care of you. But you need to summon the strength to do what I ask of you. Can you do that?" Sarah asked.

Hannah did not speak. She simply nodded the best she could. Sarah placed her hand on Hannah's belly and felt a contraction. Hannah reacted with a wince and nothing more. She had lost too much blood, and Sarah feared she would not have the strength to deliver this baby.

Sarah reached in to see if she could feel the baby. She could not feel the baby's head, but Hannah's body was fully open and ready for the baby to come. The bleeding was heavy. Sarah could feel the stream of warm liquid flow into her hand. The only hope of stopping it would be to have the baby.

"Hannah, you must push now. Push, Hannah!" Sarah screamed desperately. "Your baby needs you to push now."

Hannah nodded slightly, but could do no more. Her head fell slightly to the side. If she did not have the energy to keep her head up, Sarah knew she would not have the energy to push the baby out either. Margaret gently lifted Hannah's head and held it between her hands.

"Hannah, look at me," Sarah directed. "Look at me!"

Hannah shifted her eyes toward Sarah.

"You must push. Hannah, you have to push!"

Margaret stroked Hannah's head and hummed *Amazing Grace* to bring some calmness to the room. Florence continued to cry from her berth, but her cries went unanswered.

Hannah's eyes closed.

"No, Hannah. You must stay awake. You must stay awake for your baby!" Sarah demanded as she shook Hannah.

Hannah's eyes opened slightly. She attempted to focus on Sarah, but her stare was vacant. Sarah reached inside Hannah once again and felt nothing but blood.

"Margaret, lift her up farther and push down on her belly. Push gently toward me."

Margaret took her hands away from Hannah's head, and it fell to the side. Margaret pushed herself farther under Hannah, raising her shoulders higher. She put both hands on the top end of Hannah's belly and she pushed down. Hannah's contracting belly pushed back and Margaret pulled her hands away in shock.

"Margaret, there is nothing to be frightened of. You can do it. You must do it."

Margaret put her hands back on Hannah's belly and pushed downwards toward her mother. Hannah was not moving, and her eyes were closed, but Sarah knew that it didn't matter. She would be of no assistance at this point.

They were making no progress with the baby, and Sarah knew there was nothing more that she could do. Sarah reached up and slapped Hannah's face in one last attempt to bring her to. There was no recognition. Her eyes were closed and her cheek was covered in her own blood.

"Mama, what do we do now?"

Sarah studied Hannah's face. She was so young and beautiful. Sarah loved God, but this made no sense. It was so unnecessary and so unfair.

Sarah looked at her daughter sadly. "I do not know, Margaret. I am at a loss," Sarah whispered.

Sarah got up from the berth and wiped her hands on her dress. She was covered in Hannah's blood.

"I will be back shortly. Please tend to the young ones."

Sarah left the room, leaving Margaret in shock. She sat in the berth with Hannah's head on her lap. She had been so caught up in the emotion of the ordeal that she had not thought of how dire the circumstance was. The finality of Hannah's condition became real in one big crashing moment, and she felt completely numb. She looked at Hannah's belly and grieved for them both. Florence whimpered on the other side of the room, and it snapped Margaret out of her daze.

As Sarah reached the hospital, she pushed past the passengers waiting in line. Her pain was raw. It was visceral. It was deeply maternal. There were no tears. Tears were a release, and Sarah's emotions were bound so tightly that the tears could not escape.

"Hey, you. Back of the line like the rest of us," an incensed passenger shouted to Sarah.

As others turned to see what the commotion was, they saw a frightful sight. Sarah was covered in blood and blank in expression. They stood aside to let her pass, with no questions as to her interruption. As Sarah got to the head of the line, she remained there with no thought or focus.

A nurse came out from an exam room and saw Sarah. The nurse turned and yelled to the exam room door.

"Doctor Collins, come immediately," she beseeched. "What on earth happened?" she asked Sarah. "Is that your blood?"

Sarah continued to stare ahead, not acknowledging the nurse's question. The nurse could see that Sarah was in shock, and she shook her shoulders to bring her around. Sarah looked at the nurse and tried to formulate her words.

Those standing in line gawked at Sarah in fascination. They had been standing in line for hours, and she was a break from the boredom.

"Maybe she done in one of yer doctors for being so damn slow," a voice quipped. Booming laughter followed and rippled down the line.

"Where did that blood come from?" the nurse asked again as the doctor appeared from the exam room.

"A young lady in my stateroom. She went into labour. I sought help, but no one came. There was so much blood. I tried to help the baby, but I could not. I believe it is too late."

"Take me to your stateroom," the doctor ordered as he retrieved his bag.

Margaret was sitting on the berth opposite Mary and Florence, blocking them from Hannah. The doctor rushed to Hannah's side. He lifted her arm to check for a pulse, and after a moment or two he placed her arm back at her side.

"I'm afraid we are too late," he said.

Sarah stared at him, shocked at what she was hearing. "No, doctor, *we* are not too late," Sarah said flatly. "*You* are too late."

The doctor hesitated, not knowing what to say. "I am sorry," he offered, dropping his head. "I am truly sorry."

"If you must be sorry, be sorry for that young child," Sarah said pointing to Florence. "She just lost her mother. If she does not eat and drink something swiftly, she will be in the same state."

"Is she unwell?" the doctor asked.

"She and my daughter have been gravely ill since the storm struck. They have not eaten or drunk anything during that time and have been vomiting constantly."

The doctor reached into his bag and pulled out four pieces of candied ginger.

"If you can sit them up so they don't choke, you can place a piece in their mouths and have them suck on it. It should help with the nausea reasonably quickly, and they should be able to take some water once their stomachs settle."

"Young Florence is but two. I'm afraid she will choke."

"You can crush it. It breaks easily. Put some in her mouth a little at a time. She will swallow it. Now I must seek the assistance of an orderly to help me with…with the deceased," the doctor said, hesitating.

"Her name is Hannah Nightingale, and she should not have died."

The doctor exited the room leaving Sarah and Margaret to relive the nightmare. Margaret's stare was fixed on Hannah. She had never seen someone die, and certainly not held them as they did. Were it not for all the blood, it would seem that she was sleeping peacefully.

Sarah kneeled at Hannah's side, still unsteady while the ship continued to sway. She lowered her head and prayed.

"Our heavenly Father, may you surround Hannah with your divine love and light, and may you bless her and protect her on her journey. May you accept her with open arms into the kingdom of heaven and keep her safe always. And may you guide and protect her daughter, Florence, as she reunites with her father. In Jesus' name, Amen."

Sarah stood, lifted the blanket, and covered Hannah's head.

"I am so sorry, Hannah," she whispered. "I am so sorry this happened to you."

With one single, life-altering thought, Margaret decided she could not be a doctor. She watched her mother wash the blood from her hands, and she knew it would not wash away the pain or the memories. It was simply too much.

Sarah took one of the ginger candies and crushed it with the back of a hairbrush into a cup. "Margaret, sit Mary up and place a candy in her mouth. Watch her carefully to ensure she does not choke. I will take care of Florence."

Sarah lifted Florence from the mattress and sat down on the adjacent berth. She was awake, but very weak. She stood the pillow up against the back of the berth and leaned Florence against it. She placed one hand on her shoulder to prevent her from falling over, opened her mouth with her other, and placed a pinch of ginger candy in her mouth. Florence accepted the candy, and did not heave immediately as she had done previously with bread and water. Sarah waited a moment or two and then gave her another pinch. She continued until most of the candy had been placed in Florence's mouth. She lifted Florence up and then cradled her in her lap as she sat in the berth.

Margaret leaned Mary against her chest and put the candy in her mouth. Mary began to suck and saliva began to flow. Mary did not heave immediately, either, as she had done before. Within five minutes, Mary began to regain some colour.

"Mama, my tummy doesn't hurt as much. May I have another candy?"

"Margaret, please give your sister another candy. I will get some more from the doctor."

Margaret did as she was told, and for the first time in three days, Mary moved on her own. She remained too weak to sit fully, but she was able to shift herself to a more comfortable position.

Florence looked up at Sarah and said, "Thirsty." Her sweet, angelic little face brought tears to Sarah's eyes. Sarah poured a few drops of cold tea into Florence's mouth. She did not want to overdo it, as her stomach would still be weak. The storm was not yet over.

Chapter 32

Samuel, James, and Agnes returned to the room as supper time was approaching. They did not immediately see Hannah, nor did they see the condition their mother was in.

"Margaret, you did not come up today. Are you unwell?" Agnes asked.

Margaret did not speak. She looked to her mother for direction.

"Come here, children," Sarah said.

Sarah laid Florence down on the mattress and stood up. As they approached their mother, they saw the blood.

"What happened to you?" Samuel demanded, raising his voice sharply.

"The blood is not mine," Sarah explained. "Come with me into the hallway."

Samuel looked around the stateroom. He saw Mary and Florence, and then looked over to the other side of the room, to Hannah's berth. He saw the undeniable form of a person under a blanket. He looked back at his mother, his eyes as wide as saucers, not imagining that what he was thinking was under there was, in fact, under there.

Samuel walked to the door as he looked back at Hannah's bunk. He could not take his eyes off it. Sarah pulled Samuel through the door and closed it. James and Agnes had not seen Hannah and were focused on the blood on their mother's dress.

"Mrs. Nightingale had a bad fall. She went into labour and the baby did not come. We could not get a doctor to come and tend to her, and I tried to assist her myself. There was too much blood. I could not stop it. I could do nothing to save her."

Sarah was trembling, and her children could only gape. Sarah's words did not make sense. They had just seen Hannah a few hours before. How could something so unfathomable happen so quickly?

"Mama, how can this be? God wouldn't do this. There was a baby. And what about Florence? What will become of her? No, God wouldn't do this. You must check again. Perhaps she is just resting," Agnes said as she began to cry.

Sarah kissed her daughter's forehead. She did not want to embrace her in the bloody state that she was in.

A commotion in the hallway stole their attention. Coming toward them was an orderly pushing a wheeled stretcher. The sound of the rattling wheels echoed against the walls. A doctor and nurse followed him. As they approached the room, Sarah opened the door.

"Please let me remove her daughter first. I do not want her to see her mother this way. "

"Agnes, please carry Florence to the toilet. Margaret, you can assist your sister. Boys, please wait in the hallway."

They all did as they were told. When the room was empty, the orderly wheeled the stretcher beside Hannah's bunk. He removed the blanket. Hannah's face was devoid of any colour. Her jaw was slightly open, as though she was trying to speak her last words. Her once vibrant face was completely empty of life. Her indelible spirit was free. What was left was a shell, nothing more.

The doctor assisted the orderly in getting Hannah transferred to the stretcher. She was covered with a fresh blanket and then wheeled out of the room. Hannah's mattress was soaked in blood. It looked as though it had been the scene of a violent war. Sarah had never seen so much blood before.

"From the ship's passenger list, I understand that she travelled with her daughter, Florence, and that there was no husband."

"That is correct. She was travelling to meet her husband in Winnipeg," Sarah said.

"According to Canadian law, the girl must be released into a relative's care or must remain under the care of a government agency, which would be us at this time."

Sarah began to panic. She made a promise to Hannah that Florence would be safely delivered to her father. Sarah would not break that promise. She could not live with herself. If she did not do it herself, she would never know it was done, otherwise. There was no other way.

"I am her family. I am her aunt. Hannah was my sister," Sarah said, speaking without thinking.

"Oh, I see," the nurse said. "Very well, then, we will release her to you, along with her mother's certificate of death and a doctor's letter to clear up any questions that may arise at immigration."

"Where are you taking her?" Sarah asked.

"She will be immediately placed in a casket in storage. We are five days from port yet and have no means of preserving the body. In these circumstances, burial at sea is most prudent, but if you wish to arrange for the body to be transported to a specific destination, you may do so. What do you wish to do with the remains?" the doctor inquired.

Sarah was taken aback. She never thought she would need to answer such a question.

"Take a few moments to think about it. You may come to the hospital and retrieve the certificate and letter in thirty minutes' time."

"May we have some more of those ginger candies? They seemed to have a positive effect on the young girls. Perhaps they might be able to eat some supper."

"Take these," the doctor said as he reached into his bag. "There are four left. That should do nicely. I believe the storm is beginning to lose its strength."

"Thank you, Doctor. We will come to the hospital after supper."

As the doctor and nurse left the room, Sarah pulled the blanket over the blood-stained mattress and then ushered her children back in. The ship still rolled in the storm, but Sarah could feel that the intensity had diminished ever so slightly. It was enough to notice and Sarah was encouraged.

"Let us try and get some more ginger candies into these girls, and then we will go down for supper. I believe it is almost that time."

Florence accepted the candy without pause. Her eyes were beginning to regain their life. She was very weak from lack of nourishment, but Sarah knew she would be fine, as would her own daughter, who was sitting up unsupported.

Sarah retrieved her bag and a cloth and made her way to the toilet room to wash up. The two women who were using the wash basins gasped at the sight of the bloody clothing. They stared tentatively at her, but did not move. Sarah changed out of her stained dress and undergarments and scrubbed her body with soap and water. The tap water was frigid and uncomfortable, and Sarah's goose bumps revealed as much.

Sarah put on her only remaining dress, save for her Sunday best. She brushed her hair and pulled it back loosely and secured it. As she looked at herself in the mirror, she saw an old lady. Wrinkles lined the outside of her eyes and around her mouth. Grey lightly streaked through her wavy, brown hair. Sarah almost didn't recognize the person looking back at her. She felt her beauty had faded, but others would say it was only in her eyes it had done so. She sighed heavily and attempted to tuck her pride away. She knew God would not approve of such vanity.

Sarah took her bag into a toilet stall. As she sat there, she placed her head in her hands. "I will not cry," she whispered to herself. She needed to dig deep inside her heart and soul and find strength. She reached into her bag and retrieved her wooden box. As she slid the lid back, the smell of home filled her nostrils. She clutched her chest and inhaled a deep breath. Insecurity suddenly overwhelmed her. She had removed her family from the only home they had ever known, and at that moment they were nowhere. They had no home. They were in a place of blackness, in between the familiar and the unknown.

Sarah reached into the box and pulled out her rose. She kissed it as she closed her eyes and pictured Thomas. She reached in and pulled out her poem. She unfolded it as though it were the first time, as though what was written inside had never been read before. It comforted her, and it filled her with strength.

"Yes, I am," Sarah said to herself. She finished sorting her feelings and returned to her room.

"How are Mary and Florence doing? Are they well enough to go to supper?" Sarah asked.

"Mama, I am thirsty," Mary responded.

Sarah carried her daughter down the long hallway to the dining room, while Margaret carried Florence. Florence wrapped her arms around Margaret's neck and buried her face in it. As they arrived in the dining room, the hot food was not yet served. They took their seats at their usual table, happy to see it still empty. Sarah placed Florence on her lap to keep her steady.

"Pleasant evenin' to the Berry family. So nice to see you all here. And young Florence, too," he said with a smile.

But, as he realized the significance of Florence on Sarah's lap and not her own mother's, his face dropped. "Please tell me it isn't so."

Sarah studied Walter's face, convinced he knew something, but unsure of how that could be the case. Sarah did not know what she should say.

"Word spreads quickly around the ship. We heard of the misfortune of a young mother in childbirth. I have not seen too many women in that state on this voyage. I was so hopeful it was not Mrs. Nightingale. Please tell me she is resting."

"I wish I could Walter, but I am afraid I cannot," Sarah said sorrowfully.

"Our world is so unjust, and it makes no sense to me most of the time. No sense at all," Walter said, shaking his head.

"Walter, would you be so kind as to get us some tea, please? I believe that tea and sugar may be just what these young girls need."

While Sarah waited for the tea, she diced an apple into the tiniest of pieces and fed them to Florence. The doctor had said, "Not too much too quickly" and Sarah was mindful of heeding his advice. Sarah added sugar to a partially filled cup of tea and stirred it until it cooled. Florence took a few sips before Sarah put the cup down. Margaret did the same for Mary.

As the storm began to abate, the boat began to come alive again. It had been an unfair war waged against a much weaker opponent, but the weaker opponent persevered and prevailed...for the most part. There were always casualties of war, and in most cases they did not deserve their fate.

The line at the hospital persisted. Sarah politely squeezed her way past the line and through the door, enduring irritated stares and malicious comments. They were expected, and she tried to pay them no attention. The nurse spotted Sarah and rushed into the exam room to retrieve the doctor. The doctor emerged and motioned for Sarah to follow him into an adjacent room.

"Mrs. Berry, here is the certificate of death, and a letter of admissibility for Florence," the doctor said as he handed both pieces of paper to Sarah. "I am very sorry for your loss."

Sarah nodded at the doctor's condolences and accepted the documentation. Sarah did not look at either of them. She simply placed them in her handbag.

"Mrs. Berry, have you decided which arrangements you wish to make for your sister?"

"I have," Sarah said, swallowing hard on the word "sister." Sarah abhorred lying, but a young girl's life was at stake, as was a promise made to her dying mother.

"Doctor, cemeteries are for the living, not the dead. Burying Hannah at port would serve no rational purpose. There would be no one to visit her. And our bodies are merely vessels. Her spirit has been set free, and she should be buried in the place where it was done so."

The doctor was used to the many forms that grieving took, but he was impressed with Sarah's eloquence and her physical and spiritual practicality.

"I agree with you, Mrs. Berry. I do," he said, with a look that offered both apology and reverence. "So, the process from here is quite simple. Mrs. Nightingale's casket will be delivered to the sea. I believe it is a divine way for our earthly body to find peace. The captain is ordained and will say a few words. Would you like to be present?" the doctor asked.

"Thank you, but no. We have said our final good-byes. Her daughter is but two. She is much too young to acknowledge her loss."

The doctor's regret was amplified by his swelling guilt. Nothing more was said. There was simply nothing to say.

The ship continued to sway as Sarah walked back to her room, but it was not nearly as bad as it had been. There were no windows to the outside, but Sarah could feel her spirits lifting. Her experience had taught her that suffering was but a temporary state, and her faith carried her through.

Sarah realized that fate had brought a young girl into their lives, and she would not fail in bringing her to her father. In the room, Sarah took

Hannah's bag back to her own berth. She knew the only details as to where Florence's father was would be in this bag. Sarah held it, hesitating to open it. It felt wrong, an invasion of privacy. But it could not be helped. Suddenly, Sarah heard Florence's tiny cry.

"Mama," Florence begged as she touched her mother's berth.

She turned back to look at whomever would listen and called for her mother again. Sarah's heart broke. Florence was too young to understand. No explanations would help, no affection would suffice. She only wanted her mother, but, for the good and the bad, over time her memories of her mother would fade. Soon, there would be nothing. Sarah scooped up Florence in her arms and gently kissed her cheek.

"Your mama has gone to be with the angels, sweet girl. We will take care of you and we will take you to your papa."

Sarah handed Florence to Margaret and then returned to Hannah's bag. Inside was clothing for the two of them, tickets for passage to Québec, train tickets for Winnipeg, a small amount of money, and a Bible. There was nothing else. Sarah continued to dig, hoping that she was missing something. She was not.

She opened the Bible to see an inscription of *Nightingale Family Bible* inside the front cover. On the following page was listed:

John Nightingale, Tranmere, Cheshire, February 23, 1880

Hannah Mansfield, Wisbech, Cambridgeshire, November 28, 1881

Florence Amelia Nightingale, Toxteth Park, Lancashire, March 3, 1902

There were no other entries, nothing to provide any additional information about John. All Sarah knew was that John Nightingale worked for the Hudson's Bay Company in Winnipeg. When they arrived there, she would have to reach the company and inquire as to his whereabouts. If he was employed by them, surely they must know where he is. Perhaps he knew when they were coming and would be waiting at the train station.

As the storm continued to weaken, passengers began to return to the upper deck. There the rain had stopped pounding the windows. The clouds were still thick in the sky, but they were no longer as black as coal. As far as the eyes could see, the waves rose and fell like marching soldiers, but they no longer desired to consume the ship at each turn. They were finding a new rhythm.

Mary and Florence remained too weak to join the other children. They were content to sit on Sarah's and Margaret's laps. The ship's motion was still too exaggerated for the chess pieces to remain where they were intended so Samuel read and James worked away at his carving.

The Russian was back at the piano playing an unrecognizable piece. It was light and uplifting and entirely suitable for the circumstance. As he played, he was approached by a young child who stood off to the side of the bench. The young boy, no older than four, was mesmerized as the man's fingers moved effortlessly across the keys. As the man caught sight of the young boy, he became amused at his adoration. He stopped playing long enough to pat his hand on the bench beside him, inviting the young boy to join him at the piano. The boy looked back at his mother for approval, which he received in a nod.

The boy climbed up on the bench and watched as the pianist began to play a child's melody. In the middle of the song, he took the young boy's hand and pressed his index finger down on a key. The boy's smile illuminated the room. He continued, pressing a few keys in melodic succession. Overcome with excitement, the boy began to bounce on his seat. His squeals of joy awakened the other children, who began to gather around the piano, awaiting their turn. Parents watched on, beholden to the man for the unexpected pleasure he was bringing the children, and for releasing even the smallest burden, if only for the briefest moment.

"Margaret, why is that man staring at you?" Agnes asked.

"What man?"

Margaret followed Agnes' gaze to the far corner of the room, to the steward who stood guard. His dark, squinty eyes were fixated on her, unyielding even when they locked on hers. Margaret's heart began to race.

Samuel, who had been looking at the darkening skyline, turned to see what Agnes was talking about. The man's dark stare took Samuel by surprise. What could cause such an angry look, and toward his sister?

"Never mind, Agnes. It is nothing," Margaret said curtly.

Agnes shrugged her shoulders and looked away. Samuel was not as relaxed about it and, sensing a story, pressed his sister for more. Margaret knew he would not let it go so she leaned in to him and spoke directly into his ear to avoid being overheard. Samuel pulled back from Margaret when she was done and, anticipating his reaction, placed her hand on her brother's leg to stop him from getting up.

"Please, Samuel, let it go. You'll only make matters worse. The voyage is almost over and we shall be gone soon enough."

Samuel was sympathetic toward his sister's concerns. He knew she was right. But, while he understood, it didn't make him like it any better.

As nine o'clock approached, Sarah stood and motioned for her children to follow. Samuel had watched the steward leave the room a few minutes prior, and he was glad for that, but he had never stopped taking his eyes off her as he did. There were only four days left and Samuel would not let Margaret out of his sight.

As they exited the room, Samuel took up the rear, ensuring no one was left behind. On the main deck landing, the steward reappeared, positioning himself to oversee the steerage passengers make their way back to the depths of the ship. Samuel watched him eye his sister, who was directly in front of him. The overt display infuriated him and it took all of his restraint to not permanently remove that icy stare from his pathetic face. As Samuel walked past the steward, he shot him a glance, acknowledging that his transgression was not a secret to him.

"Cockteaser," he muttered under his breath, not intending for Samuel to hear, but Samuel heard it as plain as day, nevertheless.

Samuel stopped and turned. He walked back to the steward and looked down on him with the four inches he had on him. His otherwise squinty eyes widened in shock. Samuel's rage was as apparent as the fear on the steward's face. Any doubt as to Samuel's intentions were erased when his fist hit the steward's eye.

As the steward recoiled in pain, Samuel rubbed his fist to soothe it. Without skipping a beat, he caught up to his family. There was no notice of his absence or delay, and no word was ever spoken of it.

Chapter 33

As the breakfast bell rang on Friday, eight days into the voyage, the seas were perfectly calm again. The seasickness, which had been completely crippling for so many, had lifted, as had the thick veil of dark clouds which had choked the sky.

Appetites returned and Sarah's children made up for all that they had missed during the storm. Walter teased them that he could not understand where they were putting it all. Even Mary and Florence ate heartily. They had a ways to go before they replenished all that they had lost, but Sarah was confident they would get there soon enough.

For the first time in four days, passengers were out on the open deck after breakfast, smiling and fresh faced. The sky was intensely blue and the black waters as smooth as glass. It was chilly, not much more than freezing, but it was a delightful morning, made even more so by the contrast to the days of recent memory. Now, the sun was rising in the sky, casting a warm glow on all it touched. It felt like a new beginning.

Sarah sat on the bench and recalled her conversation with Hannah. It was very difficult to fathom how life could change so dramatically in so little a time. Now, just a few days later, Sarah was charged with finding her daughter's father, a man who was not yet aware of his unimaginable loss.

Sarah looked up at the sun and closed her eyes. It radiated a brilliant energy that she drank in. It was a simple pleasure, and yet one so magnificent that few could displace it.

Passengers milled around on the upper deck between meals, growing impatient for the welcome sight of land. The vulnerability of being at the sea's mercy with no hope for escape tested many a passenger's sanity. But, for the most part, passengers found the fresh sea air invigorating and it helped with the monotony. An unfortunate few were not afforded the same freedom. Fever had spread through the first- and second-class deck, and a handful of its passengers had become quarantined. And while Sarah felt bad for these passengers, she was relieved that, in this instance, class did not overrule sound judgement.

Life on the ship for Sarah and her family was pleasant and uneventful for the remaining few days. The monotony of consistency was broken on the eighth day when the captain sounded the horn. Its long and low blast reverberated across the deck and sent the passengers searching for the reason.

"Land! I'll be, it's land!" one Irish passenger yelled through his thick accent.

Passengers were rushing about the deck trying to catch sight of land. The ones who were inside ran out to see what the commotion was.

"Look, he's right. There it is," another said.

Far off in the distance, the contrast was faint, but sharp enough to see. The land rose out of the sea as a testament to the future. The level of energy was overwhelming. This new world that they had placed all of their hopes upon was real. Men and women broke down, falling to their knees, overwhelmed with emotion. Regrets and apprehension were buried by a flood of relief. Sarah picked up Florence, kissed her cheek, and pointed off into the distance.

"That is your new home, Florence," Sarah explained.

Florence pointed her chubby little arm and asked, "Mama?"

Sarah kissed Florence's cheek again, and looked into her innocent green eyes. "No, Florence...*Papa*," she replied.

In the dining room, Walter greeted them as enthusiastically as he always did. He was tall and lanky and had bright red hair, but he stood out amongst the other attendants in the dining room for more than just his appearance. His cheerfulness was infectious, and, despite his crooked front tooth, he had a confidence and smile that lit up the room.

"Hello, Berry family. How are you on this grand afternoon? Did my ears deceive me or did I hear the captain sound the horn for land?"

"We saw Canada. It is so exciting," Agnes said enthusiastically.

"Well, I don't know what is more exciting, seeing Canada for the first time or this?" Walter asked as he placed a swan carved from an apple on the table.

"That is extraordinary, Walter," Sarah complimented. "How on earth did you do that?"

"I'll bet that James could figure it out. I have seen his carving. But what is most appealing about my work is you get to eat it when you are done looking at it," Walter said laughing.

"Can we eat it?" Mary asked.

"Of course you can, Miss Mary. So long as you eat your dinner first," he said as he winked.

"We should be ready for inspection in a little under two days and then hopefully, you will be on your way."

"What inspection, Walter?" Mary asked.

"Before we reach port, inspectors will board this grand ship and check all of you hooligans to make sure you have brushed your teeth and washed your faces," Walter teased.

"What happens if we haven't?" Agnes asked.

"Well, they won't let you into Canada."

"Really?" Mary asked incredulously. "Where will they send us?"

"They will send you off to a faraway land filled with other filthy children," Walter said as the children's eyes grew. "They will also ask your mama if you are well-behaved children, and if you aren't they won't let you into Canada either."

Samuel, James, and Margaret grinned as they listened to the story, but Agnes and Mary looked at their mother in horror.

"Mama, what will you tell them?" Mary asked fearfully.

"Well, Mary, I will tell them that you are all the best-behaved children in the entire world." Sarah's reassurance relieved her daughter.

"In all seriousness, Walter, are you aware of what takes place during the inspection?" Sarah asked.

"The health inspector looks for signs of illness. If you are cleared, you will be approved for entry into port. If you are not, you will have to go to Grosse Île, the quarantine station, until you are well enough to pass inspection. Grosse Île is a small island in the St. Lawrence River, not far from the Port of Québec where we will be landing. We will pass by it after inspection. You will see it. You should have nothing to worry about, though. You all look healthy and shiny clean to me," Walter said as he touched the tip of Mary's nose. "There is nothing for you to worry about."

In actuality the inspection was always a cause for concern. Under the Canadian Quarantine Act, any ship carrying passengers or goods into Canadian waters was required to submit to a mandatory medical inspection. If any passenger or crew member was ill, they would be detained for anywhere from days to weeks depending on the particular type of illness. This was to prevent a repeat of the massive typhus outbreak in 1847 that killed one hundred thousand. The disease festered and proliferated on the ships, killing thousands at sea and then spreading like wildfire on land and taking the rest.

If a ship experienced an outbreak of any illness, they were expected to fly a blue flag to acknowledge such. Failure to stop for inspection could result in the quarantine station's cannons firing upon the offending ship. It would be impossible for a ship to outrun the inspectors so it would be foolish to not stop as commanded.

"In about two days' time you will be in port and then on your train bound for Winnipeg."

"Two days? But we see Canada already," James asked, believing Water must be mistaken.

Walter laughed. "If you were to travel England tip to tip six times you would still not be across Canada. She is a mighty large country, she is. We have another thousand miles to travel down the St. Lawrence before we are at port. Should be about two days."

That news took some of the wind out of their sails. They were anxious to be off the ship, and for their feet to be on the solid ground of their new home. The waiting was excruciating now that they could see how close they were, or at least how close they thought they were.

"I'd say you are fortunate, you are. Back before the steamships, it was all wind. If the good Lord decided to keep the wind from blowing, the ships could be at sea for two months or more. It was a mighty awful trip to take. We are fortunate, that's for certain."

"You are right, Walter. We are very fortunate," Sarah said as she stood to leave the dining room. "We look forward to seeing you at supper this evening."

"And I you, Mrs. Berry."

After dinner most onboard returned to the upper deck, enthusiastic and eager to see the progress that had been gained. The land that had scarcely risen from the sea, and was difficult to behold with the naked eye, now rose majestically against the horizon. The rocky cliffs were breathtaking. They were a tip of the hat to the beauty that was to come, a welcoming smile. But they were also a warning of the harshness that had birthed the rugged beauty, the endurance of a land long battered by seasons of spectacular extremes.

As the Ionian reached the Canadian shores its mighty ruggedness became clearer. Many inlets and tiny bays dotted the craggy coastline, teasing ships looking for the grand St. Lawrence, the final passage to the heart of this new country. Lonely Belle Isle stood as a guard at its mouth, granting admission to weary travellers. Beyond it the Strait of Bell Isle guided ships toward the Gulf of St. Lawrence. It was, at its narrowest point, a little more than ten miles across, providing clear view of Newfoundland and Labrador on either side of the ship.

Continuing toward the Gulf of St. Lawrence, as the northern borders transitioned from Labrador to Québec, the Gulf opened up wide. The passengers who stepped out onto the port side early the next morning were horrified to see no land, believing somehow the ship was turned around during the night. But land was clearly visible on the starboard side, as the ship hugged the northern shores.

Over the next day, the ship passed over Anticosti Island, toward the mouth of the St. Lawrence River. As it pushed farther down the St.

Lawrence, ships of all sizes could be seen littering the river. These ships, some of which carried cargo and some passengers, moved through the shipping lanes destined to or from port. The Ionian was destined for the Port of Québec, where Québec City was situated. As with all of North America, Québec City was young by European standards. It was the oldest fortified North American city north of Mexico, and was still only an infant at three hundred years old.

As the ship approached Grosse Île, it set anchor. The doctor who boarded the ship checked the passenger manifest, which listed all passengers on board and any notable information about them, looking for information about illness and death during the crossing.

Those first- and second-class passengers and crew not quarantined on the main deck were all assembled on the upper deck. Passengers were asked to remain orderly and line up. The ship was not full, which made the challenge of organizing much simpler. As passengers passed by the doctor, they received a certificate of inspection and were moved to a holding area.

The medical inspection was similar to the one performed in Liverpool upon embarkation. Sarah and her family were all certified as healthy and moved to the holding area with the other passengers who had been as well. On the main deck, the doctor determined that the fever that had forced the quarantine no longer posed a contagious threat and they were all medically cleared. The only death that occurred was due to childbirth and not from contagious disease. Upon completion of his inspection, the doctor issued the Ionian the necessary certificate to enter the Port of Québec, and the captain set sail to cover the remaining miles to do so.

Passengers were instructed to go to their decks for their final meal and gather their belongings before disembarking later that afternoon.

The familiar sight of Walter greeted them in the dining room. He had been a pleasant consistency during the trip and Sarah would miss his sunny disposition.

"Walter, did you make another carving for us?"

"Mary! That is rude. Walter, please forgive my daughter for her impertinence."

Mary looked at Sarah sideways, unsure of what she did wrong. She turned from her mother and looked at Walter to await the answer to what she thought was a perfectly reasonable question.

"Do you think I could let my favourite family leave without giving them something to remember me by?"

Mary became excited with anticipation. Whatever could Walter have, she wondered? Walter took his time, drawing out the suspense. And then when he felt he had tortured the girls enough, he placed the bag on the table.

"What is it, Walter?"

"This, Miss Agnes, is a bag of very special candy. In Québec, where it gets very, very cold, Maple trees produce a sweet syrup that is unlike anything you have ever tasted before. It makes the most divine candies, as you will see."

"Walter, how considerate," Sarah said, very taken with the gesture. "It should be us giving you a gift. You have been such a pleasure to us on this voyage."

"Mrs. Berry, your company has been gift enough. I mean that sincerely. I do not have a family and every so often I meet one that I wish were mine."

"What a kind thing to say. Thank you. You have not yet found the family that deserves you. Perhaps she is on the next voyage?"

Walter appreciated Sarah's encouragement. "Now, eat up, Berry family. You still have a long journey ahead of you. The train ride to Winnipeg is almost three days yet."

They finished their meal and one by one said good-bye and thank-you to Walter. As they were about to leave, Walter handed a sack to Sarah.

"Just a few supplies for your train ride," he said.

Sarah opened the bag and saw apples, oranges, loaves of bread and a jar of preserves.

"Walter!" Sarah was overcome with emotion. "Thank you so much. This will be put to very good use. I can assure you."

She leaned toward him and kissed his cheek. "Thank you for joining our family during the journey. May God bless you always."

Walter blushed every shade of red there was and he bid the Berry family adieu.

"Now it is time for the Berry family to become Canadian."

As they walked away from Walter, they were sad to say good bye, but happy for what lay ahead.

Sarah instructed the children to wash up for the last leg of the journey. They washed from head to toe the best they could without a shower, and when they were done they put on fresh clothes, which Sarah had washed the day before in a basin in the laundry room. She had been able to remove the blood from her skirt, but the blouse was soiled beyond repair.

The anticipation had reached a climax and Sarah and the children were ready to burst at the seams. They were cleaned and packed, but unable to disembark. The first- and second-class passengers were disembarking first and a portion of the upper deck was blocked off for steerage passengers to wait until that process was complete.

While waiting was difficult, it was a perfect day for doing so. The mid afternoon sun was starting to drop in the sky, but it was still high enough to reflect off the water. Hundreds of gulls flew overhead, squawking noisily, while a few sat perched on the railing.

It was a new beginning, a rebirth of sorts for so many. For most making the journey, there would be no life experience that would surpass the one they were living. To be removed from all that was familiar and put into a wholly unfamiliar land meant new customs, new languages and new traditions. It was a daunting prospect for even the most adventurous of souls.

The Ionian docked at the Louise Embankment breakwater wharf, which was sat at the confluence of the St. Lawrence and St. Charles Rivers. Looking out from the ship and the wharf, one could see the City of Québec rising in the distance. Smaller boats dotted the shoreline and moved freely about the port. But, above the hustle and bustle of the port activity, the city rose toward the sky, watching over the surrounding land and water like a knight guarding a castle. A stone wall protected the city from invaders in days long past, and stood presently as a testament to a rich history, a remembrance of all those who came from faraway lands before them to build new lives.

"Look at that building," James said, pointing to the tallest building on the horizon. It dwarfed all others in its vicinity. Its flag flew above its tower, rising from its sprawling base like a victor.

The Berry family gazed around, in awe of their surroundings. The colours, the smells, the sounds – it was all magnificent. As the number of first- and second-class passengers disembarking was reduced to a trickle, the stewards began to organize the steerage passengers and prepare them to do the same.

The passengers made their way to the plank and, one by one, walked away from their old lives to their new. They were all guided to a set of buildings which housed the Immigration Hall, Canadian Pacific Railway ticket office, telegraph and telephone offices, shop for purchasing supplies, dining room, and apartments for resting and washing up.

Chapter 34

The first stop was the Immigration Hall. The Main Hall within was large, housing rows upon rows of seats, enough to accommodate a thousand passengers. By this point they were filled in the first few by first- and second-class passengers who had already disembarked. The steerage passengers were directed to the seats immediately behind. Families progressed from seat to seat, crisscrossing the rows, until they made their way to the front of the line and to a waiting immigration officer. This was a frightening process for most. It was one thing to get turned down at port of departure, but to experience such an arduous journey only to be turned back now would be abominable.

A large Union Jack flag hung in the centre of the Main Hall, and a picture of the king hung on the wall. For those coming from Britain, the familiarity was comforting.

"Mama, I am hungry," Mary complained.

"Hungry," Florence nodded as she sat on Sarah's lap.

"I doubt we shall be too much longer. Once we are through immigration inspection, I must send a telegraph to Uncle Bertie and then we shall have a meal. The train doesn't depart for a few hours so we have plenty of time."

As they arrived at the front of the line, Sarah's mounting dread began to crush her chest. Every negative thought that could surface did. There was no reason that she could think of that would prevent them from being allowed further, but perhaps there was something she had missed.

As the immigration officer motioned for Sarah to approach, she gathered Florence and her children and marched them toward the officer.

"Bonjour, parlez-vous Francais ou Anglais?"

Sarah panicked, looking toward Margaret for assistance.

"Nous parlons Anglais, merci."

"Very well," the officer said smiling. "You speak French well."

"Thank you, Sir. It is a lovely language."

"Oui. Il est certainement," he said, appreciating the sentiment.

Sarah suddenly felt like a child in the group. She was overwhelmed by her daughter's maturity and wisdom, but never more so than at that moment.

"May I have your papers please, Madam?"

"Certainly."

Sarah reached into her bag and pulled out a stack of papers and handed them to the officer. As he sorted through them, he asked a few routine questions.

"Where are you from?"

"We were residing in Ardwick, Lancashire, and this young girl was residing just outside Liverpool."

"Is this not your child?" he inquired.

"No, Sir. She was travelling with her mother on the ship, but her mother died during the journey. I am taking her to her father in Winnipeg."

The officer's eyes opened wide.

"Ah, yes, I did hear about that unfortunate incident. She is fortunate to have you to care for her."

"Yes, Sir."

"What is your final destination?"

"We are going to Winnipeg...to join my brother."

"What is his name and address?"

"Albert Adamson, 106 Eugenie Street, Norwood."

The officer continued to write down information into a ledger and when he was satisfied with the responses, he provided Sarah with the necessary stamped entry documentation and wished her a safe journey. As she stepped off to the side, she closed her eyes and exhaled a long and slow release of needless worry. She could look back now and see she had nothing to fear, but in the moment rational thought is often elusive.

Sarah directed Samuel to take a seat with the children while she exchanged some of her British pounds for Canadian dollars and sent a telegraph to her brother so he would know when to expect them.

Florence was getting tired and climbed up onto Margaret's lap. She rested her tiny head against Margaret's chest and closed her eyes. Margaret wrapped her arms around her and held her tight. She felt like a doll. She seemed so vulnerable.

Sarah returned and then directed the children to the Dining Room. The room was not as large as the Main Hall, but still quite large. There were ample tables, seating for a few hundred, and on this day more than enough empty seats to accommodate them.

"It will be a few days before we have another hot meal. We shall eat well now. That should satisfy us until tomorrow. We have the food that Walter provided us with and I shall also buy some additional supplies at the shop."

The sign listed:

Tea, Coffee or Milk with Bread and Butter................*10 cents*
Full Hot Meal with Meat and Vegetable...................*25 cents*

Sarah stumbled with the new money. But she was promptly helped by the dining room worker, who was used to the confusion. She ordered the full hot meal for all. They had travelled in steerage, brought not much more than the clothes on their backs, and they were about to start their lives anew. She could not start them off with less than a belly full of hot food.

The food was inhaled, leaving no breath for conversation. Sarah would normally scold them for eating in such a manner, but she was pleased to see them eating happily and heartily. They had made it this far and they were all safe and healthy. They had much to be thankful for.

Sarah felt pangs of grief whenever she looked at Florence. She felt responsible for this young girl. She was so innocent and what had happened to her was not of her doing. For the first time, Sarah thought of what would become of her if she could not find the girl's father. But she would have to push that fear aside for the time being. Their journey was not yet complete.

Sarah cut Florence's beef into tiny pieces. It had been a few years since she'd had to be mindful of a tiny mouth. Florence ate her meal as voraciously as the rest, only stopping to take sips of milk.

"Toilet," Florence said with her tiny voice, which was barely heard above the dining room clatter.

"I think we all shall do the same. It appears as though we are done here. There is not enough left for even the birds to pick at," Sarah teased.

After they visited the toilets, the last task before boarding the train was to secure some provisions for the journey. Walter had provided them with a good start, but it would not be enough for the seven of them for two and a half days.

Sarah was told cooking facilities were available in the car, but no cooking utensils were brought so anything that needed to be cooked would not do. More bread and fruit and dried and salted meat were added to Walter's sack, as was a bag of taffy to accompany the maple candies already in there.

After the goods were purchased and Sarah had organized her bags for travel, she did an inventory of her children. All were accounted for. But something seemed out of place, and in one horrible, gut-wrenching moment she realized that Florence was not amongst them.

"Where is Florence?" Sarah shrieked as she looked around frantically.

The older children gasped as they realized they had failed in their responsibility to watch her. They, too, looked around, but Florence was nowhere to be seen. Sarah dropped her bags and rushed about the room looking for her.

"Florence!" she yelled.

Passengers looked on, recognizing the screams of a frantic parent. Many of them looked around the room hoping to spot a lonely child wandering the Hall.

"Agnes and Mary, you stay right here. Do not move! Samuel, James, and Margaret, you all go in different directions. She couldn't have gone far."

They all did as they were told, checking in the toilet room, the dining room, and every nook and cranny they could find. Sarah ran to the exit for the train, looking up and down the platform. She was nowhere.

"Sir, have you seen a small child, a girl about this height?" Sarah begged as she held her hand out.

"No, Madam, I have not," the porter said with a thick French accent.

Sarah ran back in the Main Hall and to the door on the opposite side. Her heart leapt into her throat as she thought of the water. She searched the veranda, which wrapped around the building. There were a few gulls looking for food, but no Florence. She rubbed her forehead in panic as she tried to compose herself enough to think of where she could be. As she turned to go back to the building she saw her. She was standing at the edge of the dock, watching a grey goose in the water.

People milled around her, busy with their own activities. Nobody noticed this small child as out of place.

"Florence," Sarah yelled as loud as her voice would carry.

Florence was leaning toward the goose, trying to make contact, when she heard Sarah's voice. As she looked up, she lost her balance and fell forward off the dock, slipping into the dark water and out of sight.

"Florence! No!" Sarah yelled, running as fast as she could.

Florence didn't surface. A young boy saw Florence fall in and jumped off the dock after her. He dove down into the water, disappearing as well. The water was deep, dropping off from shore with a sharp grade.

Sarah reached the dock, never taking her eyes off the spot where they both went in. The seconds felt like hours, the wait unimaginably horrible. By now a crowd had gathered behind Sarah, waiting for the boy to appear. Shortly after, he did, holding Florence by the back of her collar. As he held her high enough for her head to be out of water, she began flailing about, trying to gasp for breath. She coughed and sputtered as her body tried to expel the water from her lungs. Sarah reached down and took hold of her and pulled her out of the frigid water. A man then pulled the boy out.

Cheers erupted from the crowd as Sarah wrapped her arms around Florence. Strangers ran up to the boy, patting him on the back. A railway officer, having heard the commotion, approached the shivering boy.

"What happened here?" the officer asked.

"That boy is a hero," someone shouted from the crowd.

"He saved her," another added.

"Let's get you both inside and dried off," he said.

The officer guided them into a medical room in the Main Hall. He handed the boy a wool blanket to wrap himself in. He did the same to Sarah for Florence.

"You should be very proud of your son," the officer said to the boy's parents, who stood by shocked but proud.

The officer turned to Sarah, who had not said a word. She held on tightly to Florence, who held on tightly to her.

"Your little girl is very fortunate, Ma'am. Things could have turned out very differently if this young man had not been there. That water is very deep there and you can't even see your hand in it. God was certainly watching over her today. You may keep the blankets. You can use them on your journey," the officer offered.

Sarah knew words could never be enough to express her appreciation for the boy's actions. "I will be forever grateful to you for being there for Florence."

Sarah then turned to his parents. "The officer is right – you should be proud of your son. He is a fine young man."

They smiled and nodded, placing their hands on his shoulder.

"If you would please wait here for a moment, I have something I would like to get for you."

The boy's face brightened with childish excitement, nodding at Sarah's request.

Sarah returned to her children, who were shocked to see Florence, wet from head to toe.

"What happened, Mama?"

"I will explain in a moment. But first, I must do something. Margaret, please take Florence," Sarah said as she passed Florence to her daughter.

Sarah reached into her bag and pulled out her money purse. She pulled out fifty cents and returned to the boy.

As she handed the boy the coins, she thanked him again.

"I only wish I could give you more. This doesn't begin to show how much I appreciate what you have done. May God bless you immensely in all that you do."

"Thank you!" He was unquestionably delighted with the token.

"Yes, thank you," his mother repeated.

It was a lot of money for the boy. It was a lot of money for Sarah. But it was Eleanor's money and she would have done precisely the same thing.

The train's whistle blew, indicating it was soon time to board. Sarah rejoined her children and organized them accordingly. Florence had stopped shivering and was nestled comfortably into Margaret. The others were eager to depart, but before they could Sarah needed to change Florence out of her wet clothing.

"Mama, what happened to Florence?" Agnes asked again.

"It shows you how quickly accidents can happen. Florence became enamored with a bird and slipped off the dock into the water. A young boy jumped in and retrieved her. She was a moment from being out of reach. We almost lost her."

She leaned down and kissed Florence's wet hair. The children looked at Florence in astonishment. Blood or no blood, Florence was now part of the family. In a few short days, she had become one of them. The thought of losing her, and in such a dreadful manner, was terrifying.

Signs posted in most of the prevalent languages explained the where and how of the boarding process. And there were sufficient workers for those who could not read. One by one, the passengers were boarded onto their class appropriate cars like heads of livestock. They were packed in the car, orderly but tightly. There was no wasted space.

The third-class sleeper cars, or "colonist" cars as they were called, were boxes on rails. There was nothing luxurious about them. They were modest by all accounts. They were built simply to carry large numbers of immigrants from central and eastern Canadian ports to points west. Each car could carry seventy-two passengers. There were eighteen open sections with two simple wooden benches that folded down to make lower berths, and a single upper berth that folded down above each section from the ceiling. Gas lighting was in place in the ceiling to provide evening lighting.

Unlike the ship, there was no bedding or food provided. For bedding all they had for their journey was the single wool blanket that they had just been given. Train attendants were waiting on board with supplies – blankets rented out for seventy-five cents, as did mattresses, and pillows went for twenty-five cents. Food was purchased in the Immigration Hall. There was no dining car accessible by the colonist car on this journey and the train attendants continued to remind passengers of that as they boarded.

Above the upper berths, clerestory windows provided fresh air to the car, along with large, generous windows that opened at seat level. The cars inside were wood from top to bottom. The walls were covered with wood panelling and the floors with oiled wood planks. At one end of the car was a kitchen area for cooking. It housed a stove, which also served to warm the car during cold winter months. Water was supplied to the kitchen from overhead tanks. The same overhead tanks provided water to the toilets. The women's toilet and wash area was directly beside the kitchen, and the men's toilet was at the opposite end of the car. One toilet for each gender accommodated all seventy-two passengers.

There were seven of them, which meant that they would almost fill two sections. They would be joined in the second section by a single traveller or overflow from a family that could not fit in a single section. In either instance, it would be a stranger and Sarah was not comfortable having her children alone in that berth. She directed James to her section, which she would share with Florence. The other children would take the next section.

As Sarah sat down on the hard wooden benches, she thought of the two and a half day journey. It was a very long time to be uncomfortable, she realized. They only had one blanket between them. That would not do. They needed at least one more. With the money they saved from the food that Walter provided, Sarah decided to obtain another blanket and two pillows. She hesitantly parted with the money, one dollar and twenty-five cents, to be exact. It was a ridiculously large sum of money for basic comfort, she thought, and basic comfort that needed to be returned at trip's end. They would take turns sleeping in the upper berth with the blanket and pillow, and when below would use clothing to cushion their heads against the hard wooden benches.

As they settled into their sections, the whistle blew once again, this time as a final warning to passengers. The train attendant stepped off the car and onto the platform, waiting for the last of the passengers to arrive. The car that they were on was the last third-class car to be filled and was at slightly less than full capacity. No additional person joined Sarah, Florence, and James in their section, which was a comforting relief.

Cars were generally filled by nationality and destination. Sarah's car was filled with English and Irish destined for Winnipeg. The other colonist cars were filled with Eastern European immigrants also bound for Winnipeg. Other passengers from the Ionian who had been destined for the western provinces, beyond Winnipeg, were on a train that left not long before this one. This segregation by destination limited the movement about the cars and allowed for through-service to the end destinations. Segregation by nationality allowed common language and customs and made for a more pleasant experience for the passengers.

The children huddled around the window to watch the train as it departed from the Immigration Hall. Sarah held Florence up against the window so she could see. Florence held tightly to Sarah's neck. She was terrified from her ordeal and unwilling to let go of Sarah.

The train lurched forward as the brakes were released, and slowly the train began to move away from the platform. Every moment in motion was one moment closer to their new home, and it kindled a groundswell of excitement for the children that not even sleep could quell.

Few words were spoken as the train meandered around the City of Québec. There was too much to see to focus on anything else. It took about thirty minutes for the train to travel beyond the city and into the Québec countryside, which looked remarkably similar to the English countryside of home. It was so far away, yet so similar to the eye.

A baby began to cry at the opposite end of the car, providing a new focus for the passengers on board. The mother put the hungry baby to her breast, and her bored and unengaged toddler took full advantage of his mother's diverted attention. He wandered up the aisle looking for something of interest and he found it in Florence.

The young boy stopped in front of Sarah and felt no discomfort in staring at the two of them. He didn't speak; he just focused his full attention on them.

"Well, hello there," Sarah said.

The light was low inside the car, but his bright red hair still stood out against the wooden interior. He reached out and touched Florence's leg, as if to see if she was real. Florence looked down at him with curiosity.

"What is your name?" Sarah inquired.

The young boy did not speak. He continued to look at Florence.

"Patrick!" a woman yelled in a thick Irish accent. "Patrick, where might ye be?"

The young boy looked toward the sound of the woman's voice. He was no older than Florence, and as cute as could be. But he had a mischievous look about him. Perhaps it was the fiery, red hair.

"Is that your mama?"

"Aye," he said as he ran toward the voice.

Florence arched her neck so that she could see around Sarah. She watched the boy as he ran down the aisle back to his mother. For the moment at least, there was something to take Florence's mind off her troubles and it pleased Sarah.

The train rolled along through the Québec countryside, and the passengers settled in for the journey. As the sky turned dark, there was nothing between the tiny towns that dotted the landscape. The blackness was stark and seemingly unending.

"Mama, where will we live?"

"We will live with your Uncle Bertie to begin with. For how long, I am unsure. We cannot impose on his good nature for too long so we will find our own home as soon as we possibly can."

"Will I go to school?" Agnes asked from the next section.

"I believe so, but I am not entirely sure, my dear."

"Will Margaret?"

"So many questions...I simply do not know the answers."

"Will Florence live with us?"

That question caused Sarah to stumble. The thought of Florence leaving was a difficult one to accept. Sarah had fallen in love with her, and no amount of focusing on what was right would make it any easier.

"We will find Florence's father, who I am sure misses her desperately."

Sarah thought of the difficult discussion she would face when she had to explain that Hannah and their unborn child did not survive the journey. It was heartbreaking and there would be no way to make it less so.

As the evening progressed, and the children began to tire, Sarah prepared their sections for sleep. There was only one pillow and blanket for each section. The ceiling of the car was warmer than the lower portion as the heat from the car's stove rose, so it made logical sense that the blankets should be used in the lower berths. In the upper berths, they would use their coats for extra warmth.

"Tonight James and Margaret will take the upper berths. Samuel, you will sleep on the outside."

They were packed tightly into the car and there was little chance anything could happen, but Sarah was protective and could not forgive herself if something did.

There were no curtains between the sections for privacy. A few of the families had brought bed linens that that they used as curtains, but most did not. For the rest of the journey, there would simply be no privacy, and they could do nothing but accept the fact.

Heads were cushioned from the hardness of the upper berth by clothing that had been rolled up. Samuel realized he was not in a position to complain about sleeping on a hard bed. He had lived much worse. Time had dulled the memory, but not enough to completely forget.

In the lower berth, Sarah, Florence, and Mary slept closely together so that they could share a single blanket. The pillow was inadequate for the three of them so Sarah laid her head upon her extra skirt, which she had rolled up. Samuel and Agnes did the same with their own clothing. The train stopped for a short period in Montréal, but nothing in their car was disturbed and they slept soundly through the stop.

Chapter 35

As the morning light began to filter into the upper windows, the train made its second stop in Toronto. Passengers began to awaken, and as they did they raised the wooden window coverings for additional light. Some opened their window to inspect the surroundings.

As they welcomed in the morning, a sudden and overwhelming smell of ash and soot filled the car. It was not the smell of locomotive smoke, a smell with which they had become intimately familiar, but one that was more earthy and raw. It smelled of a fire pit whose smoking embers had been newly extinguished. It was heavy and thick and unmistakable.

Looking out from the car toward Union Station, nothing could explain the smell. There were no flames, no smoke, and no alarms. Sarah and the children were on the left side of the train, which faced south. They could see only train tracks and the train cars that blocked their view. From the opposite side, the view of the city was blocked by the station, and what lay beyond it was a mystery.

"What is that smell?" Agnes asked as she curled up her nose. "It smells as though the city is on fire."

"It is, or rather it was," the railway attendant said, happy to answer Agnes' question as he walked down the aisle.

"Half the city burned just the other side of this station, some buildings not more than a few feet away. Just a couple of weeks past. It's a bloody mess out there. Nothing but ruins."

James look down from the upper berth, wanting to make sure he didn't miss anything.

"How did it happen?" James asked, fascinated by the thought.

"Don't know. Don't think anybody does at this point. All I know is you best be shutting your windows or else you'll be smelling the smoke till you get off the train. You'd think the fire burned right up my nose. Can't smell anything else."

The worker finished his inspection of the car and upon walking back to the door stopped at James.

"We don't leave the station for another thirty minutes. You have time to take a peek, you do. You ain't seen nothing like it."

James rolled down from the upper berth in a single, fluid movement, clearing the lower berth and his resting mother.

"Can we?" James begged his mother.

"Absolutely not. You cannot leave the train," Sarah said as though it was the silliest thing she had ever heard.

"But, Mama, we are just going to step outside the station and take a quick look. We shan't be longer than a few moments. I give you my word."

"I'll go with him."

"Samuel, having you lost *with* your brother would not make me feel any better."

"Can I go?"

"You too, Margaret?" Sarah asked shaking her head.

"Mama, we shall just step outside the train station to look. We shall not take a single step farther. We must see, really we must."

Margaret's face portrayed a look of longing, of sweet, imploring innocence that Sarah, as hardened as she was, crumbled in the presence of. She remembered her own once ripe curiosity, which somewhere along the way had vanished and become locked away with life's experience. She was not so hardened that she could not remember that glorious feeling, that excitement that came with new discovery. It was exhilarating and nothing compared to it.

They held steadfast their look of longing. Sarah hesitated and her children realized that she was breaking.

"We are departing the station in thirty minutes. You must be back here in fifteen. Do I make myself clear?"

"Oh, yes, Mama. Absolutely. Thank you," Margaret said as she climbed down from her upper berth.

James and Margaret did not need to put their coats on, as they had been slept in. Samuel slipped his coat on and the three of them stepped off the train.

"Fifteen minutes!" Sarah yelled after them.

As they stepped off the train, the smell of ash mounted. The cold air was heavy and still and it locked the smell in, holding it captive. It was early and the station was not yet busy so they were able to move through the building with ease and speed, following the signs to the exit on the city side.

Emerging from the station, they stood on the street, disappointed to see the buildings directly in front of the station unaffected. As they turned to look eastward, the effects of the fire were unmistakable. Walking down Station Street toward Esplanade, the devastation in the distance was incomprehensible. The remnants of buildings destroyed by the fire rose out of the rubble, damaged beyond repair. Their walls were crumbled, and the ones that remained standing did so only in part, no longer holding anything up. The roofs were long gone. Glass had melted from the windows, leaving the openings empty and lifeless. Rubble blanketed every inch of ground. Were it not for the crumbling bases, it would be impossible to tell the roadways from where the buildings once stood.

They had all seen buildings burn, and understood the devastation fire could cause, but they had never seen anything of this scale.

"This is horrific," James said, speaking first.

Samuel and Margaret stood in silence, trying to comprehend what they were looking at.

"We must get back. Mama will have our heads on a platter if we do not."

Relief flooded Sarah as her children returned to the train. Railway companies had schedules to keep and this train would have left without them. Their welfare was of no consequence.

"Mama, you should have seen it. It was extraordinary. The city is in shambles, in utter ruin."

"Margaret, you are being dramatic. I doubt it is that dire. There is much more to the city than extends beyond the reach of your eye."

"Margaret was always a bit dramatic," James said while he rolled his eyes.

"I take offence to that," she shot back. "And you, who rolls his eyes like a child."

"That is enough," Sarah gently chided.

The train's whistle blew. It would be departing shortly and the passengers took their seats in preparation. There was no panic or running about so it appeared that all who were expected in the car for departure had been duly accounted for.

The train's whistle blew again. Beyond the station, they could see water to the south.

"Is it the ocean again?"

"I don't believe it is. We are too far inland. But it seems too large for a lake, and most certainly too large for a river."

"What is it then, Mama?"

Sarah had no idea. There was water as far as the eye could see. Ice cradled the shore, pushing out and extending the shoreline a considerable distance.

"It is much colder here than in Ardwick. Is it always this cold here? There are no flowers."

"Margaret, so many questions that I cannot answer. I do not believe it is always this cold here. Uncle Bertie tells me of warm summers with delightful lakes and plenty of swimming. I believe that winter is holding on a bit longer this year than most."

A gentleman in the section across the aisle overheard the conversation and thought kindly enough to offer his knowledge.

"Your mother is wise. It is true. It is not always this cold here in early May. But I was here in January and it was much colder. You could not be outside for more than a few minutes without feeling as though your skin were freezing like the hard winter ground. And that is not the ocean. That *is* a lake. It is one of the largest in the world, which is why it is called a Great Lake. Its name is Lake Ontario. We will go past an even larger one in a day or so."

"Where do you live?"

"Agnes, that is of no concern to you." Sarah leaped at her daughter's rudeness.

"I do not mind at all. Travelling a long way alone can get lonely. It is a welcome change to have a pleasant conversation with someone other than myself," he said with a laugh. "Although I don't want to intrude upon your family."

The man appeared to be in his early thirties, but Sarah learned long ago that guessing someone's age was fraught with error more often than with accuracy. There were too many factors that could affect how one looked and assumptions could prove harsh and cruel. He was certainly of English origin, though.

"No, that is quite all right. My children will enjoy the company."

"Marvellous," he said, addressing Agnes, "I live in Winnipeg. My parents emigrated from England ten years ago, and I just went back to visit my grandmum and granddad for the first time since. They live in Stretford."

"Stretford? We lived in Ardwick," James offered. "We were practically neighbours."

"Aye, I believe we were. And we will be again. I am assuming you are going to Winnipeg if you are on this car."

"We are," Sarah said. "My brother emigrated about the same time you did."

"Let me guess...he lives in Norwood. Most of the English live there. Feels like we never left."

"He does," Sarah said surprised. "How did you know that?"

"Seems to be the popular place for the English. Norwood is beside St. Boniface, which is predominantly French."

They were all intrigued by this man, but none more than Sarah. She wanted to learn as much as she could, knowing full well that the quality of their lives very much depended on the quality of their neighbours and of their surroundings.

"My brother tells me that the French want to preserve their heritage and feel, perhaps rightly so, that English progress is eroding it." Sarah hesitated on her words, realizing she did not know the politics of the man to whom she was speaking and didn't want to appear impertinent. "I'm sorry for my rudeness. My name is Sarah, and these are my children."

"I'm pleased to make your acquaintance, Sarah. My name is Samuel, but my friends call me Sam."

"My father's name was Samuel, as is my oldest son's," Sarah said pointing at Samuel with a smile. "I grew up in Stretford myself. 'Samuel from Stretford,' it seems we have a few things in common."

"What takes you to Winnipeg, Sarah, if you don't mind me asking?"

"My brother lives there."

"Winnipeg is a downright brilliant place to be. There is plenty of everything and in abundance...cold, warm, rain, sun, but it definitely isn't for the faint-hearted."

"Sam, what takes you to Winnipeg?"

"My parents. I work in my father's butcher shop in Norwood. The plan was to go back and take over my grandfather's shop in Stretford, as he is past the age where he should be working. The building burned while I was sailing back so it would appear that he has no choice but to retire now. He's too old to start over so I thought it was best I come back and help my father. So here I am, and happy to be."

"Patrick," Florence said, pointing up the aisle.

Sarah turned in the direction that Florence was pointing and saw young Patrick walking up the aisle. He walked directly toward Sarah and Florence and stopped and faced them. Again, he just stood there, saying nothing.

"Hello, Patrick," Sarah said.

Patrick hesitated and then nodded.

"Does your mother know where you are?"

Patrick looked back toward his mother and then shrugged his shoulders. Patrick was clearly not shy. He seemed fearful of no one, including his mother.

"Would you like to sit down?" Sarah asked.

As Patrick was about to get up on the bench beside Florence, his mother came bounding down the aisle, with baby on hip.

"Patrick, there ye be. What you think ye be doing running off like that? Yer lucky I don't swat yer behind."

Patrick's mother realized she was being impolite and appeared contrite and apologetic.

"I'm sorry for my son's behaviour, Mum. Hard to keep him close when I have this one to feed," she said, looking down at the baby on her hip. "He's a good boy, but likes to wander. Patrick, come with me and don't be bothering this nice lady anymore. Ye hear me!"

"He is not a bother to anybody. I assure you. He has been nothing but polite. Florence is quite enjoying his company and he would be welcome to stay a while longer."

"Ah, that is most generous. Thank you."

She was clearly apprehensive and Sarah could not discern her apprehensiveness for protectiveness or for her concern that he would cause her more trouble if he was out of her sight.

"Patrick. Ye behave now. Yer backside will know it if ye don't. Come back when you've worn out your welcome."

Patrick simply nodded, then turned away from his mother. Florence delighted in her new friend, who had taken a place beside her on the bench. He reached into his pocket and took out two spinning tops and handed one to Florence. Florence took it, but was unsure of what it was or what to do with it. Patrick climbed down off the bench, sat down on the wooden floor, twisted his fingers on the small knob and spun the top in place. Florence looked on in awe as it whirred and then wobbled, falling on its side as its motion slowed.

Florence climbed down on the bench and took a place beside Patrick on the floor. She placed her tiny little fingers on the knob and then twisted with all her might, but the top merely fell on its side. Florence was disheartened, but despite her disappointment decided to give it another try. The second time was not much better than the first, but it managed to spin once before it succumbed to the force of gravity and landed on its side, yet again. But that single spin was enough to delight Florence, putting a smile on her cherubic face. She bounced on the floor and clapped her tiny hands.

As they were honing their skills with the tops, they didn't notice Sam getting down on his knees in the aisle beside his section. He pulled out a bag of dominoes and began to set them up in a row, standing them on their ends. The motion of the train made it incredibly difficult to keep them standing; slight movements on the tracks caused them to fall more often than not, but Sam persisted in his efforts.

"Florence and Patrick, would you like to see a trick?"

They both turned to look at Sam, who was down at the same level as them. As Sarah looked on, they scooted over on their knees to see what Sam was doing.

"Patrick, why don't you push on this domino?" Sam said as he pointed to the lead piece.

Patrick looked at Sam. As Sam nodded his agreement, Patrick pushed the piece, knocking each one down after it in even and rhythmic succession. The children were mesmerized by the movement.

"Fun! Again?" Florence asked.

"Of course we can."

"I will show you how to do it and then you can do it yourselves. How does that sound?"

They both nodded exuberantly and then watched intently as Sam set them up again. They waited patiently as the dominoes repeatedly toppled under the train's movements, needing to be repositioned. But, when it was all complete, and the line was ready to nudge, what little patience they had vanished and their enthusiasm took over.

"Now, Florence, it is your turn."

Florence did as Patrick had before her. And, as they had before, the dominoes toppled one by one like waves on rough seas.

"Thank you, Sam," Sarah said gratefully.

Sam returned to his seat as the children played with the dominoes on the floor. And, like most children, their interest waned after a few short minutes, leaving the pieces strewn about the car floor. Sarah bent down to pick them up.

"Please, I can do that," Sam said, stopping her. "I am incredibly busy at the moment fixing this and tending to that, and I really don't have a moment to spare, but I shall do it regardless," he said in mock exasperation.

Sarah laughed at his playfulness. She did not generally laugh at so little. She was not a playful person by nature, but his humour struck a chord. And as she looked up from the dominoes, their eyes locked. His eyes were the darkest brown, like melted chocolate, and they drew Sarah in. Sarah broke her gaze and stood up.

"Well then, I best let you get back to your busy schedule."

Sarah tried to appear playful in her own way, but it was clear to Sam that she was uncomfortable. As she returned to her section and sat down on the bench, his eyes followed her.

Sarah looked out of the window and focused on the passing landscape. The sleeping fields, still full of morning frost, reached out toward the horizon, waiting for the rising sun to awaken them. The cows and horses were feeding themselves, unaware that there was more to life than the routine that they found themselves locked into.

The day passed by uneventfully. The children occupied themselves with their activities and Sarah spent her time deep in her thoughts, planning her new life. There was so much unknown and it made her feel terribly uncomfortable, but she was able to ease her discomfort with thoughts of action and of progress.

As Patrick and Florence sat on the floor playing with the tops, Sarah's silence was broken.

"May I sit with you?" Sam asked. "I understand if you would like to be alone, but I know I could certainly use the company."

Sarah hesitated, surprised by the request.

"Um, yes, that would be fine."

"It is an interesting word, 'fine,' isn't it? It could mean nice, or it could mean distasteful with a dose of good manners on top. Which is it?" Sam asked.

Sarah was taken aback by his bold conjecture. So far he seemed a reasonable gentleman, and it was doubtful he was being rude, but she had only known him a few short hours and it was difficult to form a true opinion of someone in such a short time.

"Fine is fine. It is not meant to be rude, nor is it meant to hide rude. It is just that, *fine*."

Sam laughed at Sarah's matter-of-factness. It was clear to him that she was not one for niceties or subtleties.

"Very well, then. I shall take 'fine' as an acceptance of my request and I shall sit down. I will leave it to later to decide if I am deluding myself into thinking that you are happy to do so or simply conceding to shut me up. That will give me something to ponder when I go to sleep. For then, at least, I will have my dreams to comfort me."

"You are rather shameless, aren't you?"

Sam smiled slyly. "Shameless is in the eye of the beholder, I suppose. I prefer to think of myself as forthright, with a touch of sarcastic charm."

Sarah laughed again. She did not know what to think of Sam. He did amuse her and she was not accustomed to being amused by anyone. It felt good.

Sarah reached for the food that Walter had given her and she removed the maple candies. She offered one to each of her children, along with Patrick and Florence, who were still sitting on the floor playing with the tops.

"Sam, would you be interested in a maple candy?"

"Yes, I would. Thank you."

They sat in silence as they ate their candy, both searching for something to fill the void.

"It certainly is a long journey to take by oneself. How did you handle the rough seas?"

"I am accustomed to doing things on my own. I have no siblings. I guess I ruined my mother for all other children," Sam said jokingly. "As for the rough seas, I suppose I am not as tough and put together as I look on the outside," he said smiling. "I do not think I got off my berth once the storm began."

"And you?"

"I fared better than you, by the sounds of it, but Mary here did not, nor did young Florence. They were considerably ill, and I, too, spent most of my time in the stateroom as a result."

"Well, your daughters have clearly recovered. They look robust at the moment."

"Mary is my daughter, but Florence is not. We are reuniting her with her father in Winnipeg."

"Oh. Where is her mother?"

"Florence and her mother were on the ship with us." Sarah spoke quietly. She did not want Florence to hear the conversation as she played on the floor. "Unfortunately, she did not survive the journey."

Sam listened awestruck as Sarah described the ordeal. He looked down at Florence and winced. Sarah was taken by his genuine heartfelt reaction.

"How awful. That poor child." Sam continued to look pained by the revelation.

"And for you to care for her *and* to take her to her father...that is most generous of you. How will you find him?"

"I do know his name and that he works for the Hudson's Bay Company in Winnipeg. I will have to go to them. Surely, they will have a record of him."

Sam nodded, still surprised by the information. His silence was broken by another thought.

"How awful. He will be told that his wife and unborn child have perished. I am sad for him and the anguish he will experience." Sarah nodded and continued to be surprised by Sam.

"Yes, it is a task that I will not relish. But I cannot think of that. It must be done."

"And you, where is your husband, if it is not too prying."

Sarah was not bothered by the question. She was simply unsure of how much she should say. Her hesitation made Sam sit back.

"My apologies, Sarah. I did not mean to be intrusive. Please forgive me."

He was genuinely contrite in his apology and Sarah was regretful that she had caused him discomfort. She was not bothered by the question at all.

"Please do not apologize. You were not being intrusive. It is a simple question and one I have no compunction providing an answer for. My husband, Thomas, died three years past. We are joining my brother, Albert, in Winnipeg."

"I am sorry for your loss. Under such circumstances this would not be an easy journey to make."

"Yes, well, difficult or not, we must deal with what God gives us. It is not for us to judge or question."

Sam thought to himself that she must have said that over and over to herself. It struck him as well rehearsed. He understood the pain of loss and did not begrudge her the mechanical response.

"I, too, lost my wife," Sam shared. "She died in childbirth. It has been almost ten years now."

A decade had passed, but it was evident the pain had not. Sarah did not know if she should pry, but she felt as though Sam wanted to talk and she did not want to end their conversation like this. It would have been cruel.

"I am sorry, Sam. You must have been very young."

"I was. We had both just turned twenty-three. We had been married for only a year. To lose someone you love is impossibly painful, but to lose them in such a way is even more so. I lost my entire world that day. But, as you say, we must deal with what God gives us."

For the first time, Sarah realized how trivial that could sound. Platitudes, even ones divinely delivered, do not diminish our pain nor do they diminish our need to heal.

"I lost a child as well. My Elizabeth died when she was three. She would have been ten now."

The common ground that linked them was the darkest parts of both of their lives. It was hardened ground, but it bonded them in suffering. Sarah felt surprisingly comfortable conversing with Sam. She rarely talked of her life with anyone, yet she felt at ease, almost compelled to do so with him.

He had a very gentle way about him. There was no conceit, and there was no pretence from what she could see. It was a shame that he was so scarred from his experiences that he had not found love again. There were men far worse than him who had fared much better in love and it did not seem fair.

"Well, it would appear we have much in common, Sarah," Sam acknowledged with a smile. "It is most fortunate for me that I ended up in the same car as you and was able to make your fine acquaintance."

"Indeed," Sarah replied.

The remainder of the day progressed without incident. The children occupied themselves with the passing scenery and with the activities that they brought. Florence and Patrick were inseparable with the exception of the times when they slept and ate.

"Mama, I am hungry."

She was very aware of the difficulty of a long journey on young children and she was proud of hers. They had given her no cause for worry.

"Yes, Mary, we shall eat shortly."

Sarah pulled the bag carrying the food up onto her lap. There were no tables on the train, which made eating extremely difficult, but it was for only a short period of time and she could not complain. The train, with its lack of tables and other comforts, was far preferable to the rough seas. The comforts afforded on the ship were not all that comfortable after all when the sea was in a rage.

The family dined on bread and dried meat. Had Walter not provided the cup that he did, they would have been unable to drink. It hadn't even occurred to Sarah that they would need one. Many trips to the kitchen area were necessary to allow them to each have water with their meal. But, not so long ago, they had to cart their water from a pump in the street, so this was not a massive inconvenience to them.

The bread was beginning to dry out, but the preserves helped to freshen it. Sarah completed the meal with the cake from the ship. Walter had been so good to them and Sarah thought of him with fondness as they ate.

As the evening progressed, Sarah settled her children in for the night. There was not much to occupy oneself with on the long journey and sleep seemed like the best way to pass time. Passengers found themselves in a state of slumber long before they would have at home.

Sam was sharing his section with a family of four. He took the upper berth and was at the mercy of their schedule. As they prepared themselves for bed, he climbed up into the berth and did the only thing he could...go to sleep.

Sarah and Sam smiled at each other goodnight, both tired from a long day of inactivity. There was one full day remaining of their journey and then they would be at their final destination.

As Sarah lay on her berth, she thought back on the day. She awoke in Toronto, a city in ruins, and now, as they rolled through the darkened countryside, they moved from one unknown town to another. They could have been on the moon for all Sarah knew.

But there was a single bright spot in a day of unfamiliar and uncomfortable. Sam was quite pleasant. He had a charm about him that put Sarah at ease, which Sarah admitted to herself was no easy task. Sarah was cautious and protective, protective of her family and of her own feelings. There was no room for anyone new, none at all, and Sarah made sure that every person who came close knew that. It wasn't entirely conscious, but that lack of recognition was of no consequence.

Unconscious actions speak louder than ones we purposely put in motion, and they most definitely can have a greater impact.

But as she lay there thinking about this new man with whom she had so much in common, she could not help but think about another. Sarah never saw William as anything more than a friend. But, time can change things, much like a dying flower, if watered, can live to bloom again. How obtuse Sarah had been. How blind she had been to the wonderful man he was. He had been there all the time. He had not changed. But Sarah saw him differently now, and it was too late. She knew she could love again, but the man she loved was no longer a part of her life, and it was a loss that weighed heavily upon her heart.

Chapter 36

As Sarah awoke in the morning, she rubbed her eyes and attempted to focus on her surroundings. She did not want to disturb the children so she did not sit up. She lay there looking at the ceiling and the open upper berth above that contained Agnes. Her back ached from the hard, wooden bench and she grimaced as she rolled over. Mary and Florence slept peacefully beside her, undisturbed and unaware that the berth they slept on was as hard as stone. But they were children and their bodies were far more forgiving.

Few people were moving about in the car. The sun was barely rising, and the light inside the car was dim. But, with the ceiling lanterns illuminating the aisle, it was bright enough to see Sam focused on her. He was lying on his side in his upper berth, looking down at her with a smile on his face. He felt no need to look away when he was caught. It didn't occur to him that it was anything to be embarrassed or remorseful about.

"Good morning, Sarah. Did you sleep well?" he spoke softly.

Sarah nodded and cleared her throat of her sleeping frog.

"I did, thank you. And you?"

"I think I might have been more comfortable sleeping on the top of a horse."

"Yes, I do believe that would have been an improvement," Sarah agreed, amusedly.

Sam was in possession of a mattress and pillow, but his body still ached with age. As he lay there, his brown curls fell softly on his forehead. There was not a stitch of grey. He had a youthful appearance, hardly a line, and it belied his age. Sarah thought to herself that the five years she had on him must look like twenty, for she believed herself matronly in relation. Sam, on the other hand, believed quite the opposite.

The children began to stir in the lower berths and Sarah returned them to their day state. The children in the upper berths climbed down and Sarah prepared them breakfast, which was as bland and stale as the other meals had been on the train. Sarah assured them it would only be one more day and then they would be able to cook again.

"Mama, will I be able to cook in Uncle Bertie's kitchen?" Margaret asked hopefully.

"I don't see why not. But I will not be the final word. I do not understand the workings of your uncle's home. It is your aunt's home as well and we will be respectful of that while we are staying there."

Sam overheard the conversation and interjected himself. "Margaret, do you like to cook?"

Margaret looked up at Sam and beamed. "I do. Very much."

"What do you like to cook? I, too, like to cook. My family has a butcher shop and we sell the finest meats in all of Winnipeg, if I do say so myself."

Sam pushed himself up in his berth, newly energized for the beginning of the day. As he climbed down, Margaret responded to his question with enthusiasm. Sam could see that she had a passion for cooking.

"I do not have a preference. I love to experiment with spices and sauces."

"Well, if it was the last meal you would ever prepare and you could prepare anything your heart desired, what would it be?"

Margaret felt a rush of emotion, and a panic at a question that she had never pondered before. How could she narrow it down to that one thing? It would push everything else down, and it would have to be truly special in order to do that.

"Well, that is a very difficult question. There are so many things that have appealed to me and so many things that I have not yet thought of. But I do have to say that one of my favourites is a roasted chicken with mustard and rosemary."

"That sounds tasty. Perhaps you could share the recipe with me."

"Margaret learned from a top Parisian chef when she was working at a home in Burnage. Chef Nicolas was an excellent teacher, was he not, Margaret?" her mother added.

"He was." Margaret missed him dearly. He had been kind to her and had helped make her time at Amberley House tolerable. There was another person who also made her time at Amberley House tolerable. She missed Jonathan so. She could still feel his lips on hers and the thought if it made her tremble.

"Well, perhaps you can teach me in Norwood sometime. You will have to come to our shop and see what we have to offer. I, myself, like to cook venison. Perhaps your uncle already shops with us. What is his name?"

Margaret was intrigued. "What is venison?"

"Venison is the meat from antlered animals, for instance, deer, moose, elk, caribou. It is red meat, like beef, but it has a much stronger flavour."

Sarah was impressed with his knowledge and varied interests. He was surprising her more and more with each passing moment.

"My brother's name is Albert Adamson."

"The Bertie Adamson who sells real estate?"

Sarah was awestruck. Could he possibly know her brother? "Yes, my brother sells real estate."

"His office is around the corner from my shop. His wife, Jane, buys from our shop all the time. They are regular customers. In fact, Jane and my mother are good friends."

"I do not know what to say." Sarah was completely taken aback.

"I guess we are going to be neighbours. Bertie's house is but a few short blocks from ours."

Sam smiled openly at Sarah, unable to hide the pleasure he felt upon the revelation.

"Well, it would seem you have made your first friend, Sarah Berry, and you have not yet set foot in Winnipeg. I would say that is a good start, wouldn't you?"

Sarah began to feel as though she was being conspired against, controlled by her circumstance, but she had to smile. She found it as amusing as Sam appeared to. It was comforting knowing there would be one person whose acquaintance she had already made, and a charming person at that. But, for the life of her, she could not figure out why this man, a man who lived in the same circles as her brother, a man who had his own business, was riding in steerage. Perhaps the business was not doing well.

Sarah passed the day away looking out at the scenery. The Canadian landscape was absolutely breathtaking. It was forever changing, and you could miss something spectacular if you dared take your eyes off it for even a moment. They had already passed through the sleepy farm lands of southern Ontario and were well into northern Ontario, where the rough and rocky terrain had been blasted to make way for the very tracks that carried them through.

As they ate their mid-day meal, they passed by another large body of water. This time they were not at water level, but higher up on a steep and rocky ledge. The lake, much like the one they had seen in Toronto, reached out beyond what the eye could see. And much like with the other lake, ice blanketed its shore. But here the sky was not blue. It was a dark and ominous grey. But it was not eerie. It was beautiful in a most dramatic way.

The lake was rough and the frenzied waves broke when they could rise no longer. The whites of their demise dotted the lake's monotone palette, bringing a texture that could not be imagined if it were not seen with one's own eyes.

"That is called Lake Superior. It is largest and deepest of the Great Lakes. America sits on the opposite side. You could take a ship from this point and sail all the way to England and never have to cross land."

"How is that possible? How do you know that?" James was stunned.

"To answer your first question, the Great Lakes of Canada are connected by rivers and smaller lakes that allow ships to travel between them. It is mostly to carry goods, not people. The only spot that was not naturally built for travel is between Lake Ontario, the lake we saw in Toronto, and Lake Erie. They are not of the same elevation and locks had to be built to accommodate the elevation differences. Now ships can travel through the Erie Canal all the way to the Atlantic Ocean. It is possible to sail inland in Canada, nearly 2,300 miles from Lake Superior, to the Atlantic Ocean. That is larger than most countries, and that is only partially how far Canada is across."

The children listened intently, fixated on Sam's descriptions. He had a way about him, Sarah thought. He was a very good story teller. He was animated and passionate about his topic, and it was felt by those who were listening.

"It makes you realize just how large this world is," Samuel said.

"It definitely does," Sam agreed.

"Now, for your second question, James...I know these facts because I read far more than I should, I suppose. I am a lover of geography and I like to understand the world I live in, not just the town."

Their evening meal would be the last meal on the train. It was a good thing as every last morsel of food was consumed. They were scheduled to be in Winnipeg first thing in the morning and would eat breakfast after they arrived.

"May I sit with you?" Sam asked. "I have a treat I would like to share with all of you."

Mary and Agnes heard the word treat and were at Sam's side faster than Sarah could respond.

"A treat?" Sarah repeated as she grinned at her daughter's enthusiasm. "Yes, please. Sit down," Sarah said motioning to the seat across from her.

Sam placed a bag on his lap and reached in and pulled out a slab. It looked like dark chocolate.

"This is fudge. My grandmother made it before I left. My cousin in America gave her the recipe and now her home is never without it. She sent me off with peanut butter fudge, chocolate fudge, and maple fudge. I took some maple syrup over with me. Take your time with it. Take a tiny piece at a time."

Sam pulled off pieces and began to hand them to the children. His words fell on deaf ears because Mary and Agnes didn't even chew theirs. They devoured it in a single bite.

"It is absolutely fantastic," Margaret gushed. "You must tell me how to make it. I would love to try."

"Thank you," Sarah said. "It was very kind of you."

"It was my pleasure. And now it is your turn."

Sam took a piece off and handed it to Sarah. It was softened from sitting in his warm hands and it felt sticky between her fingers.

"Take a tiny bite and let it sit on your tongue. Savour it."

Sam watched as Sarah did as he had commanded. The taste of the sweet chocolate overwhelmed her tongue, which she slowly pushed up against the roof of her mouth until the candy was gone. The taste was deep and rich, and, without thought, she closed her eyes as she enjoyed the sensation.

As she opened them again, Sam was looking at her and smiling.

"I take it you liked it?" he asked.

"Indeed I did. What is not to like? It is absolutely delicious."

The storm was clearing and the black clouds were scattering in the sky, revealing patches of dark blue. The sun cast an orange hue upon the evening, and as the train turned north the orange light filled the car. It was warm and radiant and illuminated Sam, who sat directly in its path. He narrowed his brown eyes in defence. He was a handsome man, Sarah thought, and the light made him more so. But his youthful good looks only made Sarah feel uncomfortable.

"Excuse me, please," Sarah said as she stood to go to the toilet room.

As Sarah stood at the basin, she took a deep breath and splashed cold water on her face. She looked at herself in the mirror. Her dark hair was beginning to grey. It had a while ago. But life had aged her and her smooth skin was now etched with fine lines. As she leaned in toward the mirror, she ran her fingers around her eyes, tracing the lines. Sarah was still a beautiful woman, but it was easier to believe otherwise.

When Sarah returned to her section, Sam had already returned to his. The sun had just set behind the horizon and its lingering halo was but a sliver of light. Moment by moment, the cloak of night transformed the sky from a brilliant orange to the darkest black. The last evening on the train was coming to an end and Sarah was glad for it. It had been a long journey and she was anxious to be on still ground again.

But the last night on the train did not produce peaceful slumber for Sarah. Her mind raced with every conceivable thought. Mostly, she thought of her brother. How she longed to see him again. She had been unsure if she ever would. It had been more than ten years: almost a quarter of her life. What would he think when he saw her? She must have changed so, as must he have. Would he have fully greyed like their father? Would he be thin or portly? What had his life become? She loved her brother so, but she was frightened at the thought that she might no longer know him. He might be a stranger.

She thought of her life as a child, her father whom she loved so dearly. He allowed her to wish and hope and he indulged her dreams. Her mother, whom she too loved dearly, but in a less playful and affectionate way, was much more practical and circumspect. Sarah knew of whose cloth she was cut from. There was no denying that. But perhaps it explained why she was so drawn to Eleanor. Eleanor was her father.

Thomas, her children, her life in Ardwick had been a blur of activity. Where had the time gone? She believed she had been a good wife. Thomas had told her so. But could she have been more? He was gone and she would never have the opportunity. But her children, whom she loved more than anything, were still here. She provided for her children, and she kept them safe, but Sarah felt unsure about the rest. Had she encouraged them or had she been too practical in her advice? As she thought of what she had said to her children throughout their lives, and in particular Margaret, she cringed. Margaret was a dreamer, and a skillful one at that. What would her father have done? She knew the answer to that question and she felt ashamed.

How her behaviour and her decisions had changed the course of so many lives. But Sarah realized her greatest sadness was William. She had not allowed herself to see what was right in front of her. She was too busy being strong and independent and fiercely practical. What purpose had it served? Thomas would not have wanted this for her. He would have wanted her to move on. Sarah knew that to be true. Yet she chose to hide behind her commitment to him long after his death. She did not need a man, and she proved that, but wanting and needing were entirely different.

Sarah could not control the surge of emotion that was overcoming her. Tears began to form in her eyes and they fell down the side of her face as she lay on her berth. The children were fast asleep and there was no one to witness her weakness.

She was fighting herself. Everything she knew and so stubbornly held onto suddenly did not feel right any longer. She wanted to feel, she wanted to love again. She'd had all that she could ever have wanted and she had walked away from it. She thought of William asleep on the chair as she tended to her sick daughter. He was there for her and he asked for nothing in return. As she looked back, she could now see what she could not at the time. Had she hurt him as much as she was hurting now? That thought tormented her as she lay there and the tears continued to flow.

The morning brought relief for Sarah. Her body ached again from the hard berth and standing helped relieve the discomfort. They were but a few miles from the station and the car was abuzz with last minute preparations.

There were no curtains surrounding their section so they were forced to change into their good clothing in the toilet room. The children were excited and did not pay attention to their grumbling stomachs. The room was very tight and they were forced to change one at a time. Margaret and Agnes could do so on their own, but Mary had some challenges.

Sarah sent her children back to their section and then wedged herself into the tiny room. There were only a few feet between the toilet and the wall, and the area around the basin had mere inches. Keeping her skirt from falling into the toilet was a challenging task and Sarah muttered under her breath. The clothes she took off were dirty and she had no issue simply rolling them up and placing them in the sink as she finished. She brushed her hair and positioned it neatly upon her head. She was as good as she would get given the circumstances and she would need to be satisfied with what she saw.

She was surprised to see Sam sitting in her section when she returned. He, too, had changed and looked very well put together. He grinned at her as she approached.

"Good morning, Sam."

"And a good morning to you, Madam," he said cheerfully. "It would appear we are at the end of our journey."

"It would."

"I was pleased to make your acquaintance, and I do hope that I will see you again."

"Since, by your own account, your mother and my dear sister-in-law, Jane, are good friends, I am sure that is inevitable."

Sam laughed at Sarah's pointing out the obvious. "Yes, I suppose you are right."

Sam knew what she said to be true so he did not compel her any further at this point. All in due time, he thought.

"Margaret, I have something for you," Sam announced as he stood.

Margaret walked over from the adjacent section. "You do?"

"Yes, I do," Sam said as he handed a piece of paper to Margaret.

Margaret unfolded the paper to find the recipe for fudge detailed on it.

"Thank you, Sam. I so look forward to making it. I hope I can do as good a job as your grandmother."

"You are most welcome, and I have no doubt you will."

Sarah was moved by Sam's kindness. How rare, she thought.

The train's whistle blew and the train began to slow down. The children rushed to the windows to see the approaching station.

"Mama, we are here. We have arrived."

"Yes, Agnes," Sarah said with her heart in her throat. She was suddenly terrified.

Sam could see her trepidation and he reached down and placed his hand on her shoulder.

"Do not be nervous. Ten years is not that long when you are family."

Sam winked at her. How could he know what was troubling her? Was it that apparent? His words were comforting and she appreciated them.

"Thank you, Sam," Sarah said softly.

Chapter 37

The train came to a complete stop and an attendant entered the car.

"Welcome to Winnipeg. Thank you for travelling with Canadian Pacific. Please remove your belongings when you exit the train."

Sarah instructed her children to gather what was brought and then they exited the train. As Sarah stepped onto Winnipeg ground, she realized that she did not know what to expect. Would Bertie know when the train was arriving? Were they to arrange transport to his home? She simply did not know. An overwhelming sense of fear engulfed her yet again and she wavered. Sam turned to see Sarah's hesitation and placed his hand on her back and gently pushed her forward.

As Sarah reached the station door, she saw him. It was her father as plain as day. He was standing on the platform watching and waiting for her to approach. It was as though her father were standing there in the flesh. Sarah gasped. She dropped her bag and covered her mouth with her hands. She had waited so long for this and until this exact moment, she had not realized how much she missed her brother, how much she needed her brother. She ran toward him and threw her arms around his neck. She sobbed as she embraced him. She pulled back so that she could look at his face. She touched his cheeks and kissed his face. She embraced him again, not wanting to let go.

"My dear brother, how I have missed you. And dare I say you have become our father," she said, laughing through her tears.

"And you, our mother," he returned.

Sarah turned toward her children, who were standing a few feet back. They stood together, silently watching their mother's reunion. The only children who were born when Bertie was last in England, with the exception of Samuel, were too young to remember him. To them, he was a stranger – someone their mother spoke of with immense affection, but someone they had no familiarity with.

"Come here, children. Come meet your uncle."

As Sarah addressed the children, she realized that Sam was nowhere to be seen. He had slipped away unnoticed, and she felt bad that she had not said a proper good-bye.

"Well, I do not have to ask who you are," Bertie said to Samuel. "You are a spitting image of your father."

Samuel smiled proudly. "Thank you, Sir."

"And so you must be James. Another good looking fellow. Quite the handsome sons you have here, Sarah."

"Thank you, Bertie. I certainly think so."

"And you, you must be Margaret. You look just like your mother did at your age. The resemblance is uncanny," he said as he studied her face. "And you must be Agnes. You were not even born yet when I left England, and look at you. You are a beautiful young lady."

Before Bertie could even finish addressing Agnes, Mary spoke up.

"My name is Mary. I am five."

"Why, yes, you are," Bertie said laughing. "It is nice to meet you, Mary."

Bertie's eyes fell upon Florence and he looked at Sarah perplexed.

"This is Florence. She is staying with us while we deliver her to her father. I will tell you all about it later, dear brother. For now, we would just like to get settled."

Bertie nodded in agreement. "Jane is preparing breakfast for us as we speak. Hopefully, you have arrived with big appetites. I believe she is cooking enough to feed an army."

"I am hungry," Agnes said. "I could eat it all myself."

"Well, then, I shall tell Jane to make enough for two armies. Perhaps I underestimated the appetites of hungry children. Come, let us go. We are two miles from the station. We shall be there before you know it."

They made their way to the carriage, which was waiting out front. Sarah had looped her arm through her brother's tightly.

"I'm afraid our carriage could not hold us all. It is meant for two. I have hired this one for the journey. It should do nicely. Mary and Florence will need to rest on laps, but I am certain they are accustomed to that."

The carriage driver took them down Main Street. Winnipeg did not look entirely different from Ardwick. There were electric streetcars and carriages, and people bustling about. The attire was similar, as well. Were it not for the memories of the past two weeks they could have easily imagined themselves in an unfamiliar corner of Manchester. Despite the similarities, the children looked on with unbridled enthusiasm. It was, after all, the greatest adventure in the world.

"I shall look forward to hearing of your journey, but we will be home shortly so we might as well wait until we are at the table," Bertie said.

Florence sat on Sarah's lap, clinging to her, the only comfort and safety she possessed. Sarah was attentive. She would not fail this little girl. She promised herself that.

In the distance, on the other side of the railway yard, they could see the Red River. The far shore was scattered with mostly unremarkable buildings. One in particular stood out as its steeple rose majestically above all its neighbours.

"That is the cathedral in St. Boniface," Bertie pointed out. As they continued down Main Street, they crossed a bridge. A broken blanket of winter ice, its pieces fractured from the warming air, still covered most of the river that ran beneath it.

"This is the Assiniboine River. It begins just a short distance from here, from the Red River which you just saw. We had a cold winter this year and the ice persists. As you will see in a moment, the Red River is the same. Every year these rivers rise as the ice melts. We have seen some significant flooding in this city. This year they are expecting the water to crest in a week or so. It will be high. We do not know how high at this point. It is always speculation until it actually happens, but they are guessing over twenty feet."

Within a few minutes, they were crossing another river, just as Bertie had said they would. The Norwood Bridge took them over the Red River, which snaked through the city separating Norwood and St. Boniface from the rest of Winnipeg. It, too, was covered in broken ice. The river was moving quickly and the ice, when not blocked, moved with the flow.

"We have seen ice piles so large they have taken out bridges. Mother Nature is certainly a formidable opponent, I dare say."

The children listened intently, fascinated with Bertie's narrative. Sarah's fascination was, of course, much more practical.

"What happens when the river rises? Twenty feet is very high. The banks could not sustain a rise of that magnitude, I would imagine." Sarah looked concerned.

"My dear sister, it is good to see your practicality remains intact. You have not changed for your years," Bertie said, teasing his sister. "This city has seen disastrous floods through the course of time. When anticipated, residents have taken precautions. In some cases, though, the force of the river proves too strong and the water escapes the banks and into the town. Houses are built up high on basements and the basements are rarely used for anything of value, or at least not during flood season. The river is expecting to crest high this year, but not within the city itself. We should be clear."

"*Should* be clear. That is encouraging. You, too, my dear brother, have not changed. Always the eternal optimist."

Bertie could not help but laugh. "Yes, we were always decidedly different in outlook, weren't we? Despite any threat of flooding, we must look at the positive. Winter is almost over and it will be warm shortly."

They passed by St. Boniface Hospital, which sat just inside the St. Boniface boundary. They turned down Taché, at the spot where Main Street turns into Marion Street. The two short blocks to Eugenie Street passed quickly.

"And there is my office," Bertie said pointing to a building at the corner of Taché and Eugenie. The sign out front said Adamson Real Estate.

"How exciting, Bertie. You have done so well for yourself here."

Bertie beamed at Sarah's compliment. He had worked hard to pull himself up from their life growing up in Stretford. He had seen his parents struggle and was thankful he no longer had to.

"It has been a good home, Sarah. You will see so for yourself now."

They turned the corner onto Eugenie, and halfway up the block from the office they stopped in front of a white, wooden house.

"Here is home," Bertie said proudly.

"It is wonderful, Bertie."

The house was different than what they had seen in Ardwick. First, it was wooden, not brick. Second, it had an actual front yard, with a fence that ran the full width of the yard. Third, it had a covered porch that ran the width of the house. It was grand, but not ridiculously so. It was completely comfortable looking in appearance and thoroughly inviting.

"We built it two years ago. Jane has become an ardent gardener. When we are in season, the front yard is in full bloom. The colours are beautiful, extraordinary really. We love to sit on the porch and have our tea...of course, that is when the black flies and mosquitoes are not out."

"Black flies? Mosquitoes?"

"Let us save that for another time," Bertie said with a hearty laugh.

Chapter 38

As they walked up the front steps and onto the porch, Jane came through the front door. She wiped her hands on her apron and eagerly greeted her visitors.

"Sarah! How we have missed you all these years."

Jane held her arms out for a welcoming embrace and Sarah accepted wholeheartedly.

"You look absolutely wonderful," Jane said. "And after such a long journey. It has been a few years, but I remember it not being a walk in the park."

"No, it was certainly not that," Sarah said with an expression that contradicted her tone. You look well, Jane. Winnipeg must agree with you. Words cannot describe how I have missed you both."

"Goodness, there is no sense standing out here. Let us go inside and eat," Bertie suggested.

Jane stepped aside and held the door as they all walked in the house. They stood in the foyer unsure of what to do or where to go.

"Let us take your coats. This is your home now so you must watch what we do so that you can learn to take care of yourselves. I hope you will feel comfortable here. We are just so pleased that you are here," Bertie said as he took coats and hung them up on wire hangers in a coat closet near the door.

"Come, come. Let us sit down. There is plenty of time for a tour."

Jane led the way into the dining room. A large table that seated ten sat in the centre of the room. It was simple, yet elegant, and fit the house perfectly. It was certainly much larger than the two of them needed on their own and Sarah assumed they must entertain frequently. Everything was clean and new, unlike in Ardwick, where progress had blanketed the town in shades of grey. Here, progress was different. It seemed clean. White was pure and vibrant. Colours burst from every direction. It was as though Sarah were seeing colour for the first time.

"Jane, I hope it will not be a bother, but we have a guest with us for a few days. This is Florence," she said as she ran her hand over Florence's head. "We are to reunite her with her father as quickly as we can."

"Not at all. What a sweet, precious darling. Hello, Florence, welcome to our home."

Florence tucked herself into Sarah, unsure of what to think of the events and people of the last hour.

"She is a bit shy. It has been a rather trying week for her. I will explain later."

"Of course. Let me set another place. You all may sit wherever you like. Please sit."

Bertie sat at the head of the table and Jane sat at the opposite, closest to the kitchen door. In the centre of the table sat a basket of muffins and rolls, fried potatoes, bacon and scrambled eggs. The children were salivating as they waited patiently and politely for the invitation to start.

"Please help yourself. I told you Jane made enough to feed an army."

"Yes, there is no denying that," Jane chuckled.

Jane picked up the first dish and handed it to Sarah. The dishes began to be passed around and everyone filled their plates.

"That is Canadian back bacon. It is unlike anything you have had. It is simply delicious. I like to put mustard on mine. You might prefer ketchup or simply plain."

"Please share some details with me. I am so interested in hearing about your journey."

"Well, as luck would have it, we hit what they called the worst storm in years. Florence and Mary did not fare too well, I am afraid," Sarah reminisced with the wretched memories fresh in her mind. "For half the trip, we were anchored to the stateroom. The poor girls were ill beyond belief. When the skies cleared, it was a moment for rejoicing."

"What a pity. I do remember our journey and it was just as unfavourable. I, too, could keep nothing down. I must admit I have a rather sensitive stomach," Jane confessed.

"I would like to hear about your lives in Ardwick. Please tell me. James, I hear that you are quite the sculptor. Very skilled. Your grandfather was a skilled craftsman. A friend of mine owns a cabinetry business and I am certain we can obtain some wood from him."

"Uncle Bertie, will I go to school?" Margaret asked, unsure.

"Of course, starting Monday. School is not a question. It is a must. It is not the old world. Girls are as capable as boys. Girls may do whatever they choose in life. But you must learn before you can choose properly. Margaret, what do you have a passion for?"

Margaret hesitated. What was her passion? It had definitely changed. That she knew.

"I wanted to be a doctor. Now I am not so sure."

Sarah's eyes widened. "You never told me that," she said to her daughter. Margaret's blank expression was a crushing blow to her heart.

"I am unsure of what I wish to do now. I do love to cook. That is my favourite thing."

"Yes, your mother told us that you are gifted in the culinary arts. I do look forward to learning from you. I am good with the basics, but I am afraid I have not been too adventurous."

"Aunt Jane, I do believe you most definitely have more to teach me than the other way around."

"I would not be so sure, Margaret. I did not learn from a French chef." Jane winked at Margaret, who blushed in response. She had never really considered herself a fortunate person before that moment.

"Agnes and Mary, you will go to the Norwood school, and Margaret, you will go to St. Joseph's School in St. Boniface. It teaches the secondary grades."

"James, you, too, will go to school in St. Boniface. Provencher School is a fine school. I give you the same advice as your sister. There is so much for you to learn and so much that you can accomplish with your life, and you cannot choose until you have an education. You will have to work hard to catch up on what you have missed, but I have no doubt you will rise to the challenge."

James nodded at his uncle, wide-eyed. That was the last thing James expected to hear. He had no reason to believe his life would be any different than it was in Ardwick.

"And, Samuel, you are a man now. There is no more school for you. How would you like to work with me in my office? Business has been brisk and I am in need of another office clerk. You would be able to learn the business, and then eventually work directly with clients if you chose to. Does that sound appealing to you?"

Samuel had only ever known hard labour. He had spent the last few weeks focused on less cumbersome pursuits and it suited him entirely.

"Most definitely. Thank you."

"Very well then, I think that we are mostly sorted. Well, with the exception of our dear Sarah, whom we will sort out promptly after breakfast." Bertie acknowledged his sister with a grin and continued. "Now, let me lay out the plans for the rest of the day. Once we get you all familiarized with your new home, we will get you properly groomed and attired. Samuel and James, I have you scheduled with my barber this afternoon for a haircut and a shave. James, are you shaving yet?"

James shook his head as his face turned a dozen shades of red.

"All right, then it will be a haircut for you. From there, the tailors. I know that your mother is a skilled seamstress, but it will be weeks until she will be in a position to provide you with some fresh clothing. And, for your girls, Jane will take you to the dress shop around the corner. While it is not of the same calibre as your mother's dresses, I believe it will do for the time being."

Sarah could not believe all that her brother had done. He had thought of everything. Sarah was half settled and had not needed to lift a finger to do so.

"Bertie, I do not know what to say. You have done so much for us. Thank you. But you need not trouble yourself with the expense of clothing. I will be able to sew what we need, in short order. I am fortunate in that Eleanor was able to leave a small sum to me when she passed. It will provide me with the materials I need."

"I have no doubt you can, but you are in my home and it is my prerogative to indulge my family. Is it not?"

Sarah could not disagree. Not only would it be rude, but it felt good to have her big brother looking out for her.

"As a first step in explaining the workings of your new home, let me introduce another member of the family to you. Gwendolyn, please come out here."

The kitchen door opened and an older lady appeared. She stood in the doorway, smiling at the group.

"This is Gwendolyn. She is our housekeeper, but is more like family to us. She has been with us for five years now. We could not imagine running this house without her. You will see her Tuesdays, Wednesdays, and Fridays during the day."

"Hello. I have heard much about you all. I wish you well in Canada. I believe you will all love it here as much as we do."

"Thank you, Gwendolyn. We are happy to be here," Sarah said appreciatively.

"Now let us now see the rest of the house," Bertie directed.

"Children, please take your plates into the kitchen," Sarah ordered. "Jane, thank you. It was absolutely delicious."

Jane nodded her appreciation. "You are most welcome. You have made me very happy by joining us here. A welcome meal was the least I could do. And I look forward to many more meals together."

"Well, let us tour the kitchen first then. Bring your plates in."

They all picked up their plates and made their way into the kitchen. It was a spacious room with sunlight streaming through a large window above the sink. There was a small table sitting off to the side. It was a fine looking kitchen, as far as Margaret was concerned.

"Margaret, since you will be most concerned about the workings of the kitchen, you will be pleased to know we have all of the modern conveniences. We have a double gas stove and oven. We also have an electric icebox to keep our produce and meat fresh. There is plenty of pantry space for non-perishables, and we have a garden in the back for vegetables and herbs. And last but not least we have fresh eggs daily. We keep our own chickens in the back. We shall introduce you to them shortly."

"You have chickens?" Agnes was astonished. She felt it was too fantastic.

"Chickens?"

"Yes, Mary. And there are some baby chicks out there that need naming. I should think that you and Agnes shall be well able to do so."

"Now let us show you to your rooms. Before we do, let's remove your dirty clothing from your bags. Gwendolyn will be doing laundry this afternoon and she can clean those up."

There was a small staircase leading to the upstairs, just off the kitchen, but Jane led them to the main staircase that ascended directly in front of the front door. It was a handsome staircase, and much like the house, was not ostentatious. The railing was elegant in its simplicity. On the walls along the staircase were no elaborate paintings. Hung were framed photographs, including one of Bertie and Jane at a lake. It was all quite comfortable and it made Sarah smile.

"Boys, let us show you to your room first."

Their room, at the end of the hall, housed two single beds, one on each side of the room. Beside each bed was a small table with an electric lamp. At the foot of each bed was a bureau for clothing. The bed coverings were a masculine navy blue, as were the shades covering the lamps. It was a simple room, yet comfortable and functional for two boys.

"What do you think? I hope it is to your liking," Bertie asked.

The boys turned around in their new room, absorbing its newness, and were very pleased by what they saw.

"Thank you, Uncle Bertie. This is splendid."

"You are most welcome. I am pleased that you like it."

"And girls, for you...."

Jane led the girls to the next room. It was a bit larger. And, in contrast to the boys, it was adorned in pink from top to bottom. There was a single bed on one side of the room, and on the other were single beds stacked like berths on a ship. Each bed was blanketed with a lacy pink bedcovering. Even the curtains were pink. Agnes and Mary could not contain their excitement. Margaret, on the other hand, thought to herself that she was more of a navy girl than a pink girl, but she smiled in appreciation, nevertheless.

"I will leave it to you girls to decide who sleeps on the top. Margaret, I presumed you would sleep on your own over there."

"Thank you, Aunt Jane and Uncle Bertie." Margaret kissed them both on the cheek.

"Sarah, now for your room...."

Sarah's room sat beside Jane and Bertie's room, which was across the hall from the children's. It was the smallest of the rooms, but it was Sarah's alone. She had not had a room that was not shared with a child in many years, and that thought alone transformed the tiny room into a palace. The bed was a double, not a single, and it was covered in a cream coloured duvet that looked like a cloud. It was simple yet elegant, and Sarah wanted to slide into it at that very moment. Her room also possessed another thing that the others did not...a chair. It looked indescribably comfortable, cushioned all over. It was for Sarah alone, to find peace and solitude away from the trials of daily life. That Jane and Bertie would have thought of this for her warmed her heart immensely.

"There is no need for tears, dear sister. I have not done anything for you that you do not deserve. I am happy to be able to do so."

"As you can see, we have indoor plumbing upstairs as well, which I can say is very nice during the cold winter months. And, before we go back downstairs, I have a gift for the children."

Out of the closet, Jane retrieved two dolls, one for Agnes and Mary, and journals for each of the others.

"You now have a private journal to write about your experiences. While you may not realize it now, you will cherish the memories when you are older. At some point memories fade; the written word does not. Mary and Agnes, you are too young for journals. I hope you both like dolls."

Mary hugged her doll tightly. Their smiles were Jane's answer.

"I am so sorry I do not have anything for young Florence. I was not expecting her. Hmm, let me think."

Jane paused for a moment as she thought of a solution. She could not bear the thought of the young girl going without.

"I have it. Just one moment."

Jane returned from her room with a stuffed dog. She was unclear what breed it was, but it did not matter. It was small, soft, and cuddly. She handed it to Florence, who took it gently from Jane's hand. She looked at it, turning it over to see it from all sides, and then she tucked it under her neck and buried her face in it. Jane looked down at Florence, completely taken with how precious she was. She had wanted for a child for so long and continued to satisfy her maternal longing by spending time with the children at the hospital. But, with Florence, that longing made an overwhelming sadness all the more agonizing. Sarah could see the pain on Jane's face and it broke her heart.

"I volunteer in the children's ward at the hospital and I like to take in something when I can."

"Now Jane will take you into the yard and introduce you to the chickens and horse, while I take your mother to my office. I have something to show her."

"Margaret, will you please watch Florence? Florence, I will be back shortly."

"Florence, would you like to come with me?" Jane asked hopefully.

Florence held out her arms without hesitation and Jane teared up. As Jane took the children to the backyard, Bertie walked Sarah toward the office. Directly across from the house was a large park that extended the entire block. Bertie's office occupied the corner and was surrounded by park where it was not surrounded by street.

"That is Coronation Park. It comes alive in the Spring and summer. As you can see from the temperature today, we will have a rather short Spring. Flowers will be in bloom within a week or two. You can start to see the tulips rising now. It is a bit later than usual. There are benches in the park if you are ever in need of peace and quiet."

"It is certainly larger than Ardwick Green, and from what I can see it is much lovelier. I shall look forward to seeing it in bloom."

The walk to the office took mere moments. It was Friday and the office was open for business. Bertie would usually be hard at work, but he had taken the day to spend with Sarah. As they entered the front door, a middle-aged woman with greying features stood and approached them.

"Good morning, Mr. Adamson. And this must be Sarah. Sarah, pleased to meet you. I am Mary. How was your journey?"

"Sarah, this is Mary Goodall. She is my secretary. She makes this office run without issue and keeps me organized. I could not manage without her."

Mary stood taller with pride at Bertie's words of praise. She looked at her boss with appreciation. It was clear she respected Bertie and it made Sarah proud.

"Pleased to meet you as well. The journey was good, thank you. I'm certainly glad it is over, though. We are most happy to be here."

Bertie introduced Sarah to the two other people in the office. One was a clerk and another was a sales representative.

"Business has been brisk and is growing. I will bring Samuel in tomorrow to show him around. And now I have something to show you."

Bertie took Sarah into a room off to the side, directly beside his own office. He turned the light on to a room that was mostly empty. At the front of the room was a storefront, similar to the one at the front of

Bertie's office, but much smaller. Window coverings blocked the view to the outside.

"That is what I want to show you, Sarah. That there, in the corner, is yours."

"I do not understand. What do you mean? What is?"

"It is all explained in here," Bertie said as he handed Sarah an envelope. "I will leave you to read it. I will be at my desk. You can retrieve me when you are done."

Sarah took the paper hesitantly. What could it be and why would it be for her? She saw a chair in the room and took a seat. She took a piece of paper out of the envelope and began to read.

My dearest Sarah,

I trust that your journey was comfortable and that you have made it to your brother's home in good health. I can imagine your reunion would have been a sweet one for you and it gives me great pleasure to think of your joy.

To help you get started with your new life, I have sent along a few items. A seamstress cannot be without a sewing machine, and I have made sure that you do not have to be. A seamstress can also not be without fabric, and I have provided enough to get you started. I am confident the designs of Sarah Berry will be in demand by the good women of Norwood before long.

I wish you well, Sarah. You are dearly missed.

Your loving friend,

William Markley

Sarah could not breathe. The weight on her chest was crushing, and she clutched it. She whispered William's name with the little air that she could draw in and then held her breath to stop the tears. But her desire to be strong was no match for her feelings. It had been building and a release was inevitable.

The tears poured as Sarah thought of William. How she missed him. She was happy to be here, but it did not make her loss any more bearable. She fought to compose herself, wiping her eyes with her sleeve. When she could see clearly again, she inspected the delivery. A large crate with the Markley name stamped on the side contained the sewing machine, Sarah presumed. Beside it sat a large container, even larger than the crate. Sarah lifted the lid and saw rolls of fabric. Sarah counted twelve large rolls. She was aghast at the thought of the cost, and even more so at the consideration. He was now thousands upon thousands of miles away and whatever she thought was irrelevant.

Once she felt confident that she could speak clearly, she returned to Bertie. He stood as she entered the room, aware that her eyes were red and swollen. He did not comment, but merely looked on with brotherly concern. It was clear to him that his sister was in deep pain and that

William was the reason. He could only hope that her new life in Canada would make her forget all that she left behind.

"I have made arrangements to turn that room into a shop for you. It will not take that much effort. The storefront already exists."

"Bertie, I could not impose like that. And, more importantly, I do not have the money to rent a place such as this."

"Rent? Don't be silly. I own the building. It is sitting empty now, as you can plainly see. You would be doing me a favour. When business becomes profitable, you can pay rent. Until then, you will help bring business to my office. Jane has more than enough friends who are all looking for a brilliant dressmaker. It is not a skill that is aplenty in Norwood, I am afraid."

"I do not know what to say. You are too good to me. Thank you. I will pay you as soon as I am able."

"You were never good at accepting support, were you? Your friend William must care about you very deeply, as do I. We both want you to flourish, my dear, and you will."

Sarah smiled at her brother and kissed him on the cheek.

"I love you dearly, Bertie. I do. You are a good brother and I have missed you so."

"Enough talk. Let us return home." Bertie did not want his sister to feel indebted to him. "But, before we do, please share young Florence's circumstance with me. What brought her under your care?"

"As unfathomable as it is, I did not know Florence before the journey. Her father left for Canada a few months past and she and her mother were joining him. From what I understand, he works for the Hudson's Bay Company here in Winnipeg. Florence's mother was heavy with child and the circumstance was less than favourable."

Bertie interrupted his sister. He could not believe what he was hearing. "I do not understand. Surely, you could not be telling me that she died on the ship?"

Sarah dropped her head as the memories returned. It was something she would not ever forget. She could still feel the warmth of Hannah's blood on her hands and the look of helplessness on her face.

"I wish I did not have to, but I cannot do otherwise. We encountered a bitter storm and no assistance was available."

"Surely, under such dire circumstances, medical assistance would have been available."

"You would think so, but that was not the case. Both Florence and Mary became terribly ill with the motion. We did not leave the stateroom for days. Hannah could not manage, given her condition. She went into labour, but the baby did not come. Margaret and I did the best we could."

"*You and Margaret did the best you could?!* You cannot mean that you attempted to deliver the baby yourselves?"

"We did. It was not our choice. We could not let them perish. In the end, it was God's will. And I made a promise to Hannah that I would deliver her daughter to the girl's father. I must find him."

Bertie's face was white. It was beyond comprehension that something like that could happen in this day and age.

"I will help you find him. We will go this afternoon. Their main office in Winnipeg is at Main and York. We passed directly by it this morning."

The children were helping Jane prepare lunch. Jane had advised them it was called lunch in Canada and not luncheon as it was in England. It was one of many differences that they would learn over time, she said.

"Mama, did you know that Aunt Jane and Uncle Bertie bought us a rabbit? We named it Snowflake, after Philip's rabbit."

"They did?" Sarah looked at her brother with yet another look of surprise.

"The horse's name is Teapot. She is just splendid," Agnes beamed. "I fed her an apple."

"We have certainly had our fill of excitement today, have we not? And what of Florence?"

Florence was beside Jane, kneeling on a chair against the counter, and clutching her stuffed dog. She was completely and entirely focused on Jane, who was slicing a large ham. Jane cut off a small piece and gave it to Florence, who accepted it eagerly. The look that passed between them was of absolute adoration. It was as though there was no one else in the room, as though nothing existed beyond that moment.

"Well, I would say it appears Florence is quite content at the moment," Bertie said. "And dare I say my lovely wife, as well."

Jane did not even hear her husband's comments to acknowledge them. She was too focused on the young girl who had stolen her heart.

As they finished their lunch, Bertie advised the children of the slight change of plans.

"Your mother and I have an errand to run in Winnipeg. We shan't be too long. Samuel and James, you can attend the barber shop on your own. It is but a few short blocks from here. Andrew is expecting you and he will put the charges on my account. We shall be back by the time you return. If we have time, we can go to the tailors and dress shop. If not, we have tomorrow."

Chapter 39

Bertie's backyard was surprisingly large, many times larger than the front. Teapot was feeding when Bertie retrieved her for the journey. She appeared to have a good disposition, coming without any fuss at all. Bertie led her into the carriage house and secured her to the carriage.

"The office is but a mile from here. We would enjoy the walk were it a bit warmer."

The front of the Hudson's Bay Company building was purposed for its retail business, and the rest for storage and for office use.

"I have provided location assistance for Hudson's Bay employees. There are a few people I know who may be able to assist us."

They parked the carriage around the side, on York Street, and entered through the office doors. They were greeted by a receptionist as they did. She sat at a desk, not far from the entrance.

"May I help you?"

"Most definitely," Bertie said. "I am looking to speak with Mr. Hargreaves. He is not expecting me today, but it is most urgent that I speak with him."

"May I inquire as to the business you wish to speak with him about?"

"Most certainly. My name is Albert Adamson. I have real estate dealings with Mr. Hargreaves and I am seeking his assistance with locating an employee of this company."

"Oh, I see. Please have a seat, Mr. Adamson. I will inquire as to Mr. Hargreaves' availability."

"Thank you. I would be most appreciative."

Bertie and Sarah sat down in the reception room. In front of them sat a table which was covered in copies of their current retail advertisements. As Sarah looked through the merchandise, Bertie could hear the receptionist speaking on the telephone with what he presumed was an operator. A few moments later, the door opened and a distinguished looking gentleman entered the reception area.

"Bertie, so nice to see you today. To what do I owe this unexpected pleasure?"

Bertie and Sarah stood as he walked over. Bertie shook his hand and introduced Nigel to Sarah.

"Pleased to meet you, Mrs. Berry." Sarah smiled and shook Mr. Hargreaves' hand.

"Nigel, would it be possible to have a word in private? It is a most urgent matter and we are hopeful for your assistance," Bertie asked.

"Yes, of course. Come this way."

Nigel Hargreaves was a senior employee with the Hudson's Bay Company. His responsibility was to ensure the company was supported by the right employees. In other words, if any person at the company should know where John Nightingale was it would be Nigel Hargreaves.

Mr. Hargreaves led them down a hallway and into a room with a table and four chairs. It was a simple room, and clearly one meant for business discussions.

"I hope that you and Jane are both well," he asked. Sarah could see that they were friendly, perhaps friends, in addition to being business acquaintances.

"We are. Thank you for asking. I apologize for dropping in unexpectedly like this. I understand your schedule does not allow for such drop-ins, but our matter is most urgent."

Bertie explained the circumstance as Nigel Hargreaves looked on with an expression similar to the one Bertie wore when Sarah explained it to him.

"That is dreadful. Most certainly I will do what I can. Mrs. Berry, what is John's full name, and do you know what division he is working in?"

"I am sorry to say that I do not. His late wife only told me that he came to work for the Hudson's Bay Company in Winnipeg a few months past. He came seeking work and found it here. She also said that he was with a large group of men that had found employment together. I fear that is not very helpful. I do know his full name is John Nightingale. The family Bible, which I am in possession of, shows his date of birth as February 23, 1880. That would put him at twenty-four years old at present."

"Please follow me to my office. We can search the ledgers for your John Nightingale."

Sarah and Bertie followed Mr. Hargreaves to his office. It was a large office with shelves upon shelves of ledgers. Maps covered the walls, each full of coloured pins that clearly had some significance to their location.

"Now, four months past, we hired a group of young men to help with the expansion of one of our railway lines up north. That seems like our best bet."

Mr. Hargreaves retrieved a specific ledger from his shelf and placed it on his desk. He shuffled through a few pages, running his finger down the rows as he looked for a specific name. His brow became furrowed as he reached the end of the list.

"He was not part of the group to which I was speaking. But hope is not lost. We will find him if he works for this company."

Another ledger was reviewed and placed back on the shelf. Sarah's concern mounted. Would she find John? What would become of Florence if she could not?

Mr. Hargreaves tapped on his cheek as he continued to exhaust all thoughts that would lead him to the mysterious John Nightingale.

"I'm afraid, Mrs. Berry, I do not seem to have any record of your John Nightingale, present or past. I do wish I could have been of assistance, but alas it appears I am not able to be."

Sarah was lost in despair. Florence needed her father, and he most definitely would want her.

"Thank you for your assistance, Mr. Hargreaves," Sarah said as she stood.

"Might I suggest you take out an advertisement in the local newspaper? Perhaps with some good fortune your Mr. Nightingale will see it."

"That is a splendid idea," Bertie said. "We will get right on that."

Sarah felt utterly defeated. Her heart ached for Florence and for a man whom she had never met before. But the road had led her to where she now stood and she knew she must not give up.

Mr. Hargreaves escorted Sarah and Bertie out of his office and into the reception area. As they were about to leave the building, they were stopped.

"Bertie!" Nigel shouted.

Bertie and Sarah stopped and turned. Nigel was waving his hand.

"Just a moment. I had another thought. Please allow me to check one last avenue."

Hope flooded Sarah and she looked at her brother with a renewed look of resolve. Failure be damned, she thought.

"Please have a seat. I will be back shortly. I need to visit one of my clerks who is restoring a ledger that was damaged."

Sarah's heart raced with hope. Mr. Hargreaves returned ten minutes later. His face registered neither victory nor defeat, and Sarah was forced to wait through his rambling explanation before she could determine which outcome she faced.

"Bertie, Mrs. Berry," Nigel said out of breath, "it occurred to me that a group of men that were hired to accompany shipments of supplies up north were listed in a journal that had been damaged. One of my clerks was working on it and it was therefore not in my office. It was only half restored and therefore finding the name was not easy."

"Excuse me, Mr. Hargreaves. Are you saying you found his name?" Sarah dared not hope, but hope was all that remained.

"I am, Mrs. Berry. He is currently in Churchill. He rides the line taking supplies up north and brings goods back down. He is one day gone and one day back. I can arrange for a message to be delivered to him if you like. It would be the most direct way for you to reach him."

"Thank you so much, Mr. Hargreaves," Sarah could not hide her emotion. "You have just made a father and daughter very happy. I am most grateful for your assistance."

"Mrs. Berry, I am pleased to have been able to assist. If you would like to write a message to Mr. Nightingale, you can give it to Miss Andrews here and she will have it delivered to me. I will ensure Mr. Nightingale receives it with his pay tomorrow."

Both Sarah and the receptionist acknowledged Mr. Hargreaves direction with a nod. Once Sarah completed her message, she and Bertie returned home. Finding John Nightingale was entirely bittersweet. It was with great sadness that she would say good-bye to Florence, but it was with great joy that she would have fulfilled a promise to a dying woman.

Upon returning home, Sarah was pleasantly surprised to see her sons, freshly home from the barbershop.

"Well, look at you two. Two handsome boys if ever there were any."

"Handsome? Yes, faces a mother could love or perhaps faces *only* a mother could love," Margaret teased.

James shot his sister a look of contempt. Samuel laughed, appreciating the quality of the shot. Sarah simply rolled her eyes.

As they were sitting down to their afternoon tea, there was a knock at the door. Bertie excused himself to see who was there. He returned with a parcel and an envelope.

"I was instructed that the parcel was for Margaret and the envelope was for Sarah."

Both women looked at each other with surprise. Margaret was blank in thought. Sarah wondered if it could possibly be from William. Her heart raced as it had earlier.

Margaret opened up the bag. Inside was a large chicken, a bundle of rosemary, garlic, and two jars of mustard. There was a note tucked inside. Margaret opened it, but she knew who it must be from.

"Margaret, I hope you are enjoying your first day here. I am enclosing the ingredients for your favourite meal. I told you that one day I would love to taste your cooking, and it appears I will get the opportunity sooner than expected. Your Aunt Jane has invited me to dinner tomorrow evening. I would so like to try your roasted mustard chicken. I do hope that you allow me the honour.

Your friend in cooking,
Sam

"Mama, did you see what Sam sent me? Aunt Jane, can I cook it for tomorrow evening? Sam mentioned you invited him to dinner."

"Ma, I forgot to mention that we saw Sam at the barber's. Aunt Jane invited him to dinner tomorrow evening."

"Yes, James, I just read the same," Sarah said, holding up her note. "How nice."

"What a coincidence that you would meet Sam on the train. He is such a nice man," Jane said. "And certainly pleasant on the eyes," Jane whispered as she walked by Sarah.

"Yes, of course my dear, you may cook that chicken. That is what Sam had hoped when he sent it over. We all look forward to it. You will just need to let me know what else you are in need of. The kitchen will be yours. Sam said that he would bring a dessert, so that is one less thing that you need to worry about."

Margaret felt a sudden pang of self-consciousness. Sam spoke of cooking as though he had great experience. Margaret was as nervous cooking for Sam as she would have been cooking for Chef Nicolas. She could not fail. It must be perfect.

The remainder of the afternoon was spent at the tailor and dress shops. The girls were able to find dresses that fit them right off the rack. They were bright and cheerful and precisely what they needed to welcome them to a new home. Jane spent extra time with Florence, helping her find something that was acceptable to the whims of a two year old.

And while the girls walked away with a new dress to wear for dinner on Saturday, James and Samuel required fitting and would receive their new pants, shirt, and jacket in a week's time.

After dinner that evening, once the children had retired to their beds, Sarah and Bertie shared the details of their day with Jane. She tried to remain strong and happy for Florence, but her disappointment was as clear on her face as was her desire to have children. She loved them and if there was a single person on this earth that should be so blessed, Sarah thought it should be Jane.

"It has been a very long day and I think I might retire to my room and send William a thank-you letter for his kind gesture."

"Yes, kind gesture indeed. I do not recall a *friend* ever managing such a kind gesture for me. It is extraordinarily romantic, if I do say so."

Sarah found herself blushing at Jane's comment. She dared to hope that his gesture was out of more than friendship, but she had lived her life a prisoner of her own circumstance and this circumstance was no different. She was far too practical to think otherwise, yet she could not stop herself from feeling it.

"Good night and thank you so much for all that you have both done for us."

"My dear sister, you do not need to thank me. It is I who should thank you, thank you for all that you did for our mother after I was gone. I have missed you so and having you here is splendid. It was a long and tiresome journey, but one that will be amply rewarded, I do believe."

Sarah smiled at her brother. He had always believed that, while we cannot decide on the circumstance to which we are born, we have it within our power to change it.

There was silence upstairs. Sarah peeked in the rooms to check on her sleeping children. Florence would not sleep in Sarah's room by herself and fussed until Margaret brought her into bed with her. She was nestled up to Margaret like a doll. She looked safe and loved, just the way a young child should.

As Sarah retired to her room, the emptiness was welcoming. She could not remember the last time she was able to savour solitude. She sank into her chair and began to write with the letter paper that Jane had given her.

"My dearest William,

Words cannot describe my appreciation for your kind gesture. Your thoughtfulness has warmed my heart immensely and I must thank you from the bottom of my heart.

I so look forward to sewing again. It feels as though it has been a lifetime. My brother, Bertie, has offered me a storefront in his building, and with God's blessing I shall be in business soon.

Our ship journey was dreadfully rough. Mary did not fare well, but she recovered quickly. Unfortunately, a young woman whom we shared our stateroom with did not. She died during childbirth and I am now in possession of her young daughter, hoping to reunite her with her father in Winnipeg. She is a sweet, young girl, and dare I say I have become quite attached to her.

Our train journey was uneventful. Canada's countryside is absolutely spectacular. Words cannot do it justice. It is my hope that one day you can see it.

Thank you again for your kindness and friendship. I miss you incredibly and you are always in my thoughts.

Your loving friend,

Sarah

Sarah sealed it in the envelope that Jane had given her and she planned to post it the following day. As she was changing into her bed clothes, she remembered another note. She had completely forgotten about Sam's note and she retrieved it from her pocket so she could read it again.

"My new friend Sarah,

How nice it was to meet you on the train. You brightened the long journey immensely.

I have been invited to dine with your family tomorrow evening and I hope that is acceptable to you. I certainly look forward to it myself.

And if it is not too forward to say so, I also look forward to getting to know you better.

Your new friend,

Sam Warman

So, that was Sam's name, Sarah thought. Sam's note was ambiguous. Was it merely friendship he was seeking or was it more? But Sarah began to feel as though his intentions were not the same as hers, and that his feelings were more than she could reciprocate, and she began to worry about the result.

Sarah's eyes became heavy and she climbed into her new bed. Her body and mind were exhausted from the activities of the day, yet she lay there, unable to find sleep. There was so much to do and the thought overwhelmed her. Could she manage a business on her own? She never had done so before. Eleanor was the businesswoman and she simply did as she was told.

Sarah had been too busy with the journey to think about how she would support her family once she settled in Winnipeg. The thought of her own dress shop had not even occurred to her. It seemed everyone around her had more confidence in her than she had in herself. And now, it appeared, her future was being laid out in front of her.

With the exception of William, she did not miss her old home. She had reconciled her decision and was practical in the knowledge that the memories and feelings would fade. Until then, the pain was hers alone.

Sleep did come, and when it did she slept as soundly as she had in recent memory. She awoke refreshed, unaware of the time. She dressed for the day and made her way downstairs. Much to Sarah's surprise, everyone was at breakfast and long engaged in conversation.

"Well, good morning, Sleepy," Bertie said jokingly. "So nice of you to join us."

Sarah stood there, unable to speak. She could not comprehend the discourtesy of sleeping beyond everyone else in the house. That did not happen...ever.

"I am sorry to have slept this late. It is unacceptable. What time is it?"

"Yes, it is horrendously unacceptable, quite rude in fact. She should be ashamed of herself, shouldn't she?" Jane said jokingly to Florence, who sat on her lap.

They all burst into laughter. Nothing could be funnier to Sarah's children. How fitting that their mother could be mocked for doing something so simple and completely acceptable in their eyes.

Sarah realized that she was being uptight, and was fairly certain that it happened far too often.

"It is half past eight, hardly late enough to be considered rude, and certainly acceptable considering the journey that you have just placed behind you," Bertie said, matter-of-factly. "I do hope that you had a good sleep."

Sarah took her place at the table. "I did, indeed. Thank you. Clearly, that bed is a bit too comfortable," she said with a smile.

"While there is not much food left for you, I do feel I was successful in keeping your children from eating the table. Their appetites are extraordinary," Bertie said as he winked at them.

Sarah was unsure if she should laugh or hide in shame. Bertie was clearly less formal than she was. It was his home and his choice, and she was in no position to demand otherwise. And while it was not her way, she had to admit to herself that it felt good to relax, just ever so slightly.

Later that day, Bertie showed Samuel the office. It was Saturday and the office clerical staff were not working. They worked Monday through Friday and it was perhaps one of the reasons why they were as loyal to Bertie as they were. Bertie treated his staff with respect. He did not overwork them and he respected family commitments. When Mary's son was sick, Bertie allowed her to take the day off with pay to attend to him. The others in the office all helped to cover her responsibilities, knowing that it could just as easily have been them who required the support.

Andrew, Bertie's real estate representative, was also in, preparing to show a property to a client. Bertie had Samuel sit with him, watching his activities. It was Bertie's plan to have Samuel move into that role once he learned how the office worked.

Jane walked the girls to their new school. Inside the fenced yard, there was a large field, and a playground with swings and two seesaws. It was a small school, but Norwood, by historical standards, was very young. The school was but two years old, and undoubtedly the growth of the town would force expansion.

While Samuel got accustomed to his new place of employment, Sarah spent her time in her new store organizing her inventory and equipment. It would be some time before she could entertain clients at her shop. It would cost money for racks, furniture, and construction work for dressing rooms. Prior to that, she would plan on meeting people in their homes.

Margaret respectfully declined Jane's offer to show her to her own school. She could not possibly think about that while she was so preoccupied with the preparations for the evening meal. After perusing the cupboards, Margaret created a list of what would be needed. Jane explained where the market was. It was quite simple, she had said. "Just around the corner from Uncle Bertie's office, on Taché, a mere three blocks away."

In a cluster were a butcher shop, a bakery, and a grocery store. The Adamsons had accounts with each. Margaret purchased potatoes, carrots, and dried thyme, the outstanding items she required to complete the meal.

As Margaret walked back, she stopped in at Uncle Bertie's office. Bertie heard the door chime and came out to see who had arrived.

"Hello, Margaret. There is not much going on today, but it can be positively exciting when it is busy. Would you like to see your mother?"

Bertie led Margaret into Sarah's new shop. Sarah had not told Margaret of her *delivery*. It had been a busy day and the right time had not presented itself.

"What is all of this, Mama?"

"This was a gift from a gracious friend."

Margaret looked surprised. "Gift? From whom? What is it?"

"It is a sewing machine, and enough material to help me get started with a dressmaking business...."

Margaret interrupted her mother. "Who on earth would be this generous? Uncle Bertie?"

"No, Margaret, it was not I."

Margaret looked as confused as ever. Whomever could they be speaking of?

"William Markley," Sarah divulged, shyly.

"William? Markley? *Really*?"

"I, too, am as surprised as you are, Margaret."

"No, Mama, I am not surprised. I am only surprised that you are. Did you not see the way William looked at you? Clearly, it was only you who was blind to his feelings."

Sarah was taken aback by her daughter's bold conjecture. Bertie walked out of the room, laughing as he did. He was amused by his sister's astonishment, and even more so by her daughter's confident opinions.

"Margaret, you speak of fantasy." She did not get upset with her daughter. She was too off-centre from her comments to chastise her for her boldness.

"Now, you best get back. I am sure you have much to do to prepare for dinner."

Sarah was clearly changing the subject and Margaret decided it was best to leave her mother to her thoughts. She knew enough to know that was the most prudent course of action.

"Mama, I shall see you shortly for lunch then."

As Sarah returned home, Florence was in the front yard with Jane helping to prepare the garden for the impending bloom of the season. The remnants of winter were being raked up and piled off to the side. Spring pruning was performed on the bushes that demanded it, and the grass was raked of what had not survived the previous season, protecting what lay underneath from being choked of light and air.

"It is a marvellous day for gardening," Sarah said as she entered the yard. "My mother used to love gardening. She would say that to get your hands soiled in God's earth was to get close to Him."

"I remember," Jane said with a smile. "She had a talent for gardening that I do not. I merely putter, but I do love to do so."

"And how are you doing, Florence? You look as though you have become a good helper."

Florence looked up at Sarah with a smile that only a two year old could manage. It was pure and simple. She looked as though she was right at home in Jane's yard, and Sarah hoped that her new home would be as welcoming.

"I'll be in shortly to help prepare lunch. We will eat about two. If we eat any earlier, the children will be hungry before we serve dinner. Sam is working in his father's shop until five and we won't be able to eat before seven."

"I'm assuming his parents will be joining us."

"No, they had a previous engagement. It was all rather short notice. We ran into Sam, and to my surprise Samuel had met him before. He did inquire as to how you were settling in. I thought it would be nice for him to see for himself."

Sarah knew that she should prepare herself for more of this loving and kind-hearted meddling. It was inevitable. Both Bertie and Jane loved her and they wanted her to be happy. But Sarah did not need any matchmaking in her life. She had more than enough to satisfy her.

"A simple 'very well' would have sufficed. There is nothing that he could see in person that would not have sufficed in word."

"Oh Sarah, you can never have enough friends...especially when you are new in town. This evening's dinner is no more than an opportunity for you to expand your circles."

Sarah realized her comment could have been construed as rude and ungrateful and she attempted to reverse its effect. But nothing could reverse the tone of her voice. Jane sensed Sarah's trepidation.

"You are right. Thank you for thinking of me. It was thoughtful and I do appreciate it."

It was Sarah's desire to return to Bertie's office after lunch. She wished to prepare a list of the items that she required and the tasks that she needed to complete before she could open fully for business.

"Agnes, Mary, and Florence, you girls can come with me to your Uncle Bertie's office. I do not want you to be a burden on your Aunt Jane. She is busy enough without having to worry about you."

"Nonsense. No burden at all. Bertie is going back to the office and I can spend the afternoon with the girls. We have eggs to gather and a chicken coop to clean. I'm quite confident that a certain rabbit also needs to be fed." The girls nodded with more enthusiasm and Sarah realized that she had been outdone.

"So long as long as you are not in the way. Please be helpful and do what Aunt Jane asks of you."

"Yes, Mama."

Bertie's office was quiet after lunch. Andrew had already left to tend to clients and it was only Sarah and Bertie who remained. Bertie had his own work to tend to and Sarah sat at a desk with a pen and paper and proceeded to build her requirements. She thought back to Eleanor's shop. How did it look, and what had filled its walls? Another thought overcame her...what on earth would she name it? She couldn't be so bold as to name it after herself. All these thoughts weighed her down and she began to feel that her lack of confidence and experience would be her undoing.

"How is your list progressing, Sarah?" Bertie inquired.

Sarah sighed and looked at her brother blankly.

"That well?" he questioned sarcastically. "Let's see what we have so far."

Bertie reviewed the list. He paused and then reviewed it again. He looked at his sister with a look that Sarah could not discern.

"What? Is my inexperience that apparent? Am I doomed to fail before I even begin?"

"You were always the one who was convinced it would rain, even when the sky was blue. It appears you are still the same ten year old who told me that I was wasting my time believing I could rise above Stretford. I believe your words were, 'You must know your place, Bertie – you are here because God has decided it be so.' I will never forget it. I remember clearly because I was shocked that a girl so young could be so fixed in opinion."

Sarah looked horrified, and Bertie felt bad for making her feel so.

"About your list. I must say I am impressed. It appears well thought out and, on the surface, quite complete."

Sarah brightened at his validation. She had not realized how important his approval was to her.

"I learned well from Eleanor. She was brilliant at it. I cannot take any credit. I am merely following her lead."

"There you go again, taking no credit for any accomplishment. How do you expect people to respect you if you do not respect yourself?"

Sarah dropped her head. She knew her brother was right. She had always been strong, but had lacked the confidence she needed to make her own decisions. She had always been unyielding in her focus, and believed that strength and wisdom were one and the same, but they were not. Looking back at her life, she realized that she had never made her own decisions. She had merely steadfastly administered those of others.

"Now, this is your business. It is for you to tell me how you want to proceed. They are your decisions to make. I am here to support you as you need, but it is simply that...*support.*"

Sarah felt as though she were on a ledge, about to fall, and it terrified her. She could not speak. Her throat was tight with insecurity. Bertie understood, but he did not come to her rescue. His gaze was unyielding, as if to will her to confidence. He had faith in his sister. He knew she could do this.

After a few moments, Sarah broke the silence. She drew in a deep breath, and much to Bertie's pleasure, laid out her plans.

"You can see the equipment I need. It will take some time until I can afford most of it. I will focus on what will allow me to operate at a basic level and I will expand as I can afford to do so."

Bertie smiled as his sister continued to reveal her plans.

"I have fifty pounds remaining from the money that Eleanor left me. I must save a portion of that to care for the children, and the rest will be used for the business. It is my wish to be on our own as soon as possible so that we do not intrude upon your generosity longer than is necessary."

"You can remove that notion from your mind," he interrupted. "We are enjoying having a full house. It is too big for Jane and me alone. You are welcome to stay as long as you wish."

Sarah looked back at her list and continued. "I will purchase two tables, one for the sewing machine and one for cutting. I will need sewing supplies such as scissors, markers, and pattern paper. And I will also need to build a larger inventory of fabric. Once I have a few steady clients and some income coming in, I will work on the shop."

"Well, I do believe you have a plan. Excellent! I will help you procure the tables. My cabinet and furniture maker friend can assist with that. I will take you into Winnipeg next week for the rest of your supplies."

Sarah felt empowered and confident. For the first time, she felt as though she had a path to follow that was hers entirely. She realized there was no shame in accepting support. There was more shame in not accepting support and letting one's stubbornness close doors that need not be closed.

"Thank you, Bertie. You are a good brother."

"Yes, I know," he said with a grin. "I have a few things that I want to wrap up. I will be about thirty minutes. You can go back to the house now or wait for me."

"I would like to take an inventory of the material. I will wait."

Sarah pulled the bolts of fabric out of the bin and leaned them up against the wall. They were full bolts, directly out of the factory. Some were heavier material for pants, jackets, and skirts, and others lighter materials, cottons, and silks for shirts and blouses. As the bolts lay against the wall, Sarah began to realize just how costly her gift had been. The sewing machine alone was a small fortune. It was the same type that Eleanor had in her factory, and she knew them to be the top line machine that the Markley factory produced. She was most grateful to William for his generosity and she hoped she had adequately portrayed as such in her letter to him.

As Sarah and Bertie left the office, Bertie pointed out the church across the street. The yard was bare and the building looked new.

"That is St. Philip's Anglican Church. It was completed last month. The ground has been frozen and they have been unable to do any outside work, but the inside is quite lovely. We have been two Sundays. Jane and I would like you to join us tomorrow."

"That would be splendid. We have been so busy getting settled, I had not yet thought about finding a church. It will be nice to attend together. It has been far too long since we have done so."

"Yes, when I think about how long, I have to reconcile my age. I try to do that as infrequently as possible," he said, grinning.

"Yes, I know what you mean," Sarah agreed. "But when I don't think about it, my body tells me directly."

"I'm looking forward to my niece's dinner this evening. Let us see how it is progressing."

Chapter 40

As Sarah would have guessed, Margaret was hard at work in the kitchen. Sarah had not realized how large the chicken was until she saw it on the countertop. It was the size of a small turkey. It sat smothered in mustard and rosemary and surrounded by potatoes, and Sarah looked forward to enjoying it.

Sam was to arrive in thirty minutes and Sarah would need to dress for dinner. Her clothing had been cleaned and were certainly presentable, but she would be dressed in the same dreary clothing she wore on the train. She had gone into Winnipeg with Bertie in search of John Nightingale and had not gone with her daughters to buy a new dress.

As she went upstairs to prepare for the evening, Jane and Florence came out of Jane's room. Both were dressed beautifully for dinner. Florence wore her new dress, which was yellow with large white flowers. Her hair was pulled back with a yellow ribbon. Jane, too, looked lovely in a long, grey skirt with a white and yellow blouse.

"If I didn't know better, I would say you are twins," Sarah said, teasingly. "You both look absolutely splendid this evening. I'm afraid I will dull your brightness with my frumpy frock. I did not get the opportunity to buy anything new."

Who was she fooling? Certainly not Jane. Everyone knew that Sarah was as likely to buy herself a dress as Jane was to sew one.

"Sarah, we are close to the same size. Why don't you take a look in my closet and see what might be of interest to you? You can borrow whatever you like for the evening. For that matter, you may borrow whatever you like until you can build your wardrobe again. I think it was very practical to only bring the basics with you. Now you can build as you wish."

Normally, "practical" would be a compliment. But Jane's "practical" stung like an insult, unintentional, but a blow nevertheless.

"Thank you, Jane." Sarah swallowed her pride and chose to accept Jane's kind offer, knowing she would take pleasure in the evening far more.

"Help yourself to my closet. I will take Florence downstairs and we shall see you shortly. Agnes and Mary are dressing now, as we speak."

Sarah felt as though she were in a dress shop as she looked through Jane's closet. It was neatly organized by season and colour. It seemed there was a bit of practical to dear Jane as well, Sarah mused to herself. Sarah settled on a cream coloured, raw silk skirt and jacket. It was exquisite. She had never worn anything like it before.

She stood before the mirror in her room and brushed her hair. She pinched her cheeks to bring out some colour and then she reviewed herself. She was pleased with the outfit, but it could not mask the self-consciousness she felt about the rest of her.

Agnes was trying to brush Mary's hair, and Mary would have no part of it. "Agnes, are you trying to pull my hair out? If that is the case, you are doing a very good job."

Sarah snickered to herself at her daughter's sarcasm. She was so young, yet she had mastered the art so well.

"I am simply trying to put a brush through this rat's nest that you call your hair."

"Enough, girls. Agnes, please give me the brush."

Sarah put one hand on the back of Mary's head and began to brush from the bottom, gently working through the tangles.

"Thank you, Mama," Mary said as she shot her sister a venomous glance.

"Now let me take a look at you two," Sarah demanded. "So pretty." She kissed them both on the forehead, reminded them to be on their best behaviour, and then led them downstairs.

As they descended the stairs, Bertie was walking by. He smiled as he looked up at them.

"Look at you three. You are all a vision of loveliness."

"Thank you, Bertie. You are looking rather dapper yourself this evening."

Sarah got the girls seated at the table in the kitchen with some paper and pencils. They could spend the time before dinner doing something creative. There would be less opportunity for them to get on each other's nerves if they were engaged in an activity. Samuel and James were in the study reading and carving. And Margaret, of course, was preparing the meal. The table was set, and the evening was ready to unfold.

At precisely six o'clock, Sam arrived. Sarah was surprised to find herself feeling nervous. She stood to straighten out the wrinkles and waited in her spot in the sitting room for Bertie to show Sam in.

Sarah could hear the commotion in the hallway as Bertie took Sam's coat. Jane thanked Sam for the dessert and took it to the kitchen. Sarah's heart started beating and she chastised herself for acting like a silly schoolgirl.

Sam walked into the room looking more handsome than she remembered. The curls that she had admired had been cut and his face was clean shaven. His brown eyes were even more piercing now that they were not partially blocked by his long curls. He was dressed in a stylish suit and appeared quite dashing.

"Sarah, it is nice to see you again. You look enchanting this evening."

"Thank you, Sam." She blushed as she took his hand. "You are looking well yourself. I see that you have found a razor since you returned."

Sam laughed. "Yes, I have always found trying to shave while on a moving train to be inviting disaster. I prefer to keep my skin intact when I can."

Sarah laughed as well. "I am glad that I do not have such worries."

"Sam, please sit. May I get you a sherry?"

"Thank you, Bertie. That would be nice."

"Sarah, how about you?"

"Yes, I would like that. Thank you."

"How are you settling in, Sarah?"

"Very nicely. Thank you."

The conversation maintained a staccato beat until Bertie helped it out of its misery.

"Sarah, why don't you tell Sam about the business you are embarking on?"

"Business? Do tell," he said eagerly.

Sarah shot her brother a look. She wasn't prepared to talk about it. She was nervous enough and did not need to expose herself to the attention.

"I am opening a dress shop. It will be a long ways off until I have a storefront, but it will come in due time."

"Sarah, do not be so modest. Sam, Sarah isn't just opening a dress shop to sell dresses. She is a master designer and seamstress. One of the best there is. Her designs are owned by some of the best dressed women in Ardwick. And they are surely sorry for her departure. But what the women of Ardwick have lost, the women of Norwood and St. Boniface will gain."

"Jane, you flatter me. I'm not sure I deserve such accolades, but I thank you, nevertheless."

"Flattery shmattery. I simply speak the truth."

"Sarah, you strike me as a woman who is far more capable than she gives herself credit for."

"Sam is a very good judge of character, don't you think, Bertie?" Jane said with a teasing tone.

"Come now, we don't want Sarah to feel we are joining forces against her. I'm certain she realizes just how capable she is, don't you?" he said addressing his sister directly.

"All of these compliments are going to give me a swollen head. I think it best we change the subject before it bursts," Sarah said sarcastically.

Sam was impressed with her deflection. He was intrigued with her. She was unlike any woman he had met before, and he knew he wanted to know her better.

Margaret entered the room and announced it was time to sit down to dinner. Sarah was pleased with her daughter's timing.

The table's centrepiece was Margaret's masterpiece. Steam was rising from the chicken, dispersing its enticing aroma about the room.

"Margaret, that smells exquisite. My mouth is watering."

"Thank you, Sam," she replied proudly.

"It appears you have provided the entire meal," Sarah pointed out.

"I came as close to inviting myself as good manners would allow. It was the least I could do. And, based on the smell of Margaret's chicken, I do believe it was the right decision."

Margaret smiled proudly. "Please taste it before you get too excited."

"It seems that modesty runs in the family," Sam said. "I'm sure it will taste as good as it smells."

After grace was said, Bertie raised his wine glass to make a toast to the group.

"Here's to having my long missed sister and her family here with us in Canada. May she prosper as well as we all have prospered. And here's to her first friend in Canada, Sam. Thank you for joining us this evening."

Sam smiled at Sarah as he raised his glass. Her face reddened with the attention, and he grinned when he noticed. So far, the evening was turning out splendidly, he thought.

"Margaret, this is absolutely delicious. I can see why it is your favourite meal. I think it has become mine as well. Bravo."

"Thank you, Sam. I am so happy you like it."

As the meal progressed, there was an unexpected knock at the door. Bertie excused himself, returning a few moments later.

"My apologies for the interruption, Sam. Sarah and Jane, will you both come with me, please?"

Sarah and Jane looked at each other, surprised by the request. What could it be that would take them from their guest and their dinner? Without understanding why, they did as they were asked.

Bertie had a serious look on his face, and Sarah was as concerned as she was perplexed. Inside the sitting room sat a young man who stood as they entered.

"Sarah, Jane, this is Mr. John Nightingale."

Sarah gasped, eyes widened. "Mr. Nightingale, pleased to meet you," Sarah said stumbling slightly. "You received my note?"

"I did. Thank you."

John Nightingale looked lost. He looked scared and Sarah's heart broke for him. He was barely a child himself. A man twice his age would crumble under similar circumstance. How could he have the maturity to deal with such pain? He had not yet lived.

"I'm sorry for your loss. Hannah told me that she loved you very much."

Tears began to well up in his bloodshot eyes and Sarah could see that he was fighting hard to prevent them from falling in front of strangers.

"Where do you live?" Sarah asked.

"By the station. I rent a room from a family there."

"Your daughter is doing well. We shared a room with your wife and daughter on the ocean journey."

John Nightingale swallowed hard. "Were you with her when she died?"

Sarah looked at him as a mother would look at a child. "I was."

"Oh," he said quietly as he looked down, as though this answer was the final and definite confirmation of his wife's death.

"We were told that you have a good job, but it takes you away a few days a week. Is that true?" Jane asked.

"It is."

"Who might watch over your daughter while you are gone? She is far too young to be going to school," Jane continued to question.

Sarah shot her sister-in-law a horrified look. How could she question this poor man under such a circumstance? But then Sarah realized they were proper questions to be asking. Sarah turned to John Nightingale, awaiting his response.

"Mrs. Poole, my landlord, has five children. She has said she would watch Florence during the day, and overnight the days I am away."

"Very good. The company will be good for Florence. She has come to love my children."

"She is a very resilient child, but she needs love. She needs affection. Basic care is not enough for any child, especially Florence."

Jane began to get choked up and Bertie put his hand on her shoulder. This was hard for all of them. They had come to love that little girl dearly.

"I will go get your daughter's bag. She has eaten and has already had a bath today. She will be ready for bed soon."

"And she must have her stuffed dog or she will not sleep. She needs something comforting to hold onto," Jane added, in tears.

Florence's father was trying to take it all in while Sarah went upstairs to retrieve Florence's bag. She sat on Mary's bed and looked at the stuffed bear as it sat beside Mary's doll on her pillow. They were like two friends that did not want to be parted, but inevitably must. As Sarah put the bear in the bag, a tear rolled down her cheek. She had become a part of the family, but clearly it was not meant to be forever.

Sarah went directly into the dining room. Sam looked at Sarah with confusion. The children were not quite as attentive to the shifting mood.

"Sarah, is everything all right?" Sam could see that Sarah was upset.

"It will be. I'm very sorry for this. We will be done momentarily. Children, I need you to say good-bye to Florence. Her father is here to take her home."

"What do you mean, Mama?" Mary asked.

"Florence's father is in the living room. He has come to retrieve his daughter. She will be going home with him. You need to say good-bye."

Mary put her hand on Florence's shoulder. "No, I won't let her leave," Mary said defiantly.

Florence began to cry at the tension in the room. She did not understand what was going on, but the mood had shifted and she became scared. Sarah pulled Florence's seat out and picked her up. The children began to rise when Sarah told them to sit.

"Please stay here. You will only make it harder on Florence. Come give her a kiss good-bye, but please stay here."

The girls said their good-byes. Boys being boys had not become attached and had no need. Margaret and Mary cried as Sarah took Florence from the room, but Agnes simply sat frozen. As Sarah walked Florence to the living room, Florence wrapped her arms around Sarah's neck and held on as tightly as her little arms could. Her face was buried in Sarah's neck and she could not see where she was going. Even at two, she sensed it was not where she wanted to go.

John Nightingale looked increasingly lost. He continued to stand in the same spot as his daughter was brought into the room crying. She was too young when her father left. She did not remember him. He was a complete stranger to her. But Sarah had no choice. He was her father, and he had all rights to her.

"Come, Florence. We must be a brave little girl," Sarah said.

As Sarah pulled Florence away from her, Florence spotted Jane and reached out for her. Jane took her before Sarah could stop it. It was only going to make it more difficult.

"Jane, we must let her go," Bertie said. It pained him to see his wife crying. She had suffered so much loss in her attempts to have children and this was no less painful for her. She had formed a deep attachment to Florence, and it was as though her own child were being taken away.

Jane smothered Florence's cheeks with kisses. She wanted to remember how she smelled and how soft her young skin was. She was perfection, and at that moment Jane felt as though she would never recover.

"We best be going. Thank you for all that you have done for my daughter. I am forever indebted to you."

John Nightingale seemed like a nice man. There was certainly no reason to judge him. He had done nothing wrong. He was just a man who had been dealt an unfortunate hand in life.

Sarah handed Florence's bag to her father and he held his arms out to take her. She did not release her grip from Jane, and it took some effort on both Jane and her father's part to have her do so. Florence screamed as her father carried her to the door. She held out her arms to anyone who would take her, anyone but the stranger who had her. Jane could manage the heartache no longer and she ran from the room.

As Bertie opened the door for John, John turned one last time. His eyes were red and wet with tears. "Thank you," were his last words and then they were gone.

Sarah watched as John carried his daughter to a waiting carriage. Her wailing could be heard through the closed window, and the sound was one that Sarah would never forget. It would haunt her memory as deeply and darkly as any other in her life.

As Sarah turned to leave the living room, Sam stood in the doorway.

"How are you?" he asked. His face was full of compassion for her, and Sarah thought perhaps the evening's events had dredged up some personal pain for him from so many years ago.

"I will be fine. I pray the same for Florence. I know that it will be difficult for her, but her father seems like a good man."

"Children that young are resilient. In time, this evening will be forgotten and all she will know is her father."

Sarah could not disagree with Sam. It was hard to comprehend that the memories that would last forever in Sarah's mind would fade from Florence's. But it was true and for the best.

"Come. Let us rejoin the children and finish our meal."

But they were just words. Sarah knew she could not eat. The children sat at the table in silence as Sam and Sarah rejoined them. A few moments later, Bertie took his seat as well.

"Jane sends her regrets. She is not feeling well and is going to rest in our room for the remainder of the evening."

Bertie looked at Sarah with the look of a loving husband, one in utter pain, unable to mend his wife's broken heart. He looked helpless. There was no magic in such circumstance, no substitute. Time would be the only healer.

As Sam had just said, children are resilient and Sarah's own children proved that. A serving of dessert was enough to brighten their spirits. It was Jane who Sarah worried about. It was fresh pain on old wounds that had never been allowed to heal.

As the evening drew to a close, Sarah showed Sam to the door. She felt terrible that the evening had gone so awry. Sam should never have had to witness such drama. But surely he could see that her life was much more complicated than his.

"I'm sorry the evening turned out the way it did. It was lovely seeing you again, despite the unexpected turn of events."

Sam looked at her with narrowed eyes, as if trying to understand her well enough to know what to say under the circumstance.

"No apologies are necessary, Sarah. You did an admirable thing by caring for that child during her time of need. You brought an immense joy to her life, even if only for a short time. God willing, joy will continue in her life, but it is now out of your hands. You can do nothing more for her."

"Thank you." Sarah felt comforted by his words. Sam had a calming and reassuring way about him. The tone of his voice was caring, almost loving.

Sam placed his hand on Sarah's shoulder. "Will I see you in church tomorrow?"

Sarah realized that she knew very little about Sam. She didn't know what his beliefs were, nor did she know what his religious affiliations were.

"Bertie said that we will attend St. Philip's Anglican, across from his office."

"Very good. Then we will see each other."

"Sarah, please do not worry about the evening, not for a single moment. I was happy to make your acquaintance again. So, for me the evening was a success. It is my hope that we will have plenty more opportunities to get to know each other better."

As Sarah closed the door behind Sam, she was exhausted. The strain of the evening had taken its toll. And now there was Sam. Sarah was uncertain how she felt. He was undeniably handsome and thoughtful and compassionate, but she did not feel the way she felt for William, and she was unsure if she ever could.

Once the children were secure in their beds, Sarah made herself a cup of tea and sat down in the living room. She knew she wouldn't be able to sleep so there was no use trying. She would only stare at the ceiling. As she sat alone, she felt numb. She knew what had transpired that evening had been inevitable, but, much like death, the knowledge never made the pain any easier to endure.

Sarah grasped her pendant for strength. But this time, she needed more. She took it off her neck and opened the heart. It was the first time she had done so since the funeral, and Eleanor's smiling face looked up at her reassuringly, as it always had. Sarah missed her friend. And it was a pain that was as strong as any that existed. The pain that Sarah felt when Eleanor died had not diminished. Sarah had to reconcile that it might never.

"How are you, Sarah? It was quite the evening."

Sarah stepped out of her thoughts to find Bertie standing in the doorway. Sarah had thought he retired for the evening, and she was the only one awake.

"Can I get you a cup of tea?"

"Thank you, but I am in need of something much stronger."

He poured himself a scotch and sat down beside his sister, sighing heavily as he did. He took a couple of large sips before he said another word.

"Jane will be fine. She is hurting right now." Bertie took a moment to gather his thoughts. "She so desperately wants a child, and unfortunately she attached herself to that little girl, even when she knew it was a mistake. I tried to hold her back, but she let her heart control her and not her head. I'm afraid it was bound to happen at some point."

"Have you thought about adoption? It is such a shame that you are not parents. Florence has shown you that a child need not be your flesh and blood in order for you to love it with all your heart."

"I was for adoption, but Jane was not. She was so destroyed by the miscarriages that she convinced herself she could manage not being a mother. But Florence, it appears, opened something up in her again. I'm afraid the damage this time will be permanent."

"I am sorry, Bertie. I am sorry that we brought Florence into your home. I understood Jane's circumstance and I should have known this could happen." Sarah felt entirely responsible for Jane's anguish, and she had no idea how she was going to make it right.

"Dear sister, it is not your fault. That girl was placed in your care for a reason. We will carry on."

"And, not to change the subject, but to change the subject," Bertie said with a smile, "it would appear Sam is quite smitten with you."

Sarah did not look up from her tea.

"Is that a problem?" he asked.

"To be honest, I am not certain. I like Sam very much. I am just not sure I like Sam in the same way."

"You cannot force feelings. That much I know. It is not fair to either person, but you have only known Sam for a short time. Things could change. As long as you have an open heart and an open mind, you never know."

"Such sage advice from a big brother," Sarah said, jokingly. But, all joking aside, she knew he was right.

Chapter 41

Church service began at ten o'clock and they started to make their way over at a quarter of the hour. Once inside they took their places on a single pew. Jane pointed Sam and his parents out on the other side of the church. Sam looked back and smiled at Sarah, and she returned the smile.

The minister took his place at the front of the church as the organ music stopped. He adjusted his black robe and placed his Bible on its stand. He looked from side to side, surveying his congregation with a smile.

"What a lovely day to come together to share in the joy of Christ. We have so much to be thankful for. For one, we have this cherished church that God has provided for us...along with a few generous parishioners," he said with a grin. "We are happy to be in our new home, and we look forward to many, many years of worship here."

Sarah thought the minister had a nice way about him. He spoke confidently, but not arrogantly. He was at ease in front of a group and he made those who sat before him at ease as well.

"And, while we are all new to this church, most of us are not new to Norwood. I wanted to take this opportunity to welcome a new family to our family. Mr. Albert Adamson's sister, Mrs. Sarah Berry, has joined her brother from Ardwick, in Manchester, and we are pleased that she has done so. And I understand from a good source that Mrs. Berry is an accomplished seamstress. She will be opening a new dress shop in her brother's building across the street in the coming months and we look forward to it. Sarah, may God bless you richly as you make your new home here in Norwood."

Sarah smiled at the minister in appreciation. What kind words, and completely unexpected.

"Mrs. Berry, please stand so that everyone will recognize you and can make your acquaintance later."

Sarah hesitated and Jane gave her a gentle nudge to move her off her seat. As Sarah stood, her face turned crimson with the heat of the embarrassment. All eyes were on her and she forced a smile to hide her fear.

"Thank you, Mrs. Berry. And I have one other request of this fine congregation. There is a young girl who recently lost her mother. Her name is Florence and she has just been reunited with her father. I ask that you pray for her and ask for God's blessings and protection as she makes the transition to her new life."

Anticipating Jane's pain, Sarah took her hand and gave it a light and reassuring squeeze.

At the end of the service, as they gathered for coffee and cake, many parishioners introduced themselves to Sarah and welcomed her to her new home. There was none of the guardedness or fear that so plagued people back home in Ardwick. Everyone was friendly and kind and Sarah was filled with a resoluteness of purpose, a rejuvenated confidence that made her stand taller and brighter. Sarah could not have imagined a more different world than the one she left.

As Sam approached with his parents, Sarah found herself getting nervous. Sam's mother was a striking woman who looked no older than Jane. Her skin was flawless and her chestnut hair had no grey to be seen. Sarah could see where her son got his good looks. She must have had her son when she was fairly young, Sarah thought, because the calculations in her head made no sense otherwise.

"Sarah, I would like you to meet my mother and father, Lydia and Percy Warman."

"Mr. and Mrs. Warman, it is very nice to meet you both."

"I understand you kept my son company during your train travels across our great country." Lydia Warman's smile was warm and friendly.

"I believe it was he who kept me company, Mrs. Warman. He is an accomplished conversationalist."

She laughed at the compliment, which she could clearly see was wrapped in playful sarcasm.

"He is at that. I hope you are settling in nicely in your new home. I know Jane was so looking forward to your arrival. I heard nothing else for a solid month."

Sarah caught Jane's eye, and she looked back with a warm and loving glance. Sarah did so love her sister-in-law. Her brother could not have chosen better.

"I find it fortuitous that you have joined our great community when you have because I am in need of some new Spring garments. You have saved me a trip to the Winnipeg stores. Are you ready for business yet?"

Sarah was not expecting the question. She hoped her look of surprise was not disconcerting to Sam's mother, and it appeared it was not. Mrs. Warman's warm smile never ceased. This was the beginning, Sarah thought to herself, only the beginning.

"I am indeed, Mrs. Warman. I am still organizing the shop, but I would be happy to come to your home to discuss particulars."

"I have a better idea, Sarah. I am having afternoon tea with Jane at your home tomorrow. We can discuss particulars there."

"Thank you, Mrs. Warman. I look forward to it."

Sarah was beaming, and through the entire conversation she did not notice Sam had been as well.

"And, Sarah, please call me Lydia. Mrs. Warman is much too formal and stuffy."

Sarah left church with a new spring in her step, anxious to get her new business off the ground. The most difficult part would be customers and it appeared that it might not be as difficult as she had feared. She laid out her plans in her head as she walked back home.

Sarah was so taken by the lightness of mind and spirit amongst the people in her new community that she felt inspired to create clothing that reflected as much. One by one, ideas flowed from her head and onto paper. Sarah used the crayons that Jane had bought the girls to add a splash of colour to the pencilled drawings. She was thoroughly pleased with the end result.

The next morning, after the four youngest were settled in at their new schools, Bertie took Sarah into Winnipeg to buy her initial list of supplies. Bertie had first taken her to convert her British pounds to Canadian dollars. It was a bittersweet endeavour for Sarah, the last of her old life gone. She thought of keeping a small amount for nostalgia, but realized the money would be better spent on her new life. British pounds would serve her no purpose.

On the return trip, Bertie took Sarah to Barrett's Furniture and Cabinetry. Sarah needed to procure her tables, the last items on her immediate list, and then she would be ready for business. Nothing elaborate was required, just two simple utilitarian tables of a certain size. Sarah provided the required measurements and was told delivery would be made the day after next.

"Wednesday? This Wednesday?" Sarah was shocked. She had not contemplated being able to start so soon.

"Mrs. Berry, they are simple tables, and I have the wood ready. They simply need to be assembled. And, most importantly, I understand any delay in their delivery will only impede your ability to do business. We can't have that now, can we?" Mr. Barrett said as he smiled at Sarah.

After lunch Lydia Warman arrived for tea. She looked as beautiful as she had the day prior. She was put together in such a way as to look elegant without being "done." Sarah found herself nervous as she prepared for her discussion with her first customer.

"Lydia, you mentioned you were looking for a few Spring items. Do you have anything in particular in mind?" Sarah asked. She did not want to present her ideas until her client had presented her own.

"It has been a long and harsh winter. I would like a few 'cheery' pieces, something to welcome the sunshine and warmer weather."

"Very well. I would like to show you a few sketches that I have done. If none of them is of interest to you, we will work on some new ones together."

Lydia reviewed the sketches one by one, not saying a word, only offering a quiet "hmmm." Sarah began to feel self-conscious. If they were terrible in Lydia's eyes, she might not get a chance to create any more. She would lose her first customer before she even was a customer.

Lydia looked up at Sarah as she put the designs down on the table. "I think these are absolutely exquisite. So different from all the drab designs that we are so accustomed to seeing. They are fresh and vibrant."

"Thank you, Lydia. I appreciate that."

"I am being truthful. These are very good. I like that dress in particular," she said, pointing to Sarah's favourite. It had a slight scoop neckline, elegant but not so daring as to draw negative attention. The horizontal navy and cream stripes were broken by a thick navy waistband that buttoned in the back, and a simple lace tulle completed the bottom of the dress.

"Lydia is right," Jane said to Sarah. "And how fortunate for her that she saw it before I did. I think I would have chosen that for myself had I seen it first."

Lydia settled on some of Sarah's designs as they were presented. Sarah also spent some time sketching as Lydia discussed her own ideas. In the end, Sarah had an order for two of Sarah's dresses, a few skirts and blouses, and a summer evening cover.

Sarah would have her tables on Wednesday. She also knew where the supply store was so she could go there on foot without troubling her brother. She was making her way to complete independence and it felt freeing.

Sarah told Lydia she would have the costing to her the following day, and would take measurements at the same time if all was acceptable to her. Sarah planned to keep her profit margins low while she built her customer base. She could raise her prices in due time, when her customers felt the increase was warranted.

The following day's session turned out as Sarah had hoped. Sarah provided her pricing, and after agreeing that it was more than fair, Lydia provided Sarah with a deposit for half the cost. Sarah did not ask for the deposit, as she was confident that Lydia would honour her commitment.

But, Lydia insisted, saying she understood that supplies would need to be purchased and a cost would be incurred for them. Sarah accepted the deposit with much appreciation, and told Lydia she would be ready for her first fitting the following Wednesday.

With deposit in hand, Sarah floated home. Her feet barely touched the ground for the elation that filled her. Her confidence was increasing by the moment. She only wished she had William to share her progress with. When she arrived at home, she would write him a letter, she thought.

In Norwood, the weather was warming quickly. The tulips and hosta plants were well out of the ground and the sound of singing birds began to fill the air. Sarah looked forward to the summer, to seeing the beautiful lakes that she had heard so much about. The previous year the trains began delivering people to Winnipeg Beach, and Bertie and Jane spent their summer vacation on its shores. They expected to do the same this year.

As Sarah arrived at home, she settled into her room to write William a letter.

My dearest William,

I so wanted to write to you and tell you of my progress here in Norwood. We continue to settle in nicely. The children are attending school. Even Margaret is able to attend here, which is making her very happy. She is a keen student. She spends all her spare time dreaming about how she will spend her life, and what great accomplishments she will achieve.

Samuel is settled in nicely at Bertie's office. He is managing basic office chores, but it is Bertie's wish that he increase his responsibilities over time. It appears to be to his liking.

As for me, I am delighted to report that I have my first customer. I received an order just today and I will be hard at work over the next week getting ready for my first fitting. I receive my tables tomorrow and I will be ready to begin fulfilling my order. It is all very exciting.

I do hope all is well in Ardwick.

I miss you so.

Your loving friend,

Sarah

As Sarah began to place the letter in an envelope, Jane called to her from downstairs. Sarah went downstairs to see Sam sitting in the living room.

"Sam," Sarah said surprised. "What brings you out on this fine day?"

"Precisely that. This fine day is too fine to spend inside. I thought I would see if you were interested in joining me for a walk."

Sarah was surprised, yet again. And while the thought of a walk on a sunny day was appealing, she couldn't possibly. She had promised Mary and Agnes that she would walk them home from school.

"Thank you for the offer. It is very tempting, but I cannot today." Sam could not hide his disappointment. "I promised my girls I would walk them home from school today. I must leave in a few moments."

Sam's dimpled smile returned. "Well then, all is not lost. If it would be all right with you, I would like to join you. Whether we walk in the park or walk to the school, we will enjoy this glorious day together and I will be able to delight in your company at the same time."

"Yes, please join me. I welcome your company."

It was a ten minute walk to the girl's school. Margaret's was in St. Boniface, about five minutes farther. The air was brisk with a cool breeze, but the freezing temperatures were now gone. And, when the breeze decided to take a rest, the sun felt delightfully warm on their faces.

"Are you not working today?"

"My father let me off my chain for a short break," Sam teased. "I started earlier than usual as we received a delivery. He felt that I deserved some fresh air. There are some advantages to being related to the boss."

"I'm sure they too can boast advantages, as you work harder than most. Loyalty and hard work seem to be becoming more the exception than the rule, unfortunately. For children today, it seems more about 'how quickly can I get the job done than how well can I do it?'"

Sam nodded in agreement. He enjoyed hearing Sarah's opinions, and the enthusiasm with which she expressed them. Sam could see that she was intelligent and full of conviction in her beliefs. He would have been disappointed if she had not been so.

"I understand you have decided to make my mother some new dresses. She seems quite excited to be the first. You need to prepare yourself for the Lydia Warman level of enthusiasm. Everyone in Norwood will know that she had the first Sarah Berry design," he said jokingly. "You will have no need to advertise. She will do it for you."

Sarah smiled at Sam. "I will take all the help that I can get, even if it is unintentional," she laughed. "Your mother seems very pleasant. I am happy that Jane has such nice friends."

"My mother thought you were nice, too. I told her I agreed."

Sarah blushed at the compliment, and Sam seemed amused that his comment brought on such a reaction.

"If I had known it was so easy to make you blush, I would have tried much sooner."

"I am not blushing. It is the cool air," Sarah quipped.

Sam and Sarah arrived at the school as its large bell was ringing. Within a few minutes, children began to exit the door, and Agnes and Mary were in the middle of the mix. They were excited to see their mother waiting, and even more so to see Sam with her.

"Hello, Sam. It is nice to see you," Agnes said politely.

"It is nice to see you as well, Agnes. How was your day?"

"Fantastic," she said enthusiastically. "We are learning about how the railroad was built and how far it goes. I talked about our train ride."

"How timely. That *is* fantastic." Sam was truly interested in how their day went and Sarah was pleased for it.

Sam took both girls' stack of books like the gentleman that he was, and the girls ran off ahead.

"So much for walking home with my daughters," Sarah said laughing.

"It is nice to see that they are settling in so nicely. It is a testament to good parenting, I would think."

Sarah smiled at the compliment.

"Perhaps it was the wind earlier. That compliment did not bring about red cheeks," he teased. "Uh, I spoke too soon. They are turning red now as I speak." He winked at Sarah.

"You are incorrigible. You must know that?"

"Am I? I have never noticed." Sam spoke in a playful way that was endearing to Sarah.

As they rounded the corner onto Eugenie, Bertie's fenced yard came into view. "Well, we have arrived. Thank you for allowing me to join you on your walk. It was a nice break from work. I must return now, as my father will be waiting to put my chains back on."

"It is a good thing for your father that I know you are merely joking. I would have to go to him and give him a piece of my mind."

"Good to know," he said with a smile. "I will ensure that you always know when I am merely teasing...well, most of the time anyway."

"Good. And I will endeavour to ensure that you will almost always know when I am amused."

"Very well then. I believe we are both understood. I wish you a pleasant evening, Sarah Berry."

"And I you, Sam Warman."

And with that, Sarah walked up the path to the house and Sam down the street toward his father's shop. Sarah truly enjoyed Sam's wit and charm, as he did hers. He was delightful and she was happy to have become friends. As they glanced back at each other, they caught each other's eye. At the very least, it was a matching of wits, and that presented both intrigue and excitement beyond their daily routines.

As Sarah entered the house, Jane stood by in full smirk.

"What?"

"What do you mean *what*? Do I really need to account my perceptions in painful detail?" Jane quipped.

Sarah walked past her sister-in-law. She knew no words would suffice. A discussion would be purely a waste of time. She still was not sure how she felt so how could she speak of feelings not yet defined?

Despite it being a school night, Margaret prepared the evening meal. She had decided on a cassoulet, a French white bean stew with pork and garlic sausage, which she had learned from Chef Nicolas.

"Margaret, you need to stop cooking like this or we will never let you leave," Jane teased.

"Yes, Margaret, you could have your own restaurant one day," Bertie beamed.

"I would love that," Margaret said enthusiastically. "I love cooking as much as Mama loves sewing."

Sarah looked at her daughter with a boundless love. She finally understood the depths of her daughter's heart. How she had condemned her for her dreaming. She was so ashamed of herself.

"Margaret, you can do anything your heart desires. You are smart and talented. If you want to cook, I have no doubt you will be the best cook in the world."

Margaret looked as though she were going to crumble under her mother's words. She had never heard the like coming from her mouth.

"Thank you, Mama."

As they continued their meal, there was a knock on the door.

"It is probably Andrew. He showed a property to a client and may have an update. Samuel, I will want you to listen in. It will be good learning for you."

Bertie reappeared in the dining room, all colour drained from his face.

"Bertie, what in heavens is wrong?" Jane asked her husband.

"Sarah and Jane, please come with me. Children, please wait here."

Sarah and Jane followed Bertie to the living room. Standing in the middle of the room was John Nightingale. He had his daughter in his arms. As soon as Florence saw Jane, she squirmed in her father's arms, holding her own out to whomever would take her. John looked pale and drawn.

"Mr. Nightingale, what is wrong? Is Florence unwell?" Sarah asked.

"She is in good health, but she is not happy," he said, his voice breaking up.

"It will take time. You were a stranger to her after all that time and it will take time for her to get to know you again," Sarah continued. "You must be patient."

"I cannot do it."

"Cannot do what?"

"I cannot care for her. Mrs. Poole will not watch her any longer. Florence has not stopped crying the entire week. Mrs. Poole has other children and it has been such a disruption to her home. And I must work. If I do not, I simply cannot afford to live. None of this is fair to my daughter."

Bertie, Jane, and Sarah were speechless. The momentary silence was deafening. It felt as though time stood still, thoughts swirling to dizzying effect.

"What are you suggesting, Mr. Nightingale?" Sarah asked, interrupting the silence.

"I do not know what I am suggesting," he said, hesitating. "No, yes I do. She deserves to be where she is happy and well cared for and that appears to be here. I know it is a lot to ask for, but if you could find it in your hearts to welcome her into your family for a time, you would be answering a prayer. I would pay for her care."

Bertie did not need time to consult with his wife. The tight grip that Jane had on Florence, and the tears that were flowing from her eyes, were enough approval of his intentions.

"Mr. Nightingale, we care for your daughter very much, but we cannot simply be her caregivers. We opened up our hearts to her already and it pained us greatly when she was taken away. If we are to welcome her into our home again, it must be permanent. It must be legal. We will not allow her to leave again. You would be welcome to see her anytime you wished, but she would become our daughter."

John Nightingale looked at his daughter and then shifted his glance to Bertie. He sat silent in his thoughts for a few moments. His eyes welled up and he drew a long, deep breath.

"I understand. I must do what is best for my daughter. She deserves better than what I can give her on my own."

John could not bear to stay a moment longer, and stood to leave. He did not look at his daughter; he simply turned and walked to the door. Bertie followed behind and walked through the door, closing it behind him.

"I am very sorry for all that has happened to you. You are a good father, Mr. Nightingale, and I pray that you are blessed in your life. If you are able to return Saturday evening, I will have a lawyer present, along with the proper documentation. Will that be acceptable to you?"

"Yes."

"Saturday at seven o'clock. Thank you."

John Nightingale rushed down the walk and disappeared into the darkness. There was no waiting carriage that night. Bertie turned and joined his wife and sister inside.

"Bertie, is it true?"

"I believe it is." Bertie was stunned. He was in a state of shock as well.

Jane gasped. She could not believe what she was hearing. She was going to be a mother? Florence was going to be her daughter? Through her tears, she kissed Florence's cheeks.

"Florence, I am going to be your mama."

Bertie had the most serene, satisfied look on his face. Sarah was witnessing the deepest and purest kind of love. Bertie was falling in love with his wife all over again. Sarah had never been happier for anyone as she was for the two of them at that moment, but her heart pained for John Nightingale.

On Sunday, Florence Nightingale Adamson was introduced to the congregation. She looked deeply content as she sat on her mother's lap. Her doting aunt and cousins watched on proudly as Florence was baptized before them all.

"Well, this certainly is a surprising turn of events," Sam acknowledged to Sarah as he joined her after the service ended. "I am happy for them both. Jane looks utterly blissful."

"She certainly does."

"And how are you these days? Are you utterly blissful as well?"

Sarah was used to Sam's wit and sarcasm, but she didn't sense that in his tone this time. She was unsure of what he was getting at, and her uncertainty forced a hesitation in her response.

"I'm well. Thank you."

"That certainly was formal, Mrs. Berry. I thought we were more casually acquainted," he said, his teasing tone returning.

"I'm sorry," she said with as much facetiousness as she could muster. "I'm absolutely, utterly fantastic. Is that better?"

"Now, that is the Sarah who I have come to know and love."

Sarah looked at Sam in response, unsure if she had heard him correctly. His smile was unwavering and was enough to confirm to her that she had. Anxiety began to build, pulling across her chest in one tightening squeeze. She did not feel as she should with such a heartfelt revelation. There was only unease. She cared for Sam, but she did not love him in that way.

"I believe your mother is trying to get your attention, Sam," Sarah said, relieved to have been saved from the conversation.

Sam turned to look. "I believe she is trying to use me to get out of a conversation. I must go be the dutiful son. Please excuse me."

"Of course. We must be leaving ourselves. I'm sure Florence is exhausted with all of the attention."

"I hope to see you during the week. You'll never know when I just might pop out of nowhere, perhaps from behind a shrub or a tree. I do have an air of mystery that I must maintain, you know."

Sarah laughed. "Understood. But forewarned is forearmed, and I do have an air of composed sophistication that I must maintain."

Sam thoroughly enjoyed bantering about with Sarah. It was a playful repartee that, to him, was a welcome match of wits and spirit. But it had grown beyond innocent fun; he had come to crave it, to crave her.

Chapter 42

Sam's words hung in Sarah's mind, echoing and reverberating, undiminished. What could she do? The last thing she wanted to do was hurt Sam. That would break her heart, but she could not break her own by pretending to feel something she did not. She was still in love with William. Her heart still ached for him. When she wanted to share her thoughts and feelings with someone, it was William she thought of. She was not ready to let him go, not yet.

With the children off to bed, Sarah sat down in the sitting room with a cup of tea, trying to unwind before putting herself to bed. Jane joined her from upstairs.

"It was an eventful day," Sarah said with a smile.

"It certainly was. I'm exhausted."

"I'm sure you wouldn't have it any other way." Sarah's grin made Jane laugh.

"That is true. I am completely and totally happy at the moment. My dreams have finally come true."

"I am so happy for you. God brought the two of you together, and He could not have done a better job. She will always know that you chose her. She could not be more loved."

Jane closed her eyes as she contemplated the thought. Her smile lit the room in a burst of incandescent warmth.

"Speaking of 'could not be loved more,' how are things with Sam?"

Sarah commended Jane for her skillful segue. Sarah was not surprised. In fact, she expected as much. Between Jane and Lydia, Sarah was, in effect, under emotional attack. She paused as she thought of a response. There was no sense offering any witty retorts. The truth was all that was required. It was all that made sense under the circumstance.

"Today in church, Sam all but told me that he loved me."

Jane gasped, covering her mouth. "He did? Then why do you look so gloomy? Does that revelation not make you happy? How could it not? I have seen the two of you together. You look positively happy when you are with him. You are radiant."

"I am happy when I am with him, but merely as friends are happy to spend time together. I do not feel the way that he does, and I cannot pretend to."

"Hmm, what is it? Is it Thomas? Do you feel that you cannot move on?"

"No, it is not Thomas."

Sarah was not offering Jane any more than was directly asked of her and Jane's frustration was mounting. She could not understand how Sarah could not feel that way about Sam. He was everything that a woman could want in a man, and he clearly adored Sarah.

"Well, what is it? There must be a reason. There are many women in Norwood who have tried to secure his affections, but he has had no part of them. He has not been interested in anyone…until now."

"I am too old for him."

"That is ridiculous, and you know it."

"I know no such thing. I have five children, and the wrinkles and grey hair to prove it. Sam needs to be with someone younger. He has plenty of years to build his own family, his own flesh and blood."

"Maybe he doesn't need that. Maybe you are all he needs. Do you forget his sorrow? Do you not think that he wants to be with someone who understands his pain, someone who has lived a life as fully and harshly as he has? Come now, Sarah, you must realize that. He knows what is important in life. He knows what he wants."

Sarah was growing as frustrated with Jane as Jane was with her. She desperately wanted her to drop the subject.

"If not Thomas, is it someone else?"

Sarah turned away, unable to look Jane in the eye.

"So, there we finally have it. Sherlock Holmes has cracked the case of the stubborn widow."

Jane's attempt at humour did not amuse Sarah in any way. She wanted the conversation to end, but Jane was not willing to let go until she understood.

"Who is holding the heart of Sarah Berry? Surely, he must be someone extraordinary to keep you from loving such an incredible man as Sam."

Sarah knew that Jane was not going to let up. She could get up and walk out, but the interrogation would merely continue the next day. She needed to face the assault head on.

"It is true. I do love another and my heart belongs to him."

Jane chastised herself for not thinking of it sooner.

"William Markley. It is William Markley, isn't it? Why didn't I see it sooner?"

Sarah's look confirmed Jane's suspicions. Of course it was. Sarah's reaction to his gift, the letters back to England…they all made sense now.

"Clearly, your heart belongs to him, but does he know this to be true? And what of his heart? Has he offered his in return?" Jane asked pointedly.

"I do not know," Sarah said as the tears began to fall. Jane felt terrible for nudging her so hard, and her harsh mien turned softer.

"Might it be possible that you are holding on to something that cannot be so that you can be excused from having to face what can? Do you not believe that you deserve to be happy? Do you feel it is a right and prudent thing to allow someone to hold your heart who does not know he does or might not even want to? Do you want to throw something wonderful away that is within your grasp for something that might never be?"

Sarah could think no more. Her head hurt and her eyes burned. She gave Jane a kiss on the cheek and said goodnight. She wanted to be alone, without anyone to answer to, so she could go to sleep and make the suffering stop.

As she lay in bed, she relived Jane's words. Could Jane be right? Sarah knew that Sam was remarkable, and she fully understood what was at stake. She also knew that William was a world away and that was not going to change. But what Sarah knew more strongly than anything was that, despite all of that, she still loved William. She longed for him. She desired for him to touch her, to kiss her, to hold her in his arms. She could not give herself to Sam knowing that she felt this way about another. She could not do that to him. It would be cruel and selfish. He deserved infinitely better.

When Sarah woke the next morning, her heart felt the same. Sleep did nothing to ease her torment. But, it appeared, it softened Jane.

"Sarah, I am deeply sorry for being so harsh with you last evening. I only wish for your happiness. You must know that."

Sarah embraced her sister-in-law in an act of understanding. She never felt any ill will toward her, only frustration because she could not give her what she was looking for.

"Of course I know that. And I thank you for it. But I can only speak what is in my heart," Sarah repeated.

"I realized last night that I should know that better than anyone. I could not change my own heart, and I should not expect you to change yours either. If it is meant to be, love will change it."

"Thank you, Jane. Your support means the world to me."

"Jane, I do have one question for you. It has left me quite perplexed. Why would Sam journey in steerage when clearly he could have afforded not to?"

Jane's response was curt and stinging. "For the same reason that you did not when you could afford to. While Sam may more easily demonstrate his feelings than you do, he remains entirely as practical. You really are very similar."

Sarah's heart was heavy and she desperately needed a diversion. It was a pleasant morning and she decided to walk to the supply store rather than take the carriage. It was only a mile and she thought the fresh air would do her good. As she crossed the Norwood Bridge, she could see the cresting water. Ice was still blocked from moving freely in places and it gathered at the river's edge, which was now substantially farther in than it had been previously. Buildings along the edge of Norwood were flooded. Bertie's home was out of the danger zone, but there had been fear before the river crested. Bertie said it was the price they paid for living where they did. They were grateful that it was not as bad as it could have been.

She required only two bolts that day and decided to carry them herself. She returned to her shop just before noon. As she laid out her fabric and organized her receipts, there was a knock at her door. She kept it closed so the sewing machine whir did not bother the office staff. She opened the door and was surprised to find Sam standing there.

"Sam, what brings you by today?"

"It seems I had all this extra food and I thought it would be a dreadful shame if it went to waste. I have to eat and you have to eat and I thought that perhaps we should just eat together. What do you think? Do you have an appetite for me...uh, I mean do you have an appetite for my food?" he said with a sly grin.

Despite Sarah's misgivings, she could not help but smile.

"I do have to eat, I suppose. And I suppose it would be cruel to leave you to eat by yourself. So, yes, I accept your invitation. Thank you."

"Excellent. It is a pleasant day, and surprisingly, a blanket just happened to appear in my basket. Perhaps we should eat in the park."

Sam led Sarah outside, and they found a nice spot in the park beside a bed of tulips of purple and yellow. The colours were lovely and reminded Sarah of a bolt of brilliantly hued fabric that she had admired in the shop that morning.

Sam laid out the blanket and took Sarah's hand to help her down. He opened the basket to reveal how full it was. He began to lay it out in front of them. There was roasted chicken, paté, French cheeses, quiche and devilled egg sandwiches.

"It appears you brought your entire kitchen."

"No, I left the stove and sink. I thought that would just be plain silly."

Sarah surrendered. She would not worry about what would happen. She decided she would enjoy Sam's generosity and wit and think about nothing else.

"This was thoughtful, Sam. Thank you. I was destined to have dry leftovers for lunch."

"Well, I'm glad this is better than dry leftovers," he teased. "How are my mother's dresses coming along?" he asked with interest.

"Very nicely. I am meeting your mother for her first fitting the day after tomorrow."

"Excellent. I'm confident your business is going to do marvellously well. There is always a need for quality. We seem to be in a diminishing supply of it these days."

Sarah and Sam paused long enough to eat some food and gather their thoughts. Sam appeared to have something on his mind. He was not as chatty as usual and seemed preoccupied.

"Is everything all right, Sam? You don't seem yourself."

Sam looked at Sarah with a long, thoughtful gaze. How astute she was, he thought. Sarah could feel Sam's nervousness. It thickened the air and brought a level of discomfort that had not been there moments earlier.

"Sarah, I would like to speak with you, if I may?" he asked, almost pleaded, waiting for an invitation.

Sarah swallowed hard, sensing with dread what was to come. But there was no avoiding it any longer. The time had come for Sarah to be honest with Sam.

"Sarah, I am sure you know that I care for you very deeply. And I have come to care for your family as I would my own."

Sarah's tension was rising. A lump was forming in her throat and she could not breathe.

"But I also sense that your feelings are not the same."

Sarah's widened eyes locked on Sam in surprise. She was not expecting such an admission. It was the furthest thing from what she expected.

"In the short period of time that I have known you, I have come to love and admire you as I have never loved and admired a woman before. I thought I knew what love was, but I realize now that I did not. I knew it when I first met you on the train. You stirred my heart and I am afraid that it remains so. You are everything that I long for in a woman. You make me feel whole...complete. You challenge me, amuse me, but most of all you fill my heart with such joy. You are an angel to me."

Sarah continued to sit wide-eyed, her own silence deafening in her ears.

"I know you care for me. I do. But I long for more than the caring one has for a friend. I long for you to love me as I love you."

Sarah could see that Sam was hurting. He was opening his heart to her utterly and completely. She wanted to comfort him, but she held back. It would only hurt him more.

"We have not known each other a long time, Sarah, but to me it has been a lifetime. I pray that time will bring me your heart and make me the happiest man alive. I will wait for you."

Sam looked lost and deeply pained. He had found what he longed for, but it was not his to take.

"I'm sorry," Sarah whispered.

She dropped her head in shame. What was wrong with her that she did not feel the same? She was hurting him and it grieved her. Would she over time? Her head was spinning with thoughts and feelings, but she could not speak her mind for her thoughts were yet unclear to her.

"I care for you, Sam. I do. But my heart still belongs to another and I do not feel I am ready to move on. Perhaps over time I will, but I cannot ask you to wait for me while I sort out my feelings. You deserve so much better."

Sarah's admission of attachment to another was a crushing blow to Sam, his fragile heart already breaking. How could he compete against a faceless stranger, an enemy he knew nothing about?

"You are not asking me to wait. It is my choice and my choice alone. In the same way it is not for you to decide what I deserve."

Sarah shuddered at Sam's admonishment. "You are right. I am sorry," she said, sincere in her apology. She wasn't going to try and relieve his pain for fear of hurting him more, but she could not stop herself. She was sincere in her hopes. "It is my greatest desire that my feelings do change, Sam. I mean that with all my heart."

Sam was gutted. His smile was forced and was hollow as he felt.

True to his word, Sam gave Sarah space and time. For the next few weeks, Sarah found herself busy with her new business. Lydia Warman had loved her dresses, and as Sam had suggested she would, she told everyone who would listen. Her days were filled with appointments and she spent the rest of her time sewing and buying supplies. She did not have a moment to spare, and it was just what she needed. But she did miss her friend Sam.

As May gave way to June and then to July, the summer heat set in with an intensity that Sarah had never experienced. Nothing in England rivalled a Winnipeg summer. As Bertie had teased, the black flies really were voracious and the mosquitoes the size of small birds. But, despite that, they managed to enjoy their summer. Weekdays were spent working indoors, trying to remain cool, and the weekends were spent at Winnipeg Beach. The lake was always a welcome respite from the city.

And despite the intensity of her new life, Sarah enjoyed it. She had her family and her customers. And on a lovely July morning, a few days after Sarah had opened *Sarah's English Garden* to the public, she had an unexpected visitor. She had not heard the voice in over a month and she turned in surprise when she did.

"Sam, what an unexpected pleasure." It was then that she realized how much she had missed his company.

"Hello, Sarah. It has been a while. I hope you are well."

Sam was uncharacteristically monotone and serious and it caught Sarah off guard.

"What is wrong? Are your parents well?"

"They are, thank you. Do you have a moment? I don't want to interrupt you while you work."

"Of course. No interruption at all. Please come in the back. Sit down."

Sam took a moment to gather his thoughts. It was apparent to Sarah that he was in an emotional state and it made her uneasy.

"Sarah, my feelings toward you have not changed. But what has changed is my willingness to wait. I cannot do it any longer. I see you at church, I see you out walking, I see you in my shop and it tears at my heart like nothing else. I cannot continue to torment myself. I must move on. I am getting older and I want a family," he said as his voice trailed off. "I want a wife."

"I understand," Sarah said. "I do."

"I am not going to ask you if your feelings have changed. Surely, you would have told me if they had. But I will beg of you to search your heart one last time to see if there might be room in there for me. If there is not, you will never hear me ask again. I can promise you that the subject will be dead. I'll give you two days and at such point I respectfully request a response."

Sam didn't wait for Sarah to say anything, nor did he say good-bye. He simply walked out of Sarah's shop, leaving her completely speechless.

For the next day, Sarah thought about nothing else. She tried to imagine her life with Sam, but she continued to come back to the same person, to the same conclusion each and every time.

Just before noon, Bertie popped his head into Sarah's shop. He wasn't aware of Sam's ultimatum, but he could sense something was amiss. He tried to cheer his sister up with his good humour and her favourite food.

"Jane has made you your favourite today for lunch."

"And what favourite would that be?" Sarah said amused. "She makes so many things that are my favourites."

"Your favourite favourite, I suppose...toasted peameal bacon and tomato sandwich."

"Yes, you have me. That is my favourite favourite."

"And there is a letter for you. Jane put it on the chair on the porch. You can read it before you go in."

Sarah wasn't expecting a letter from anyone and her curiosity had the best of her. She told her assistant, Matilda, that she would be back after lunch and she left for home.

As Bertie had said, there was a letter on the chair. Sarah sat down and opened it. It was from William.

My dearest Sarah,

You are often in my thoughts and it is my greatest wish that you are happy and healthy.

Business is good here. My father is expanding and has put me in charge of the factory. Hopefully, one day I will do something more interesting, but for now it keeps me satisfied.

I am writing to share some news with you. I am engaged to be married....

Sarah dropped the letter to her lap. She could not believe what she was reading. This couldn't be. She picked up the letter and continued to read while her tears blurred the ink.

I am writing to share some news with you. I am engaged to be married. I will be married the Sunday after next, although by the time you receive this I will already be married, I suppose.

Sarah's heart was not breaking. It was broken, fully and irreparably, she felt. Sarah could read no more. She stared off in the distance as the letter lay on the porch. As Jane emerged to invite Sarah in for lunch, she saw the letter.

"Sarah, what is it?"

Sarah did not respond. She continued to stare blankly into the distance. Jane reached down and picked up the letter and read it. She understood immediately. Jane sat down beside Sarah.

"I am so sorry, Sarah."

Sarah still did not speak. Jane hesitated, but she felt the need to make her opinion clear.

"Sarah, I love you and I know this will hurt, but this is truly for the best. You will see in time. You turned William into a dream, a vision of a life that wasn't real. William has moved on and now you must do the same. One day it will be too late and you will be sorry for it," Jane said, pointedly. "Your sandwich is on the table when you are ready."

Jane left Sarah sitting alone on the porch. Her words played over and over in Sarah's head until Sarah realized that she was right. It wasn't that William was marrying that bothered her; it was that the fantasy she had created, the fantasy that she had used to keep the world away, was shattered. She used Thomas to keep William at a distance and now she was doing the same with Sam. How could she not have seen that?

She was happy for William. He deserved love and a life full of blessings with his new bride. She did love William, and she always had, but she knew it was never truly in that way.

When Sarah arrived at her shop the next day, there was a large bouquet of flowers at her desk. A note rested against the vase. It said, simply, *I'm very sorry, Sarah. I am thinking of you. Sam.*

When Matilda arrived, Sarah excused herself and walked to the butcher shop. Sam was behind the counter arranging the daily specials when he noticed Sarah walk in. He wiped his hands off on his apron and stepped out from behind the counter.

"Thank you for the flowers. They are lovely, and incredibly thoughtful."

"You are welcome. How are you?"

"Do you have a moment to talk?" Sarah asked.

"I do. Just give me a moment to take off my apron. I'll attract the flies outside if I don't," he quipped.

Sam joined Sarah and they walked outside. It was going to be another blazing hot day, but it was early and still quite comfortable. They walked the short distance to the park where they stopped and sat down on a bench.

Sarah did not look at Sam. He sensed her uneasiness.

"Sarah, you need not say anything to me. I understand how you feel and can see that nothing has changed. Please do not worry about me. We Warman men were bred to withstand the pain of heartbreak." Sam forced a smile through his anguish.

A tear rolled down Sarah's cheek as she looked up at Sam. He wiped it away with a sympathetic look. Even when he felt she was breaking his heart, her feelings were still paramount.

Sarah focused on Sam's face. How beautiful it was. How comforting it was.

"Sam, I do love you." Sarah drew in a deep breath. "Not as a friend, but as a woman loves a man. And not because I can't have William, but because *I love you.* I understand now that it was England, that it was my life back home that I could not let go of. I held onto my feelings for William because to me they were one and the same. But Canada is my home now. I have no intention of going back. Not now, not ever. My life is here. My life is here with you, if you will still have me. Nothing could make me happier."

Sarah's words cleared away the heaviness that had burdened Sam's heart and they lifted him to a place where he had never been before. No woman had ever been more beautiful to Sam than Sarah was at that moment.

He took Sarah's hands in his and looked deeply into her eyes. Her heart was aflutter and she knew that she was madly in love with the man who sat beside her.

"I prayed that our hearts would come together and my prayers have been answered."

As Sam leaned over to kiss Sarah, the woman who had captivated him body and soul, she let go of her own burdens, burdens that had so long held her captive, and her heart was freed to love again.

Research Acknowledgements

1. "Ardwick: Districts and Suburbs of Manchester," Copyright © John Moss, Papillon Graphics AD 2013 Manchester, United Kingdom <http://www.manchester2002-uk.com/districts/ardwick.html>

2. "Life in Victorian Manchester: Working, Health, Housing & the People of Manchester," Copyright © John Moss, Papillon Graphics AD 2013 Manchester, United Kingdom <http://www.manchester2002-uk.com/history/victorian/Victorian1.html>

3. Higginbotham, Peter "The Workhouse" <http://www.workhouses.org.uk/> consulted 5 May 2012

4. <http://www.britishtelephones.com/histuk.htm>

5. Types of Graves in the Cemetery - <http://beckettstreetcemetery.org.uk>

6. Life in Industrial Towns - © 2000-2013 HistoryLearningSite.co.uk <http://www.historylearningsite.co.uk/industrial_revolution_towns.htm>

7. The Manchester Tramways (Yearsley and Groves, TPC 1988)

8. Hanna, Jonathan. "Colonist Cars Helped Build the West," Momentum." Fall 2008. <http://www.okthepk.ca/dataCprSiding/cprNews/cpNews90/08090100.htm>

CPSIA information can be obtained at www.ICGtesting.com
Printed in the USA
LVOW12s2352210114

370378LV00001B/6/P